## A RELUCTANT BRIDE

Eleanor Archebold will stop at nothing—
even a marriage of convenience—to keep
her family estate from being sold to the
highest bidder. And when her young siblings attempt to cast a spell to find her a
husband, Eleanor is astonished by the arrival of the young English baron with
whom she had spent one recklessly passionate night. In that night of soul-searing
passion, he had stolen her heart. Now he
has arrived to take possession of her home.

## A DETERMINED KNIGHT

Sir Garrett Neville has never wavered in his
desire to claim the land he believes to be
his birthright. But he never expected that
Eleanor might be part of that desire. Yet
the dazzling intensity of her determined
green eyes enflames his deepest passion
and adds a new quest to his life's ambitions. She promised to marry him—in
name only. Yet Garrett is determined to
take her wild heart and claim her as his—
body and soul.

# NANCY RICHARDS-AKERS

# SO WILD A KISS

*An Avon Romantic Treasure*

AVON BOOKS ◆ NEW YORK

AVON BOOKS, INC.
1350 Avenue of the Americas
New York, New York 10019

Copyright © 1998 by Nancy Richards-Akers
Published by arrangement with the author
Visit our website at **http://www.AvonBooks.com**
Library of Congress Catalog Card Number: 98-92776
ISBN: 0-380-78947-7

First Avon Books Printing: November 1998

AVON TRADEMARK REG. U.S. PAT. OFF. AND IN OTHER COUNTRIES, MARCA REGISTRADA, HECHO EN U.S.A.

Printed in the U.S.A.

WCD 10 9 8 7 6 5 4 3 2 1

*To all those women down through Irish history who have aided the Queen on her way to Freedom, especially to the memory of those whose lives inspired this work: Eleanor, Countess of Desmond; Eibhlin Dhubh ní Chonaill; Lady Wilde, Maud Gonne; Mairead Farrell; and Constance Markievicz.*

*To the centuries of poets, who, in daring to open their hearts and souls, have preserved moments in time too precious to be forgotten, and especially, to the poet king.*

You are one of the little stones on which the feet of the Queen have rested on her way to Freedom.

Maud Gonne

# Author's Note

## On Resource Material

In researching the times and people and places for my books, I use a range of material far beyond traditional history texts. One of my favorite resources is poetry. The body of written Irish lyrics and poems over the past 1,200 years is rich in detail, commentary, and vernacular.

Pick up almost any anthology of Irish poetry and you will find *Cill Chais*, or an excerpt from it. Originally composed in Irish, I am the proud owner of several translations of this mournful, yet hopeful poem.

In my opinion, *Cill Chais* is the most beautiful of the *filíocht na ndaoine* (poetry of the people)—verse which insists that in spite of all oppression the men and women of Ireland are irrepressible. While much is known of the terrible strife that inspired *Cill Chais*, its author remains unknown . . . thus it was that my mind, always seeking answers, began to spin its own explanation.

*So Wild a Kiss* tells how and why and by whom this poem was written, and while my story is fiction,

I encourage you, dear reader, always to believe in possibilities and miracles.

## On My Use of Language

In *So Wild a Kiss*, I use less Irish than in *Wild Irish Skies* and *The Heart and the Holly*. Instead I incorporate numerous aspects of English as it was and spoken in Ireland as well as that spoken by the English in the mid-seventeenth century. Many current grammar rules did not apply, and in an effort to lend a ring of authenticity to my prose and dialogue, I often elect to ignore them. Specifically, adverbs without the "ly," adjectives used as adverbs, redundancies, emphatic pronoun with *self*, mixed verb tenses to avoid perfect and pluperfect, double constructions, and *do* as an auxiliary verb are not errors overlooked by the copyeditor, and I direct readers to the following for further background: P.W. Joyce, *English as We Speak It in Ireland*, Dublin, Wolfhound Press, 1910; McCrum, Cran and MacNeil, *The Story of English*, New York, Viking Penguin, 1986; E.L. McAdam, Jr., *Johnson's Dictionary: A Modern Selection*, New York, Pantheon Books, 1963.

## On Basic Definitions

| | |
|---|---|
| bawn | an enclosure near a farmhouse for livestock, or a farm yard |
| *bodhrán* | hand-held drum which is played more like a tambourine |
| bonnyclabber | thick milk |
| booley (as a verb) | annual practice of moving cattle to the high hills for summer grazing |

*brine-oge*      a young fellow full of fun and
                 frolic

brohoge          small batch of potatoes, roasted

byre             barn or shed for cows

*céilidh*        a social evening with music and
                 dancing

*dánta grándha*  courtly love verses

dullaghan        a hideous hobgoblin who lurks
                 in churchyards, and takes off his
                 head at will, and substitutes it
                 with a human head

*duthracht*      tender care and kindness

drugget skirt    woman's multi-purpose garment
                 made of coarse wool; large and
                 voluminous, it tied about the
                 waist like an apron or could be
                 worn over the head as a cloak

*mucais*         pigsty

raif             a pejorative reference to the En-
                 glish; a play on the common
                 Anglo-Norman name, Ralph

*sidhe*          a faery or faeries; often referred
                 to as *them* or *they*

*Tain*           *Tain bo Cuailnge* ("The Cattle-
                 Raid of Cooley") the great cen-
                 tral epic of the legends of the
                 Red Branch warriors (the ancient
                 Cuchulain sagas)

thewes           manners

tory, tories     from the Irish word *toraidhe*
                 meaning *raider*; during mid-
                 1600s it referred to those Irish
                 who fought the English employ-
                 ing guerrilla-type raids (not to
                 be confused with a political
                 party or with those Colonists
                 who allied themselves with Brit-
                 ain during the American Revo-
                 lution)

# Prologue
## A Cradle-Tale Begins

**O**ut of the mist, a maiden emerged. Black as raven wings her hair was, and though she moved with the light steps of an airy spirit, she was human. O, how human she was, owning a tender heart and trusting nature. She was Órla, daughter of the O'Toole chieftain at Castlekevin, and to the people of the glen she was as exalted as any princess of Windsor could e'er be.

Crouching beside the man, Órla set fingertips to his brow. His crashing through the underwood had been a hullallo to wake the dead. He must be one of the strangers who would steal her family's land, and whose king enacted laws against Irish civilization. His name was Henry, that king of the English, who despised the people of these hills that he ordered his earls to steal Irish children for adoption in England.

Órla's family guarded her well. To be sure, this was the first stranger she had gazed upon, and he was a clever man to her eyes, tall and straight and fair-favoured in his making. Not so different from one of her brothers or cousins, she was thinking, for she saw nothing to affright her. Sooth, the grief that had marked his countenance upon being trapped in the bog had touched a chord within her.

This stranger must love the world as much as myself, thought she, and the Lord would not be wanting me to let such a rare man perish.

1

* * *

Adventure. Enchantment. Pure love.

That was the stuff of which legends were spun, and it was such a cradle-tale that had long held Garrett Neville, Baron Aylesbury in its thrall. Forsooth, his earliest memory was of listening to this particular one whilst sitting in Lady Olivia's garden.

For twenty-three years, Lady Olivia had recited it for Garrett in a like manner. She had repeated the tale as her mother had recounted it to her, and as her mother's mother had recited it almost a century afore. The language was a charming fusion of Irish and English as spoken during the reign of the Tudors. Nary a syllable differed from the first telling, and despite Lady Olivia's advancing years, the same captivating quality infused her delivery. She whispered in a voice most soft, yet certain, so full of suspense it seemed she was sharing a secret of such power, such sorcery that its mere telling could be fatal.

This was the last time Lady Olivia would tell the story, and she motioned for Garrett to sit beside her. On the morrow he would be gone, and this time their parting would be forever. Garrett was as dear to Lady Olivia as any child of her flesh, perhaps dearer, and she had promised herself no tears. She had always known this parting would come, and intended to see him go forth with naught but the joy of promise in his heart. She would not weep until he was leagues gone.

The cradle-tale continued.

*The young man stared. The maiden had not the yellow hair of the mystical* sidhe, *but whether she was mortal, he was not certain, for he had ne'er seen such a maid of grace. How entrancing were those ebony curls. He did not stop himself reaching for them, and he smiled, for they were as soft to his fingers as they looked to his eye. His other hand moved to where she touched his brow, and threading fingers through hers, he brought them to his lips. Soft, he kissed her fingertips, the top of her hand, the inside of her wrist.*

*'Tis said the music of flutes and harps filled the misty glen as they lay upon a bed of sweet clover-grass and moss. The hawthorn shuddered, its white petals spilling to the ground, and nine months later a babe was born at Castlekevin. Wee Órla, she was called after her mother, who waited patient to introduce her lover to his child, but wee Órla's father ne'er held his daughter. Pestilence took him before he might return to the glen, and her mother— that girl who had given pure love to the young stranger of the English—died of a broken heart when she saw her newborn growing not into the image of her lover, but of her own good self.*

"The babe was a dark child of the hills," said Garrett.

Lady Olivia knew why he spoke. She understood Garrett not because she had raised him. She understood because of the kinship betwixt their souls.

In the both of them character, desires, and ambitions had been dictated by the generations that had gone before, and while they were both descended from noble English families, that ancestry accounted for only a portion of their genealogy. Indeed, their Anglo-Norman seed was thin. Unenduring. Passionless.

'Twas Irish blood in their veins, flowing hard and fast, that nourished their souls. Irish seed from which sprang a certain character that could never be mistaken for English. In Lady Olivia it was termed whimsy. In Garrett it was foolish daring. His tendency to observe the world through the eyes of a poet, and the deplorable habit of measuring one's fellow man with an impartiality that defied English notions of social order, had been marked by more than one gossip. Lady Olivia smiled. She was rather fond of those tendencies herself.

"You intend to finish the story for me, do you not?"

"I would have it no other way." Garrett smiled, and set his lips to the top of Lady Olivia's head. Her hair was faded, yet he would remember always how dark it had been in his youth, so dark that he had only to gaze upon her to envision Órla of the glen. He would never forget Lady Olivia, or the treasure she had given him.

Garrett must finish the tale this night, for on the morrow what came next would be his story. He had never recited it aloud, but the words flowed most easily.

*The strangers searched for the child of an English knight who had one time lost his way in the hills, and they found Órla. The lass was stolen from beneath a hawthorn tree at the edge of a bright green bog. Alack, Órla was taken against her will across the sea to be civilized, and in time, made to wed a Turbeville cousin. But she ne'er forgot Ireland.*

*In time wee Órla, far from her beloved home and living among the English, had a daughter, and she named the child Órla, not for herself but for everything she had lost. In time, she told that child about the glen and the O'Tooles, about Castlekevin and the sidhe, the hawthorn in spring, the flutes and pipes, and she taught her daughter the language she'd learned at her grandfather's knee.*

"You will write?" Lady Olivia asked.

"Every fortnight." He heard the tears she tried to stifle, and gave her forearm an affectionate hug. The debt he owed Lady Olivia could never be repaid; a few missives were the least he might do. Garrett had the world and a thousand tomorrows before him, while she would be left with naught but memories. Guilt pricked at him as if to sap his elation, to blunt his anticipation; he tried to ignore it.

"And you must tell me everything. Leave nothing out." Lady Olivia managed a smile, holding Garrett's hand in hers, and gave silent thanks to God the Father for His mercy and generosity. She had invoked the same prayer a hundred thousand times before, and would continue giving thanks until her final breath. Like herself, Garrett was a lost child of the hills, and it was to him she had passed on Órla's memories, for she had not been blessed to marry and have a child of her own. The treasury of memories had been preserved for another generation; they had been passed on and had become his, as had a truth known to no other living soul save Lady Olivia.

Garrett Neville, Baron Aylesbury, was the great-grandbabe of another stolen Irish child.

"You have my pledge that I shall write every fort-night," vowed Garrett.

"I would hear every single detail. Omit not a mote of dust, not a blade of grass. I would know every sight that passes before your eyes, every sound that reaches your ears. Do not fail me."

"Fail you? Am I not a gentleman of honor in word and deed?"

"Of a certainty, dearest boy. I do not question whether you will write. 'Tis the nature of the news. Pray do not disappoint me in that."

"I will do my best." Garrett knew she spoke of the life he would make for himself. His future.

"Tush! You have always been much dedicated to your aspirations. There never was a more single-minded gentleman. To be sure, your correspondence will overflow with splendid accomplishments. My fondest wishes will be realized when I read of a family and home, and of your future brightened with a fair Irish bride of the hills."

Garrett frowned. Guilt pricked him again. Would

that Lady Olivia might be with him at his journey's end, instead of hundreds of miles away. Would that she might witness his future rather than read of it after the fact.

"Something troubles you," she said.

"I will worry for you, Livia," came his half-truth of a reply. Indeed, he would think of her every day. She had not been well of late. Something smothering had settled upon her lungs, and each time the physician came to bleed her, she did not revive, but worsened. A different man would stay through the winter. A more better man would wait until spring to leave her, but Garrett was not that man. He could not wait.

She was correct. He was determined and single-minded.

Garrett would reach his journey's end.

He had lived his entire life for what was to come next. He had read the law, invested and reinvested his inheritance, and finally, sold Aylesbury Manor in support of his ambition. Over the years, he had avoided entanglements of the heart; indeed, he'd endured loneliness in order to remain free to pursue his ambition.

Nothing would stop him, not even consideration of Lady Olivia, whom he held as dear as his own life.

"It is time," said Garrett, when a servant informed him the carriage was ready. He offered Lady Olivia his arm, and together they walked the length of the long gallery one last time. He would travel through the night and the better part of tomorrow to sail some twenty-four hours hence on an evening tide.

Lady Olivia's story was ended.

It was time for Garrett's to begin.

Lady Olivia Turbeville, daughter of Órla, descended from the O'Tooles of Castlekevin, had been

born among the English and she would die among
them, but Sir Garrett Neville, born at Aylesbury
Manor and raised at High Knole, was bound for Ireland.

# Part I

# Chapter 1

~~~ᴑᴑᴑ~~~

**B**iddy O'Fierghraie lived in the fold of the mountains below Brockagh Hill. She was a wise woman, trusted and depended upon by many for her cures and charms. From as far away as Imail on the other side of the mountains, or from Clonegal to the south, high-born ladies as well as common folk made their way to her cabin. This afternoon Biddy had three callers knocking at her wicker shutters. It was Eveleen and Grace, youngest daughters of the dear-departed Lady Moira Archebold come from the big house with their brother Rory, who had been taken with fever whilst his sisters had made the trek to Baravore to bury their mam.

" 'Tis glad I am to be seeing ye're better, Rory Archebold."

Rory grinned. He was a wee lad, not even as tall as the shaggy wolfhound at his side.

Eveleen was the eldest of the three. At eight years of age, she was almost nine, which was almost ten. She rolled her eyes. "And with more energy than a bag of fleas, 'tis our Rory."

Biddy regarded the children with a kind smile.

11

"Ye must tell myself what brings ye to visit ould Biddy this fine day." Although the English might call her witch, Biddy O'Fierghraie had not a harmful bone in her body. Her solicitude was genuine, especially for these weans. It was less than two months gone since they had buried their mam, and there was suffering at the big house no less than in the poorest bothy in these hills.

No town or village, big house or cottage had been untouched. Old-English or Irish, the English under Cromwell cared not for such distinctions. One might travel a full twenty miles and see not a single living creature. The slopes and fields did not glow purple this harvest time with bog cotton and heather. Even the *jack, jack* of daws was rare heard on the wind, for there were few birds and even fewer trees in which they might perch. Daily the strong were taken by the English, the weak by pestilence. Indeed, that was what had taken Moira Archebold.

"We've come for a charm, Biddy O'Fierghraie," said Eveleen. She nudged Grace in reminder, and the younger girl held forth a basket to the wise woman.

Biddy leaned out the window, took the offering, and peered inside the basket. Two hen's eggs were a precious token in these times of want. Their need of a charm must be a mighty need, to be sure. "A charm, is it now? And which of ye is it that finds yerself in need of charming?"

"Oh, not us, Biddy O'Fierghraie." Grace giggled.

" 'Tis for our Eleanor," Eveleen clarified.

Eleanor was their older sister, less than three months shy of her twenty-first year, and mistress of the demesne of Laragh, its woods and tillage, hills and valleys. Since her mother's death, and since her brothers had gone into the hills, the welfare of her siblings and the household retainers, the tenants in the Vale of Clara and villagers in Annamoe—some two score persons, mostly widow-women and orphans—was Eleanor Archebold's.

"And what kind of charm would ye be needing for Eleanor?"

"A love charm."

"A love charm? Does yer sister have an eye for a particular fellow? I have not heard of any bachelors in these parts, lest ye be counting the English soldiery, and not a one of them would do for the mistress of Laragh, I'm thinking. Pray who can it be that's caught yer sister's eye? For 'tis a rare man who wins the heart of a *bean-draoícht*, and yer sister ought not to be working charms on some undeserving fellow."

Since the time before Saint Patrick there had been *charming women* in these hills; women about whom ballads were sung, poems recited, and tales of their comeliness whispered to lads who might dream of falling under their spell. Some believed they were faery women come to live amongst mortals, and that when their time was passed upon the earth they returned to *Tir n-an Og*, the Land of Eternal Youth.

'Twas said the *bean-draoícht* were the incarnation of the past, the guardians of the present, and the bridge to the future. 'Twas said Eleanor Archebold, with her glossy black curls—unruly some called them, wild—and her eyes as green as the ancient Irish wilderness, was one of them.

"That's the problem," said Grace. "That's why we need a charm."

"To bring him here to Wicklow. He must needs come to our Eleanor."

Biddy O'Fierghraie was intrigued. "And who might *he* be?"

"He would be a fine loving man to cosset and protect her, and to take upon his shoulders the great responsibilities she carries," Rory quoted his mother almost word for word. He had been hiding beneath Lady Moira's deathbed, and had harkened everything their mother had said to Eleanor, the whole of which he had reported to Eveleen and Grace as soon as they had returned from Baravore.

"Do not be anxious, my daughter, 'tis what I heard our mother say. We are the both of us ready for what is to come next, she said to Eleanor, she did, and her voice no more than a thin whisper, but I heard each word sure and distinct. The time arrives, she said, and you'll be caring for the weans and the people of Laragh with dignity and *duthracht*. And though our Eleanor did not seem as certain as mother, Mama reassured her. I have no fear, said she, and one day the *tender care and kindness* you show to others will come back to you in abundance. This is my wish as sure as I wish your brothers return to Laragh. There will be someone for you, my daughter, our mother said. A loving man to cosset and protect you, and to take upon his shoulders the great responsibility you are ready for this day."

It was a serious mission upon which they were embarked, for the children were determined that their mother's dying wish for their sister be fulfilled. Eleanor must have a husband.

"Can you help us, Biddy O'Fierghraie?" Rory tugged on her shawl.

"Love charms," the old woman muttered a few times, wondering how to deal with this situation. It had never happened before that someone came asking for a cure she could not give, and she had not the heart to tell the Archebold children the truth. Her skills were devoted to curing. She had little knowledge of love potions, and even if she did, most such charms required the name of a particular young man, or at the very least, the cooperation of the girl who wished to wed him.

Gazing upon their earnest, innocent faces, and hearing the affection in their young voices, Biddy O'Fierghraie could not turn them away empty-handed. Theirs was, to be sure, a goal most worthy. Eleanor Archebold had heard the keening of widows far too often for a young woman who ought to be better acquainted with flirtation and stolen kisses than with tragedy. A wee charade could do no harm, she decided, thinking it better they return to Laragh this night secure in the hope of a better future. Aye, a charade was the right course. Besides, she did not wish to give back those eggs.

"Seven fistfuls of bogbine blossoms and two valerian stalks, I'll be needing," she told them, trusting the list sounded appropriately mysterious.

"Gathered beneath a full moon?"

"Nothing so dramatic as that. Take yerselves down to the bog on the other side of the ridge and bring some back fresh this same afternoon." She handed them their basket, emptied of its contents, and off they scampered.

When they returned, Biddy welcomed them into her cabin. Even the great wolfhound was ushered within. The little room was dark, and smelling of tansy and smoke; it was an odd, but cozy abode owing to the assortment of items she had received over the years in payment for her cures. Hanging on the stone walls were sconces too grand for a cabin no bigger than a bothy, two reflecting glasses, and a needlework carpet.

The space was crowded with more chairs and chests than a woman living on her own could ever need. Benches piled with books were flush to one wall, and against another was a cabinet displaying an hourglass, spectacles, two fiddles, and a child's puppet. Instead of a sleeping pallet, Biddy O'Fierghraie was the proud owner of a narrow bedstead topped with an abundance of blankets and bolsters. But her greatest pride and joy were the two-handled pewter cups she had received from Lord Chambre the year she'd cured his lordship's bride of her fright of the marriage bed. There had been six cups, each in a small velvet bag, and each etched below the rim with a delicate strand of ivy; but two of the cups had disappeared the same night as Biddy's husband thirty years before, and now four was the perfect number to be bringing them out of their little bags to entertain her young guests.

"Ye're sure to be needing a bit of nourishment before ye start back to the big house," said the old woman. Courtesy, hospitality, and generosity were natural to Biddy O'Fierghraie; she was an Irishwoman first, a poor woman second. Biddy set aside the basket of roots and blossoms, then spooned a portion of bonnyclabber into each pewter cup, and set out a wooden platter of brohoge. "Come up to the table now, and be having a seat."

The children clambered to the table. It pleased Biddy to see they were glad for the thick milk and roasted potatoes, and it pleased her all the more for their thewes, for they thanked the Lord and herself, and did not eat like piglets but as proper mannered children of quality.

"If you please, would you tell us now what we must do?" said Eveleen when she finished.

"Och, let myself be thinking," mused Biddy. "Now it comes to myself. Ye're listening, are ye? Good, for 'tis important ye get the whole of this, and do not be disremembering a single step, else the charm won't be working. First, ye must sprinkle salt at each of the four corners of yer sister's bed, then at each of the four corners of her bedchamber, and last, at the end of the lane, where the track from the big house meets the Annamoe road. Do this for six nights," she instructed, thinking six nights made it seem a powerful charm. Then to make certain they would not be venturing out in the dark, she added, "Mind ye must be doing this each night before the ground is moist with dew."

"Is there something special we must say?"

"A verse, mayhap?"

"Do we recite a *Paternoster* backward?"

A verse? Biddy had not thought of that. "Och, I do have it. *Salt, salt, I salt thee in the name of God in unity. May Eleanor's man be coming whether by land or by sea.*"

"Does it work?"

"Margaret Quinn's mother used the same when she was wanting a husband for Margaret, and it was this exact charm that brought Margaret's Seamus from Cork." It was a bold-faced lie, but Margaret Quinn's mother was long gone. None but the good Lord and Biddy knew the truth, and there were times such as this that Biddy believed the Lord was most generous with His forgiveness. The children were satisfied. The Lord would be, too.

"And the bogbine blossoms and valerian?"

"Aye, Biddy, tell us what are they for, if you please?"

"On the sixth day, ye must put the blossoms in yer sister's shoes—divided equal between every pair she owns. That will signify a journey, that someone is coming to Laragh. On the seventh day, put the valerian stalks beneath her mattress, and on the eighth day . . ."

"The gentleman shall arrive at Laragh!" Rory exclaimed in jubilation. "On the eighth day our Eleanor will have a husband."

Biddy cautioned, "Not always on the eighth day.

'Tis not always as easy as it sounds. Moretimes ye must gather new bogbine and start anew. But whatever comes to pass ye must not tell anyone what ye're doing. There's to be no idle chatter of charms and such, or of yer visit to myself, else ye could be making *them* angry." Biddy was a wise woman, and never did a thing to cross the *sidhe*. Although Biddy never knew why the faeries had bestowed the skill of curing upon her, she didn't doubt that this dabbling with matters beyond her skills could displease *them* as surely as it might distress Mistress Eleanor to learn someone had been encouraging her brother and sisters to charms. "Ye'll not be wanting to bring *them* knocking on the door of the big house."

The children nodded in grave understanding.

"Be off with yerselves now, and good cess, says I," Biddy O'Fierghraie bade them good luck and success. She stood in her door until they disappeared down the valley toward Laragh. "The Lord between us and harm," she said aloud, and crossed herself.

It was not, however, faeries she feared most, but Cromwell's English.

It was three strong miles from Brockagh Hill to the big house, and the children hastened on their way, reciting Biddy's verse as they went so as not to forget a word of it. At the Glendalough crossroad, they espied a crowd gathered at the foot of a great tree, and they slowed their pace.

"What do you think happens?" Grace whispered.

"I see Sean Rian the blacksmith, and Aidan Lawless. There's the young widow-woman Róisín O'More. And one of the Puritan soldiers."

Rory cut off Eveleen. "Nay, 'tis no soldier, but a psalm-singing coward looking like an old gray rook."

"Whist!" the girls admonished him to silence.

" 'Tis what Conall calls them. I've heard him."

"That may well be true, but you need not be repeating everything you hear, Rory Archebold, especially not in such a trumpet-tongued voice. Behave yourself, now, unless you wish to be forced into hiding with your brothers."

Their approach had been noticed. The people acknowledged them in silence with naught more than a nod or discreet smile. This was not their usual welcome for the children from the big house.

Something was not right.

It never was when one of Cromwell's soldiers of God was present.

"Do not stop," came Eveleen's urgent order. "But do not forget to salute as courtesy requires."

They were halfway past when the soldier called out, "Why such haste, little nits?"

Like the majority of his comrades-in-arms, he was a rude man hailing from the lowest order of English society, a fanatical man firm in the belief that God had cursed the people of Ireland, and an ambitious man for whom the prospect of landownership in Ireland with its attendant elevated social status was a heady intoxicant.

"Bastard," the curse came in Irish from one of the men beneath the tree.

Rory's wolfhound growled and put itself before the children.

"Speak up, little nits." This soldier was not the first Englishman to level such an insult upon an Irish child. It had been more than a decade since Sir Charles Coote had commanded the English in Ireland, but it would not soon be forgotten how his army had been ordered to dispatch every Irish enemy, including women and children, for "Nits will be lice," Sir Charles had explained to his reluctant army.

"Do not be talking to the landlord's family like that," the widow-woman O'More dared speak.

"Landlord's family?" In two steps, the soldier was in the roadway, moving toward the Archebold children. The wolfhound's low growl turned to a snarl. The soldier stopped a few paces away. "Not for long, little nits. Not for long. In short time thou won't be the landlord's family, for thou and thy beast will be off this land and far gone from here."

Eveleen started to tremble. She longed to reach out to hold Grace's and Rory's hands, but dared not risk twitching so much as a single muscle.

"Here, little landlord. Take notice." The soldier ripped a broadsheet from the tree trunk. It was perhaps a foot wide and two feet long with printing in large black letters; at the top was drawn the official seal of Ireland. He commanded Rory to step forward and take it from him. "Carry this home, little landlord, and make certain to tell thy papa-landlord to be heeding it, else we'll be using this tree for more than posting notices."

The children tore down the road with the faithful hound at their heels, not daring to look back, not daring to slow their pace until they had reached the lane to Laragh. Despite her fear, Eveleen remembered to hold close the basket of bogbine blossoms and valerian stalks to keep its contents from spilling. Rory clutched the piece of paper. Quick, Grace darted down the lane.

"Does anyone follow?" asked Eveleen.

Rory peered behind him. "Nay."

They scrambled into a thicket of sheltering boscage to catch their breath. The dog crawled after them on its belly.

"Give it over here, Rory. I would look at that broadsheet," said Eveleen.

"I can read it," Rory protested. Their mother had

taught all of her children to read and write in English, Irish, and Latin. Their father had been a poet of decent reputation, and learning and literacy were greatly valued in the Archebold household as they had been in Ireland for centuries.

"I'm eldest, and should be first."

"Oh, cease your squabbles." Grace, who was in the middle, put out her hand, and Rory passed the paper to her. She scanned the bold black letters, saw the loathed named of Cromwell, and began to read in silence: 15 OCTOBER 1653, ORDER FOR FORFEITURE FOR THE GREAT TRANSPLANTING. She had intended to read it aloud a second time, but could not bring herself to utter its contents, and instead, passed it to Eveleen.

It was the proclamation they had feared, yet about which they had held out hope might never come to pass.

Henceforth all estates, farms, and fertile fields of the Irish were declared the property of the English soldiers, who had won them by the sword, and of the English Adventurers, who had financed the military expedition into Ireland. The Irish must repair themselves—landowners, their wives and children, their cattle, servants, and possessions—into Connaught, and under penalty of death no Irish man, woman, or child was to let himself, herself, itself be found east of the Shannon after May 1 of the next year.

"What is it?" asked Rory. "Why do you cry, Grace? You must let me see for myself."

Eveleen clutched the basket tighter. "We visited Biddy O'Fierghraie none too soon."

"Aye." Grace swiped at her tears with her tabby petticoat. " 'Tis more important than ever to be bringing our Eleanor's husband to Laragh."

# Chapter 2

**G**arrett had never liked London—a noisy, fetid, and overcrowded city, in his opinion. He liked Dublin even less. It was twelve hours since he had disembarked at Ringsend wharf on the Liffey River, and already he was eager to complete his business and depart. The narrow streets were dirty, congested, and dangerous, and they made him uncomfortable A pall of evil hung over the coney-warren of back lanes as Garrett hurried along Dame Street in the direction of Castle Street and the residence of Lord Egerton, Esquire.

Many gentlemen of the most highest standing lived along these densely populated lanes within sight of Dublin Castle. Here much of the old, medieval city remained as it had been three hundred years afore. Signs identified private homes, taverns, coffeehouses, and guild businesses. The board hanging over Egerton's stoop depicted the three sister goddesses of Greek mythology: the Three Graces. That was what had brought Lord Egerton to Ireland in the first place. Not the goddesses, but the concessions King Charles had granted Irish landowners, and at the king's request, Lord Egerton had gone to Ireland to defend the Crown's title to Irish lands. That had been eighteen years before, and Egerton had never left. Like countless English over the centuries, his lordship had been beguiled by Ireland. To live in Ireland and know the Irish had revealed the soul he'd never known was his; Egerton had been captured by Ireland, and hadn't been willing to leave.

Garrett found his lordship's large half-timber house at the sign of the Three Graces, and banged the heavy knocker thrice. *Patience*, he could almost hear Lady Olivia's cautionary whisper. *Patience.*

The door opened. A plump woman, shy and gray as a dunnock bird, peered out at him.

"Sir Garrett Neville for Lord Egerton," he announced.

"Lord Egerton is expecting you, Sir Garrett." The woman ushered him inside and secured the door. The interior of the dwelling was stifling. Windowless and heavy-scented with anise and boiled cloves, it was not so different from many London homes. A corridor led to the rear of the house, where the woman indicated a door. "In here, sir."

Garrett entered a gentleman's study.

"Aylesbury!" exclaimed a man standing by the hearth with three others.

At once Garrett recognized Lord Egerton. Once upon a time, the solicitor had been a regular guest at High Knole, and Egerton's robust form, bald head, and hearty, exuberant voice were unmistakable. He had not changed in the years since he'd left England. Garrett liked that.

The older man crossed to embrace Garrett and clap him on the back, as had always been his customary greeting. Egerton's gregarious personality dominated the room. He was an imminently likable man.

"Welcome. Welcome. Excellent to see you. Excellent. Trip was uneventful, I trust. Come over to the hearth. Warm yourself. Join us. You must meet these gentlemen. Never know whom you needs turn to one day. Never know. Gentlemen, I present Garrett Neville, Baron Aylesbury.'' The men executed perfunctory bows. Egerton rambled on, ''Old family friend. I was his father's solicitor, and continue to advise Sir Garrett. Young fellow disembarked on the last tide at Ringsend.''

Egerton introduced his other visitors. The first was Miles Corbet. Garrett knew the name at once. Corbet was one of the four Commissioners of the Parliament of the Commonwealth of England for Ordering and Settling the Affairs of Ireland. A barrister from Norfolk, he had been one of the judges who had signed Charles I's death warrant; he was a regicide, though most dared not say such aloud. The two other men were not so infamous. One was from Boston, a merchant and ship owner, by the name of David Selleck; the other was a Captain Bingham from the Virginia colony.

''This is thy first visit to Ireland, Sir Garrett?'' inquired Commissioner Corbet.

''Aye, sir, it is.''

''And what thinkest thou? First impressions are always enlightening, if thou would share them with us.''

Garrett considered his answer with care. Corbet, the regicide, was one of the four or five most influential men in Ireland, and while Garrett had no respect for such a man, nor any desire to seek his favor, he owned a mighty desire to avoid provoking him. ''I have not seen much of Ireland to commend it.''

''Well spoken, Sir Garrett. Well spoken. The country is rife with cankers.''

''Which you intend to cure through ordering and settling,'' quipped Egerton. However, whether he

jested in friendly admiration or had dealt Corbet a
barb of mockery, Garrett could not discern.

"Indeed, Lord Egerton, daily do I endeavor to effect a cure, and God willing, I will succeed." Corbet's expression was unperturbed, self-satisfied. He
focused on Garrett. "The Commissioners have
granted licenses to our good friends Selleck and
Bingham to export some of our problems to the
Americas."

Garrett angled his head to one side in query....
*Export some of our problems* ... The words repeated
themselves, taunting Garrett, who wondered if he
understood, and he glanced toward Egerton. *By
heaven, Corbet cannot mean* ...

"Aye, 'tis as distasteful as you imagine," Egerton
replied, as if Garrett had voiced the question aloud.
"Downright fiendish. 'Tis no wonder they seek my
counsel, and asked me this day to draw up indem-
nity papers. The gentlemen trade in human cargo,"
his lordship clarified. "Irish."

"*Rebels*," Corbet corrected. "And a wise man
spares not a shred of pity for such lawless creatures.
Thou go soft with age, Egerton. Soldiers who refuse
our generous terms of surrender and foment civil
unrest deserve the gallows. I ask, are we fiends to
let them live? Nay, 'tis mercy we mete to undeserving troublemakers, malcontents, common thieves.
Thou will soon learn, Sir Garrett, that the Irish are a
race of felons. Defiance is as natural to them as obedience is to an Englishman. Captain Bingham pro-
vides a valuable service, and aids our efforts to
purge Ireland of felons, while Selleck will abet our
cleansing the island of paupers. 'Tis not only felons
infesting the countryside, but homeless and destitute
whose numbers increase daily, and they swarm
through all parts of the nation in multitudes too
plentiful to tolerate. They are a threat to public

safety and a most dangerous source of disease, I'm sure thou art aware. Not to mention what an unsightly spectacle they present with their begging and dying by the wayside at any place they might choose. Passage with Selleck is much for their own good, that they might be given lives of purpose and honest labor. His license specifies four hundred children.''

*Four hundred children.* Bile rose in Garrett's throat, while he managed a thin smile.

"Come, Sir Garrett, what we do is not fiendish. 'Tis a reprieve we offer these simple folk from certain death.''

Garrett struggled for something moderate to say, something that would reveal none of his true feelings, his foul scorn and loathing. Something that would thwart his instinctive reaction to dispute Corbet. The Commissioner was a swine. A powerful swine who could, no doubt, be a relentless adversary. It was best not to say anything, more best to remain quiet, but knowing the wise course made little difference when Garrett's outrage overwhelmed common sense. Time and again Lady Olivia had warned him; this tendency was perhaps his greatest weakness. Still he could not keep himself from addressing Corbet. "While I have no desire to offend yourself, sir, I am not certain God's will blesses endeavors the likes of which you embark upon with Captain Selleck.''

Corbet's gaze narrowed. "Prithee, Sir Garrett, what are thy politics?''

"I have none.''

"What say thou? No politics? Are thou not an Englishman?''

"Indeed, I am, sir.'' Garrett infused his reply with the conviction and dedication of a zealot. Whereupon he launched into speech, trusting the Lord would forgive his lies. "You are correct—I *am* an Englishman, and I do admit my error in neglecting to account my most foremost allegiance. I meant no disdain or disrespect, and should have been more thoughtful in my response. Although I claim no particular political alliance, I am English. And while I do prefer to stand alone and follow no man, I do follow the Lord's path. Since I would never elect to be one of Captain Selleck's cargo, I would not be true in my faith were I to consign another man to that fate. Is it not written, *Do unto others as you would have others do unto you?* I would that you understand, sir, I cannot serve two masters, and if must choose between heaven and earth, I choose heaven."

Corbet grinned. "Again, well spoken, Sir Garrett. Thou art a thinking man like myself. Nothing wrong with that. A thinking man who reads the Scripture. I do approve, and 'tis well spoken indeed. Godliness is worthiness, and thou art worthy, to be sure. There should be more fine young gentlemen of solid English stock like thine own self come to Ireland to school these heathens in proper ways." He shook Garrett's hand, wished him luck, and encouraged him to seek his assistance, if need be.

The Commissioner and his associates stayed a few moments more, then bade farewell, and left the study in the escort of the housekeeper.

"Not a trace of your mother or father about you," were the first words Egerton spoke when they were alone. He saw nothing of the Nevilles in the young baron, whose father, Sir Charles, had been a weak man—kind and honest, but lacking in any conviction of his own. His son, to the contrary, had a palpable strength of character. He'd held his own with Corbet and had made a favorable impression. Sir Garrett Neville was not a man who could be influenced or intimidated. There was something in the way he held his tall frame, intensity in the glimmer in his eyes, and confidence in the measured manner of his speech; he had the look of a man who seldom made mistakes.

Egerton poured a glass of port and handed it to Garrett. "Nothing like your mother or any of the Nevilles, but can't say it surprises me any more than the night your father summoned me to Aylesbury Manor to amend his last will and testament. Uncommon for a man as young as Sir Charles to amend his will. Seemed peculiar at the time. Later I couldn't help but wonder if he'd had a portent. Divine guidance. Some such thing. Lady Olivia's told you the whole story, I do suppose."

"She has." Garrett knew he'd been orphaned whilst in swaddling. His mother had perished at the hour of his birth, and his father less than four months later, whereupon Lady Olivia, a neighbor and family friend, had been named his guardian. He knew that and more. Much more.

"Never did make sense of it, myself. But no matter. My duty wasn't to understand, but to make certain the stipulation was legal, and to stand firm behind your father's wishes, should it be necessary to enforce them. Hardly expected him to die. Can you imagine the stir when the will was read? Gossips were twittering from Canterbury to Grinstead, and then there was your mother's brother come down from London to contest the arrangement. "Sir Charles couldn't have been sound of mind," the transparent fellow declared, and whilst Uncle towed along some female to coo over you, he was more concerned with the Neville assets than your well-being. Nothing wrong with your father's mind. Perfectly lucid. Myriad witnesses agreed. Nothing to question. No grounds for challenge, and you were delivered to Lady Olivia Turbeville of High Knole. Remarkable woman, Olivia Turbeville. Embraced you into her heart and home without a moment's hesitation. Ever hear from the uncle again?"

"Nary a word."

"By the rood, 'tis a long time. How many years now? Fifteen? Sixteen? And without fail, Lady Olivia's kept me apprised of your progress. Prodigious letter writer, and she boasts as much as any parent might." From the hundreds of missives, one comment in particular had impressed Lord Egerton. *Neither a Royalist, nor one of Cromwell's Puritans, Garrett has managed to distance himself from the turmoil of English politics*, Lady Olivia had written whilst the young baron was reading the law. Now his lordship studied his young guest, recalling again his exchange with Corbet. No follower was Garrett Neville, but an independent man, rare in his willingness to stand alone. Egerton saluted him with his glass and an appreciative smile. "You are aware, I trust, how remarkable it is that you've managed to keep your handsome head affixed to those shoulders."

Garrett grinned. "So Lady Olivia tells me."

"Which brings us to her latest correspondence. She writes, you've a mind to acquire land and plant in Ireland. No better time nor place for shrewd investors, and there's land to be had aplenty. Believe 'tis near thirty thousand soldiers to be paid their arrears in land. 'Tis said an enlisted man's debenture can be bought for about one hundred and thirty-six pounds. The trade is already brisk, and numerous small holdings are being amassed to make larger ones."

"That is what I hear, and would like your help and counsel."

"Help is easy. You'll require an agent. Someone

who knows his way through Dublin's lowest quarters and can make queries in your behalf. I can recommend such a man. As for my counsel, it would be negligence if I did not ask: are you certain of your desire to plant? Planting is a hard life, and these days more uncertain than ever. For the most part, 'tis land-hungry grocers and carpenters, butchers, drapers, and the like who fancy themselves the future feudal aristocracy of Ireland. You already possess wealth and a title. No need to build a fortune or reputation from lording over a parcel of land. 'Tis murderous hard work and risky."

"I have always enjoyed a challenge, the riskier the better for it. And I've never shied from hard work."

"You may then be intrigued," said Egerton, thinking again what a remarkable young gentleman Lady Olivia had guided to manhood. "There are other opportunities for those not opposed to a little risk, and who, like yourself, have access to a ready source of funds. Do not forget that hard work and perseverance are no guaranties of success in Ireland. 'Tis money. That's the ticket, and you've more than enough to finance whatever endeavor suits your fancy. More than enough to secure whatever approval and favors you require. The timber industry is yet to be claimed, and I know of several abandoned ironworks that are available. Indeed, there is one just south of Dublin in the Wicklow Mountains."

*Wicklow*. The mention of Órla's mountains caught his attention. "Such a project as the ironworks may be of interest to me. First, let me plant. Once I'm established on my land, I will consider the other."

"Take heed. Do not allow too much time to elapse. You may have more cash now than most, but soon profiteers will have fortunes to rival yours, and such opportunities as I mention will be gone." Egerton set down his empty glass. "Will you stay and dine with me?"

"I would like that."

"Good, and you can tell me how Lady Olivia gets on. Scarce mentioned a word about herself in all those letters. Enjoyed them, you know. Her letters. Rather like herself, they were. Full of excitement. Remarkable woman, Lady Olivia. She was quite the beauty in her day, you know. Had a flock of admirers eager to pledge their troth, but she wouldn't have a one of them, and least of all me. Accepted an Irish earl, but the fellow died before the nuptials, and she never would consider anyone else after that. Poison, 'twas the rumor. A terrible business. Terrible business."

"I knew nothing of a betrothal," Garrett remarked. Lady Olivia had told him so much, yet she had never revealed much of herself. He'd always been aware of her beauty, and once or twice had asked why she'd never wed, but she'd never said a word about any Irish earl.

"Such a tragedy." Egerton shook his head.

*Tragedy*. Egerton didn't know the half of it. Lady Olivia had lost more than the young man she was to marry, and Garrett alone could imagine the depth of her pain. She had lost a future in Ireland, endured loneliness, raised another woman's son, and then bidden farewell when that child, grown to man, had embarked on the journey that might have been hers.

"Such an awful tragedy. All alone until your father's will. Suppose she must have been destined for other things. And, tell me, how about yourself? There's no Lady Neville on your arm. Do not suffer from a broken heart, or have an aversion to marriage, do you?"

Garrett laughed. "No broken heart, nor any particular aversion to marriage. 'Tis entrapment with a wife not of my choosing I do spurn." Or anything else for that matter which might have obligated his future in England. He'd been scrupulous to avoid ladies of good birth, and had sought his pleasure with women who posed no threat to his future. Nothing had been allowed to impede his ambition. His hearty appetite for bed-sports had been sated with seamstresses, ladies' maids, serving girls at the village tavern, butcher's daughters, brewer's wives, and courtesans, playful punks and jaded queans from London to Rome, but never with a gentle-bred lady.

"Fortune-hunting papas and scheming mamas tested your patience, did they? Suppose that comes with being an heir. But not to worry. You'll find no conspiring parents once you leave Dublin. Irish girls are sensual above measure. Uncommon winsome creatures, and they enjoy fleshly pursuits as much as any man. Mind, though, not to let Corbet and his cronies catch you, if you dally. That's another thing the Commissioners think needs ordering and set-tling. Fornication betwixt the races. Many a man has fallen under their spell, and whilst 'tis only the sol-diery who are fobidden by law from taking an Irish wife or mistress, the rest of us risk disapprobation or fall from grace. And in a land where bias and bribery rule, that can be a fate worse than the exe-cutioner."

# Chapter 3

"**O**ch, Mistress Eleanor, how my heart lightens to gaze upon these," spoke Father Netterville. With the sweep of one hand, he gestured at the books and manuscripts spread across the writing desk in Laragh's library. "Feiritéar. Your worthy sire, Sir Thomas. Céitinn. Mac Giolla Phádraig. They are with us in this room. Our patriot poets. To my shame, I had forgotten how remarkable was your father's library. 'Tis an immortal treasury, Mistress Eleanor."

Eleanor's smile was pensive. Nostalgia laced her voice. "You speak true, Father. They are here, every single one of them, for those of us who know for what to look, and how to listen."

The library was Eleanor's retreat at Laragh. She had always loved this dark, paneled room, where the air was heavy with oiled wood, ink, and leather, and where she had passed many an evening with her father. This library with its shelves reaching to the ceiling, and with books upon every shelf, had been her father's special place whilst the small parlor had been her mother's. This was where Sir Thomas had put his poems to paper, where he'd taught Eleanor about the ancient bards, and where she'd composed her first joyful lyrics under her father's

33

watchful eye. Sir Thomas had entertained Ireland's noblest poets in this room and had allowed his daughter to sit in the window alcove to harken their conversation, animated, robust, quick-witted, and flying back and forth from English to Irish to English.

"You must guard these manuscripts well, Mistress Eleanor. This conquered land is ruled by men who would delight in their destruction. Not many days apast, I heard a gentleman in Ossory mourn how none of these works had survived Cromwell's onslaught. It appears he was mistaken. Mayhap these are the last."

"Such rare manuscripts would fetch a substantial profit in Dublin, would they not?"

"To be sure, they would. Whilst the trade in published books is profitable, hand-scribed manuscripts such as these command even higher prices."

"By my faith, Father, 'tis most shameful to admit, but I have not the fortitude to sell them, no matter how dire our needs," Eleanor confessed. "To part with them would be like losing my father a second time. I could not bear to give them into the hands of persons who would not understand their worth."

Sir Thomas and the others had given not only their pens for Ireland, but their swords and their blood. She remembered the last time Piaras Feiritéar, the Kerry chieftain, had been to visit. That night the two landowners of Norman lineage, both poets, scholars, and warriors, had talked not of their latest compositions or literary acquisitions, but of their decision to resist the English and fight with the native Irish. From that night onward neither man had composed another of the classic Irish *dánta grádha*; instead of *courtly love verses*, they wrote of politics and the events sweeping Ireland. Eleanor would never forget Feiritéar's lamentation, *The barbarians are in the*

*beds of the Irish.* Nor would she forget how the decision made in this room that night had cost them
their lives; Sir Thomas had been executed last year
at Kilkenny, and Feiritéar, this year at Killarney.

"You need not summon the strength to sell them.
Indeed, you must not take them to Dublin, nor mention their existence nor whereabouts to anyone. To
do so would draw unwanted attention to your good
self and Laragh," was Father Netterville's advice.
The priest had come to Laragh at Eleanor's request
to inspect the condition of each printed volume in
Sir Thomas's library. Those of highest value were
being set aside for sale, and before inspecting the
next lot, he had helped Eleanor return the hand-
scribed manuscripts to their proper places upon the
shelves.

In addition to contemporary Irish poets, Sir Thomas's library boasted earlier Irish works, lays and
lyrics of the *Fianna* as well as lives of the Saints, monastic poems, and illuminated manuscripts. There
were published books of Doctor Donne, Machiavelli,
and Shakespeare, and by the dozens there were
pamphlets on various and sundry topics.

"Do these have any value?" Eleanor examined one
of the pamphlets. They satisfied the English appetite
for advice manuals on everything from warnings for
whoremongers to dream interpretation. "Father and
I used to laugh over these. *A Treatise of the Cumbers
and Troubles of Marriage,*" she read aloud a title. "*A
Godlie Forme of Householde Government.* Do you suppose English wives follow such admonitions to the
letter? Pray, listen, *the duty of the husband is to deal
with many men; and the duty of the wife's to talk with
few. The duty of the man is to be skillful in talk; of the
wife, to boast of silence.*"

The priest sighed. "Mayhap it is adherence to such
advice that accounts for the woeful state of affairs in

England. Whilst the value of their content is disput-
able, they are first editions, and should command
four or five times their original price.''

Eleanor looked at the growing stack of books.
Among them were two hand-scribed manuscripts,
illuminated by the monks of Glendalough. It was a
sorrowful thing she must do, for they had been
among her father's favorites, but there was no other
choice. They needed money to survive the coming
winter; the larder was near empty, and there was
little to barter hereabouts. On occasion supplies arrived at the Arklow quays to be had by those with
ready coin, and the sale of a few volumes might see
them through the winter. Eleanor's need for cash,
however, went beyond surviving the coming harsh
months. She had a plan to save Laragh; it was a
suitable strategy, but required money, and the good
priest had recommended a thousand pounds.

"So much?" Eleanor had asked, upon recovering
from her initial shock. It was a staggering sum. She
couldn't recall her father ever having that much coin
at once, not even in the days when Laragh was self-
sufficient, and they had traded wolfhounds and
wool for wines and spices, silks, and other luxuries
from the Continent and the East.

"Aye, *that much*. And even one thousand pounds
may not be sufficient," the priest had said. Eleanor
had found him posing as a blind harper in a village
south of Clara, and they had talked whilst sitting on
an outcrop above the Black Water, keeping watch all
the while for English dragoons. " 'Tis a sound plan
you devise, Mistress Eleanor, and the more coin at
your disposal the more greater will be your chances
for success.''

"It is not possible to save Laragh," Eleanor had
said, stricken. "My plans fails ere it begins, for I ken
no way to raise such an enormous sum.''

"There is one avenue to pursue. Sell some of your father's books. Nothing else commands such prices these days in Dublin, where the trade in books is brisk and lucrative. Dealers flood the coffeehouses, come from cities as far afield as Bremen and Prague. Even agents of the Swedish queen, Christina, bid at auction. A recent traveler through Carlow told of a Dutchman who spent three thousand pounds in a single day."

"Your counsel is appreciated, and I thank you for showing me the course I need to pursue. I will take books from my father's library to Dublin." Eleanor had made a pledge on her mother's grave to save Laragh, and she would see that pledge fulfilled.

Once before, the English army had passed so close to Laragh she'd heard their hymn singing as they marched into battle, so close she'd heard their screams mingling with cannonade across the ford at Seven Churches, where they'd fought the O'Tooles and O'Byrnes, and had lost. An O'Toole had even managed to steal Cromwell's horse during the fray, whereupon the Lord General's wrath upon the countryside had been merciless. By some miracle, Laragh had been spared.

This time, there would be no army. The enemy would be one man owning a powerful piece of paper, and there would be no miracle to save Laragh, only Eleanor and a large enough pile of ready coin to tempt that man to sell his debenture. If he wouldn't sell, Eleanor intended to bribe the precinct commissioner in charge of exemptions. Given how corrupt and greedy were the new English, one of those two individuals was bound to be seduced by a thousand pounds in ready cash.

Father Netterville selected the final book and added it to the pile. "You're certain you do not want company on your trip, Mistress Eleanor?"

"I would not put you at such risk." These days the price for a priest was the same price set for the head of a wolf, and hunters combed the hills and bogs eager to collect the bounty for flushing out priests who had defied the order to leave Ireland. Dublin was especially dangerous. *Terra Pacis*, Land of Peace, the Pale, as Dublin had been variously called over the centuries, had always been an English stronghold. These days it was a capital crime for any ecclesiastic to enter the city, to offer the Holy Sacrifice, or administer the sacraments. "You have already put yourself at peril in my behalf more than once. I could not ask for more."

"I do nothing except my duty. Now, you must let me help you wrap these." Father Netterville did not like to hear Mistress Eleanor speak as if he were doing anything extraordinary. Although many priests had left Ireland, many more had stayed. Like Peter Netterville, they refused to leave their people, and continued to serve their parishes as best they might, hiding in the hills and caves, always on the move, conducting Mass in secrecy, and venturing forth on missions of charity despite the hazard of arrest and execution. "In Dublin, you must seek a man by the name of Whalley. He conducts business on Skinner's Row at Dick's Coffee House."

"Whalley. Skinner's Row." Eleanor nodded. She had been to Dublin as a girl, and would find her way. "I will ask for him by name. Thank you."

In silence, they readied for travel the books and manuscripts with rags and string. Outside the night wind moaned. It was a low, steady wind, rattling the shutters and making the ancient trees creak. Always the night wind. Sooth, this land would not be Ireland without the night wind. All else might change, but each night when darkness fell over the countryside there would be the wind.

The bundles were secured, and Eleanor embraced Father Netterville as he prepared to leave. "Though you do not like it said, you are a true friend to stand by us as you do. If there is ever anything I might do in your behalf, you must not hesitate to ask."

"There is one thing. I have heard tell of an old thatcher, a native of Enniscorthy, who wanders the countryside in search of shelter. 'Tis said his master was evicted and he did not wish to serve the new one."

"I understand," Eleanor whispered. It was no thatcher of whom Father Netterville spoke but a Jesuit, mayhap, or a Franciscan or Capuchin in hiding. Usually such men could be found among the peasantry disguised as beggars, ploughmen, faggot dealers, or carpenters, and whosoever received them in his dwelling committed a capital crime. Eleanor knew what Father Netterville was asking of her, but she did not hesitate in her reply. "There is always shelter at Laragh. I would not turn away this thatcher, nor any other wanderer who knocked upon our door."

"Bless you, Mistress Eleanor. You have your mother's heart. And her courage. I do wish you a safe journey and good cess to yourself."

There was a scurry and a scuttle in the corridor as the three youngest Archebolds darted behind a decorative screen. They were out of sight none too soon. Not more than a few heartbeats passed before the library door opened and Eleanor exited with Father Netterville. The weans held their breath as the pair passed, and Eveleen was the first to speak once they had moved into the reception hall.

"What did you hear, Grace?" she whispered. "What were they discussing? Tell us."

"Eleanor is going to Dublin."

Eveleen groaned. "What did I tell you? Something has gone awry with the charm."

"Do you think we have done something wrong?" wondered Grace. "Forgotten some of the verse? Mayhap omitted a step?"

"It would seem that way, for I do not recall Biddy telling us anything about *Eleanor going* on a journey."

"At least *someone* is going on a journey," said Rory, who had already been blamed for leaving the valerian roots where one of the dogs had chewed them to useless, unrecognizable pulp.

Another groan issued forth from Eveleen.

Grace frowned. "I've told no one of what we've been doing. Exactly as Biddy O'Fierghraie instructed us. I've heeded her caution word for word."

"And myself as well," said Eveleen.

As if on cue, the girls turned their heads at once to gaze upon their brother. They each pinned the lad with a ferocious probing stare.

"Not fair," Rory protested. He knew what they were thinking. " 'Twas but a wee mistake I made with the valerian—"

"And with the salt when it was your turn to sprinkle it at the end of the lane. And with the bogbine, crushing it. And —" Grace was quick to remind him of his other mistakes.

"Honest mistakes, all of them," he retorted.

At this his sisters had the decency to relent. Rory might be young, and he might lack even the vaguest shard of any natural talent for casting love charms, but he was honorable.

"A setback or two is naught to be stopping us from trying anew, says I." Rory looked at his sisters with his ever hopeful smile. "What say you, Eveleen? Grace? We will start anew, yes? And this time we will get it right."

"Aye, Rory, we will start anew."

"But we'll make certain to say a little prayer as we do, asking the good Lord to delay any eligible bachelors from coming a-calling at Laragh whilst Eleanor is in Dublin."

Their sense of purpose as strong as ever, the three prepared to begin once more. Rory headed to the kitchen to replenish their salt supply; Eveleen hurried outside, across the lawn and down the hill to the lough, where she might find more bogbine before dusk gave way to night; and Grace proceeded upstairs to Eleanor's bedchamber, determined to locate every single pair of shoes, boots, or slippers belonging to her sister that they might be set in a row.

# Chapter 4

A single white blossom on the floor caught Eleanor's eye, and she bent to pick it up. Bogbine. She recognized the tiny star-shaped flower, and her brow knitted in concentration as she tried to discern how a lone bogbine blossom had found its way to her bedchamber.

She espied another one, a third, a fourth, another and another, and like a bird following a trail of crumbs, made her way along the path of tiny flowers to the tall clothes cupboard in the far corner. There the trail stopped. She turned round twice, but saw nothing more.

This was not the first time Eleanor had discovered a stray blossom in her private chamber but could not account for how it might be there. Curious, she opened the cupboard, aware of the familiar aromas that had been her mother's. Woodroof and lavender—not bogbine—and for a moment she imagined her mother was beside her. Stored in the cupboard was the gown Eleanor had worn to Baravore for her mother's funeral; it had belonged to her mother, who had been wont to scatter sweet-scented dried petals in her chest of drawers. Eleanor intended to wear the gown to Dublin, much for the same reason she had consented to wear it to her mother's funeral.

"You're not to be wearing black when you bid me farewell," her mother had instructed Eleanor. "And you're to make certain your sisters wear their better frocks."

"But —"

"I'll not be having my daughters looking like Puritans. I would hear your promise."

How cold her mother's flesh had been when Eleanor bent to kiss her cheek and seal her promise. "Aye, mother, I shall do as you wish. Do not vex yourself. We are the daughters of Sir Thomas Archebold, Lord of Laragh, poet, officer, and proprietor; we are the granddaughters of the O'Connor chieftain who defended Baravore against Ireton; and we will never look like Puritans."

"Well spoken, my daughter. Well spoken. Tell me, which of your frocks will you be wearing? What of your scarlet dancing dress? 'Tis your favorite, is it not?"

"Aye." The nostalgia in Eleanor's voice had been tempered by her more practical nature. Three years the scarlet gown with silver silk bodice had been at the bottom of her clothes chest. It had been that long since a suitable occasion to wear it, and even longer since Eleanor had had anything new. She had glanced at her day dress, its dimity faded from cockle blue to dull gray; its seams had been let out last summer, and its hem twice lengthened. "Aye, the scarlet is my favorite. Although it may not be fitting me quite as it used to."

Her mother had been unperturbed. "You will wear something of mine, then. Go to my chest, and let us decide together, as we used to do."

Long ago when Eleanor had been Eveleen's age, when her father and older brother, Ciarán, had been alive, in the time before Cromwell and Ireton, Eleanor's little world in the hills below the high Wicklow Mountains had been a different place. The Archebold family had celebrated the changing seasons with their neighbors, friends, and tenants; they had gathered to rejoice marriages and births. The Wicklow gentry had feasted at Christmas and on All Saints', reveled on May Day and Midsummer's Eve and Harvest Home. How well Eleanor treasured those memories of helping her mother select a gown for each occasion, watching as the maid had dressed her mother's hair, and being allowed to lift her mother's jewels from their velvet-lined boxes. This time it had been her mother who had watched and offered suggestions whilst Eleanor delved through the chest, holding up first one gown, then another.

"The emerald brocade. Aye, that is the one. With your coloring being like mine, the green will be perfect. Your father always said it made my eyes flicker with the enchanting light of a faery bog. *I'll not resist your charms, a chuisle mo chroí,* my Thomas would say to me. Our darling Grace was born some nine months after I wore it last. Och, I've been missing your father, I have." Her mother had sighed as if knowing the end was nigh and soon she would be with her Thomas again. "There will be someone for you, Eleanor. Fear not. One day someone for you, as your father and I had each other. There will be a steadfast and brave man, especially when you wear the emerald brocade. You promise to wear it often, do you not? 'Twill go well with your eyes, and there's no man who'll be turning away from a sight so fair, and the pulse of his heart ye'll be."

"I will have Grace and Eveleen and Rory and the household to occupy my time," Eleanor said. *And little time for emerald brocade or turning men's heads.*

As if reading the direction of Eleanor's mind, her

mother had added, "A loving man is always needed, and a woman always has time."

Her mother's words had made Eleanor think of Hugh MacMurrough. He had been Ciarán's friend, and part of her childhood, of the lost times. Indeed, the last night she had worn her scarlet gown, Hugh had flirted with her. He had even stolen a kiss. Now, like tens of thousands of Irish swordsmen he was exiled to the Continent; his choice had been military service on the Continent, or death, and he had chosen the Spanish army. Eleanor's fondness for Hugh hadn't been that of a maiden for a suitor, but he had been close and dear, and that he was among the many familiar faces never to be seen again was sorrowful. She had lost her father and both sets of grandparents, Ciarán, and a younger sister, cousins, and friends, and soon her mother would be gone. Eleanor did not think she could endure the pain that must surely attach itself to coming to care for anyone other than those who were already a part of her life; there would be more than enough pain in losing them. That was more than anyone should have to endure, and she would endure it, if need be, but that was all. She *would never allow* herself to care for anyone else. Eleanor had told her mother there would be no man because she had not the time; in truth, there would be no man for her because she would not allow it.

She closed the cupboard and glanced down at the bogbine blossoms in the palm of her hand. Most of life, she was discovering, had no rhyme or reason, and this latest riddle was just one more thing to fill her head with thoughts when she ought to be sleeping. Tomorrow, Eleanor would leave for Dublin, but with her mind being a-churn with bogbine, and green brocade gowns, and memories of her father and the other warrior-poets, it was useless to try to sleep. Instead, she made her way to her father's library.

She pulled a thin volume from the shelf. *The Green Woods of Laragh*. It was her favorite of the numerous verses she'd composed with her father. On her own, and to her father's delight, she had written *Blackberry-Flower*, *Long Dances in Moira's Garden*, and *Dreams Under a Quicken Tree*. But what was there to write of now? She dreamed no more. There were no long dances in the garden, Moira was dead, the blackberry bushes were withered, and there was little of the green woods that had escaped scorching by Cromwell's soldiers when they had been ordered to burn the fields and forests. Eleanor did not think she could ever write again.

Outside the wind howled. Shutters banged against the wall. A branch scratched against a windowpane.

Eleanor went to secure the shutters, and glancing into the darkness, saw a pale face framed in the black night. She opened the sash. "Nuala O'Byrne," she declared with evident excitement, though she did not raise her voice above a whisper. " 'Tis near two months gone since your last visit. Let me look upon you."

"Aye, Eleanor, it is myself," Nuala said in Irish. "Same as always. Though a bit more of a reed than a young lady ought to be. My curves are lost, I do fear, and those who once knew myself often pass by without a word of recognition. There's a price on my head, did you know? *Five pounds for the lad, Ned O'Byrne*, I'm told the handbill reads." She tried to make light of her situation. "There is some blessing, it would appear, in going to skin and bones, if it confuses the English and saves me from the hangman."

"You must be cold. *Tar asteac sa teanra. Fan tamall.*" Eleanor switched to Irish. *Come into the room. Stay awhile.* She understood the need for caution.

" 'Tis not possible to linger, though I do thank you most kind. The others wait for me in the orchard, then we must hasten to the pass at Mullacor, where we meet Liam and Cahir."

The others of whom Nuala spoke were her sisters. Isobel, Cait, and Aislinn. Liam and Cahir were her brothers. The last of the O'Byrnes of Aghavannagh. For more than four hundred years, indeed, from the first trespass the Anglo-Normans made into Leinster to claim the land for their own, O'Byrnes had been fighting the invaders. Theirs was an ancient family, large and powerful, and for centuries O'Byrnes had been a particular enemy of many an English commander. As numerous as the many pricks of a white-thorn there had always been an O'Byrne to pierce English pride, always until Cromwell, who had set aflame every single one of their fortresses and had ordered that the charred ruins be dismantled. Last year, the chieftain at Ballinacor had gone to Spain as had many other earls, landholders and their followers, but Nuala's brothers, Liam and Cahir, the O'Byrnes of Aghavannagh, had not left. They were in the hills with the tories, and the four sisters, having no home or haven on O'Byrne land, would not be parted from their brothers even if it meant going into the mountains.

"*Súil ar charaid an tsuilse,*" said Eleanor. *My eyes rest on a friend.* She leaned out the window to pull Nuala's hood closer round her face. Even though Nuala was less than a year younger than herself, and hardly in need of a mother, Eleanor couldn't stop herself. Once a slip of a girl, Nuala had blossomed into a lovely young woman, but now the child returned. Eleanor had a vision of her own brothers in the chapel at Baravore; while the mountains had aged Luke and Conall, they had robbed Nuala of her womanhood, and left instead a pale, raw-boned child of no particular age or sex. *"Bhfuil tú go maith?"* she asked. *Are you well?* "And Isobel? Cait? Aislinn? How do they fare?"

"Everyone is safe. We remain together, but needs be moving constantly to evade dragoons and hunting parties." Even though Nuala spoke Irish, she whispered as if the stars had ears. "It has been weeks since we were last near Laragh. Would that I might have come sooner to deliver these into your safekeeping." Nuala reached beneath her mantle, brought forth several sheets of paper, and thrust them through the window.

Eleanor accepted them, noticing that every bit of space on the top sheet had been written upon; no doubt the same was true for every other piece. She turned away from the window and went across the library to where a section of the paneled wall opened to a cabinet. Quick, she opened the cabinet, lifted down a large metal box, and having set the box upon a nearby table, unlatched and raised its lid.

Inside were four sheets of writing paper resting atop a richly bound book. Bronze clasps fashioned as birds held it closed, and in turn, this treasure sat upon a plump leather pouch; Eleanor lay Nuala's sheets on top. They were the latest entries in the *Annals of Finnén*, a historical chronicle that recorded the births and deaths, marriages, victories, accomplishments, and defeats of the people of Aghavannagh, of the Wicklow high hills and Leinster, and of Ireland.

The O'Byrnes of Aghavannagh were scribes and historians, and the stewardship of these annals had been passed down through generations, sons and daughters receiving equal instruction in its care and the art of scribing. The first entry in the bound book was dated 1399, while the earliest event recorded on the vellum pages kept in the leather pouch had occurred more than four hundred years before Strongbow and the Anglo-Normans had landed at Waterford. Nuala's father had been the last steward of the annals, and he had passed them into his eldest daughter's care.

That the O'Byrne chieftain of Aghavannagh might perish in battle had not been unexpected, but that Aghavannagh, hidden in the shadow of Croaghanmoira Mountain at the remote end of a glen called Farbreaga, might ever be destroyed had been unthinkable. But the inconceivable had happened, and now Eleanor kept the annals until such a time as Nuala might keep them once again. Neither young woman would allow the story of almost nine hundred years to be lost.

On her way back to the window, Eleanor paused at the writing table and took two blank sheets of paper and several quills from a drawer. She gave them to Nuala.

*"Taim buideac duitse,"* said Nuala. *I give you thanks.* "Tell me, now, you keep up with your writing, do you not?"

*"Mo léan,"* came Eleanor's reluctant admission. *"Alas,* I can't."

"Because the world round is laid low and oafs enter the homes of poets, and you say there is nothing in that about which to write."

*"A mhuire!"* Eleanor exclaimed on a whisper of astonishment and sorrow. *Oh, Mary!* In her grief, she invoked the Blessed Virgin. "You know."

"The same thoughts have been mine. Can you not imagine the difficulty and pain I endure to put pen to paper and record another death or loss, another execution? But I carry on and must tell you the reason why.

"Once there was a time when I too believed I could no longer write, and it was then I found myself, instead of writing, reading through the annals. They were not always in the care of my family, you know, but came to us from St. Finnén's Monastery at the edge of the Shillelagh wilderness. There is nothing there now; the church and its relic of the True Cross were destroyed by Richard II's army more than two hundred years afore. Were it not for the annals, we would have no record of that holy house, nor of the dense wilderness that once covered these mountains, so thick of leaf and underwood the sun did not reach the forest floor; we would have no record of the cruelty the English Richard inflicted upon the women and children of Leinster in the summer of 1399. Do you not see?" Nuala looked at Eleanor and implored, "You must try to understand.

"The people of these hills are born and pass on, yet the annal endures. Time and again the strangers in our land do their worst to conquer us, yet the annal endures. If we fail in all else, our words put to paper remain; they will be the evidence, the truth we leave behind, and with such a legacy there can be no such thing as failure. You must try again, Eleanor. And remember that poems of dancing and feasting, of bells calling us to Mass and plentiful harvests, are a reflection of other days. What you write now should not be of times past, but a mirror of the true world about you."

"I will endeavor." Eleanor leaned out the window to embrace Nuala. "Do not leave right away. Wait." She hastened to fetch a few handfuls of beans from the larder. It was the most she could spare with ten mouths to feed at Laragh, not to mention the people coming to the door. Sometimes they came to share, and sometimes to ask for a wee bit of help, although they knew the landlord's family had not much more than they.

"Will you and the others come to Laragh for the winter? We would like your company, and surely Liam and Cahir would be at ease to know you were warm and sheltered."

"You are too generous. Do you dare forget there is a price on each of our heads?"

"Didn't you say they search for lads? Pass the winter here with us, Nuala, you and your sisters, and be girls again. No one will know."

For a moment, it seemed Nuala smiled. "I will tell them of your offer, and we will decide together."

"That is fair."

"*Slán agat,*" Nuala bade Eleanor farewell.

"*Slán leat,*" was Eleanor's proper reply to one who was departing.

Nuala disappeared into the night, her footfall on dried leaves swallowed by the wind.

Eleanor secured the window and shutters, then went to the cabinet behind the paneled wall from which she removed the large metal box. She carried it to the writing desk, sat down, took out the *Annals of Finnén*, and began to skim the entries.

*A.D. 831, Muireen, princess of Leinster, abbess of Kildare, and sister of Fínnechta, king of Leinster, dies. At Arklow . . . a large Viking fleet anchors. Also in this year . . . a solar eclipse, and a storm of lightning accompanied by a rain of blood . . . a great wind lifts wooden churches from their foundations. 917, Battle of Cenn Fuait, near St. Mullins . . . the Bishop of Leinster and 600 others were slain by Vikings . . . A.D. 1030, Flann, abbot of Glendalough, dies whilst on pilgrimage at Clonmacnoise . . . A.D. 1097, An abundance of acorns choke the streams in this Year of Fair Nuts. . . . A.D. 1119, A relic of the*

*True Cross is given this year into the custody of St.
Finnén's Monastery at the edge of the wood called
Shillelagh . . . A.D. 1152, Diarmait Mac Murchada
abducts Derbforgaill, daughter of Ua Máel Sech-
lainn, and wife of Tighernán Ua Ruairc. . . .*

*A.D. 1170, Anglo-Normans capture Waterford,
Dublin, and Ossory . . . A.D. 1171, Diarmait Mac
Murchada, king of Leinster, dies at Ferns . . . is succeeded by his son-in-law, the Anglo-Norman
Strongbow, Richard de Clare. . . . A.D. 1290, Queen
Eleanor establishes a royal forest at Newcastle
McKynegan from which timber was taken for her
castle in Haverford, Wales. . . . A.D. 1398, English
soldiery burns the monastic settlement at Glendalough. . . . A.D. 1407, Rian O'Byrne, son of Ronan,
and grandson of Cathal, is this year affirmed as
chieftain of the O'Byrnes of Aghavannagh.*

*A.D. 1540, The child Órla, granddaughter of the
O'Toole chieftain of Castlekevin, is taken. . . . A.D.
1542, An infant boy is stolen from the O'Byrnes,
and the noble line of descent from the firstborn son
of Rian O'Byrne, son of Ronan, chieftain of Aghavannagh, was ended. Mayhap not English, but faeries
took the child. All this summer and harvest time the
hills are full alive with stories of faeries carrying off
mortal babes, many a child having disappeared. . . .*

*A.D. 1581, O'Byrne fortress at Ballinacor is burned
by the English . . . A.D. 1641, The English outlaw-
ries list Phelim O'Byrne and his sons, nephews,
cousins, and kin, plus the noble names of Archebold,
Cavanagh, Clare, O'Connor, MacMurrough and
Lawless . . . A.D. 1653, Fever sweeps the countryside
claiming many lives, and in August, Moira ní*

*O'Connor, Lady Archebold of Laragh, is buried at Baravore.*

Nuala was right.

Eleanor must at least try to continue writing her poems, for they were as valuable a means to preserve truth as were the annals.

What if the annals were somehow lost, or did not survive? If such an unspeakable disaster were to occur, there might be no memory. And without memory there would be no past for the generations of Irish children to come, no path between past and present, no way to the future.

# Chapter 5

"**M**aster Petty, what business have you found for me this night?" Garrett remarked to the agent Lord Egerton had recommended to him. As had become their custom since he'd engaged Edwin Petty to seek out soldiers wishing to sell their land debentures, the two men met each evening at a coffeehouse on Skinner's Row. This night the public room was crowded with the regulars who gathered for light refreshment and conversation.

"Only one, sir, but it will please you well." Petty motioned the soldier to present himself before Garrett. "Fletcher, wasn't it? Step up here."

"Aye, Titus Fletcher is my name, your lordship."

"Do you come before us of your own free will, Titus Fletcher?" Garrett inquired.

"I do, my lord." The soldier held forth a piece of paper.

Garrett took the paper. It was the debenture, which had been issued to Fletcher in payment for his arrears, and Garrett scanned the specifics. Fletcher had been in the service of the Army of the Commons longer than other soldiers, making his allotment no mere parcel, but a noteworthy holding. Garrett nodded in satisfaction, then signaled to Master Petty, who set two leather pouches on the table along with another piece of paper. "Do you read, Fletcher?"

"Nay, my lord." Titus Fletcher did not look at Garrett. His regard was fixed upon the plump pouches.

It was the same even when a single pouch was displayed. While the prospect of landownership had been sufficient to appease the discontented, unpaid army, instant possession of ready coin was much more attractive for a man whose life before military service had been a constant battle between paupery and meager subsistence.

"Allow me to explain the legalities of the business we conduct this night," Garrett began, although he knew Fletcher was not paying heed to what he said. No doubt his thoughts focused on the countless gadgets and commodities, the rents, the foodstuffs, the apparel and horseflesh heretofore beyond his means. Or if he'd left a wife and children in England, mayhap, he was anticipating a homecoming whereupon he might deliver such a ransom to his family rather than send a clod of dirt from Ireland with no more than the promise of reunion, if he planted well and was successful on his new-owned land. "This legal document conveys one man's rights to another. At this moment, your debenture is your right to the parcel of land referenced therein, but you may transfer that right to me through fair sale. Once the paper is executed by our signatures, and there is an exchange of coin for debenture, the transaction is completed, such a sale being an irrevocable alienation of your right to the land in question. Do you understand?"

"I can't change my mind. Is that what you're saying, my lord?"

"Precisely."

"Not to worry none, your lordship." Titus Fletcher took a quill from Master Petty and put his mark to the legal document. "I'll be leaving Ireland on the next tide and never looking back."

Garrett added his signature. Master Petty served as witness.

" 'Tis done?" the soldier inquired.

"Aye, that's the whole of it. The money is now yours, the debenture and the right entailed therein are mine, and I thank you."

Titus Fletcher mumbled a quick reply, snatched up his money, and hurried from the coffeehouse.

"Another commendable night's work. I am more than satisfied with this latest acquisition." Lord Egerton had been correct; Edwin Petty was well acquainted with persons in all quarters of the town, and it hadn't taken long for Garrett to acquire numerous entitlements, some of which he'd retained, others which he'd already traded to the purpose of amassing one large holding. As for Edwin Petty, who received a three percent commission on each transaction, he was becoming a rich man.

"Two additional debentures have come to my attention. They are, like this one, for landholdings in the specific area in which you've expressed interest."

"Do we know who possesses them?"

"Aye, I did meet the men earlier this afternoon on Wood Quay."

"They're willing to sell?"

"Not yet. But come morn, when they learn four of their former comrades are returning to England with more coin than a prosperous brewer might save in a lifetime, they'll no doubt reconsider the benefit of planting in countryside infested with tories and bogtrotters. You're not worried about the rebels, Sir Garrett?"

Edwin Petty knew nothing of Garrett's ancestry,

nor of his motivations. No one but Lady Olivia knew his secret, and he was considering an appropriate reply when a glimpse of black curls tumbling over green brocade distracted him. His attention shifted to the far side of the coffeehouse, where a man and woman were exiting a private room. Garrett recognized the porcine man by name and reputation. Joseph Whalley was a usurer who dabbled in book trading and pawnbroking, and pity to the poor soul reduced to doing business with him; Whalley's interest rates were those of a pirate, and he owned the deplorable habit of fleecing, cozening, and otherwise stealing legacies from the desperate and destitute.

Whalley was grinning. Indeed, even at this distance, Garrett imagined a glimmer in those beady eyes, for his expression bespoke much satisfaction, and by the look of the woman in his company, Garrett ventured it was not Whalley's regular business that had been transacted in the private room this night. The usurer draped the woman's mantle round her shoulders, but not before Garrett had had a good look at her gown. Made of rich green brocade, elegant, expensive, and stitched to flatter the female form, it was not the sort of gown a right-minded Puritan would wear.

"Trow, are you interested?" inquired Master Petty, always vigilant to his employer's every need. "They say she is young, and fair of face, with no mark of the pox."

"Nay, not this night." Garrett frowned. The woman might be as comely as the goddess Aphrodite, but he didn't favor the notion of being second after Whalley.

"You can afford her, of a certainty."

"While 'tis true, it does not —" Garrett began to reiterate his disinterest when the woman turned, giving him an unobstructed view of a startlingly beautiful face framed by glossy midnight curls, and whatever else he'd intended to say was forgotten. She radiated a freshness the high-priced courtesans of London and Antwerp lacked, a subtle yet simmering sensuality he did not often encounter. She had the sweet face of an angel, but the full, inviting form of a woman. There was nothing Garrett appreciated more than female pulchritude, and it was a pleasure to gaze upon such loveliness, such enticing charms, and upon something more elusive. There was about this woman a certain fragility Garrett found appealing. Desire stirred within him. It would be a unique indulgence to pass a few hours with a whore who had not lost touch with the woman she'd been before taking to backsliding.

"Me thinks you may have denied in haste, Sir Garrett. Would you like me to approach her in your behalf?"

"Aye, if you would." It was an impulsive reply, mayhap one to be regretted on the morrow, but that was often the way of the flesh. Garrett set another pouch of coins atop the table.

Master Petty crossed the room. He gave a perfunctory bow to the pair, addressed the woman, and motioned toward Garrett.

Joseph Whalley burst into coarse laughter.

The woman pulled up her mantle hood, and without offering a reply to Master Petty, or a parting word to Joseph Whalley, she walked away from them. Neither did she acknowledge Garrett, but went straight toward the door.

Turned down by a whore. Now, that was something new. Garrett reached to retrieve the pouch, but his hand halted mid-motion when she turned from her path toward the coffeehouse exit and came instead toward him. Renewed desire coiled through him. Could this be part of her play? That despite the youth he'd glimpsed upon her features, she was a woman with much experience in the ways of luring and pleasing men. Garrett's regard did not stray from her; closer she came, softly as if she were floating, so slowly he held his breath in anticipation that was almost unbearable. Then she stood before the table, and he found himself gazing upon eyes as green as the faraway glen of cradle-tales. Something jolted within him, a memory, mayhap, or an association, he knew not what precisely, and for the space of a heartbeat he was standing at the edge of a bright bog where hawthorns shuddered.

With neither a word, nor even a silent nod of acknowledgment, the woman took the pouch. She slipped it beneath her mantle and turned to leave the coffeehouse.

Garrett followed her into the night.

Eleanor's humiliation was complete. Soon it would be absolute.

Since arriving in Dublin she had been threatened, insulted, propositioned, cheated, and disgraced. She was a failure. The loathsome Joseph Whalley had not paid even a third of what Father Netterville had told her the precious volumes from her father's library were worth.

Over the stinging memory of Joseph Whalley's mocking laughter, she heard the man's footsteps following her down Skinner's Row. Tears stung her eyes, but she did not cry. That someone would think Eleanor Archebold of Laragh was a trollop defied every notion she held of the world and herself. It was appalling, incredible, but no more so than her acceptance of his offer, and what she intended this night.

Her initial reaction had been automatic. She had not thought twice when she had turned to leave the coffeehouse without dignifying the man with a nay-word. He was *one of them*. An Englishman, a speculator and profiteer as despicable as the predatory Joseph Whalley. It had been obvious to Eleanor that he'd been buying debentures, or more accurately, stealing land he'd no right to claim, no matter how many pouches of coin he might offer. It was unthinkable that Eleanor Archebold would stoop to accept such a low proposition, and certainly not one from a man who revolted her as much as did Joseph Whalley.

But with each step toward the coffeehouse exit, each step, as it were, closer to home, Eleanor had found herself reconsidering the proposition. She could not return to Laragh with anything less than the full amount of funds she'd intended to raise. Upon her mind's canvas she saw Rory and Eveleen and Grace waving farewell when she'd set off for Dublin; she thought of the Cavanagh children, who slept in the pantry on pallets, of her brothers and every tory, who risked their lives in defiance of the English, she thought of Nuala and her sisters, and of Biddy O'Fierghraie and the others who were already weary and stretched to their limits. Many of them were not strong enough to survive the journey into Connaught, let alone the future that awaited the dispossessed in that bleak, rocky land to the west.

Eleanor had sworn on her mother's grave to do *anything* to save Laragh, and if it meant *this*, so be it. It was *her choice* to turn away from the door and take the offered money. This Englishman's purse was much heavier than the one from Joseph Whalley, and selling her virtue to this Englishman was the "anything" she must do to save Laragh.

*Besides, what difference did it make if she sold her virginity to a stranger?* an inner voice taunted. All the young men she knew were exiled or dead or gone into the hills; no suitors waited for her at home. There was no more dancing in the garden. She had no future as a bride. Sooth, without the money she could earn this night, there might be no future at all.

The great bell of Christchurch Cathedral marked the hour. Two beadles patrolled the dark lane, rapping upon doors where householders had neglected to hang a blazing lantern outside their dwelling as required by city ordinance. Soon the streets would be deserted.

"Mistress, will you not slow your pace to walk with me?"

Eleanor forced herself to pause. His voice was refined, educated, and he did not infuse his speech with *thy* and *thou*. That much, at least, confirmed he was a gentleman, and she dared to hope that as a gentleman he would be clean and possess some measure of civility. She attended his approaching footfall; with such a firm, even cadence, he must be a large man, and her heart began to race. He had almost reached her, and the reality of what she had agreed to do made her tremble. It would be quick, she tried to calm herself. No more than a matter of hours, mayhap a few minutes, for she'd heard it could be as fast as that with some men—and by this time tomorrow she'd be halfway home, with sufficient funds to save Laragh.

He walked in front of her and stopped; silence closed round them as his final footsteps faded into the night. Eleanor took a deep breath, and peeking from beneath lowered lashes, she saw the silhouette of a tall man, who was wearing not the plain black felt hat favored by Puritans, but a graceful, plumed Cavalier hat. A second peek, more of a lingering glance, revealed broad shoulders—confirmation that he was, indeed, a striking large man. In the dim light, she could not see his face beneath the hat, but she sensed he was staring down at her.

" 'Tis glad I am you accept my proposition, mistress, for what I saw in the coffeehouse enticed me greatly."

His voice was rough, deep, but the way each word seemed to melt one into the other had a liquid quality Eleanor did not associate with Englishmen, and she quivered no less at the rhythm of his words than at what he had said. *Enticed me greatly.* Another quiver darted through her. She trembled, confused. He was one of them. A stranger. The enemy. It must be fear and loathing that made her react this way.

"Pray, sweet mistress, do not be shy." His murmur fell low, and when he stepped toward Eleanor the scents of sandalwood and tobacco wafted round her, filling her senses. There was another aroma she did not recognize; it seemed exotic, foreign, like spices from the Holy Land, and the rich, sharp perfume made her head swim. Closer he moved, closer until his body brushed against hers.

"Look up at me, if you please," he murmured. "Allow me to see more close what I own this night."

... *What I own this night.* His deep whisper repeated itself in her head, a dizzying, sensual dance she did not understand. ... *what I own this night.* He was too close. There was not enough air, each breath drowned her in sandalwood.

"Look up at me," he murmured a second time.

She raised her face, hoping for a breath of fresh air, hoping that she might see him, and mayhap understand what was happening.

He grinned down at her. "My thanks, sweet mistress. To sport with a biddable woman is always a pleasure, but with one as sweet as yourself 'twill be no less than an unexpected treasure." He doffed his hat in an affectation of a playful courtesy, then set it back on his head at a jaunty angle that revealed a bold, handsome face.

His manly features and brash nature were a potent mix of charm, and Eleanor's dizziness worsened. She had grown up surrounded by vigorous, good-looking men aplenty, and was accustomed to hard men whose rugged, oft-scarred features bespoke virility. The Irish were a fiercely attractive race, but she had never seen a man who possessed such a dark male presence as this Englishman who had paid for her, and who stood too close to her in this deserted, shadowy lane. Faith, he was compelling, with a full mouth, and hooded eyes. His high cheekbones, strong nose, and sculpted jaw, his heavy brows and golden brown skin, were dangerous handsome. He was sensual in a way that was as masculine as it was beautiful, and Eleanor couldn't stop staring up at him, nor could she resist when he propelled her backward with his thighs, his chest, until she was pressed flat against a wicker wall.

Of a sudden, his grin faded, his hands rose to cup her face. They were warm, his hands, large and gentle, and Eleanor drew in her breath when his fingertips brushed along her jaw. She dared not exhale as the pads of his thumbs made tiny circles at the corners of her mouth. He was caressing her. No other word could define the way his fingers skimmed across her cheeks, along her brow, down the slope of her nose. He outlined her mouth, and had scarce gone round once when her lips parted to his touch.

Eleanor blinked up at him as amazed by his tender touch as she was by her reaction to him. She tilted her head to one side, and his mouth closed over hers in a kiss that was nothing like the youthful kiss Hugh MacMurrough had stolen behind the screen in her parent's banqueting hall. This was a man's kiss, demanding and hard, and she did not tremble in reaction to it. She quaked. The Englishman's body enveloped hers, his muscular arms enfolded her, his chest and thighs molded to her; he held her as if they might be one, leaning into her, pulling her to him.

Eleanor sensed all of it, every ripple, every muscle, every hardened sinew, and though she had never experienced anything like this before, she knew the bulge pressed against her woman's place was his swollen man-sword. Eleanor's mother had told her how a man's parts became enlarged with his desire to couple, and Lady Moira had assured Eleanor that when love flowered between a man and a woman there could be great pleasure in coupling her woman's place with a man-sword. Her mother had described how a woman's body readied for such a coupling; she had spoken of melting sensations, a quickening, a flowing moisture, and she had assured Eleanor, "You will know when it happens, my daughter."

The Englishman pressed his swollen man-sword against her. It mattered not that several layers of fabric were between his flesh and hers, his touch was like liquid fire. There was a quickening in Eleanor's blood. She grasped his shoulders to control her trembling, but it worsened, and she knew—to her shame—'twas not fear that caused such quivering.

"Let me rock into your woman's cradle, let me sense how the fit will be between us," he murmured.

There was no affection between herself and this man. Eleanor did not even know his name, yet the sensations swirling through her were most pleasant. Indeed, they beguiled her, and she did as he asked. She parted her legs to him, finding it was most pleasurable when he rocked into her. A tiny, breathless moan escaped her.

By the tears of the martyrs, her humiliation was

going to be thorough and unforgettable. This man had stripped Eleanor of every vestige of dignity; he had stolen her very control. Eleanor tilted her hips to meet his male parts, and silent cursed him for the thief and predator he was. She was melting, throbbing, and floating in dizzying circles all at once.

At least, it was only her body. Praise the angels and archangels, it was not her mind or heart she could not control.

At least, she would never have to see him again once their business was done.

*No one else would ever know her shameful humiliation this night, and when she went home to Laragh she could forget any of this ever happened.*

# Chapter 6

"**M**istress, your eagerness is potent. This interlude promises to satisfy my appetites beyond expectation," Garrett whispered against her soft lips. It was no wonder she could afford brocade gowns. "Put your arms about my neck."

She raised her arms, shifted slightly, and a dart of lantern light fell across her eyes to reveal not only arousal, but unguarded astonishment. This fast-rising passion between them was spontaneous, not play-acted. Garrett grinned, a little wicked, a little knowing. She returned his smile, somewhat shy, somewhat beckoning. Desire thickened his voice. "I want you to kiss me."

She rose on tiptoe until her lips brushed his, so smooth, delicious, and he felt himself harden even more. She was his for the night, his with whom he might fulfill his every desire, and the possibilities enflamed him. "Will you do as I ask of you, mistress?"

She nodded.

"Let me hear your answer."

"Aye," she whispered.

"You will do all that I ask of you?"

"I will do all that you ask of me."

He heard the quiver of passion in her voice. He

66

needed more of her, and fast. His hold on her tightened, and he growled, "Kiss me deep and hard as I kissed you. Deep. Inside. As a man goes within a woman."

Her tongue flickered along his lower lip, the warm moist tip teasing, tasting. Garrett groaned. He could not wait for her kiss, and thrust his tongue into her mouth, probing, stroking.

When he'd followed her out into the night, he had assumed he would take his pleasure in one of the alleys off Skinner's Row. It wouldn't be the first time for such a hasty out-of-doors tryst; it was not only paying customers lingering with pretty quearns who enjoyed such profligate delights. Many a maidenhead had been pricked in a pristine garden; many a husband might blame his own boxwood maze for his being a cuckold; many a noblewoman, her identity protected behind a velvet mask, had wandered the back alleys of Paris or London in search of a few moments ecstasy with a stranger.

Now Garrett did not think such a quick encounter would suffice with this woman. He wanted her behind the closed door of his private chamber; he wanted her beneath him through the night, matching him, and doing all that he would ask of her.

"Come with me to my lodgings, mistress mine. I'll make it well worth your while. Does two pouches of coin entice?" It was a ridiculous offer. Far too much money for a whore, who probably would come anyway, if he led the way, but he did not want to leave anything to chance. Garrett never depended on luck or the vagaries of fate; he had always endeavored to conduct himself with purpose and logic. It was said that Sir Garrett Neville, Baron Aylesbury, had never embarked upon a course of action he did not achieve; indeed, it was a matter of pride, although he was loath to admit it even to himself, for he didn't consider himself a vain man otherwise. Garrett had never risked failure. "Bide with me until dawn, mistress, and there will be a third pouch for you."

Eleanor reeled. Had she heard correct? Was he offering her another pouch to accompany him to his lodgings? And a third to stay the night? Could it be this easy? A vision of Laragh tumbled through her mind. She recalled the near-to-empty larder; she saw the people when they had come with no offering to lay at her feet save the promise of honest labor from their good hands. Daily the situation worsened. In another fortnight or two, it would be desperate.

"Aye, milord," she agreed to his conditions. " 'Til dawn at your lodgings for three pouches."

Once more his lips claimed hers, hard, demanding.

Once more a swirl of sensations whirled round Eleanor, making her light-headed, dizzy. An unfamiliar emptiness, an urgent need was spreading through her, and she closed her eyes as if to deny this, as if to stop it, but there was no controlling any of it, no making it go away. Indeed, it seemed as if she were melting into him, as if this alone might assuage her, save her. Eleanor heard herself sigh, sensed herself welcome the thrust of his tongue, the rocking of his hips. No man had ever aroused such sensations in her. She remembered her father's battle-honed strength, and how he'd embraced her in greeting; she had always experienced security and comfort in his arms, but this was different. This was far from safe, far from comforting. This was reckless.

"That's right," she heard the Englishman say. "Keep pace with me. Stay with me, sweet mistress mine. Come with me."

Next, she heard, "The devil take it! What happens here?"

He said something more, but it was not clear to Eleanor. His words were fading in and out. Of a sudden, her knees were weakening, her legs were unable to support her, and she clutched at him, but it was too late.

Garrett swore a string of oaths.

The woman had fainted in his arms.

Eleanor nestled deeper into the featherbed. Soon her maid would enter to pull back the window hangings; the morning sun would fill her chamber, and the pair of linnets in their wicker cage would start to sing. But for now she wanted nothing more than the simple comfort of resting one's cheek against such fine, fresh bedlinens, soft as silk. Eleanor sighed. From afar came the lovely music of her mother's humming, and the memory of Lady Moira sitting cross-legged on the bed, sipping morning chocolate and talking of the future.

"Pray, daughter, what manner of man do you wish to wed?"

It was a question her mother had asked a hundred thousand times, and Eleanor had never faltered in her response.

"I would have a husband who is steadfast and brave, tender yet strong. I would have a horseman, a poet, and a warrior."

"Is that the whole of what you desire?" Lady Moira had always asked, knowing full well Eleanor had not finished.

"I would have a man who might risk his life for mine as did Bran O'Connor for his Aislinn." As a wee girl Eleanor had dreamed of marrying her ancestor, that long ago chieftain of Baravore, who had defied fate and death to rescue his beloved Aislinn when the English held her hostage in Dublin town.

No one but an Irishman like Bran O'Connor would suffice for Eleanor Archebold.

Eleanor sighed, and breathing deep, she caught an unexpected scent. It was masculine, sharp. Sandalwood, mayhap, or something else? Who might be in her chamber? She opened her eyes, and encountered the chill of reality.

This was not home. This wasn't her featherbed. The furnishings of wainscot and heavy walnut were unfamiliar. Neither was it morning. Candles flickered throughout the chamber, and the greatest single source of illumination was a fire before which a man was standing. Eleanor did not need to look twice to recognize the tall, lean form, and the strong, masculine features in profile. It was the stranger, the Englishman who would own her until dawn.

She tried to recall everything that had happened since she'd made her decision in the coffeehouse, but her memory was foggy. Too foggy.

One question required an answer: Was *it* done?

"Sir?" she managed to speak.

Garrett glanced over his shoulder.

"What has happened?" Her voice was no more than the breath of a whisper.

"You fainted."

*Fainted.* Eleanor did not know whether to laugh or scream. *Fainted.* Then *it* was not done, and she had failed in this as well.

"These are my lodgings in High Street," Garrett said, restrained and tactful that he might ease her confusion. She was beautiful, sensual, and sweet; beguiling enough to have blinded even a man of his experience to reality. Her charade had been near perfect. She had almost succeeded. He frowned. "When was the last time you ate?"

"Ate?" Eleanor could not gather her thoughts to remember. Faith, she could think of nothing beyond her multiple failures this night, and the dreadful prospect of returning home empty-handed.

Garrett took a wooden bowl from the chimney-piece, and went to sit on the edge of the bed. He held a spoon to her lips. "Come, you must eat. This is warm yet."

A beefy, salty aroma assailed Eleanor. Nausea wambled in her stomach. She shook her head. "No, thank you, sir." Solemn, she added, "By the by, I do not intend to take your money."

"It is yours," he said, touched by the dignity in her voice.

She forced herself to sit straighter. "Then I would fulfill our bargain, sir."

He studied her face, the clear, wide eyes, the luscious mouth slightly red, slightly swollen from his kisses. She was as pale as the moon, and though he sensed her fear, he saw naught but courage.

*A perfect sacrificial virgin.* Of a sudden, the whole of this night seemed to Garrett some macabre theater. He set aside the bowl, and spoke, "You are new to this particular commerce."

"Aye," Eleanor whispered. She lowered her lashes. To confess such a thing to this Englishman—this profiteer and thief—should not matter, yet somehow it was the crowning blow to her humiliation. This stranger knew her worst secret, and yet he knew nothing about her. She wanted to tell him she had been a good daughter, chaste and obedient, a devoted sister, generous hostess, and dependable neighbor; she wanted to assure him she possessed an admirable knowledge of the skills a lady required to run a large estate; she wanted him to know she had been educated in four languages, could play several musical instruments, was an accomplished horsewoman and poet, and that for the past three years had taught reading and writing to any child who wished to sit at her feet. Her lower lip trembled. She held it steady between her teeth. There was a burning sensation in her eyes.

Garrett raked his fingers through his hair. *Hell's scorched bones*, he had a definite aversion to women and tears. "Here, now, you must not weep," he said.

She raised her face to his, tilted her chin upward. "I never weep," she declared, in a voice that dared the world to prove otherwise. "And I would fulfill our bargain, sir."

He said nothing, her words tumbling through his head, taunting him, beguiling. *I would fulfill our bargain, sir*. It was a mighty temptation, and for a moment, he considered how easy it would be to take up where they'd left off. She was the kind of woman who would give as much as she took, a woman willing to surrender one moment, take control in the next. She was the kind of woman men spent their lives remembering and regretting.

"I would do anything you asked. Anything."

That sweet, trembling voice tugged at Garrett. She was lovely, and to be sure, he still wanted her, but it was not to be. Garrett had never taken his pleasure with a gentle-bred lady, never with a maiden, and that would not change tonight.

"You are obviously a lady, and whatever brought you to accept my proposal, I would not abuse to my advantage," he said with utmost sincerity. What could be so compelling that she would barter the one commodity most women valued above all else? He thought of the myriad parents in England who would have him standing at the altar, if she were their daughter. "You must take the one pouch, for you have come to my lodgings as I requested. 'Tis only fair. I have occupied your time. Please." He held forth a pouch. "You must."

"I *must*?" Eleanor pushed his hand away. The

pouch fell to the bed, its contents spilling across the blankets, and she stared at the abundance of rix dollars, ducatoons, and Portugal royals. She forced herself not to seize the gold and silver coins, forced herself to look away as if they were of no consequence. "I do not take charity."

Garrett scowled. "But you sell your body to a stranger," he retorted. She needed someone to protect her. A lady should have someone watching over her, caring for her. He gentled his voice to try again. "Consider it a gift from a gentleman to a lady."

"No, thank you."

Her polite refusal provoked him. "You reject my gift, but would spread your thighs—"

Eleanor slapped him. " '*Tianam 'on diabhal.*"

He grabbed her wrist. Lady Olivia's instruction in the Irish language had been thorough, and he understood with no trouble. *Your soul to the devil.* Garrett didn't like being cursed, and tightening his hold on her, he said, "Guard your tongue, mistress. 'Tis certain your lady-mother must have schooled you better."

"Do not speak of my mother." Bitterness sharpened her words. "You know nothing of my family. Sooth, you own little knowledge of anything, it would appear. 'Tis obvious you are no soldier, and thus know nothing of war. 'Tis obvious you are no Irishman, and thus know nothing of Ireland. 'Tis obvious you are a rich man, and know nothing of want." Her pain was a raw, open wound, and she directed her anger at him. "I have heard it said most rich men attain their fortunes by the suffering of others. Pray, what manner of man does that make you, sirrah?"

"And what manner of lady durst insult the gentleman?" He gave a jerk to her wrist, and pulled her off the nest of pillows, bringing her toward him until their lips were almost touching. Their breaths mingled. He saw light flash in her lush green eyes, heard her sharp intake of breath, and he smiled, not in joy, but more a knowing, assured grin. Despite the contemptuous words, she wasn't immune to him. "I have shown you naught but kindness, have I not? Yet you deal me insolence."

"Kindness!" she spat back. "Kindness from the likes of you! 'Tis not insolence I dispense, but truth. I do dare— I dare—" but she could not remember what she intended to say. Frustration overcame her. "I do dare to wonder if you are a man at all." The words had barely spewed forth when Eleanor knew she'd gone too far.

"Oh, I am a man in every way, and well you know it, mistress," he drawled, allowing his mouth to brush against the corner of hers, then he pulled back. He stared down at her parted lips, saw red suffusing the cream of her cheeks, and watched a convulsive swallow move down the slender column of her neck. He grinned as before. Aye, making love with her would be exquisite, explosive, memorable. Aye, she was the kind of woman men never forgot.

Garrett stared a moment longer before releasing her wrist. He stood to snuff out the candles throughout the chamber, and when that was done, he returned to the bed. She was watching him like a little hedgepig that hid quills beneath a tempting coat of fur.

"Go to sleep." He eased his tall frame onto the space beside her, crossed his legs at the ankles, supported his head on folded arms, and closed his eyes, trying as he did to pretend he didn't see Órla's bright glen, trying to pretend none of this bothered him. "Go to sleep," he said, as much for his own benefit as for hers, trying to pretend it would be easy to forget.

\* \* \*

She was gone when Garrett awakened.

The first light of dawn seeped through the shutters, and he noticed the three pouches of coin he'd left on the oak chest were gone as well. Those pouches were, however, the only thing to which she was welcomed, and he rose to determine whether she had helped herself to anything more.

The pair of black hide saddlebags was where he had left them. The debentures remained inside. Safe. Untouched.

It was early yet, and he lay back down, but could not sleep. Lavender and sweet woodroof lingered on the pillow; he recalled the scent of her hair, the softness of her dark curls, and his mind crowded with sensory memories of the lovely maiden who might have been his. Mayhap he had been the fool to let her go. After all, this was Ireland, where he was meant to live life instead of waiting for the future, and Garrett toyed with the notion of asking Joseph Whalley where to find her. Only then did he realize he didn't even know her name.

Garrett closed his eyes and welcomed a vision of lush green eyes. He remembered the taste of her lips, the sweetness of her sighs, and how she had let him rock into her, how she had put her arms around his neck and welcomed his deep kiss.

Whoever she was, Garrett hoped she was gone from Dublin, and out of harm's way. And while Garrett was not a praying man, he found himself hoping that if the three pouches were not enough, there would be someone to watch over her.

# **Chapter 7**

❧ ⟶∘◦∘⟵

It was past midnight. Eleanor waited in a doorway, exhausted and disheartened. She had yet to accomplish her purpose in Dublin. The three purses of coin she'd taken before dawn from the English stranger were heavy, but not heavy enough, and so she waited. The lane was silent except for the creak of painted signs in the wind, silent except for the pounding of her heart. The watch called out the quarter hour. A dog barked, a baby began to cry. Someone approached.

Eleanor held her breath, then peered from the shadows.

At last. She exhaled, but did not know whether to be pleased or terrified.

There was no mistaking the tall, lean form, or the elegant plumed hat worn too much to one side. It was him, and Eleanor stepped forth from the doorway. She had made a vow.

Garret noticed the figure lurking in the entranceway to his lodgings.

"Bloody hell," he mumbled, for at least the eighth or ninth time in as many hours. It had been an over long and most unfavorable day, beginning with the matter of his unsated lust, a most unusual predicament that had failed to diminish with the passing hours. Indeed, each time his thoughts had strayed to the previous evening, desire had licked at his innards, tormenting him, reminding him the green-eyed lady would not be easily forgotten. Then there were the London grocers who held debentures for Castlekevin and adjoining lands called Tomdarragh. Despite Master Petty's efforts they had declined to hear Sir Garrett's proposal and had refused to meet with either of them; Petty had promised to try again, but that had not blunted Garrett's disappointment. Lastly, there was the dinner engagement with Lord Egerton, which had promised to be an agreeable diversion, but had become most unpalatable when Miles Corbet had joined them. By the time Stilton and dried fruit had been served, Garrett's temperament had been thoroughly curdled by the Commissioner's righteous talk of cleansing and purging.

Now some ragamuffin, no doubt a pickpocket, wished to waylay him.

"Sir," said Eleanor.

Garrett's reaction was immediate. His heart thudded against the wall of his chest. His loins stirred. It was the gentle-bred lady who played at whoring. She had not left Dublin; she wasn't out of harm's way. He tipped his hat in courtesy. "Never thought to see you again," he remarked, as if he had already forgotten her.

"May I talk with you?"

"You are all right?"

She nodded.

He knew relief, but hid it well. "Say away, my lady."

"In private, if it would please you, sir."

. . . *If it would please you.* . . . Desire thrummed through him. It would please him to have her naked beneath him, to feel his bare skin against hers, to have her moaning at his slightest touch. Would she faint to hear him speak of such things? Would she flee and never look back? He cocked his head to one side, and wondered what her game might be this night.

Eleanor stared up at his handsome face, but it was too dark to read his expression, and she was frightened. She had been afraid he would not return; now she was terrified he would not hear her out. She heard herself plead, "Please." *Do not make me fail at this as well.*

Whatever she wished to discuss, Garrett knew he should send her on her way. He should send her from danger's path, but he didn't. "Come along. Out of the night air."

He held the door. She went up the steep stairs before him.

"I did take your gift," Eleanor said, upon entering the parlor.

He said nothing as he dropped his Cavalier hat to a table. Only one taper lit the room, and after using it to light several others, he secured it in a sconce, then faced her. She was lovelier, far more fragile than he recalled. In the flickering candle glow he saw all too clearly that she was a young woman who had been forced to grow old beyond her years whilst remaining young, for having never truly lived. Once again she presented the picture of a sacrificial virgin with her hands clasped before her, standing in the middle of the chamber. That she was a maiden somehow made her all the more desirable, and longing roughened his voice. "What have you to say?"

Eleanor bit her lower lip, stared down at her folded hands, at the floor. She thought of Laragh, of her brother and sisters, of the people who now looked to her for reassurance, for survival, then she raised her head and spoke in a voice that was no more than a whisper, "I am here to make a proposition, sir."

"What manner of proposition?" He took a step toward her, curious.

She met his gaze. "I would be yours."

" 'Tis not necessary. The pouches were yours to take. A gift."

"That is not my meaning, sir."

He took another step closer, his gaze narrowed.

"I would strike the same bargain, sir, for this night. I would be yours. Here. In your lodgings. Until dawn."

Garrett wasn't certain what he'd expected her to say, but it had not been this, and he shuddered. He closed the distance between them, set one finger beneath her chin, and raised her face to his regard. Hers was a portrait of beauty and courage. Her loveliness enticed him, her bravery intrigued. It was a tempting offer to consider, especially when a man stood close enough to catch the lavender and sweet woodroof that clung to her clothes, her hair, her skin; it was a seductive invitation, especially when a man had tasted the sweetness of her response. Garrett fancied he might delve and dive for hours with a woman like her. Indeed, he might very well enjoy such a woman as this lady and not get bored for many months.

His hand fell away from her chin. So, too, was she an innocent.

What had begun in his youth as a way for Garrett to guard himself from marriage had become in manhood a preference for women as decadent and abandoned as himself. He had come to patronize women who were eager for a man of his appetites and could match his pace, his endurance; women for whom carnal sport meant nothing beyond the moment of pleasure. He raked back his hair with both hands.

Until now, sex had always been uncomplicated and easy. Until now Garrett had never been responsible for anyone other than himself, and that was not going to change.

He made as if to turn away from her.

"Please." She set a hand on his forearm. "If you naysay me, I must find another man, who would be willing. There must be such a man to be found on Skinner's Row."

It was not the soft touch of her hand that stopped Garrett from moving away. It was the quiet desperation of her words. "True enough, plenty of men would be more than willing to accept such a proposition. Men like Joseph Whalley," he said, finding it pleased him to see her revulsion at mention of the man's name. "To be certain, there are willing men to be found anywhere and everywhere, but not many who would pay as generous as I did last night."

"Pray, how much would most men pay?"

"In these times?" He paused, considering not his answer, but his sudden need to discourage her from the course she was contemplating. He did not understand this urgency to deter her. "A few pounds. Mayhap four. Five, at most." Every trace of color drained from her face. He knew an odd satisfaction. If she was as horrified as she appeared, he had succeeded.

"What then explains your improvidence of yestereve, sir?"

"I am a very rich man," he said, but it explained nothing at all.

Eleanor trembled. She required a few moments before she might speak. "It would take twenty or thirty men if I wished to earn the same amount as in one of your pouches."

"Aye, that many." *It was almost done.*

On a deep sigh she said, "I will do it."

"Do what?" he shot back.

"Conduct business with as many men as I must to raise the funds I do require."

"You need money?"

She nodded.

"Is there no one—"

"No, there is no one else."

There was a tightening in Garrett's chest accompanied by the fleeting impression of finding himself in a corner with no way out. There should be someone to shield her from want and distress, to guard her from men such as himself. "Tell me, mistress, if I were to agree to your proposition—your body at my whim and disposal for a night in exchange for the money you required—would you not be frightened? Would you not have regrets on the morrow?"

"Regrets? Nay, I would have none. Despite what else you might call me after the business of this night would be done, I'm not a fool, and would spare no time for things that cannot be undone. As for fear. Fear is an altogether different matter, and 'tis why ... 'Tis why I came here this night. *'Tis why I came to you.*" Her voice trembled like a quicken tree before a summer tempest. She shivered. Fear was cold, deathly. "I am told there is pain for a woman in her first coupling, but my mother said it need not be that way. Pray, you must understand ... it is the prospect of such pain that frightens me, and after much consideration, it seemed to me that you, sir ... that you would—"

Garrett watched her tease that lower lip as she was wont to do, and the solution came to him. It had been there all along. There was no need for this discussion. No need for her fear. No need for the tightening in his chest, nor the cornered feeling that had come over him. If she needed money, she could have it. He was, as he'd told her, a rich man.

"You need not fear any pain, mistress."

"I know." Eleanor struggled for the right words to describe the acts of which her mother had spoken. "I—I believe I do trust you to sheath your man-sword within me, and to make that first time not as painful as 'tis said."

He reeled. A fierce response pumped through his body.

*. . . I trust you to sheath your man-sword . . .*

God's wounds, *that* was not what he'd meant when he said she need not fear, but what he'd intended mattered not. Arousal rocketed through him. It was too late to suppress his hunger for her, too late to send her away. In another moment, he was going to take her to the bedchamber, he was going to kiss her, stretch out beside her on the bed, and caress her with his mouth and hands slowly, thoroughly, entirely. "I have no practice with maidens."

"It matters not," Eleanor whispered. There was no mistaking the ribbon of tenderness in his low voice. Her fear ebbed. The chill in her hands, her arms, her legs turned to slow burning heat. "I do trust you, sir."

" 'Tis a rare commodity, trust, and I will honor yours." Garrett reached for her hand, and with that first moment of physical contact, something leapt between them. It was like the crackle of lightning against an ink black sky, sharp and sudden. Blazing. There was no name for this thing that heightened his awareness of her, that clenched at his gut, at his chest, and he stared into her eyes. *Did you feel it, mistress mine?*

*Aye, sir, that I did.* Eleanor trembled with awareness of the fire that shot from him, that flowed through her, and back to him in an unbroken circle of energy. *What is it? What is this thing that steals my breath? Suspends my heart?* She was aware of the heat in her cheeks, the change in her breathing. Her hand trembled in his. *Pray, you must tell me, sir, what happens betwixt us?*

She watched his fingers entwine through hers, watched as he raised her hand to his lips, watched the outline of his jaw muscle as his lips worked their way across her palm to her wrist. A little noise escaped her at the sensations this wrought, while her free hand rose of its own to caress that strong, hard jaw. He turned his face into her open hand, his mouth continuing its roving, its nipping, and when he reached the tip of her first finger, he took it between his lips.

"Oh," she whispered, more of a moan than a word. There was a quickening at her core.

Their gazes fused, and this time the rush between them was like a spark to dry gorse. With a ragged groan, Garrett pulled her against his chest. He wanted to be gentle, to kiss her tender and slow, but the thought of what was to come enticed him to abandon such control. Swift, fierce, his lips claimed hers.

It was a wondrous kiss that seemed to have no end. Breathless, deepening, it went on and on, and at the invasion of his hot tongue the most astonishing, most delicious ring of fire skated its way round her belly.

Somewhere in the back of her mind, where conscience and sanity dwelt, a wee voice called out to her, reminding, cautioning. *This English stranger is your enemy. Ireland's enemy. Do not give more than you agreed.* She moaned as his hands massaged her shoulders, then trailed down her back to cup her buttocks, bringing her body in contact with his. Her cries drowned out everything but this man, his mouth, his hands, his firm male body against her;

indeed, those unbridled sighs of delight grew louder, fueled by the fire he lit within her, and she kissed him back as if she had always known how to give as well as receive.

Garrett shifted his stance to accommodate his increasing desire. His body swayed, his arms holding her close, moving her with him, thigh on thigh, torso to torso, and in a fluid, sensual dance he brought the both of them gradually downward until they were kneeling in their embrace. His lips drifted away from hers. He heard her sigh as he nuzzled her neck, as his hand slid beneath the hem of her gown, as he caressed her calves, and when his hand, following the curve of her leg, went higher, she quivered. His mouth brushed against her earlobe. He murmured, "In exchange for your trust, I intend to bestow what pleasure might be yours this night." He heard another little sigh.

The Englishman's hand was large. Eleanor sensed his strength, yet his touch was soft, exciting, and when he went higher, when first the tips of his fingers came in contact with her inner thigh, Eleanor's heart did that peculiar little leaping thing. His hand slid upward, and the higher it went the more sensitive she was, the more responsive. There was moisture in her woman's place, intense throbbing in her breasts, and along her inner thighs where he had touched her skin it tingled, burned. Her body was awakening to his every caress, and when his hands reached her woman's place, her legs parted for him.

*This stranger is your enemy*, the distant voice tried to warn Eleanor, but she was beyond range. His hand brushed across her mons, his fingers drifted between her legs, then pulled away in wicked, sensual play. Her woman's place was the center of her, the whole of her. She could not stop her sighs. She was beyond return, and longing for nothing more than a lingering caress between her legs, she tilted herself upward, searching for him, wanting him to find her.

A finger skimmed her sex. She gasped at this loveliness, strained for more, but he pulled back. Somehow both hands were at her waist, and he was holding her at arm's length. Eleanor blinked and tried to catch her breath, tried to fight back a host of trepidations.

"What?" she whispered her confusion, knowing this was not the whole of it, knowing she could not, must not, fail this night. The expression upon his face was as hard as the granite Wicklow peaks. "I trust I do not displease you."

Garrett stared at her. *Pray, mistress, who are you?* The question swirled through his mind, over and over. He could not credit the way he was being swept away. This passion was beyond his experience; it was like nothing he had ever known before. "You do not displease me, mistress," was his gentle reply.

"What is wrong then? You must tell me, sir. I would do as you bid."

*How to tell her?* She had not the experience to understand fully what was happening between them; he had not the words to explain, for he had not made sense of the whole of this. Garrett shook his head. His gaze moved about the dark, sparse room, then back to her. It seemed as if she had always been a part of him. Faith, he could not shake the impression that something beyond his comprehension was at stake this night.

He motioned about the drab chamber and spoke the only answer he had, "A lady such as yourself deserves more than this." More than a hard, fast coupling on a cold, bare floor, he thought, but kept the unfortunate truth to himself. *More than myself.*

Whereupon Garrett scooped her into his arms. He knew what he must do, and he carried her over the threshold to the bedchamber.

# Chapter 8

T he English stranger set Eleanor on her feet and removed her cloak. "Come, mistress, I would be your lady's maid this night," he whispered.

Firelight suffused the bedchamber in a golden glow. Sandalwood clung to the warm air. Eleanor's outer garment fell to the floor. The quiet sounds of their breathing and her rapid heartbeat swirled about her, but the Englishman's words didn't register. It was his presence, his male person that commanded her full attention. He loomed over her; he held her gaze as he set a finger beneath her chin, brushed his lips across hers, and she shuddered. Heat bled down her spine. His effect upon her was potent; her eyelids closed of their own accord.

*Who are you?* Her soul begged to understand why he was affecting her in this way. She intended to do what she must this night; she would give her body to this man, but she had not imagined it would require anything more of her than passive surrender. She had not imagined she would accept his kiss. Indeed, she took it gladly. She had not reckoned with her own need, or her inability to restrain a little cry of frustration when he lifted his mouth from hers.

Her eyes opened as he reached beneath her gown. The fabric fluttered, grazed her knees when he lifted each foot to slip off her shoes and roll the woolen stockings down her calves, over her ankles, off her feet. It was such a simple act, yet this man made it fascinating, made it erotic. He cupped the heel of one foot. Her breath caught. He set a kiss to the inside of her ankle, and a flash of heat coiled through her belly.

That done, her feet and legs bare, he turned her round to face the bed. His hands sought the lacing that ran down the back of her gown. "My job is not yet done."

She heard her mother's voice. *There will be a stead-fast and brave man, especially when you wear the emerald brocade.* The stranger was unlacing the ribbons that held her gown together. *There's no man who'll be turning away from a sight so fair, and the pulse of his heart ye'll be.* The stranger was pushing the bodice off her shoulders, pulling her undersheath with it.

The air was cool against her breasts. Of a sudden, there was a desperate ache in her heart, and her hands rose as if to cover herself, as if to protect herself.

Garrett dropped the bodice and undersheath. They slid over her hips to the floor, and he savored the sight before him. The slight curve of her spine, the hourglass shape of her waist, the smooth hips, rounded buttocks, and flawless skin were bathed in firelight. His erection was fierce, straining with his desire to be sheathed by her soft warmth, and he began to disrobe.

The thud of boots, the metallic clang of a buckle were discernible to Eleanor. She knew what was happening; he would soon be naked, and she wrapped her arms tighter about herself to stop her trembling. He moved nearer, she sensed his heat. His hand slid beneath her elbow, flesh against flesh, his touch was warm, and the same energy as had ignited between them in the parlor shot through her. She swayed, her knees weakened, and as if sensing her lassitude, he helped her onto the bed, to lie on her stomach with her head resting on the pillow of her arms.

When he joined her on the bed, Eleanor couldn't see him, yet a potent awareness of his size, his strength, enveloped her as the mattress gave beneath his weight, and more of that heat, more of that energy transmitted from his body to hers. Her heart skipped a beat, then it seemed to stop altogether when he kneeled over her, straddling her thighs. She tried to swallow a little moan, but it was impossible to stifle his affect upon her. To feel his bare skin touching hers was a most vivid sensation, and of a sudden, the whole of her body yearned for similar contact.

It was not enough to feel his legs against her outer thighs, and she wondered if he would lower his body to rest upon hers. It was not, however, his thighs she next felt against her bare skin, rather it was several drops of something warm and smooth; he drizzled this liquid across her back from one shoulder to the other, and while it reminded Eleanor of the oils her mother had used to keep her hands smooth, it was heavy with an exotic scent she didn't recognize.

" 'Tis oil from essence of cardamom, feverfew, and sandalwood," came his whispered explanation, as if he could see into the quiet corners of her mind. He began to massage her shoulders in a circular motion, his large hands going round and round with a touch that was firm, masterful, yet tender. Inch by inch, the circle expanded, the oil, the warmth, and the intense friction all conspiring to heighten Eleanor's senses as never before. Each of his fingers was kneading her, his hands were molding her; she could feel the pad of each palm gliding over her slick skin. His hands pressed along the length of her spine, they played over the twin rounds of her buttocks, teasing lower into the cleft until for the briefest moment his fingertips passed between her legs. Enthralled, she sighed.

She was as responsive as Garrett had hoped she would be, and he lost himself in the pleasure of exploring her smooth skin, discovering every curve, lingering in every hollow. With each sensual advance down her back and across her buttocks, his fingers went a little lower until he almost touched her sex. She quivered beneath his hands, and Garrett knew it was time to change her position.

With his large, strong hands at her waist, he coaxed Eleanor to roll onto her back. Her pulse raced. There was that energy again, that irresistible heat. She lay back against a nest of pillows, aware of an altered state of reality in which she and this man were cut off from the rest of the universe by a shimmering wall of haze. It was a carnal universe in which she did not hesitate to allow him to bend her legs at the knees until her feet were flat on the mattress; a fiery universe in which she willingly allowed him to part her legs and reveal her most private woman's place to him.

He slipped a pillow beneath her, tilting her higher, opening her wider, and she closed her eyes as if to pretend he was someone else, anyone else, but an English stranger. Mayhap if she closed them tight enough she might sleep, and upon awakening, find herself back at Laragh in a time when her parents lived and young gentlemen might come to call upon her.

Garrett reached between her legs, and slid a single finger along that wet seam. Her eyes flew wide open; she stared up at him, her gaze clouded with arousal. He smiled at her innocent passion, at her beauty, her trust, and gradually inserted his finger within her, delighted by her little moans as he stroked her once, then again. Her dew was increasing. He used two fingers now, and his hard, swollen shaft throbbed to plunge where his fingers delved. *I do trust you, sir*, the memory of her sweet-whispered words awed Garrett, and he took a steadying breath to force himself to patience. He would not have his pleasure from this woman until he had fulfilled hers.

He leaned down to kiss her belly. Deliberate, his lips feathered their way lower, across her hip and down to her inner thigh. Decisive, his hands grasped her beneath the buttocks; hungry, he lifted her sex toward his mouth.

"What are you doing!" Eleanor gasped at the shock of it. She tried to back away, but his hold was firm.

"I mean to pleasure you," his reply mixed with a rough groan. With his thumbs he parted her folds, and in the next instant his mouth claimed her, his tongue gliding over her netherlips, then probing, flicking, teasing. He inhaled the fragrance of her, absorbed her heat, indulged in the silky flesh.

Eleanor cried out at this intimate invasion. Her skin warmed not once, but twice with a violent heat. Her hands clenched, her back arched, and she tossed her head from one side to the other, black tresses trailing on the mattress. Deep inside her body something tightened, then relaxed only to tighten again, making it seem as if her body was about to be stolen from her. She whimpered at this mounting loss of control, and found herself breathless as some great force seized her, making her inner muscles quiver, making her skin tingle. She was being swept away by a mighty current, and her body undulated as if tossed upon the waves of a stormy sea. She cried out again and again, then the storm began to recede.

When it was done, Garrett slid his hands up her back, and sitting up, he brought her with him, cradling her shoulders, holding her in his embrace, their legs each entwined about the other's hips.

"This is not what I expected," she whispered. Too easily did her gaze meet his; too eagerly did she welcome his embrace. "I—I never imagined . . . I have never heard of such things between a man and a woman. I did not know the English were different in this way."

"They're not different. Not at all." He could not resist dropping a single quick kiss on the end of her nose.

"But my mother told me nothing of this." She wondered if he heard the fear mixed with her confusion. It was not this intimate act nor the extent of her pleasure she had never imagined, it was the accompanying sentiment that perplexed her. There was no logic to the sense of connection she felt with this man, this ability to trust someone she did not know. It was not right, yet she could not deny it any more than she could deny the impression that somehow in some way she did know this man.

"Is that the whole of what worries you?" he said on a tender hush, as if the soft-spoken words alone were meant to comfort. His smiled at her. "There are some things a mother may blush to tell a daughter just as there are some things men never dare to play with their lady-wife."

"And I am no lady-wife, but your whore."

"Nay, sweetheart, you are a virgin pure, and I seek nothing more than to assure your pleasure. I do not treat you like a whore, but a lady. Some men never give a moment's pleasure to their lady-wife, most men never give any to a trollop, but I will give you pleasure in abundance before this night is

spent." He kissed her on the brow, the lips, and
again upon the end of her nose. "You are a beauty,
you must know. In every way. A woman to be
prized by the man who would pledge his life for
her."

Eleanor's heart contracted at this hint of what it
might be like to be adored by a man. This was, she
imagined, the sort of intimacy that must pass between lovers. A lock of raven black hair fell across
his forehead in strange imitation of an Irishman's
glib, and Eleanor knew the impulse to smooth it
away, but she held back. He was her enemy, and
despite his words, despite her own odd emotions,
she was naught but his whore. Breaking away from
his gaze, she looked down and for the first time saw
his fully aroused man-sword.

He saw where she glanced, but could not discern
her reaction. " 'Tis my hunger for your sweet self."

"You are . . . enormous, sir." It was thick and
large, and stood out before him. She had seen her
brothers, but they had not such rampant tools.

"Do I affright you?"

"Nay, I am not frightened, but I do not think 'tis
possible to fit—"

"Oh, 'tis possible, I do assure you," Garrett murmured, as he raised himself between her thighs to
position his turgid desire. With one hand he lubri-
cated himself with her warm, ready moisture, recalling his first encounter with a woman when
anticipation turned mere seconds into years. It had
been ages since he'd thought of that, ages since he'd
experienced such expectation, but now it was the
same as that first time; Garrett was certain he might
perish with yearning in the space of a heartbeat. He
leaned forward, parting her dewy entrance. She
shuddered when the tip of his manhood parted her,
she cried out when the head of his shaft entered her,

and he groaned at the delicious agony of her flesh closing round him.

Eleanor's body opened to his, and gasping, she surrendered to her natural instincts, arching upward, bringing him deeper. He was filling her, there was no pain, only a sort of taut, thrilling glory, and then there was no more. He stopped, but she knew not why. She wriggled, overcome by craving. This could not be all there was. There had to be more.

"Careful." His voice was little more than a growl. He moved as if to kiss her, his lips brushing hers. "You must let me do this."

He kissed her then, open-mouthed, hard, demanding, and when the kiss began to spin out of control, his body moved again. His hands found hers, his fingers entwined with hers. He extended her arms on the pillows above her head, capturing her thus as he devoured her mouth with his, pinning her upon the bed to rise over her and embed his sex in hers.

A sudden, sharp sensation tore through Eleanor. His kiss deepened; he swallowed her cry as his mansword filled her to the hilt, and her cry of discomfort melted to a long, high keen of discovery. A great burst of heat was radiating through her, into the core of her belly, down her legs, and over every bit of her flesh, inside and out. He began to move in a slow, urging rhythm, and she rocked upward to meet his strokes.

"Aye, sweet mistress, that is the dance. Come with me now. Stay with me." The words rumbled forth from his chest as his pace quickened and he kissed her anew.

Eleanor writhed beneath him, his tongue branded her mouth, and his swollen sex plumbed her. The sensitivity of her inner walls surprised Eleanor, for she could feel every inch of him; he was vibrating within her, and she could feel her responding contractions. The fire ringing her belly was consuming her. Tension was building in her. Yearning. Craving. Need. They were the focus of her body and soul as he pounded into her, each time going deeper, joining more thoroughly with her than in the moment before.

She had never imagined such power, such oneness, such momentum betwixt a man and a woman.

Her fingernails raked his back. She clutched at him, and when he raised her shoulders, tilting her, filling her with more of him than she thought possible, Eleanor knew a night such as this would never come again. She heard him yell, a sort of ragged growl. His pace was furious now, wild. He thrust deep into her, once, twice. Again. Again. She heard herself scream, heard him reply with a jubilant noise that sounded part laughter, part untamed beast. Something exploded within her, propelling her through the clouds, past the moon and stars, racing into eternity, and with a terrible frenzied shudder, it was done. The English stranger collapsed atop her, then rolled to one side.

It was a while before Eleanor's heartbeat returned to something akin to normal, and she might speak. Indeed, she needed to speak. "You honored my trust."

"On the morrow it will be even sweeter," his whispered reply came out of the darkness.

"What say you?"

"You do not think I will let you go?" His lips brushed her temple.

"I do not know what to think." Eleanor was confused. So many things bewildered her this night.

"Pleasure's kingdom is vast, and a mere passing dalliance does not satisfy." Garrett was flirting. It was the most surest way to disguise his real emotions. This moment, this ending was the corner he'd dreaded, and it was as bleak as he'd known it would be. In silence, he got a soft cloth and washed her with warm water, rearranged the pillows, then got back into the bed to hold her in the cradle of his arms.

His embrace offered a tranquility Eleanor had forgotten existed, and in his arms, she didn't worry about the morning or the meaning of his words. She drifted to sleep lulled by his breathing, her senses drenched with warmth and sandalwood, and her dreams filled with memories of the Irish boys who had gone to Spain, of dancing in her mother's garden, of someone to watch over her, and all the things that would never be hers.

She was dancing in her mother's garden with a tall, beautiful man.

*"Avourneen, as m'aisling, tháinig mo ghrá-sa, lé mo thaobh, guala ar ghualainn, agus béal ar bhéal,"* she heard him murmur. *Sweetheart, out of my dream, my love came near up to my side, shoulder to shoulder, and mouth on mouth.*

It was her English stranger, holding her safe, smoothing her hair, and speaking tender in Irish, *"Fógraim an grá, is mairg a thug é do mhac na mná úd ariamh nár thuig é."* Eleanor had never heard anything so sad. *Love I denounce: God help who gave it to a man who could not appreciate it.*

They were the soft-whispered words of a poet and lover whose heart knew more grief than joy, and she was glad it was nothing more than a dream.

Had it been real, Eleanor might have cried for the first time in many years.

She was gone before daylight. Garrett hadn't really expected anything else.

In the gray small hours of dawn he rose and went

to the saddlebags as he'd done the morning before. This time he didn't check their contents. This time it was emptiness that compelled him to look.

Last night he had not been alone. For the space of a few hours, there had been someone for him. Until now Garrett's loneliness had been merely physical; now it assumed another, more painful embodiment. Already he missed that sense of fulfillment, that sense of never needing to look any farther for that one soul who might complement his, but it had been fleeting, and Garrett was alone again with nothing save his wealth, the contents of those saddlebags, and the journey ahead of him.

This was how it had always been for him.

Lady Olivia had once said he had never really lived yet. It was true. Always he'd been waiting for the future, and for the first time, he regretted there was no one to accompany him to his journey's end. Garrett took out the debentures, unfolded the one from Titus Fletcher. He perused the particulars.

*"the demesne of Laragh comprising a great house, a village called Annamoe, woods and tillage in the Vale of Clara, and a tract of high ground in the mountains at Baravore."*

While this place called Laragh was not Órla's Castlekevin, those names—Annamoe, Baravore, and Clara, oft-mentioned in Lady Olivia's tales—were a part of the memories entrusted to Garrett. He had never been to Laragh, yet he knew the river flowing from nearby Lough Dan teemed with salmon. A mile from the village of Annamoe stood Castlekevin. He didn't have to close his eyes to picture the ancient fortress with its deep fosse, four massive towers, ramparts, and barbican with iron portcullis. Órla's wilderness crowded his mind. The woods echoed with the cascade of waterfalls, the whisper of furze grasses in wind, the cries of finch, and the trill of redpolls. He knew the hills and moors, the purple thistle, and heather, and the fruit of wild plum trees and whortleberries. He knew the heights of Lugna-quillia, Mullacor, and Kirikee that guarded bogs where pipistrelle glided in summer twilight. More than once his imaginings had taken him along the narrow track from Glenmalure through the schist and granite fastness to Imail, where O'Tooles guarded the western slope of the mountains.

This was the Ireland for which Garrett had yearned since boyhood. He would stay in Dublin only so long as it took Petty to arrange a meeting with the grocers, but no longer than that.

Garrett's journey was almost ended.

# Cradle-Tale
## *The Beginning*

❧

"**C**ome hither, handsome sir. Won't ye be dancing?" a chorus of pretty voices beckoned. "A fine night for frolicking, it is. Won't ye be coming closer, now?"

The young man tried not to listen.

A dust cloud whirled past his good self. The nearby hawthorn shivered. He had heard tell Irish faeries had a fondness for hawthorns. Mayhap 'twas nothing more than the wind in the trees turning the merlin's cry to girlish voices, stirring up the dust and making the branches tremble. 'Twas dusk, and in the gloaming light the tangle of brambles and sloe-bushes took on the shapes of creatures come out to make mischief. In the high hills a wolf called to its mate. The young man durst not tarry lest the forest spirits cast their spells upon him. Irish faeries were skilled at seduction, and 'twas dangerous love-games they were wont to play with mortals.

"Take our hands, gentle sir. Say ye'll stay . . . say ye'll play," the pretty voices called. Enchanted voices, they were, sweet as the song thrush, musical as a distant waterfall. The most gentle voices in all Innisfail. "Come hither," they whispered. They taunted, beckoned, and teased, "Hither. Hither."

*The young man trembled and could not but wonder which of his sins had condemned him. His life had not been a particular bad one. Faith, he'd had selfish moments, and ofttimes he had used profanity, but he was honourable and honest, and certainly not an evil man. Overall, the Lord could not be displeased with his conduct. Besides, he was too young to depart this mortal realm. His heart had ne'er admitted pure love.*

*There were sidhe in the glen, their spirits as untamed as the thick wilderness that cut them off from the mortal world. O, what beautiful maidens they were with tresses the colour of sunbeams and skin as fair as pure creamery butter.*

*The most beautiful women in the whole of Leinster, fair of face and form, bewitching, beguiling, and the glen was thick as grass with them, though there's ne'er been a soul to attest to the truth of this. Ne'er hast a man set his mortal eyes upon the feadhree and lived to speak of what he's seen come daylight.*

*O, how they loved dancing, those beautiful sidhe. And every night they would rise from their palaces beneath silvery pools; they would come forth from their lisses within the hills and forths to spin and twirl, dainty feet capering through dew-moist grass, lithe bodies swaying, hair flying about them to the music of flutes and harps. Such sensual music it was to lure mortal men to join the sidhe in their abandon.*

*They were faery women: fallen angels cast out of Heaven as a punishment for their pride. Not good enough to be saved, nor bad enough to be lost. Under their influence, a man would commit any transgression, and when his soul was blackened to the core, the faeries would carry him away for eternity.*

*The young man this night was of the English. He was a light horse officer in service to King Henry VIII, and he'd ridden out of Arklow Castle that morning bound for Wicklow, but had lost his way. Twice he'd passed another* traveler, twice he'd asked the direction to the coast, and twice he'd taken a path leading not to Arklow, but deeper into the fastness in which faeries dwelled.

He had no wish to dally in that glen, where mist curled up from the earth, and the night beasts were stirring. He quickened his pace. His heavy sword thumped against his thigh, and he crashed through knotted branches making for the bright open space afore him.

Then the ground gave way beneath him. He cried out in alarm.

Ankles, knees, thighs were swallowed, and he was held in that moist, treacherous land the Irish called bog. He cried out again.

There was water all around. Bottomless 'twas said to be, oozing, and able to swallow man and beast, to devour wagons, even mighty war cannons. He was sinking. Sinking fast. The black water was up to his waist. He tried to paddle through the surface greenery that glowed an eerie hue in the twilight. He thrashed at the water . . . and was sucked deeper, deeper.

There was nothing for him save to call upon the Lord. The end was anear. He ceased his struggles, savoured one final look at the world, and sorrow-stricken, closed his eyes.

The end was upon him, and he had ne'er known pure love.

"Good sir, yer hand, over here. . . ."

# Part II

Part II

# Chapter 9

The candle was near spent. Its circle of light was scarce large enough to illuminate a piece of paper.

Eleanor stared at a blank sheet. She had been sitting in her father's library for nigh on two hours. Sitting and staring and knowing Nuala O'Byrne was correct. She must do what she might to preserve truth, and she must do her best to make up for the treasures that were no longer in this chamber. Nuala would record to paper the facts of history in the annals, whilst Eleanor would do her best to capture to paper the soul and spirit of these times.

*. . . darkness failing from heaven . . . not even the song of birds there . . .*

Phrases crowded her mind. *. . . . the crown of the forest was withered . . .* Phrases inspired by the images and events around her, that which she saw and experienced each and every day.

*. . . the pasture's rock and stone now . . . and the young men gone away . . .*

Every sadness, every question, each doubt, each hope and fear, and every last regret filtered through her heart and soul until the phrases began to flow.

*. . . the great earls, where are they? . . . beaten into the clay.*

It was there, every word, and the myriad images that might become a whole, if she only knew where to start. If she but knew how to order them. How to convey truth so that others who would live in far-off times and places yet to come would be able to understand what had happened here.

She whispered a few lines to test aloud the sound. She played with the words, the rhyme, the balance, and tried them in English as well as in Irish, for whatever she composed must please the ear in both tongues.

Time passed.

The wolfhound by the hearth stirred. The fire was low, naught but embers. Cold was settling over the room.

Every night since her return from Dublin, Eleanor had sat before this desk, but each night she had left her father's library without putting pen to paper.

Each night it had not been poetry that had filled her thoughts, but memories of the English stranger.

*Do not give more than you agreed*, Eleanor had warned herself. She had been aware of the need for caution, yet still she had failed to protect herself. By her own design, she had bartered her virginity, but that was all she had intended to relinquish. She had not imagined how the bargain struck might rob her of something more. Too late had Eleanor come to understand there was some part of a woman's soul which could be given only once and only to one man, too late for Eleanor to prevent that precious bit of her soul from being taken by a man who in all likelihood did not even realize what had come to pass.

Which seemed to Eleanor all the more reason that she must record the truth, for in doing so, mayhap she might save some piece of her soul for eternity.

At last on this, the twelfth night of sitting and

musing, this twelfth night since Dublin, she began to write.

> *Cad a dheanfaimid feasta gan adhmad?*
> *Ta deireadh na gcoillte ar lar;*

Eleanor read the lines. A glow warmed her heart. She translated:

> *What shall we do for timber?*
> *The last of the woods is down.*

That was a fine beginning.

She dipped the pen into the inkwell, the lines began to flow from her head to her hand to the paper, and she worked without cease until the candle sputtered. The room fell into blackness, but it mattered not. Already she knew those first sixteen lines by heart. Two stanzas were completed this night, and she would never forget them.

She whispered into the dark.

> *What shall we do for timber?*
> *The last of the woods is down.*
> *Kilcash and the house of its glory*
> *And the bell of the house are gone,*
> *The spot where the lady waited*
> *Who shamed all women for grace*
> *When earls came sailing to greet her*
> *And Mass was said in the place.*
>
> *My grief and my affliction*
> *Your gates are taken away,*
> *Your avenue needs attention,*
> *Goats in the garden stray.*
> *The courtyard's filled with water,*

*And the great earls, where are they?*
*The earls, the lady, the people*
*Beaten into the clay.*

For the time being, Eleanor would be satisfied, and until another night the lines would be kept secure in a tin box much like the one in which the Annals of Finnén were stored. She set the box upon the highest, most out-of-the-way shelf. Her father would have been pleased, and as Eleanor went upstairs to her bedchamber, she indulged in the fancy that he was watching her from Heaven and smiling down upon her. Her mother and brother, Ciarán, were by his side; Nuala's mother was there, too, and the last O'Connor chíeftain of Baravore, and Piaras Feiritear, and all the poets and warriors, all the mothers and brothers, the fathers and sisters, sons and daughters who had left Ireland against their will. She would write her poem for them.

Biddy O'Fierghraie listened for the low, quivering cry that had awakened her.

Such a mournful wail could not have come from beast or fowl. To be sure, it was the lament of a spirit condemned to wander forever in darkness, and Biddy whispered a fervent prayer to the Holy Virgin that if one of the *bhean-sidhe* was abroad this night, the little woman would not stop at this cabin.

There it was again. A long, drawn-out moan coming from outside, and upon hearing the haunting noise a third time, the wise woman rose from her mattress. Dragging the woolen bedcoverings about her shoulders, she padded toward the door to see what she might in the clearing.

Silent it was o'er Brockagh Hill save for the clacket of bare branches in the treetops. There were only ghosts in the scorched gray hills. Ghosts and *tóraídhe*. This land was theirs, and from their hiding places in what remained of the ancient wilderness, the *tóraídhe* continued armed resistance against those who would take the land from them. Young men of the old English gentry, remnants of the Irish army, royalists, Confederates, farmers, scholars, tenants, and poets united in their refusal to submit to Cromwell's thieves and butchers. They were called *tories* by their English enemies, *raiders, thieves,* and condemned as common felons, hunted like wolves. They might as well be ghosts.

There was no moon this night. The conditions were perfect for a raid upon the English. A gust of night air buffeted the cabin, rattled the wicker door, and swept the unmistakable scent of smoke through the hills. Biddy widened the shutters to stare down the valley, focusing on the northeast horizon where a thin line of golden red light stretched skyward.

Fire. It was a large blaze, by the look of it, mayhap it was the barracks at the Baltynanima crossroads, where some two score English soldiers had occupied the abandoned village since early summer.

A few yards from the cabin a twig snapped. Biddy turned away from the valley. She glanced to the shadowy woods rising beyond, and smiled to herself. They were out there. *Tories.* Ireland's brave sons and daughters had indeed been abroad this night, and she sensed their passing through the woods. They were returning to the caves in the high hills above the upper lough at Glendalough. Another twig snapped.

Biddy squinted into the dark, and imagined a small, pale face staring at her from a sheltery nook under an old thorn.

"*A geluin tu me?*" an odd, shrill voice spoke from

beneath that thorn. A chill skated along Biddy's spine, and as her eyes adjusted, she knew it was no *bhean-sidhe*, but a living lass whispering, *"Do ye hear myself?"*

"Aye, I can hear ye, child. *Cia an tabair a bfuil tu ann so?"* Biddy replied. *"Why are ye here?* Why do ye linger, instead of hastening after yer companions?"

"We've need of yer healing skills, Biddy O'Fierghraie. *A dtiocfa tu liom?"* came the answer. *"Will ye come with myself?* I will show ye the way to those in need."

The wise woman nodded. "Wait but a moment whilst I gather my supplies." Her druggit skirt hung on a nearby peg. She put on the garment, tying it about her head like a cloak; she filled a large basket with her healing salves and tinctures, plus assorted leaves, dried flowers, roots, and berries, then exited the cabin.

*"Deanam."* She secured the door behind her. *"Let us set out."*

A slender figure crawled out from beneath the thorn, and Biddy O'Fierghraie recognized one of the O'Byrne lasses. It was Nuala, the eldest of the pretty girls who had greeted her with smiles and laughter when Biddy had visited the fortress at Aghavannagh. Nuala O'Byrne, she was of a like age to Eleanor Archebold, and as Biddy followed her up Brockagh Hill into the black night, she could not help wishing there was a charm to bring back the joy and hope that belonged to innocence and youth.

Garrett and his agent, Edwin Petty, were searching the Liffey waterfront for the pair of adventurers, grocers from London by the name of Waring and Powell, who owned the debentures for Castlekevin and Tomdarragh. Twice they had sat face to face with Methusaleh Waring and Thomas Powell, and twice Garrett's generous offer had been refused. Indeed, Sir Garrett Neville's interest in their property had seemed to increase its value in their eyes. It was now near a sennight since these tradesmen had last been sighted in Dublin.

"I begin to suspect Waring and Powell have quit Dublin to begin the business of planting," Garrett remarked. "What think you, Edwin? Have we had enough work for today? Would our time this day be better spent with a pitcher of ale and a platter of plum cakes at the Essex Bridge?"

Petty agreed with a companionable laugh. The relationship between the men had evolved beyond a business arrangement to one of friendship. Edwin Petty was no longer of the singular purpose of leaving Ireland; indeed, Garrett had almost convinced him to invest as his partner in the Wicklow ironworks of which Lord Egerton had spoken.

"There is a crowd," Petty remarked, as they neared a low, half-timber building. Located adjacent to the customs house, the Essex Bridge Tavern was one of Dublin's older establishments. It was known for its fine fare and the quality of its imported wines, and as always, gentlemen were gathered outside its entrance.

" 'Tis Commissioner Corbet and some of his cronies." Garrett slowed his pace, hoping the gathering of somber, black-clad Puritans was about to disperse. He had no wish to exchange false pleasantries with the Commissioner, or to be introduced to any more of his so-called associates.

"Cronies?" Petty did not hide his contempt. He and Garrett had ceased walking toward the tavern. "They are merchants. Out of Bristol and the Americas, and no doubt vying for Corbet's signature on one of the special licenses to be had these days."

"You are right, Edwin. They are merchants. In

fact, I had the dubious honor of meeting one of them at Egerton's, first night I was in Dublin." Garrett indicated which of the men garbed in near identical black coats and felt hats was the one of whom he spoke. "Captain Selleck from the Massachusetts colony has already won favor with a special license. You would not be pleased to hear him speak of trafficking in human souls as if it were the Lord's will."

Edwin Petty shook his head. "Come, let us dine elsewhere."

They were about to turn away when a well-dressed gentleman approached the tavern from the opposite direction. Waving a gold-tipped cane and calling out for Commissioner Corbet by name, he resembled a peacock coming to roost among so many crows. His doublet with wide-slashed sleeves was of the finest linen, his jacket was stitched with colored threads, his buttons were polished to a shine, and his periwig was impeccable, showing not the usual signs of overpowdering. He carried his tall, trim figure with confidence; indeed, the manner in which he flourished that gold-tipped cane could almost be termed pompous.

"And who is that?" Garrett could not suppress a grin.

"Of a certainty, he's a prominent landowner, of the old English, no doubt; mayhap a Protestant. Dublin is overrun with ten score of his type, all who come to plead their rights as landowners," replied Petty. "There are some landowners whose estates, being situated east of the Shannon, were included in the forfeiture; such men are here to present their case for an exemption from resettlement to Connaught. While the landowners from the west, who the Commissioners have promised to reimburse for the use of their land, have come to make certain their new estates will be of equal value to those the government takes to accommodate the resettlement."

"And what might you suggest his particular business would be with Corbet?" he asked, but already suspected the answer, and frowned.

"I would venture he seeks Corbet's favorable treatment in return for helping Selleck acquire cargo. I imagine a man can obtain an exemption in exchange for twenty-five or thirty healthy young women."

"To save his land, he will sell his neighbors. That is what you are saying?"

"Lo, Sir Garrett. They depart the tavern and come this way."

"Then we hie ourselves in the opposite direction. I've no stomach for the company, even in passing, of such men."

# Chapter 10

〜⁀⁀〜

"**A** visitor, Grace! Eveleen! Someone approaches," Rory shouted from the ramparted roof of Laragh's tower-house. Since the days of Murchad, high king of Leinster, a stronghold had stood sentry on this gentle rise. Tall and gray, Laragh's solid walls had never been breached. This tower was where the household had sought shelter upon the approach of Cromwell's Ironsides, and it was from this roof that the Archebold children and their mother had watched the countryside burn. Rory had been a babe and didn't recall those terrible times himself, but he'd heard tell how fire had gutted a nearby fortress, and flames had lit the sky for two nights, how the heavens had turned black as pitch, and cinders had fallen like soiled snow upon the landscape.

"What say you, Rory?" Grace poked her head through the trap door. It was a cold, overcast afternoon, and while Rory took his turn as watch, Grace and Eveleen huddled out of the wind in the uppermost tower chamber. "Is someone coming?"

"A rider's coming down the lane from the Annamoe road."

The girls crawled outside to peer over the rampart. A rider, swathed in a mantle, was cantering toward the big house.

"Do you suppose 'tis *him*?' wondered Grace.

"Who else could it be?" asked Eveleen.

"Another gardener sent by Father Netterville?" Rory wondered. A few days after Eleanor's return from Dublin a gardener by the name of Ambrose had knocked on Laragh's door, asking for work and saying Father Netterville had told him to speak to the young mistress herself.

"Nay, a gardener would not ride such a fine horse." Ambrose had been on foot, hungry and ill-clothed, and Eleanor had welcomed him to Laragh, given him a room above the stable, and set him to work.

The children studied the approaching rider.

"It must be *him*. Come at last."

"At least he's Irish."

"How can you tell?"

"The mantle," explained Eveleen. "You've never seen one of Cromwell's English wear an Irish mantle, have you?"

"Enough chatter," said Rory, all boyish impatience. He led the descent into the tower and down narrow stone stairs. Once this fortification had been where the men-at-arms loyal to the lords of Laragh were quartered, but the brave fighting men were gone, and no one but the children ventured through its dank, deserted chambers anymore.

Having descended to the next level, the children jostled one another to get through the passage to the brighter, roomier residence where the family lived and entertained. The "big house" had been built by their father's father and his grandfather. Less than half a century had passed since its completion, and it was as stately as any English palace, Sir Thomas's mother had been wont to boast. As a new bride she'd visited Somerset and Surrey, and had returned to Ireland determined that her home would have the same wall panels, painted chimneypieces, and fretted wooden ceilings as those gracing the finest English estate. On the ground floor were a banqueting hall in the old tradition, a small parlor like the women's bower of old, Sir Thomas's library, and a long gallery. On the first floor were six sleeping chambers, each with a small closet, and on the uppermost level were the schoolroom, storage lofts, and a guest chamber.

The central corridor ran the length of the house past the sleeping chambers. Its walls were hung with rich damask, and at the far end there was an enormous window, more glass than wall, that offered a plentiful source of light above a formal staircase. The Irish oak floor was matted with woven rushes, and the children dashed headlong down this corridor.

"Slow yerselves to a walk!" Old Sibéal appeared in a doorway. She was folding linens, and her fluid motions continued even as she spoke. " 'Tis not the racecourse at Taillte. Are ye listening to myself, now? Ye're not to be running indoors."

"Where's Eleanor?" Eveleen panted. All three children were out of breath.

"Here with myself readying the winter bedding," said Sibéal. The old woman had been Lady Moira's nurse from childhood, born and bred in the hills at Baravore like her mistress; she had come to Laragh nearly a quarter century before, when her chieftain's daughter had wed Sir Thomas Archebold and her role had changed from nurse to housekeeper. It was the same each autumn. Sheets, blankets, and woolens were taken out of summer storage, inspected for moths and other vermin, then shaken, aired in strong wind and bright sunshine, and finally distributed to the household. Sibéal had always assisted the mistress of Laragh with this task; it was one of the few things that had not changed. "And what would ye be wanting with yer sister?"

"There's someone coming from the Annamoe road."

"Do ye tell me now?"

"Who is it?" called out Eleanor.

The children scrambled into the chamber, where the air was sharp with costmarie and camphor oil. Their sister was kneeling before a cedar chest, and having shut the lid, she stood to ask again who was coming down the lane.

"Do not know." Grace was the first to speak.

"But you've got to hasten, Eleanor," came from Eveleen.

"Aye, Eleanor, you must bestir yourself." Rory tugged on her skirt.

"Nay, Rory, she can't go yet. Oh, Eleanor, your hair! 'Tis an awful sight," Grace declared. "Won't you be tidying it?"

"And your face, too," Rory added, once he'd had a good look at his eldest sister.

"There's dirt on your forehead," said Eveleen.

"Listen to yerselves, carrying on like it was the noble Ruaidhrí Ua Conchobair himself come to call," Sibéal teased. The legendary O'Connor ancestor had been part of their childhood tales. Ruaidhrí Ua Conchobair was the high king who'd twice defeated Dermot MacMurrough, and the children, especially Rory, delighted in hearing how their kinsman had—in these very Wicklow hills—fought the traitor who'd betrayed Ireland to the Anglo-Normans. "Who is this important personage that yer sister must primp and tidy her good self, I'd be wanting to know?"

A secretive glance darted between the girls. Twice

they'd performed the whole of Biddy O'Fierghraie's love charm, yet Eleanor's husband had failed to come knocking upon the door at Laragh. Rory said it was because a fierce rain had washed away the salt on the lane; Eveleen blamed Grace for five times reversing *by land or by sea* while reciting the verse.

Whatever the cause, they had not lost hope. They'd returned to the bog below the wise woman's cabin for more bogbine blossoms and valerian, and had started anew. This time they were being extremely careful, extremely precise. Perhaps, just perhaps, the visitor was *him*, at long last come to knock on the door of Laragh. No one had ever claimed enchantments ran like clockworks.

"Och, something's fermenting betwixt the three of them," clucked Sibéal. "Do ye not see that, Mistress Eleanor? Scheming they are!"

Eleanor was looking elsewhere, and she was frowning not at the children, but at the melancholy encircling her. It had accompanied her out of Dublin and home to Laragh, this rather dazed sense of walking round in a cloud, as if she were lost and might never find her way home.

"*Eleanor!*" Grace stamped her foot, and her sister responded.

She peered at her image in a reflecting glass. There was, indeed, a sooty smudge upon her brow. Quick she rubbed it off. "Who did you say it was?"

"We didn't."

"But he isn't English," Eveleen assured her.

"Lord bless us for small miracles!" Sibéal crossed herself. An English stranger at Laragh would mean but one thing. Dispossession. It was going to happen, but better that it might be later rather than sooner. Better that they might pass the coming winter's cold beneath a roof familiar and secure.

"Hasten, Eleanor!"

The children hurried on, and Eleanor smiled. It gladdened her to see excitement upon their faces.

"Off with yer good self. 'Tis enough work for this day," said Sibéal. It was sorrowful how rare was a smile upon Mistress Eleanor's pretty face. She was a good, courageous lass. Not a word of complaint was to be heard from her, nor did a single tear flow from her eyes. It was not right that she'd had to go to Dublin and sell her father's treasures. Few things were right these days. Mistress Eleanor ought to have a man and be starting a family of her own. "I'll finish here, mistress. Go on with yerself, now, and greet yer guest."

Eleanor said a quiet thank you and was halfway down the broad wooden staircase when wee Maeve Cavanagh lifted the beam to open the front door. A whirl of twigs and leaves blew inside, next came the visitor.

Rory's voice bespoke his eagerness. "I'll take your mantle, my lord."

But there was no husband for Eleanor beneath the yards of black wool, not even a man.

" 'Tis only Rosanna Clare," exclaimed Rory in disappointment, which caused wee Maeve Cavanagh— who was not a proper maidservant, having come with her brothers to live in the big house since her mam had died—to giggle.

"Rory Archebold!" Eleanor admonished. The boy appeared penitent. Wee Maeve ceased giggling. "Only Rosanna Clare, you say. She's a guest nonetheless. Have you no manners? Are you not a gentleman like your father and his fathers afore?"

"Good afternoon, Rosanna," Eveleen and Grace chimed in one voice. They never missed an opportunity to shine when Rory had blundered.

"*Dhia duit*, mistress." Wee Maeve bobbled a curtsey of sorts. *God save you. Good day*. She was eager to be a proper maidservant in order that she might remain a part of this household. The big house was much nicer than their cabin ever was. Not that she didn't sore miss her mam, but having slept in a room where the rain didn't ooze through the ceiling and walls, she never wanted to go back to a place such as that where she'd been.

Rory glared at the girls. The *three* of them. Eveleen, Grace, *and wee Maeve*. Sisters were bad enough. Did he now have to contend with Maeve Cavanagh? He didn't mind having her brothers in the big house. They had a fondness for the same grand pursuits as himself, and Rory was happy to have companions for wrestling and climbing trees and spying on the dragoons as they patrolled the Annamoe road. But Maeve? There was no use for her.

"God save all here," Rosanna returned their greeting, and gave Rory a wink. " 'Tis sorry I am to have disappointed you, Rory lad." She was a comely young woman, admired for her natural grace and the abundance of rich auburn hair she always wore in a single heavy plait. Her eyes were shaped like a cat's, and they were the same verdant hue as Eleanor's. Rosanna was a cousin, Clare bloodlines having mingled with Archebold and O'Connor ancestry for generations, and both young women had been blessed with the O'Connor eyes.

"Rosanna, how glad I am to see you. How truly glad." Eleanor embraced her dearest friend. They had been playmates since childhood, and in the days of girlhood past, constant companions when the gentry visited back and forth throughout Wicklow.

"You are cold frozen, Rosanna. Winter comes early, I do fear."

"Aye, the people say Biddy O'Fierghraie divined

a harsh season. 'Twas the clouds racing over the last full moon that proved it.''

"The weans were to see her, and heard the same from her very own mouth."

Rosanna smiled, and chatted as they walked down the gallery. "Do you recall how we used to visit her cabin?"

"To beg that she would teach us the arts of charming?"

"Until her hair went gray."

"Ah, yes, the coming of the gray hairs, for which she blamed us, and vowed to cast a spell on us, if we didn't bring her a fat hen."

"So now she has Rory, Grace, and Eveleen to blame in our stead."

They were laughing as they entered the small parlor. Lady Moira's embroidery frame was positioned in the light of a tall window; there was a chest filled with children's toys, and an octagonal table painted with a gameboard. Near the fireplace was a long bench and two armed chairs with velvet cushions. With its southern exposure, colorful tapestries upon the walls, and carpets covering the floor, the small parlor was an inviting chamber.

Eleanor drew Rosanna hearthside, and bade her sit while she stoked the fire. "Now tell me what possesses you to ride forth from Killoughter on such an ill-favored afternoon as this."

Rosanna did not answer.

"It isn't bad news from the hills?" Eleanor worried about her brothers. It was a miracle they had survived so long. The perils for tories were constant. If it wasn't soldiers and their dogs searching out Irish for the hangman, it was the bone-chilling cold that brought on fever and consumed a man's lungs; if it wasn't gnawing bellies, it was hungry wolves on the prowl for creatures weaker than themselves. "Nothing has happened to Roger, I do trust."

"I've heard naught from Roger since he joined your brothers, and can only assume my prayers for his health and safety are answered. Have you any word?"

"None." Eleanor didn't like the misery in Rosanna's eyes, and wished there was a message for her. Roger was Rosanna's uncle, but they were more like brother and sister since he was less than four years older, and had been raised by her mother. Eleanor saw the trembling in Rosanna's hands, and took them in hers. "You must tell me what troubles yourself. Surely there is something I can do."

A sigh escaped Rosanna. "I do not think there is anything for anyone to do. We have a visitor at Killoughter."

"A stranger?" Eleanor's voice was as soft as Rosanna's. It was as if they whispered a terrible secret.

"*One of them.*"

"Sweet angels in heaven. It cannot have happened at Killoughter."

"A new owner has arrived," was Rosanna's awful confirmation.

"I do not believe it. 'Tis not possible. Your uncle is a Protestant and did not fight in the Confederacy. His properties are not subject to the Act of Forfeiture."

"Which is what Uncle William contends, but Master Stubbs—that is his name, *Nehemiah Stubbs,*" Rosanna uttered the name with the somber, over-serious accent that was intoned by the stiff-necked people come from England. They were a dour lot, those Puritans, who made even the merest utterance sound like a sermon from the pulpit. "He holds a debenture for the land which he asserts is as good as any forfeiture order against us."

"It is a mistake and will be remedied."

"I pray you're right," she said. In every province in Ireland similar "mistakes" were being made. From Munster to Ulster, Protestant landowners were finding they were not safe from forfeiture. Loyal English subjects were being ordered from their homes, for although confiscation and resettlement were meant to cleanse Ireland of English enemies, they were also intended to provide land to pay English soldiers their back wages, and the arrears owed the army were far greater than imagined. Old English or Irish, Protestant or Catholic, Cromwell no longer cared for such distinctions; he needed land. Rumors of what had happened to the Spensers of Kilcoman, Cork, were proof how grim was the situation. Spenser's grandfather had been one of Queen Elizabeth's favorites and Edmund Spenser was not remembered in these parts for *The Faerie Queene*, but for his virulent anti-Irish historie. A family such as the Spensers ought to be above Cromwell's reach, yet everyone had heard stories to the contrary.

"Uncle William has written to the Commissioners and goes himself to Athlone to present his case before the Committee on Transplantation. He reminds them of his loyalty to the Commonwealth of England and its Parliament, and of his mother's lineage."

Sir William Clare was another uncle, but a much older man than Roger, more of an age to be Rosanna's grandfather than her father's brother, or to be exact, her father's half-brother. Sir William was the only child of Sir Walter Clare's union with Lady Jane Stratford, who had been the granddaughter of one James Stratford, counselor to Thomas Cromwell, Henry VIII's head monk-killer and the current Lord General's great-great-great uncle.

A tear slid down Rosanna's cheek. "How strange

is the road I find myself upon. I used to cringe when uncle spoke of his mother's family, and over the years I have spared no affection on him. To my shame, I have cursed him to hell and back, and have gone weeks without exchanging a single word with him though we sit at the same table and pass each other on the stairs. Now I do pray each night for his success, and when he departed for Athlone I actually wished him good fortune."

The parlor door opened. It was Sibéal come to greet Rosanna. She bustled across the room.

"The weans told myself it was Mistress Rosanna, her good self, come to call like the ould days. 'Tis news as welcome as the flowers of May, and it set—" She was brought up short by the sight of Rosanna blotting her eyes. "Do not be saying sadness pays a visit upon us this day. Is it tears upon yer sweet face?"

Rosanna sniffled, but could not stop the trickle from giving way to weeping.

"Och, *leanbh.*" Sibéal called Rosanna *my child* and rocked her as she used to rock her babes. In a way they were every one of them her babes—Eleanor and the weans, Rosanna Clare, the lads in the hills, even the Cavanaghs sleeping in the pantry—for she was the only one left for them. Sibéal used to mourn that she'd survived her husband and twelve bairns. How deep had been her pain to watch the others buried before her—the chieftain at Baravore, Sir Thomas, Ciarán, and Lady Moira, whom she'd tended from birth. Now she understood, and no longer wished to join them. There was gentle wisdom in this madness, and despite the misery inflicted upon this land, the Lord had seen fit to nourish the love in her heart. They were all hers now, and there was more than enough mothering in Sibéal for every single one of these children.

"Ye must tell ould Sibéal what brings on this misery." She kissed Rosanna's brow and held her at arm's length to see what her expression might reveal. "Yer uncle has not had words with Roger again? They have not come to blows, God forbid?"

"Nay, for once 'tis not Roger who makes the blood rise in uncle's face."

The animosity betwixt the half-brothers was well known. Sir William had loathed Roger from his birth; he'd loathed all the boys born of the Irish bride his father had wed after Lady Jane's death. Now William and Roger were the last Clares of Killoughter, who might pass on the family name, and William's loathing was sharpened with resentment. Their father's will obliged him to accept Roger as his heir, and to maintain the lad in his household. It mattered not that William had no son of his own. Killoughter was meant to be his, not to be shared with some Irish whelp, and to his dying day, Sir William would always believe his father had penned his will in malice. Sir William Clare, who had never been guided by fairness or good conscience, seldom attributed such motives to others, not even his own father. "I do not think Roger knows of our troubles at Killoughter," Rosanna said, in preface to telling Sibéal everything she had already told Eleanor. She ended with her uncle's trip to Athlone.

"Sir William will set matters right," assured Sibéal. "Though he is careless, says I, to be leaving a gentle maid as yerself with a stranger. Ye must stay at Laragh until he is returned."

Eleanor agreed, and invited Rosanna to stay as long as she wished.

"You are kind, the both of you, and I know there is always a welcome for me here. But 'tis not necessary, for I do not reside beneath the same roof as Master Stubbs."

"*Buiochas le Dia.* Master Stubbs is a gentleman. *Thank God.*"

"Nay, Sibéal, he is no gentleman, but a candle-stick-maker by trade, and a most insistent fellow." Again Rosanna affected a sober accent. "*Master Stubbs, the candlestick-maker* would not be denied his rights and has already taken up residence in Kil-loughter. He sleeps in the master's chamber, dines at the family table, drinks uncle's wine, and rides his best stallion whilst he inspects the property he durst call his own."

"Do you say he forced you out?" Eleanor's stom-ach churned. It was like hearing news of pestilence and knowing it would spread to Laragh, but there was no way to predict when, no way to ward off its advance. "If not at Killoughter, where do you re-side?"

"Oh, do not misunderstand. I have not left Kil-loughter. I would never abandon the people on our land. If my father and his brothers were alive, they would not forsake them, and one day Roger will re-turn from the hills. Until then, I do act in his stead." It was the same all over Ireland, daughters and wives, sisters and mothers carrying on in the ab-sence of men.

"Where do you reside, Rosanna? You have not an-swered."

"William Groome's widow has made space for me in her quarters above the stable. It is remarkably comfortable, and Master Stubbs did allow me to take a few of—"

"Oh, Rosanna, I could never imagine," Eleanor whispered. "He *allows*!"

"It is the same at Dunranhill, where the widow Plunkett coshers with a tenant, and the Ridelsford sisters at New Castle reside in the old tower." Rosanna didn't mention the old tower had no roof, nor that these situations were only temporary while the ladies made arrangements to leave for Connaught. She didn't want to reveal how truly hopeless was the situation, and how little confidence she held for her uncle's success. She couldn't bring herself to tell them the widow Plunkett, seventy years old and suffering the palsy, had applied for an exemption from transplantation and had been denied.

Sibéal crossed herself, invoking the Lord's guidance and the Virgin's protection upon herself and the two gentle bred young women, and upon all the women of Ireland. "Ye're a rare girl, Mistress Rosanna. And yer good self, Mistress Eleanor. Ye deserve better than Cromwell and Fate are dealing in these times. What say ye, Mistress Eleanor, to a rousing *céilídh* on the morrow?"

"A *céilídh*!" Eleanor shunned the notion of a *social gathering*.

"Aye, tomorrow eve. No elaborate arrangement, mind ye, merely gathering with folk ye have not seen in a while. A little dancing and piping in honor of our visitor from Killoughter."

"Dancing?"

"Aye, dancing, says I."

"And who would we dance with?"

"Rory, for one. Can the lad not dance? And Sean Rian the blacksmith still lives in Annamoe, does he not? He was always a quick one with a jig, I do recollect."

"Pray, what would we celebrate?"

"Life. 'Tis yet ours no matter how many edicts are imposed upon us. But whoever said there had to be a reason? A little dancing and piping would cheer the weans and tenants, the village folk and anyone near enough to join us. Do ye forget it is already the middle of November, but there was no harvest home this autumn to celebrate bringing in the sheaths?"

"I warm to the notion myself. What think you, Eleanor?"

"That Sibéal speaks true." It had been too long since the people had gathered for anything other than a funeral. The Puritan soldiers had threatened to punish anyone who celebrated All Souls. There had been no dancing at crossroads, no bonfires on hilltops, no perambulations through fields. *Bastard witchcraft*, the soldiers called such merrimake, and the mere mention of the fate reserved for witches was enough to terrify folk into obedience. Sibéal was right. " 'Tis not only bellies in need of nourishment, but hearts and souls. A *céilídh* it will be. But is there time to prepare for tomorrow eve? What should be done about the—"

"Whist, now. I'll be in charge." Sibéal tossed up her hands to silence the young mistress. "There's time and enough, and plentiful helping hands, says I, so yerself does not worry about any of it. Indeed, I'll start now and set the weans in charge of the hall, moving benches and hanging what bit of greenery they might. The Cavanagh lads can run round to tell the people we'll be gathering in the big house and all are welcome." Whereupon Sibéal excused herself and went to inform the household of the *céilídh*.

"How went your visit to Dublin?" Rosanna asked Eleanor, when they were alone.

Eleanor had expected this question, but that did not make answering any easier. That did not prevent the sudden flow of warmth that went through her from head to toe.

*No one need ever know.*

But she knew, and would never forget. Sooth, she

knew of things Rosanna could never imagine. She knew about failure and carnal pleasures, about falling asleep secure in someone's arms only to awaken to loneliness and shame.

*The English stranger is your enemy. Do not give more than you agreed.* Near a fortnight had passed, and in that time she had managed to forget his face. It was almost as if she had never set eyes upon him, almost as if they had never met. But his voice had not faded from her memory. His voice was always with her, especially late at night when she was alone. *You are a beauty, you must know . . . a woman to be prized. . . .* Sometimes when she closed her eyes his lips brushed against her skin, such a tender caress that the whole of her body would glow as if wearing a halo, and her heart would clench tighter, tighter.

Something had happened to Eleanor in Dublin, but she could not explain it to Rosanna, for she did not understand it herself. She would tell Rosanna no more than what she had told Sibéal and Father Netterville. "I did not return empty-handed."

"I am glad. You are braver than myself to have gone among them. Dublin is more evil than ever these days, I have heard it said."

" 'Tis behind me now." It was a bold-faced lie. That night in Dublin would never be far enough behind her. A thousand times each day Eleanor told herself to be satisfied with the coins in the strongbox beneath her bed. She should forget the English stranger, who had promised pleasure and been true to his word; she must not allow her nights to be visited by visions of the man who had taken away despair for the space of a few hours. *No one need ever know.*

Outside in the yard the children and hounds erupted in another frenzied commotion, and, grateful for the distraction, Eleanor went to the window. One of the Cavanaghs was leading a horse to the stable. "Someone arrives. I cannot see who."

"Is it Elizabeth Corballis from Tanseyclose?"

"Perhaps. Though I do not recognize the horse. Or it might be someone come from Sir Nicholas Comyn, who sends one of his people to check upon us every now and again."

Wee Maeve burst into the small parlor. Her eyes were wide with alarm, her face was pale. "'Tis a stranger, my brother, he says." She spoke on such a keen of terror Eleanor and Rosanna could not understand her.

"Calm yourself, Maeve. You're not injured? Is the house afire?" asked Eleanor. The child was really too young to be helping in the kitchen, but she was a determined wee thing and would not be deterred.

"A stranger, mistress," Maeve said on a huge gulping breath, then curtseyed and endeavored to speak with a bit more servant-like decorum. "What shall ye want myself to be doing?"

"Why, let him in, of course. Strangers have always been welcomed at Laragh. That hasn't changed. Show him into the library, and prepare a tray. We shall share what little we have with any traveler who stops at our door."

The children were cheering. Huzzahs reverberated through the house.

"Come along, Rosanna. Let's see for ourselves what the cause of their merriment can be."

In the long gallery, Grace was standing outside the library door. "'Tis Eleanor! I see her. She's coming with Rosanna. Eleanor is coming."

The two young women exchanged glances.

"Are you thinking what I am?"

"Need you ask? There are only one or two persons

who might throw this household into such tumult."

"Trow, which one of your brothers would be so bold and clever to visit Laragh disguised as a stranger?"

# Chapter 11

The *Prestissimo* coasted south through choppy water. Sea-spray made the deck slick, Garrett's cloak was wet, the clouds overhead made the sky gray, yet it was a fine day. In fact, there could be no finer day. He stood at the rail of the three-masted cog and stared at the shoreline.

A verse learned from Lady Olivia tumbled through his mind. It was called "An Exile's Dream" and had been written more than a thousand years before by the saint, Colum Cille, royal son of Tir-Conaill and founder of the Derry monastery. Exile was the worst sentence against a patriot of Éirenn, and as penance for having caused the battle of Cuildremne, Colum Cille was ordered to go forth from his country and behold it nevermore. The holy man had settled on the Scottish isle of Iona, where he had founded a monastic community and devoted his life to teaching and writing, and upon his death at the age of seventy, Iona was where he'd been buried.

"An Exile's Dream."

So too had it been Garrett's.

*It would be a pleasure, O Son of my God,*
*in wondrous voyagings*

> *to travel over the deluge-fountained wave*
> *to Ireland.*

As a boy Garrett had shed a child's tears for Colum Cille. Through Órla's tale, he'd come to understand the loneliness and heartache of exile, and he had pledged that one day he would sail over those waves to Ireland. The verse no longer saddened Garrett. He was triumphant.

Soon he wouldn't depend on cradle-tales and ancient poetry to envision the countryside around Castlekevin. *Wilderness abundant with yew and oak and hazel. A dark green fastness wherein faeries dwelt, and fox and stoat, stag, boar, and songbirds flourished,* he whispered the words that he'd learnt as a lad. *Forests fruitful with mast, honey, whortleberries, and leeks, sweet apples and haws; meadows colored with the blue splendor of speedwell, the red of wild campion, the purple of star thistles; fine booley-land aplenty for kine and cattle, hillsides where the air blew crisp with the scents of pine and moist earth.* His journey was near ended, and he would be able to see and touch for himself, to inhale and fill his lungs with fresh, moist air, to hear the waterfalls and birds, the wind in the wildwood.

His senses reeled at the prospect. Soon he would disembark to ride into the countryside from which Órla and his grandfather's father had been taken.

Young Órla's last sight of Ireland had been of Black Castle perched on the headland outside Wicklow harbor. *A three-sided fortress, solid and conforming to the outcrop like a well-made tunic sleeve, with two towers rising above a high curtain wall and rock-cut steps going into the sea.* That was how she'd described the landmark to her daughter; that was how the memory had been preserved and how Lady Olivia had described it to Garrett.

The castle came into view, and Garrett knew a skirl of excitement.

There was Órla's three-sided fortress with steps disappearing into the sea. Garrett saw the loopholes in the curtain wall, the two towers. His chest contracted. It was a miracle how a young girl's memory had been passed down with such accuracy that he might recognize those towers and that wall in her stead. A fleeting image passed before his mind's eye. A child, black curls blowing about her tear-streaked face, onboard a Bristol-bound ship; she was the image of everything resolute and stoic, and Garrett had always imagined her wee mind fixed on one goal and one goal alone. *Cuimhneamh*. She must never forget. *Remembrance.* That would sustain her. Every sight and sound, each leaf, every thistle and blade of grass, every sprig of heather, and each and every dear face. She would keep them with her for always.

The cog sliced through the sea, canvas snapping, rigging clanging. Approaching the shore, closer to the yew and oak and hazel. Waves slapped at the hull. Near to the meadows colored blue with speedwell, a stone's throw to booley-land aplenty. The quayside came into focus. Of a sudden the breath was seized from his lungs, and in a single moment, the images he'd held dear were shattered. It was almost as if the vessel had hit a shoal, or a galloping horse had refused a hedge. Garrett grabbed hold of the railing to maintain his balance.

Wicklow was no bustling waterfront of carters, haggling merchants, and piemen hawking their wares. Garrett saw no inventory of timber, no bundles of hides and raw wool, no caged hawks awaiting the next ocean-going vessel. No piglets running loose, no housewives hauling water, no laundresses balancing linens, no lads at play, no pony carts or wagons, no o'erflowing handbarrows. That the Liffey quays resembled the Thames waterfront had not surprised Garrett, but that this town some thirty miles more or less from Dublin resembled no village or settlement of his experience was a shock.

"What happens here?" Garrett turned to the ship's master, a Venetian named Frescobaldi.

"*A righteous judgment of God.* Those were Oliver Cromwell's very words read before your Parliament." There was no mistaking the animus in Frescobaldi's voice. "After Drogheda the Army of the Commons headed south, following this coastline on its way to Wexford. It was the same everywhere in that autumn of forty-nine. None were spared. No distinction was made between armed men or women and children, between Catholic and Protestant, Irish and old English. All were put to the sword. More than three thousand were slaughtered in two days at Drogheda, where the commander was no Irish chieftain, but the most venerable Sir Arthur Aston." The ship's master from Venice shook his head. Grief mingled with respect upon his features. Sir Arthur Aston's distinguished reputation was well known on the Continent; the English officer and former governor of Oxford had served in Poland against the Turks, for which all of Europe, and especially Venice, remained most grateful, and Cromwell's actions in Ireland were viewed with much contempt. "At Waterford 'twas two thousand in a single day. As for this smaller place, I do not know how many souls once called Wicklow town their home, but my recollection of a more livelier settlement has not faded."

"God's mercy!" Garrett invoked on an underbreath. He could almost hear the cries of terror.

" 'Tis blasphemy, I do think, that the man dares to call himself a servant of the Lord," said the Venetian. "Those not butchered have struggled against pestilence and famine in the three years since. Each season their numbers dwindle evermore lower, leaving the young and weak to fend for themselves. 'Tis a crime against heaven and humanity, though I have never heard it spoken of as such.''

A horrific chill pierced Garrett, a sense of death and evil, and of spirits roaming without peace. Four years had passed, but that wasn't long enough. Perhaps it would never be long enough. God forbid that in another century the Irish would still be seeking justice against the English. Garrett invoked a silent blessing. *God save all who might live and die here.*

''Are you certain you wish to go ashore, milord? There are tories in the mountains, and it will be a mighty struggle to plant this land with English virtues.''

''I will not turn back.'' Garrett reaffirmed his original intention.

*Tories.* Dublin's coffeehouses were rife with fearful talk of these rebels. *The dispossessed.* Mayhap his great-grandfather's descendants were among them. The possibility of reunion with blood kin had not been lost on Garrett; if he was fortunate, if he was blessed, he might find family therein.

That his great-grandfather had been taken from this countryside called Wicklow was, however, the sum of his knowledge about his ancestors.

That and a name. He knew his grandfather's name. *Cahir O'Byrne.*

*Cuimhneamh,* Órla had told herself the first time she'd heard mention of another child taken from Ireland. *Remembrance.*

And the story had been passed down to Garrett.

Órla had been living among the English for two years when there occurred an incident which was at once as horrifying as it was strengthening. An infant had been delivered to a neighboring estate in Kent, and the adults had discussed the arrival of this child, the son of an Irish chieftain, as if the lass from the faraway hills could not hear. The English lady and gentleman, who called themselves Grandmother and Grandfather, had been kind and generous; they had indulged and spoiled Órla, and as each day, each week, each month had gone by, they'd acted more and more as if she possessed no memory of the truth, no remembrance of the past. But she had not forgotten, not a leaf or thistle or blade of grass, not a name or a face, and when the babe arrived at Aylesbury Manor in that third year of her exile, the memory of her own journey to Kent was as fresh as it had been on the afternoon when she'd been stolen from the glen.

She never forgot the day their neighbors came to call and show off the babe. Her recollection of how the English couple had boasted was exact; she never forgot a word of their telling how the wee one had been stolen from his father's fortress, and how they intended to raise him to be a proper Englishman. They had spoken of these things in Órla's presence as if she would not have had any curiosity in another child taken from Ireland. But she had cared, passionately, and had harkened when they'd spoken of changing his name to something *more English, more civilized*. Best to wipe away any trace of the past. He would take the name of his adoptive father, they had agreed. He would be Charles Neville, and little Órla, listening in the corner, had made out his Irish name when it was uttered for the last time, and thus she'd added Cahir O'Byrne to her memories never to be forgotten.

Bitterness had seethed in Garrett since Lady Olivia had told him of his right to a name other than Neville. It had been a constant struggle to pretend he didn't know the truth of who he was, that he didn't know how his grandfather's father had come to be an English milord. Garrett's right to Aylesbury Manor and his title were genuine, but his maternal bloodlines were only half of who he was. By virtue of omission, his identity was a fraud, and he intended to right that deceit.

Garrett had no intention of planting so-called English virtues in those hills. He intended to take possession of his new home, to seek out his kin, assume his rightful name, and do what he might to preserve Irish virtues. *Cuimhneamh.* In his own way, Garrett would carry on in Órla's and Lady Olivia's stead. He would not allow the past to be forgotten. Cromwell might hold the land and transplant the Irish, but Garrett was going into those hills, and he would safeguard the truth. *Remembrance.*

Quick he disembarked and bade farewell to the ship's master. Swift he made his way out of Wicklow town, urging his horse to a gallop as if to escape the moans of the dead. Nothing must be allowed to ruin this day. His journey's end must be as perfect as he had always imagined. In the years to come he would remember his arrival at Laragh as an hour of joy and triumph. Garrett wanted no part of ghosts or misery or anything else that might stand in his way. He had already waited a lifetime for this. No more.

The furlongs raced by, but the scenery along the sharp course of the Vartry water didn't improve. By Jesu, it worsened. As far as the eye could see, the landscape stretched gray. Trampled. Bleak. From the rise of each new hill, Garrett discerned another skeleton of a demolished dwelling. Where once a tower-house had stood guard there was naught but rubble. Farther along, Garrett came upon a burned church. On a nearby hill a solitary chimney reached toward heaven. Lo, the dense, fast wilderness was naught but a grave garden of wanton destruction. In the woods a massive fall, left to rot and decay, was the forlorn remains of the verdant canopy through which sunlight had once been unable to penetrate. Oliver Cromwell was not the first ruler to pursue a scorched-earth policy against Ireland. In the previous century Henry VIII and Good Queen Bess had torched the countryside and ordered the waste of the Irish wilderness. It appeared Cromwell—the regicide—had realized their goal.

One thing hadn't changed: the pattern of the land.

River, mountain, valley, waterfall, loch, plain, and bog remained as they had since the days when the warrior kings of the Uí Brúiun Cualann and Uí Mail drove their chariots through the passes and over the river-crossings.

Young Órla had done well in regard to the lay of the land, and the paths and roadways winding their way through this countryside. Her memory had been vivid and precise. The track along which Garrett rode was the same over which Kevin's followers had traveled on pilgrimage to Glendalough. He made his way to the crossroads at Garryduff, where the roads from Ballylusk, Castlekevin, Glendalough, and Ballinacor converged. There, almost at his journey's end, he turned toward Castlekevin, squinting and straining as if he might conjure up the fortress of Órla's fathers.

Two days past he'd met the grocers. Methusaleh Waring and Thomas Powell were strutting parvenus, and although they had refused to sell their debentures, Garrett had not finished with them. Somehow he intended to wrest Castlekevin from the pair of clownish upstarts. They were going to be neighbors, and in time, a way to deal with them would present itself to Garrett. He would be patient and wait; he was not finished with them.

Guiding his mount along the bridle path, Garrett

noted more trees hereabout, more color, more vegetation, and after a distance of three or four furlongs he came upon a standing dwelling. It was a cabin with a thatched roof, one door, and no chimney or windows. A woman of indeterminate years stood outside. She could have been young, his own age of one score and three, or mayhap she was as old as Lady Olivia. Garrett couldn't tell.

"Ho, friend, is it almost to Laragh?" he called out.

The woman stared at him. He knew she'd heard for the way she focused on him. Mayhap she even understood his question, but there was no response in her eyes, no expression upon her face. He asked again, and still she spoke not a word.

"*Cá fada ó so e?*" Garrett tried a third time, this time in Irish. *How far is it from here?* The woman transformed before him. Her thin body relaxed, her face brightened; she was young with a shy, gentle smile.

"*Agus te sios a bóitairín beag, a dhuine uasail,*" she said, and pointed a few yards ahead. *Go down the little lane, noble sir.*

"*Go raith maith agad,*" came his reply. *Thank you.* He reached into one of the saddlebags, withdrew a piece of wrapped sausage, and held it forth to her.

Without hesitating she crossed the hard ground to Garrett. Her feet were bare, a hint of faded blue petticoat peeked from beneath a red woolen skirt. "*Go mbeannaid Dia duit, a dhuine mait uasail,*" she thanked him. *God save ye, good noble sir.* It was customary among the native Irish for the recipient of goodwill to extend a blessing, and she added, "*Go meádaighe Dia dhuit,*" which meant, *God increase your stores.*

"*Go mbeannaid an ceadna duitse.*" Garrett tipped his hat in farewell. *May the same bless you.*

He rode on, wondering for the first time if the Army of the Commons had passed this way. The debenture told nothing of Laragh's condition. Would the big house be fit for habitation?

Upon reaching the lane, he dismounted.

It was an intoxicating moment, to pass onto the land that was Laragh.

*My journey's end. My future.*

He led his horse through knee-high yellowing sedges, savoring as he went this place that was his. This was Ireland. His lungs filled with the clean scent of moist earth, a hint of pine. Garrett triumphed in the undulation of the land and the quince orchard on the other side of the hedgerow that marched beside the lane; he could almost hear the bees in summer, the linnets on a spring morn, the merry cries of children at play, and the trill of pipes, the beat of a bodhrán, the laughter of dancers circling round a midsummer bonfire. This was where Lady Olivia's tales melded with reality, and he listened to the wind in the trees, heard the rush of a nearby stream. Mayhap the past could become present, and the future would be Garrett's at last.

The lane was in some need of attention. There were ruts that wanted smoothing, rocks that needed to be removed. It curled past a clump of gorse that required pruning, and Garrett had a glimpse of roof and chimneys peaking above a gray twist of treetops. He hurried now around another clump of gorse, down a hollow. The lane sloped upward, and there before him was a splendid and most stately dwelling.

Laragh appeared to be intact.

Cromwell and his Ironsides must not have come up this lane.

Garrett noted the comfortable blending of an old tower with a newer residence. There were stables and a large kennel, and while the yard had become an oversized mud puddle and the dependent buildings were somewhat shabby, their condition was not unexpected, given the circumstances of war and abandonment. It was nothing that hard work and ready coin couldn't remedy. None of the roofing had visible gapes, every wall was standing, the windows of the big house were in good repair, and the chimneys . . .

A faint wisp of smoke was rising from one of the chimneys.

"By all the devils," he swore, loud and clear.

Could it be the family was still in residence? Garrett hadn't considered the prospect, and in a blink his triumph and perfect journey's end were tainted. God's lid, he hadn't considered anything or anyone other than himself. He stopped in his tracks as the horror of what he'd done revealed itself to him. He had not spared even the most fleeting consideration for the people whose property he was claiming as his own. Far too readily had he devised the fiction that whoever might have once called Laragh home, they must have been long gone from the neighborhood, perhaps away to Spain or Poland.

In an act of supreme conceit Garrett had cast himself Robin of Locksley. The land belonged to no one, he'd reasoned with an arrogance of which his English forefathers would have approved; the property would be vacant, idle, and waiting for a master. Waiting for *a proper master who would respect its past*, he'd told himself more than once, and followed his presumptuous logic to the conclusion that *Laragh was in need of a master such as himself*.

"God's nails! God's belly!" he swore again and again until he'd execrated the Lord from brow to toes. He stared at the rising smoke, and his expression buckled with rage toward the men who would steal babes, at Cromwell who would resettle the whole of Ireland, and with himself for having failed to consider every detail of this final, most important step toward the future that was meant to be his. He ran a hand across his eyes. Perhaps he'd imagined the smoke. After all, it had been a long day, and hattered men were known to see things that weren't there.

He looked again at the house, this time to see the front door opening.

Several shaggy wolfhounds burst forth from the elegant dwelling followed by a lad and two girls dressed in smockets befitting offspring of the gentry. Garrett's dismay was profound. His mind conjured an image of standing waist high in a rushing stream, yet dying of thirst as torrents of water swept past him.

No doubt these children had been born at Laragh. Mayhap the lad had been told the house would be his when he was grown and wed with a family of his own. The thought was sobering. Heretofore, there was nothing Garrett wouldn't do if it brought him closer to this journey's end. Now he sensed an unfamiliar weakening, a faltering in the resolve that had sustained him these many years. In its place there was nothing but emptiness, vast and hollow, and Garrett was a lad again, lost and alone.

The dogs were leaping and yapping, creating quite a din. A small boy, having the appearance of a servant's child, came from the direction of the watery stable yard to lead away Garrett's horse while the children from the house approached without any trace of apprehension or suspicion.

"How do you do, sir?" The boy, though the smallest of the three, was the first to speak. "I am Rory Archebold of Laragh."

"I am Eveleen, sir."

"And I am Grace."

They lined up one, two, three as if expecting his approbation, and for some reason he tilted his head as if inspecting them. Garrett was not certain why he did such a thing; mayhap it was the way they seemed to be studying him that had prompted him to do likewise.

One look at the trio confirmed they were siblings. Indeed, each was a somewhat smaller replica of the other, beginning with the girl called Eveleen, who was tallest, then Grace, whose head came to Eveleen's shoulder, and then the lad, Rory, whose head topped at Grace's shoulder. They had yellow hair, straight and thick, without the slightest curl whatsoever, and three sets of eyes that were an astonishing bright blue. Their near identical features were fine, aristocratic; their cheekbones were high, the noses delicate, the lips nicely drawn. Garrett gazed upon their trusting, merry faces and knew there would be no triumph for him this day, no joyous memory to hold dear in the years to come. For a long, agonizing moment he felt sick. There was a churning in his chest, an unfamiliar burning in his nose and eyes. He forced himself to reveal none of this, forced himself to breathe slowly, steadily.

The lad gave a gentlemanly bow. The girls curtsied.

" 'Tis a pleasure to welcome you to Laragh," they said in unison, as if the greeting had been rehearsed with the utmost of care.

"Thank you." Garrett bowed. He tipped his hat. There did not seem to be much else he might do. Besides, it was better than standing there feeling ill and no doubt looking most uncomfortable.

"How worried we were that you wouldn't come to us in time," said Grace. "But we are blessed. At last, you are arrived, sir. 'Tis not too late. Now everything will be set to right."

"Blessed?" Garrett repeated. "At last, arrived? Not too late?" They weren't making any sense, and he couldn't quell the impression of being swept into some macabre stage drama. A farce, to be certain. He had always known who he was and where he was going, but there was no logic to this. "Do you mistake me for someone else, mayhap?"

"Nay, 'tis no mistake," insisted Rory. Here, he paused between each word to pronounce most emphatically, "You. Are. The. One."

The girls nodded in most earnest agreeement.

"But you do not even know my name."

"It does not matter," declared the younger of the girls. "Nothing matters."

"Excepting that you are here. That is what matters."

"At last!"

"Come along!" The lad tugged at Garrett's breeches leg, where it ballooned forth from the cuffed top of his bucket boot. "You must meet our older sister, Eleanor, who is mistress here."

"Has she, too, been waiting for me?" Garrett wondered aloud.

"Oh, nay, milord," said Eveleen, who appeared to be the most serious of the trio. "She knows nothing of this. Nothing at all."

"But oh, how surprised she will be!" enthused Grace. "How perfectly wonder struck!"

# Chapter 12

~~~~⌒◯◯⌒~~~~

"**W**ill Eleanor find him pleasing, do you think?" Grace whispered to Eveleen.

"His eyes are nice. She will favor their color, I ween."

"And he isn't lame, which is certain to please her."

"Nor is he missing any teeth. Another point in his favor."

"Or—"

"Whist, the pair of you. Say not another word. Do you want to send him running?" Rory admonished his sisters, then turned to the gentleman. "My apologies, sir."

Garrett nodded in acceptance, thinking this must be the sort of moment when an older gentleman might remark to a younger one on the tediousness of sisters, but Garrett knew nothing of sisters, tedious or otherwise. He was out-of-place in more ways than one. A *stranger* in their midst, and if these children had any knowledge of his purpose, they wouldn't be greeting him with such enthusiasm.

"By the by, sir, what is your name?" inquired Eveleen.

"Sir Garrett Neville."

Her gaze narrowed, perplexed. "You're not

146

Irish?" she asked. Neville did not ring like an Irish name, nor did his accent sound like one born on this island, but he had the look.

"I was born in England," Garrett answered with slow deliberation. "At a place called Aylesbury Manor," although he was not sure why he was compelled to supply this detail. These children would not know Aylesbury Manor from Sudbury Hall or Cheddar Down, nor did the place name of his birth change anything.

"Oh," Eveleen uttered.

Her surprise was echoed by her brother and sister.

"Then I'm not the gentleman you were expecting."

"To the contrary, sir, we have been expecting a gentleman to arrive, and you are him."

Garrett imagined his smile must be very thin.

"Come along, Sir Garrett Neville. You must come out of the wind. Eleanor will scold us, if we do not treat you like a proper guest." Grace tugged at his breeches with such vigor that the fabric came out of one bucket top boot, but she was oblivious to the disarray she caused as she pulled him up broad granite steps.

"Aye, come into our home." Rory hurried to keep pace with them. "And a hundred, thousand welcomes to you."

Inside the big house, warmth and calm enveloped them. Garrett recognized the lingering scents of polished woodwork and tansy, the odors of wet dog and damp wool, the welcoming comfort of hearth smoke. Another child entered the receiving hall, her eyes as big as saucers, and she stared at Garrett as if gazing upon Beelzebub himself.

"A *raif!*" she squeaked the byname. *Raif* was a play on the common Anglo-Norman name Ralph or

Rafe, used by the peasant folk in derogatory reference to English Colonists.

"Nay, wee Maeve, he is not called Rafe," corrected Eveleen, "but Sir Garrett Neville, and he is a gentleman and our guest."

Maeve shook her head and wrung her hands. Mistress Eveleen might have a fancy name for him, but it made no difference. He might be as tall and braw a figure of a man as her own dear da had been, but he was still a stranger, and while her mam and da might be gone to join the angels, wee Maeve had not forgotten their warnings.

*Watch yer fields else they'll burn yer harvest. Watch yer cow else they'll steal her from the byre. Watch yer petticoats else a rutting raif will help himself to yer virtue.*

Although wee Maeve wasn't certain what her virtue might be, she knew better than to smile and chatter with a *raif* as did these Archebolds. Mayhap living in a big house kept the soles of your feet from going hard and your nose from running, but by wee Maeve's reckoning, it didn't appear to make a body all that clever.

"Och, to be sure, a stranger, he is. That's what my brother said when he came from the stable, and what I told the mistress. No doubting it. A stranger, and a *raif*." Wee Maeve pushed herself flat to the wall. "The mistress says ye're to be showing him to the library."

"This way, then, Sir Garrett," said Eveleen, and she led the way.

They proceeded down the formal gallery, a long corridor with an imposing array of oil portraits and tapestries displayed upon the inner wall, and opposite, a dazzling expanse of widows with a view to lawns sloping down to a lough. Garrett noticed a pair of massive freestanding candelabra and an ornate table that served little purpose other than to display a fine gilt clock. Laragh was as refined in its design and appointments as the foremost English estates. This wasn't the lair of savages who must be tamed and schooled in higher virtues, better taste, gentler ways. Garrett wondered how it was Cromwell and his Godfearing Commissioners had lied with such ease about the people of Ireland.

Halfway down the gallery, they entered a high-ceilinged oak-paneled chamber. Garrett was drawn to the nearest shelf. He scanned the gold lettering tamped into each leather spine and recognized many titles as well as authors.

One manuscript in particular caught his eye. It was a collection of poems in Irish by Padraigin Haicead. Garrett had heard of this Dominican priest from Cashel, and he took the leather folder from the shelf. His hands near trembled at sight of the poet's own hand. *Rise up my country with God's aid: be roused up by the Son of Mary; may an angel, above the land, protect your high places.* He translated the first stanza in silence, but read no further. Waves of emotion crashed over him.

Grief, confusion, a dreadful loneliness, and an awful sense of futility.

Garrett shut tight his eyelids and required a deep breath before he might speak. "This is a remarkable library. Your father is a scholar?"

"Our father was a poet," said Grace. "Over there was where he put his poems to paper."

"Was?" Garrett opened his eyes and glanced where Grace was pointing. Nearby a writing table was positioned to benefit from the early morning light. An inkwell, portfolio, and several new sharpened quills sat atop a leather tablesquare creating the impression that someone was soon to open the portfolio, soon to remove a sheath of paper and begin writing. "Your father does not compose anymore?"

"Not anymore. Never again."

"He was a poet. And an officer with the Confederate army," said Rory. The youngest Archebold child, he had scarce known his father, yet he spoke with authority of things that had happened before he was even born. "He commanded one of Preston's brigades before fighting under the command of Hugh Duff O'Neill and the Royalists at Clonmel. A colonel, our father he was, with three hundred pounds on his head. Little more than a year past, he was executed at—"

"Whist, Rory," scolded Eveleen. "Hush. You know better than to talk of such things. Do you want to upset Eleanor?"

"She's not here," he replied, defiant.

"But will be, and you know it grieves her to be reminded—" Eveleen broke off at the sound of muted voices.

Grace peeked into the corridor. " 'Tis Eleanor! She's coming with Rosanna. Eleanor is coming."

Rory and Eveleen positioned themselves on either side of their guest. They were proud of their accomplishment and bursting with anticipation to witness Eleanor's reaction. Biddy O'Fierghraie's spell had succeeded; a husband had come to Laragh for Eleanor.

Grace held the door. Rosanna entered first.

"May we present our cousin Rosanna Clare from Killoughter?" Rory announced. "Rosanna, this is Sir Garrett Neville."

"Mistress Clare." Garrett recognized the surname of the Norman knight, Richard the Strongbow, who had led the first English army into Ireland, married the daughter of the King of Leinster, and been granted heirship to his kingdom. He bowed before a young lady in a handsome riding outfit.

"And this is our sister, Eleanor, the mistress of Laragh."

He looked to the sister they called Eleanor, and saw black hair, green eyes as lush as Órla's glen. Recognition slammed into Garrett. He recalled lavender and sweet woodruff, and her gift of trust; he recalled how irresistible had been the attraction between them, and how sensual had been her body's reponse to his. He had never expected to forget her; she had indeed been the kind of woman men regret leaving behind. He had never thought to see her again, yet she was standing before him. He had found her at this journey's end, and he wanted to laugh aloud, to grab her hands and spin her in circles.

This had almost been the most accursed day of his life, but in an instant, everything had changed.

Curious, discordant emotions rushed through him, yet he managed to suppress any reaction out of the ordinary. There was nothing in his demeanor to suggest he'd ever before encountered Mistress Eleanor Archebold. Nothing upon his face to hint he knew her more intimately than many husbands did their brides. Nothing to reveal that he was—at that precise moment—considering how delicious it would be to reach beneath her skirt, run his fingers up her inner thigh to caress her, and see how quick he might stir her.

She opened her mouth, but not a sound came forth. A fierce blush scalded her cheeks, and Garrett could not help being pleased. It suited him to fancy she was remembering every passionate detail of their time together. Then every trace of color drained from her face. She swayed.

"Mistress?" Garrett reached her side in time to catch her limp form.

Once again she'd fainted into his arms.

He stared down at her, but needed no reminders. He hadn't forgotten the way those dark lashes feathered against skin as fair as cream, nor her habit of chewing upon her lower lip. Often in the past weeks, his thoughts had been interrupted by an unbidden vision of the unguarded arousal he'd seen upon her delicate features, of the trust and curiosity her eyes had revealed when she'd been lying upon the pillows, speaking soft to him. The calculated chill he'd seen in her eyes at the coffeehouse was a distant memory.

"Sir," came her faint whisper. She had opened her eyes, and was trembling. "Sir. I—I do not make sense of this. You cannot mean to—"

"Hush." Garrett grinned. He leaned close and murmured against her ear, "You must promise me you'll never change, Mistress Eleanor. I rather enjoy this habit you possess of falling into my arms. 'Tis most charming. Has anyone told you what an enchanting female you are?" His voice dropped lower until the husky rasp seemed to taunt her in caress. "Verily, it would appear you've cast your spell upon me."

Whereupon Mistress Eleanor emitted a tiny gasp, and for a third time she swooned into his arms.

The first thing Eleanor saw when she opened her eyes was *him*. Compelling, dangerous, and virile. It nearly took her breath away.

He was real, flesh and bone, not some figment of her imagination come to torment her, to remind her of how low she had stooped, and of how she had failed even in that. He was sitting beside her bed, having made himself most comfortable in the privacy of her chamber. Much too comfortable. Verily, he wasn't sitting. He was lounging. His long legs were stretched before him, his feet were resting on a stool, and her heart seemed to stop completely when she met his gaze.

He had the satisfied expression of a man who has won a great victory. It was a look which Eleanor didn't like, a look which reminded her of when he'd said, *You do not think I will let you go?* It was almost as if he'd come to claim the rest of her.

A flash of heat touched her belly. A sort of panic swirled through Eleanor, and she forced it down, tried to concentrate. That was not what was happening here! Though how it was that he'd come to Laragh, she could not fathom. He'd already taken everything she had to give, and more. What could he want? She tried to remember what Rory had said his name was, but instead of recalling his name, her mind conjured up images of warm hands exploring her, of his mouth seeking, his tongue stroking, and . . . of loneliness and dreams that would never come to pass. *Sweet company of heaven, my brain is addled.*

"Pray, sir, what is your name?" she asked, in a stilted voice that must belong to another woman.

"Garrett," he said. His voice was quiet. His intense, hooded eyes didn't waver from her face.

Eleanor felt like a butterfly about to have her wings pinned back. It mattered not that she had once trusted him. This was different. This wasn't Dublin, far from home, where she might be nameless, and might never concern herself with the consequences of what she had done. This was home, Laragh. Indeed, this was her very bedchamber. Everything was changed, and she was terrified, confused. "Garrett what?"

"Neville." He continued to lounge. "Sir Garrett Neville."

Eleanor closed her eyes. *Sir Garrett Neville.*

She heard the rising wind and knew nightfall was nigh. Outside, the immense holly tree scratched against her window as it did every night, and the wind whistled through the yews that grew round the walled garden. Her chamber was warm and secure from the elements, smelling as it always did of lavender and sweet woodroof. Eleanor should have felt safe, but she didn't; she felt threatened, betrayed, dishonored. She opened her eyes. "What are you doing in my private chamber, Sir Garrett Neville? Where is Sibéal? Rosanna? Explain yourself."

"Harbor no fears, mistress. I've not harmed your family, nor do I own any intention of ravishing you." He leaned forward, those dark eyes holding her in their thrall. "Your family trusts me. What has happened to your trust?" he whispered.

She continued to glare. Anything to hide the melting, quivering sensation his soft words wrought upon her. "Explain yourself, sirrah."

He sat back. "You fainted in my arms."

"That explains nothing," she snapped, defensive, and caring not how froward she might sound. He shouldn't be in her chamber, shouldn't be sitting close to her bed, nor whispering like that, nor gazing upon her with such bold regard. She recognized the penetrating gleam in his deep, dark eyes, and knew the direction of his thoughts. No doubt he saw her exposed upon a mound of pillows, sighing, wanting; no doubt he remembered how she had rocked upward to meet his thrusts. She was naught but a whore in his eyes. A blush colored her face. Eleanor essayed a cough. "I haven't been well, sir. My throat. The fever returns, I do fear. I am not well."

"Ah, is that what you call it?" he drawled. "That must explain your fainting in my arms. Twice this day. There you were, pale as a ghost and oblivious to the pandemonium you'd created in the household. I'm told 'tis quite unlike you to keel over. *Mistress Eleanor has never fainted*, your old nurse assured

me, which your cousin confirmed, whereupon your
brother boasted of your stalwart and practical disposition. *Not in the least hen-hearted*, the lad declared
more than once, which your sister Grace assured me
was a fine thing. I can't imagine why they made no
mention of your illness." He noticed the way she
was nibbling on her lower lip, and finding it ach-
ingly familiar, he grinned. "Sibéal suggested I carry
you upstairs, Grace and Rory showed me the way.
I brought you here as any gentleman would do, and
have waited whilst you regained yourself."

Eleanor wanted to scream, *Wipe that grin off your
face!* The matter-of-fact way he talked about her sisters and Rory, Rosanna and Sibéal, infuriated her. It
seemed as if she had somehow lost control, as if he'd
of a sudden put himself in charge. This was not his
home; it was hers. And while he might have owned
her for a night, that would never happen again.
"You call yourself a gentleman?"

"Have not my past actions proven I am a gentleman?"

"Surely, you do not dare to speak of—" she faltered. Thick lashes lowered over her eyes, then
lifted.

He finished for her, "Of our previous encounter?
Or should I say, encounters? Indeed, 'tis precisely
what I dare."

"Then you answer your own query in the nega-
tive. You are no gentleman, but an arrogant cad. A
gentleman would never remind a lady of such an
unfortunate incident."

"Unfortunate, you call it?" He arched an eyebrow,
gave his best rakish expression, and was rewarded
to see the color upon her cheeks deepen. But there
was no hint of the sacrificial virgin he'd once seen
in her blush; rather, it reflected awareness of her
own sensual nature and the pleasures shared betwixt

them. All Garrett could think was how he wanted to take up where they'd left off in Dublin. He wanted to kiss her, to lie back with her upon that bed, to feel her heated, inner velvet, hear her moans, and behold the passion swimming in her eyes, the play of arousal across her lovely face. "By my recollection, that *unfortunate* incident concluded most profitably for you. Nor was it altogether unpleasant for either of us, I might add. Though our parting was disappointing. Suffering from a fever, you say?" His grin broadened, and his voice dropped to a husky whisper. "Truth to tell, Mistress Eleanor, *I haven't recuperated myself.* You left me in a state of frustration, quitting Dublin in such haste. I had hoped you would stay longer or at least would have bidden me a proper farewell. Slipping away whilst I slept and without so much as a parting kiss caused me much discomfort, you must know."

Eleanor forced herself not to react. She didn't gasp or look down her nose in indignation, but stared at him with a cool, unwavering gaze while wondering if she'd misunderstood him, wondering why he was here, and more important, when he was leaving. *Tomorrow will be even sweeter. You do not think I'm going to let you go?* It could not be that he'd come after her. Men did not do such things except in childish cradletales. Could it be he wished his money back? Eleanor's gaze narrowed with suspicion.

Laragh was leagues from Dublin. Back of God speed, it was, and miles from the coast highway. It wasn't on the road to anywhere but the mountains. No one journeyed through this country unless they had a reason; travelers didn't arrive at Laragh by accident. "What business brings you to my home?"

" 'Tis not what you might imagine." Garrett did not like the sudden chill in her eyes. The woman with whom he'd made love owned no such frosty, passionless stare. It reminded him of how calculated she had been in the coffeehouse, how guarded, and he didn't like that. He preferred the woman who'd given him her trust.

"You presume too much, sir, to know what I imagine. And I would ask that you cease your riddles, and speak plain and true. Why are you here? What do you want?"

Garrett heard her questions, but was not prepared to answer.

Until a mere quarter hour past, he would have had a ready answer, but no longer.

Until today he'd always known what he must do next, for everything had always been another step closer to the future. He knew why he'd made the journey to Laragh, but he wasn't certain anymore what he intended, and Garrett, once a man of careful purpose, found himself in the peculiar and unexpected situation of being unable to focus on anything beyond the immediacy of Eleanor Archebold.

There was a reason to stay at Laragh, but it was not sensible, practical, or worthwhile. It was not what had brought him through the hills and up the lane. It was tempting and selfish. To be sure, it was the very thing he'd avoided those many years in England.

Garrett wanted Laragh, and along with the land, he wanted its mistress. He knew what he wanted; still, he was not certain whether to laugh or to frown.

He plowed his fingers through his hair, and, needing time to think, he stood to leave the chamber. "Lie back, Mistress Eleanor. Go to sleep. Rest for now. I would not want your fever to return. We can talk on the morrow. There will be time then, or the day next, or thereafter. For you must know, Mistress Eleanor, there is much for us to discuss."

"The day after morrow? Or the next! Do you not need to be on your way? Surely you must be continuing on to somewhere else."

"There is nowhere else of which I know." He grinned in earnest. Despite the unforeseen circumstances at his journey's end, Garrett was certain of one thing. He was going to stay at Laragh to claim this land and its mistress for his own. Eleanor Archebold would be his. "I have no need to be on my way. At least, not for a day or two. Besides I've been invited to your *céilidh*."

"Do not tell me you intend to stay!"

"Oh, but I do, Mistress Eleanor. I've heard much of Irish revels and jigs and the sort of dancing music that rouses faeries from their hill forts, but I've had no experience of such delights," Garrett said, low and teasing. He bowed in farewell, wished her a proper good night, but could not control the impulse to wink at her. "A plague of a thousand devils could not drive me away from your *céilidh*."

# Chapter 13

〰️〰️

**"'T**is high time ye were pausing to catch a breath, Mistress Eleanor," declared Sibéal. "Like yer own dear mam, ye are this night spinning in circles, raven hair flying round yer shoulders, and a sparkle in yer eyes. Ye've not ceased since Cormac MacMurrough took up his flute, and yerself, the one who said there wouldn't be enough menfolk for proper dancing!"

"Do not remind me of my foolish reluctance. A *céilidh* was a grand idea, Sibéal." Eleanor hugged the old woman. " 'Tis a joy to again behold mirth in my father's hall."

This night Laragh was not a place of ghosts and souls given to mourning, but a place of laughter and voices joined in song. Bog deal glowed in the massive hearth, sweetening the air with the fragrance that came from burning ancient pine roots embedded in turf. The lofty hall was ablaze with tapers, rush-candles, and lantern-lamps like the countless stars in the sky. 'Twas a night for the living. Nearly three score had come to the big house. There were villagers from Annamoe and Clara. From neighboring estates came Elizabeth Corbellis of Tansey Close with her maid, and Sir Nicholas Comyn from New Castle with the last of his tenants, fourteen souls, where once there had been more than eighty. Brian the piper and his auntie had come the farthest, all the way from the pass at Knockreagh, playing his pipes as he walked, and calling forth the widow-women and orphans from their cabins and cottages; young Róisín O'More, who lived in the cabin beyond the Laragh gates, had joined them as had Biddy O'Fearghraie.

Eleanor smiled. "In reply to the unspoken question etched upon your face . . . aye, Sibéal, 'tis a wonderful time I'm having."

*Almost perfect* were it not for Sir Garrett Neville. It was not right that he should be here, instead of her parents and brothers, instead of the husbands and wives, sons and daughters, who were absent. Eleanor had tried her best to ignore him, but it was impossible, especially when his laughter rose above the music or when she overheard one more female singing his praises. Róisín O'More, who hadn't spoken more than a few sentences since her Declán had been shipped to the Indies, volunteered to walk him through a long dance while Elizabeth Corbellis and Rosanna had been fluttering about his person like bright moths to a flame.

"Merriment is a fine tonic, says I. 'Tis no harm for a body to be forgetting the troubles a spell," said Sibéal. "Och, look behind yerself now. Sir Garrett comes this way. Himself is a fine, braw gentleman, and a *brine-oge*. Most popular with the girls, being such a *young fellow full of fun and frolic*. Likes to dance, he does . . . though I do not believe he's had yerself on his arm yet."

"He did not ask." In truth, Eleanor had been staying as far away from him as was possible, and while she had evaded dancing or conversing with him, the banqueting hall was not large enough to escape his scrutiny. All evening she'd been aware of his gaze.

Like a wolf stalking its prey, he had been watching and waiting that he might catch her eye. As for the expression upon his face, it was far too knowing, far too hungry.

"Didn't ask, is that the way of it? Och, himself'll ask now, I'm thinking."

Indeed, that appeared to be his intention. Eleanor looked where Sibéal pointed, and saw Sir Garrett cutting across the hall. Eveleen, Grace, and Rory were at his heels.

"Smile, mistress," whispered Sibéal in encouragement.

Eleanor did not wish to smile. Of a sudden, she was distempered, impatient, and more than a little warm.

"Good evening, fair ladies." Garrett stopped and bowed to each of them. "Mistress Eleanor. Dame Sibéal."

Eleanor acknowledged him with a curt nod. Perhaps if she said nothing he would go away, and perhaps geese laid golden eggs or Brian the piper might tame the whole English army with a single tune. He did not leave, but took her hand and raised it to his lips.

"You're a lovely sight this evening, Mistress Eleanor." He grinned at her. " 'Tis a most becoming gown. You should always wear green."

Eleanor suppressed a grimace. Sibéal had insisted she wear her mother's green brocade this night, the very dress she'd taken to Dublin, the very dress Sir Garrett had unlaced and slipped off her shoulders. Heat warmed her face at the memories. More than likely Sir Garrett construed it as an open invitation, but Eleanor managed to return his far too knowing look with one of mild indifference.

Grace and Rory were standing on one side of him; Eveleen was on the other.

"Go on, Sir Garrett. Now," they chimed in encouragement. "Ask her now, sir. Now."

"You must make haste before she scurries away from you again," said Eveleen.

"And do not allow her expression to discourage you, sir," advised Rory. "She is never half as cross as she makes herself appear."

"Nay, Rory, Eleanor's not cross. Merely upset, I do warrant, for two years have passed since our last *céilidh*, and after all that time, she remains unwed," was the opinion of Grace, who gave excessive overemphasis to the final two words. *Remains unwed.*

"Grace Sorcha-Rose Archebold! A lady does not discuss such private matters with strangers," Eleanor scolded, but it sounded too indignant to be a decent reprimand. What was wrong with her brother and sisters? They'd made any number of peculiar references this day to weddings and bride grooms. Not to mention their secretive whispering, and the unusual quantity of dried roots and wilted bogbine blossoms the girls insisted upon keeping in their bedchamber.

Garrett met her gaze, pulled a face, and grinned. "I do believe your sister is as cross as a bag of cats."

"Never!" proclaimed Grace and Eveleen.

"Ah, Miss Grace, Miss Eveleen, you must never say never." Garrett spoke in his most charming manner, and while he addressed the younger sisters, his gaze never wavered from Eleanor's. "I trow Mistress Eleanor has not yet forgiven me for breeching the privacy of her chamber."

"Och, there's naught to be forgiving, Sir Garrett. Breeching the privacy of her chamber, is it now? Don't ye believe such a thing. The young mistress is as grateful as the rest of us for yer being there to catch her, and carry her upstairs. Now and again we all need someone to watch o'er us, says I. Isn't that right, mistress? Tell Sir Garrett that's the way of it."

Eleanor remained silent. She struggled not to reveal how deep Sibéal's words cut.

"Go on, says I, reassure him. Dance with yer guest, and be enjoying yer young selves."

"The good dame Sibéal speaks true, Mistress Eleanor. I would be much reassured, if you would dance with me. But only if you are well enough, of course. Your fever does not return, I trust? Your lung inflammation is cured? I would not want to be the cause of a relapse."

"Fever, do ye say? Lung inflammation?" Sibéal exclaimed, in a voice that revealed her confusion. "The young mistress?"

Eleanor shot Garrett a look so quick and deadly it could have been fired from a musket.

"Say you will, Eleanor." Grace gave her a nudge. "Do not be shy. Dance with him."

Rory grabbed Eleanor's hand and held it out for Sir Garrett.

"Sir Garrett is the most handsome man here," sighed Grace. "Do you not agree, Eveleen?"

"Aye, he's the handsomest. And also a gentleman and a scholar and a bachelor of considerable estate," waxed Eveleen, who had devoted the better part of the afternoon to quizzing the bridegroom about his qualifications. Biddy's charm might have brought Sir Garrett to Laragh, but that did not mean he was deserving, or that they couldn't employ another charm to send him back to that place called Aylesbury. Biddy had said it was a rare man who won the heart of a *bean-draoícht*, and after several hours' questioning, Eveleen had decided Sir Garrett was, indeed, a rare and worthy gentleman.

"Why, 'tis nothing less than magic how he came to Laragh in time for our *céilidh*. 'Tis almost like the old times, and he would be a gallant come to call upon you, Eleanor. Oh, you must dance with him. You must. Then everything will be perfect.''

Eleanor studied Grace. She had never witnessed such pleading from the girl. And then there was Eveleen, prattling about scholars and whatever else! Could it be that wicked faeries had cast a spell over the weans?

"Surely, Mistress Eleanor, you will not disappoint your sisters.'' Garrett took her hand from Rory, and threaded his fingers through hers as he stepped closer. Syllable by syllable his voice fell until she was the only one who could hear his smooth coaxing, "Say aye, Mistress Eleanor. Allow me the honor of dancing with the most beautiful woman to grace this hall. The most beautiful woman I've seen since coming to Ireland. *And that includes the whole of Dublin's fair city.*''

He was flirting with her! Standing too close, towering over her, and whispering in a voice that was far too smooth, far too deep. His smile was restrained, but the glow in his eyes was intimate, hungry. Eleanor had seen that look before. He was trying to make it impossible to ignore him, but she wasn't going to play rabbit to his stoat. He did not own her this night, and never would again. Indeed, Eleanor intended to make that point. She would dance with him, but afterward, he would still be hungry.

"Aye, Sir Garrett, I will dance with you.''

Cormac MacMurrough had again taken up his flute to play a lively old song. He was accompanied by Brian the piper, and a tenant named Aidan Lawless, whose quick fingers and callused knuckles marked the tempo on the hide stretched across a *bodhrán.* Garrett and Eleanor joined the couples in the center of the hall, where a large ring was being formed.

"You had a smile for your other dance partners, Mistress Eleanor. Do you not have one for me?" Garrett asked as he bowed.

Eleanor curtsied. The dance required it, but she didn't smile. "I do not like you, Sir Garrett, and do not wish to smile."

"You hardly know me well enough to dislike me," he replied, thinking that while she no doubt lied to herself, that was not going to make this any easier.

They linked arms to spin in a tight circle, and having spun round thrice, separated to face one another with their hands positioned at their hips.

"Hardly is more than sufficient."

"Faith, mistress, do not tell me your trust wavers. Can it be you are uncertain what you might discover?" He studied her with a measuring glance before adding, "Be assured, the full history of Sir Garrett Neville is not any worse than what you already know."

"I harbor no such concerns regarding your history, sir. Rather it is a matter of interest. I harbor no interest regarding yourself."

His dark brows knit together as if he were pondering what next to say. "Tell me, Mistress Eleanor, have I ever hurt you?"

She knew what he insinuated. No doubt this veiled innuendo was intended to provoke her, but she paid no heed, and instead said, "You are one of the English; you are not one of us. That suffices. There is no need for me to know you any better."

To her ear, Eleanor sounded composed, cool, and convincing, and pleased with herself, she tossed her head in a sort of definitive gesture that declared, *And there's naught else to discuss.* The women were forming an inner ring, and she took several steps away from Sir Garrett.

The tempo quickened; the *bodhrán* beat harder.

This was the faery music that stole men's breath away, and while the inner circle of women danced around the hall, shaking their flounces and twirling their skirts, the men remained in place clapping their hands and stomping their feet until the rafters shook.

Garrett scarce realized how the floor quaked beneath him. He was focused on Eleanor Archebold, mistress of Laragh, as she twirled round the hall, making the green brocade skirt rise and fall about her slender calves, offering glimpses of a frilled linen petticoat, and resembling the froth and waves in a stormy, untamed sea. He admired the way her dark hair tumbled down her back, cascading, curling, unbound and natural. This spirited creature was neither unexpected, nor unappreciated. Garrett knew how she could blossom, and his loins stirred. He remembered how those silken tresses felt against his face, the smell, the texture, and he knew a vivid memory of sweet lips, full breasts, and eager moans. Yet even more vivid, brighter, clearer he remembered her trust, her honesty, and her surrender. He'd enjoyed full breasts aplenty, he'd heard scores of breathless moans, and partaken of countless delicious lips, but Eleanor Archebold offered something more, something valuable and irreplaceable. There had been a vulnerable quality about her he would never forget; a vulnerability that went beyond the loss of her virginity. It was as if she'd been taking something that wasn't meant to be hers, and he couldn't shake the impression that she'd been afraid of being caught before she'd had her fill. She held nothing back, and that aroused him as no other woman had ever done.

As soon as the women completed the circle, Garrett lost no time linking his arm through hers. He would try again and again, if need be. She was going to be his. He whispered, "Who I am does not seem to matter to the others."

"They do not open their eyes wide enough to see beyond the man who rescued the mistress from cracking her head upon the hearth." They were spinning, and Eleanor had to lean close, if she did not want the whole hall to hear her every word. "They see a man who spent the morning helping Ambrose ready the winter garden, after which he extracted a thorn from a hound's swollen pad, then endeared himself for eternity to Sibéal by hauling her bathwater, and did not rest until he'd made himself of further use by plucking several plump salmon from the stream. They know nothing of the man I encountered in Dublin, and lief believe your arrival at Laragh owes to some mysterious whim of chance." She paused in the hope he would explain himself, but he said nothing.

As if to emphasize his silence, the *bodhrán* missed a beat.

"You will not be long in our company, I trust," said Eleanor. Her remark, however, went unheeded, for Sir Garrett's attention had shifted.

Aidan Lawless missed another beat, Cormac MacMurrough hit a series of wrong notes, and Brian the piper stopped playing altogether. The dancers came to a sudden standstill; their movements were frozen in mid-air. The onlookers ceased their chatter to stare at the silent musicians, the motionless dancers. There was no clapping, no music, no stomping or twirling.

It was an eerie quiet hanging o'er them, and then an audible quaking rippled through the hall as if a colossal blast of thunder had rent the heavens. Brian the piper cocked his head to one side and frowned.

The thunder rolled closer. In automatic reaction to danger, Eleanor glanced about the hall for her father,

her brothers. It was almost upon them, and she recognized the galloping approach of many horsemen. She trembled. The riders were in the stableyard, but her father and brothers were gone from Laragh. She saw the people looking to her as she had sought the reassuring sight of her father. The weans rushed to her side, and at the far end of the hall, the massive double door burst open.

# Chapter 14

**B** itter night air wailed over the threshold, a whirl of straw and dried leaves followed, and throughout the hall rushlights contorted against the violent wind. The wolfhounds growled, low and menacing, and several persons muttered, "God bless them," thinking it was a faery host passing in the spinning straw and leaves.

The noise was deafening as some dozen or more men invaded Laragh's banqueting hall. Not content to remain in the yard, they rode their horses up the steps and through the doors. They were English dragoons, full armed, and from the looks of their frothing, heaving horses, they had ridden hard this night. Sir Garrett moved to shield Eleanor's body with his own, the weans pressed close, and the horsemen broke into two groups, making way for the ranking officer who walked his mount to the fore.

The officer held up a single gloved hand to still the other riders, and when the jangle of bridles and clatter of hooves had subsided, he addressed the crowd. "I am told this be the home of the felon Thomas Archebold. And I am here to see the widow Archebold who calls herself mistress of this place."

Eleanor's hands clenched together to still her trembling. She recognized the officer; he had been at

her father's execution, he had been present when her
brothers had been declared outlaws, and it appeared
he was to be the instrument of this final heartache
as well. Laragh's new owner had arrived with a
troop of armed men to enforce his right to seize her
family home. Of a sudden, it seemed to Eleanor that
her plan to save Laragh was doomed to failure.

"Come, Lady Moira, I would ask that thou present
thyself before me, if thou wouldst be so kind."

She heard the English officer ask for her mother
by name, and knew that she should step forward in
her stead. Eleanor made to step from behind Sir Garrett, but he leaned ever so slightly to one side to
block her way.

"Stand fast," he whispered without looking at her.

It was warning enough. She hesitated, and
glanced sideways at him, but he was looking
straight ahead, giving no hint he'd spoken a word,
and from beneath lowered lashes, her gaze went
round the hall. No one was looking at her. Not a
man, woman, or child among them intended to identify her, nor from their expressions did they expect
her to welcome these English soldiers.

"You people do speak English, do you not?" came
the officer's insult after a lengthy silence.

Still not a word was uttered in reply.

"Townsley?" The officer addressed one of his
men.

"Yes, sir," replied the dragoon.

"Tell me, Townsley, dost thou not burn with curiosity to know what cause these folk have for celebration this night?"

"Aye, sir, I do wonder. Mayhap they welcome the
arrival of a new landlord."

Eleanor gasped beneath her breath, and Sir Garrett
took hold of her forearm. The soldiers enjoyed this
cruel barb while the tenants and village folk, the

widow women and children, the orphans, mothers, and old men continued to stare, unflinching, unwavering. Their expressions were hard, narrow, unforgiving.

"If not the Lady Moira, then, I would know who amongst you stands as head of this household. Speak up. Have you no respect for authority?" the officer demanded, but it was a question which needed no reply. He had been in Ireland too long and had seen that loathsome expression many a time before; he knew hatred seeped through the veins of these rebellious insolent people. So, too, did he appreciate the difficult and righteous task it would be to school them in proper manners. He pulled on his reins and began walking his horse around the hall. At his progression, mothers gathered their children close. Elizabeth Corbellis and her maid shrank as near to the wall as they might.

The officer stopped before Elizabeth and raised one gloved hand to the brim of his black felt hat where a small Bible was thrust behind the hatband; it was a gesture meant to intimidate. Power and right were his, the gesture indicated, for he was a soldier of God. "Good evening, mistress. I am Captain Rowlestone from the New Castle barracks, and we are abroad this night on Commonwealth business. We pursue vermin."

"Vermin," repeated Elizabeth Corbellis, in a thin voice of confusion.

"Aye, mistress, vermin most foul. We respond to a report that a popish felon, a priest, who would defy the January sixth edict to surrender or leave Ireland, has been seen on these lands."

Eleanor swayed. Her relief that these soldiers were not here to enforce an eviction was fleeting. She forced herself not to pale, nor make a sound; she knew the man for whom they searched, and did not allow her gaze to settle upon anyone in particular in the banquet hall.

The captain continued round the hall, reciting as he went the fate that was meted out to priests in Cromwell's Ireland, or to any among the citizenry who might be foolish enough to harbor such a felon. He peered at each person, leaning down in his saddle to scrutinize anyone who might try to hide from him. Halfway round the hall, he came to another halt, and pointed at an elderly man. "Seize him!"

Two dragoons dismounted to advance upon the man known as Ambrose, by whose side Garrett had worked that afternoon in the winter garden.

"Nay! Stop!" Eleanor broke away from Sir Garrett and rushed forward to place herself before the dragoons. Father Netterville had sent the man to her; she could not fail to protect him.

"Who dares to impede Commonwealth business?" The officer wheeled his horse round, and upon seeing Eleanor, the fury in his voice only abated somewhat. "Mistress Archebold, is it not? Do not arrest him, thou sayeth, but he fits the description. Pay heed, Mistress Archebold. Pay close heed." From the depths of his coat he produced a rolled broadsheet which he unfurled, then began to read aloud, "Stephen Kirwan, a priest of the order of Capuchins, and a native of Enniscorthy, graying hair, middle stature, advanced in years. Tell me, Mistress Archebold, how you might argue with that?"

"I do not argue, sir, but hasten to assure you that despite the similarities there are many men of middle stature of advanced years with graying hair to be found anywhere in Ireland, and in this particular instance, there must be some mistake. You cannot want this man."

"Ah, but I do," the officer affirmed. He nodded to

the dragoons, and they pulled Ambrose away from
the others; the man stood tall, but did not struggle.
"My orders are to pursue this popish vermin, to arrest him, and deliver him to Kilkenny, which is what
I intend, and I would advise that neither thyself nor
any of thy people try to stop me in any way. Thou
dost not forget the punishment for harboring a
priest, I trust? The Lord High General's judges make
no distinction between men and women. Justice is
fair and equal in Cromwell's Ireland. Thou would
hang as easily as any man, I warrant."

"I'm certain, Captain, none of us fails to appreciate the Lord High General's justice." Sir Garrett
spoke. The ring of authority in his voice was as confident as was his aristocratic English accent, and
while this did not surprise Eleanor his moving to
stand beside her did. Indeed, it produced the most
inappropriate fluttering in her heart. She stared at
him as he went on, thinking that she ought to let her
gaze drop, thinking of the danger he could bring
upon himself for speaking so bold.

"And by that same token, sir, none amongst us
must need be reminded of that justice in a manner
that might be construed as threatening. Mistress Archebold is correct, Captain, and I regret that you are
mistaken. This man is in my employ and cannot be
the man you seek. We arrived only yesterday from
Dublin. I know of no Stephen Kirwan, a Capuchin.
He is Ambrose Talbot."

Sir Garrett was lying. Eleanor knew this as surely
as did every man, woman, and child in the hall, yet
not a single one of them raised an eyebrow. They
were each well practiced in those arts of deception
required to protect priests, practice their faith, and
survive from one day to the next.

"Sir Garrett?" queried one of the men who rode
with the soldiers. " 'Tis thou, my lordship, is it not?"

Garrett glanced toward the horsemen and noticed for the first time that several of their number were not in uniform, although they wore the same black felt hats and plain coats, and were as heavily armed as the others, with leather bandoliers hanging across their chests.

"A pleasure, my lord," a second man spoke up. "And an honor it would appear."

"Aye, gentlemen," Garrett replied, and having acknowledged by name the London grocers, Methusaleh Waring and Thomas Powell, who had refused to sell their debentures for Castlekevin and Tomdarragh, he turned his attention back to the officer. "I assure you, Captain, to arrest this man for a priest is altogether impossible."

The officer ignored Garrett and addressed the grocers. "Thou knowest this man?"

" 'Tis Sir Garrett Neville, Baron Aylesbury. Aye, we met him in Dublin, sir, that we did."

"And thou can vouch for him?"

"Nay, we did not move in same circles, but if what we heard is correct, 'tis Corbet thou should be asking to vouch for him."

"Thou speakest of Miles Corbet, the Commissioner?"

"Aye, we do, sir," confirmed the grocer, whose gaunt face was dominated by a long, questing nose. "Did not know we were to be neighbors. We are honored, my lord. Honored."

Garrett heard Eleanor's tiny gasp. His arm went about her shoulder, he pulled her close, held her firm, and whispered in a voice that could not be overheard, "Faith, mistress, do not faint on me now."

"I trust thou will accept my apology, Sir Garrett. It is difficult to know whom to trust these days." The captain motioned to the dragoons to release the man, who went to stand at a proper distance behind Sir Garrett; the two dragoons mounted their horses. The captain scrutinized Sir Garrett and Mistress Archebold. "Thou art the new landlord here, my lord?"

In haste, Garrett whispered to Eleanor, "Protest not my reply," then, in a voice to be heard by all, he declared, "Aye, Captain Rowlestone, I am come to claim this forfeited estate, and I celebrate this night with the good people who will be my tenants and neighbors." He anticipated Eleanor's reaction even before he heard her short gasp, before her shoulders stiffened. It was to be expected, and he knew this was not going to make it any easier to tell her the truth. He did not remove his arm from about her shoulder, although he suspected it annoyed her as much as it appeared to garner the disapproval of Captain Rowleston, and forcing a pleasant tone, he added, "Captain, you and your men are welcome to join my other guests."

"English soldiery do not consort with heathens and papists."

"I am neither, sir, and having been told the people of this land have a proud tradition of hospitality, I would not want it said the English were poor hosts by comparison."

"And any Englishman making such a comparison would be a poor Englishman, indeed." Captain Rowlestone raised one glove in signal for the riders nearest the entrance to begin exiting. A horse snorted, bridles jangled, and the first of the dragoons went into the night. "Thou had best keep a watchful eye o'er thyself, Sir Garrett. A piece of paper is no guarantee of thine interests, nor would it matter to some that thou art no papist, and are English by birth. Verily, we are not so near to Dublin and thine influential friends as thou might believe, and I wouldst caution thee to heed the fate of the Spensers of Kilcolman, County Cork."

The last of the dragoons was leaving. The sound of hooves beating the lane to the Annamoe road echoed through the night. Without another word, nor formal farewell, the captain gave spur to his horse to join his men.

An odd quiet settled over the banquet hall. No one spoke nor moved while the noise of the departing dragoons faded away. Even the dry leaves skittering through the open door made not a sound. Garrett imagined Eleanor must be holding her breath; she had not moved a muscle since he'd declared himself the new owner of Laragh.

"Come, someone shut the doors. There is dancing yet to be done this night." Garrett was the first to speak. He glanced round the hall and saw he was the focus of every pair of eyes in the chamber; it was almost as if after he'd declared himself Laragh's new landlord, the people waited for him to take control. He essayed a smile, and nodded toward the musicians in encouragement that they begin playing. "You must not let them ruin a grand *céilidh*. You are safe, no one is taken from us, and they are gone."

Brian the piper began to play a tune. Two little boys broke away from their mothers and dashed across the open space where the dragoons had been.

" 'Tis a brave and noble gentleman you are, Sir Garrett," said Ambrose. He offered his hand. "You have my deepest gratitude."

Garrett embraced him. He was not in the habit of accepting appreciation, and instead remarked, "You do not think my soul will burn in hell for the stories I have told this night?"

"Och, now, 'tis not myself you should be asking." He winked at Garrett. "For I'm not in business of tending souls, but saving turnips from weeds, or is it your bidding I'm to be about?"

"My bidding," mused Garrett. A sober mood continued to hover over the banquet hall despite the music that quickened as Aidan Lawless and his *bodhrán* joined the song. "If you would dance with Mistress Eleanor, then I might partner Sibéal, and we could do our best to restore this gathering."

Soon the two unlikely cohorts in merriment, an English milord and a renegade priest, had the assembly dancing and twirling, clapping and stomping, but it was not the same as before. Indeed, it would never be the same again. For many weeks, Eleanor had presented a confident face, and the household had followed her example. Now such confidence was forced; indeed, it was altogether false. English soldiers had come up the lane to Laragh, up to the great doors of the big house, but those doors had not stopped them, they had not even paused to knock. They had invaded her family's home, threatened, insinuated, and insulted, and Eleanor, finding herself helpless against this violation, had been rescued by the last man to whom she wished to owe anything.

Nothing would be the same. The man she had hoped, indeed, the man she had believed would be leaving Laragh as soon as possible was instead being embraced by her friends and neighbors, not to mention by every member of the household. Indeed, their remarks made it seem to Eleanor that they might actually welcome him, should he declare that he was, in truth, the new lord of Laragh. He was not one of them, he was one of the English, yet he had been elevated to a hero by everyone present this night, and along with that elevated status came acceptance and trust.

Nothing would be the same, for Eleanor, who had

thought she could protect herself from this man, was no longer certain of her feelings. She was not certain of anything, and from beneath lowered lashes, she studied him, wondering at what he'd done and why. It was no little risk he'd taken to step forward and lie to protect Ambrose. The penalty was death.

The whole of her life these days, the whole order of the universe, defied logic. There were a hundred thousand riddles of which Eleanor could make no sense, and one enigma above all haunted her: Sir Garrett Neville was not one of them, yet he'd chosen to behave in such a way that his own people now considered him askance. He had given up much this night in defense of Ambrose and herself, and she could not help wondering what he might expect in return.

# Chapter 15

**"Y**ou must come again soon. Afore Christmas, to be sure," Eleanor called to Elizabeth Corbellis, as the pony cart from Tansey Close rumbled down the lane. She stood atop the massive granite stairs that ascended to the front door of the great house, where Laragh's mistress always bade farewell to her guests. Eleanor smiled and waved, and gave no hint this might be the last time she saw Elizabeth.

"Aye, before Christmas," came Elizabeth's faint reply.

The pony cart disappeared round the first bend.

Eleanor did not move for several minutes. She watched the dust settle upon the lane and listened to the fading rumble of the cart. It was mid-morning, and the other guests had departed except for several men, who remained to help with some repairs. Eleanor heard their voices in the bawn rising over the pounding of hammers and the gabble of geese. Somewhere the hounds yapped in play, children's voices drifted on the wind. It was an uncommon fine Irish day. At last, she descended the stoop to walk in the direction of all the noise. Afore sunrise there had been wolves in the yard, worrying the horses, sniffing at the stable doors, pawing at the cracks in the timbers. The men were reinforcing the gates and doors, and dismantling two interior stalls to supply planking for any folk who wished to replace a woven rush door or otherwise make their cottage more secure against the bold beasts.

*Bold beasts.* There had been more than one sort of danger abroad last night, and Eleanor gave yet another silent prayer of thanks. Last night had been but a prelude, she thought with a chill, of what was to come, and she did not deceive herself; they were fortunate Sir Garrett had been among them. Eleanor full well intended to thank him when he left Laragh, but not afore that time. He had already received enough praise. She was astonished at the ease with which he had been accepted at the *céilidh* by even the most wary and distrusting among them. Indeed, she was astonished and irritated, for it gave Eleanor the sense of standing alone, and she did not like that isolation, especially when it was the English stranger taking something more that was hers.

The stables were adjacent to the round tower, and Eleanor passed through an opening in the old defensive wall to the open space that had once been a bailey, but had over time transformed to bawn or stable yard. Sir Garrett was working alongside the other men, and the sight of him brought Eleanor to a sudden stop. In part, it was unexpected to see him thus engaged, but that was only a portion of her surprise; more than anything, it was his imposing, handsome person that made her pause and stare. In the warm, mid-morning sunshine, he wore no coat, and his white linen shirt, open at the throat with sleeves rolled past his elbows, accentuated his broad shoulders, his lean strength, and the midnight black of his hair.

He turned as if he'd sensed her gaze. A slow smile played across his face. He said something to the other men, then cut across the yard. He was coming to her, straight to her, as he had in the banquet hall last night. Something tumbled inside her, warm and quick.

"Good morning, Mistress Eleanor." He stood before her, a grin upon his bold, handsome face, and he swept her an elegant bow.

"Sir Garrett," she replied, wondering if her voice revealed her fascination, wondering if he had caught her staring at him in the yard, and if he knew the color upon her cheeks owed to more than fresh air and bright sunshine.

"Your last guest has departed?"

"Mistress Corbellis returns to Tansey Close," she replied, and tried to stop herself from staring at his face, but failed. Unbidden, the thought came to Eleanor that this was the first time she had seen him in the bright light of day. He had the most uncommonly beautiful green eyes, and she could not look away.

"You are finished then with your obligations as hostess, and may enjoy some time for yourself." He offered his arm to her. "I would be honored, Mistress Eleanor, if you would walk with me."

This elicited another tumbling response inside Eleanor. She blinked and stared back into his eyes. O'Connor eyes, they were, lush as the wilderness beyond Baravore. A vision of Bran O'Connor, the long ago chieftain of Baravore, swam before her; she remembered her dream in which the English stranger had danced with her in the garden and whispered in Irish, *Sweetheart, out of my dream, my love came near up to my side, shoulder to shoulder, and mouth on mouth.* A flash of heat went straight to the core of her.

Of a sudden, Eleanor had a keen sense of danger. Walk with him? To the contrary, she must stay

away from this man. "Nay, I cannot walk with you,
Sir Garrett."

"Come now, 'tis a lovely day," he coaxed. "Your
guests are gone. Sibéal attends to the household with
numerous eager small hands to help her whilst you
should allow yourself a moment away from your
concerns." A breeze teased her long tresses, soft
curls blew across her face; they had escaped the silver bodkin shining like a star in her ink black hair,
and he watched as she raised one slender hand to
brush away those stray curls and resecure the bodkin. He wanted to walk with her, to hear her laugh,
make her smile, mayhap steal a kiss; he wanted to
be with her this morning, for many mornings to
come, and he knew that unless he told the truth
now, those mornings might never be possible. He
offered his arm again. "Come. You should not be
shy with me."

"And you, sir, should not make this difficult. I do
not wish to walk with you."

"Which no doubt you believe to be the truth," he
said, as if she'd paid him a glowing compliment. He
slipped a hand beneath her elbow. "Come now, mistress, the skies are clear. I am told the weather is
soon to turn, and it would—"

" 'Tis not possible that I might walk with you.
What will they say?" she cut him off, grasping at
any excuse she might. Her gaze focused on the men
in the yard. "What will they think?"

"That the mistress is a fair lady to catch a gentleman's eye. Come, I wish to talk with you, and if you
care not for walking with me, then let us sit on the
terrace above the lough."

She did not want to sit with him where the lord
and lady of Laragh had received their tenants. That
was her parents' place; it was not for a stranger such

as this Englishman. "I do not wish to bide my time with you, Sir Garrett."

He observed her. She was the picture of propriety. Her expression was thoroughly distant and entirely cool, reminding him of that sacrificial virgin. She was guarding herself, and he wondered if it was already too late to claim Eleanor Archebold along with this land. His roguish grin became a frown. Hard truths never got easier with the passage of time, and he must not put off telling her why he had come to Laragh, but he could not tell her here. They must have some little privacy.

"You must tell me, mistress, which would be worse—to bide time in my company or to become the object of speculation?" He altered his tone as if addressing another person who had joined them. *"Ambrose, do you hear how the lady protests? Given the history of our acquaintance, do you not find her refusal to be in my company most curious?* To which the loyal Ambrose would of a certainty query, *History? Sir Garrett, do you tell me you are already acquainted with the mistress? How can that be?* And I would reply, *Indeed, Ambrose, need I remind you of the visitor who twice passed the night in my Dublin lodgings?* Of course, the man owns no such remembrance, and would be quick to tell me so. Whereupon I would turn to yourself, Mistress Eleanor, and suggest you might be able to refresh his memory."

*You would not do such a thing!* was on the tip of Eleanor's tongue, but she said nothing, and stared at Sir Garrett. Had she misunderstood? His smile returned, confident, subtle, and she dared not ask, dared not risk a wrong choice, nor even so much as a wrong word. While she had been willing to raise the funds for her plan to save Laragh, she was not willing that the means she had employed be known to one and all. She could not bear the certain scorn and pity, if household, friend, and neighbor were to know of the business she had transacted with this man whilst in Dublin.

There was no choice for her but to reply, "I accept your invitation, Sir Garrett. Come along this way, I would show you Laragh's walled garden, if you please."

They strolled along a path that led to a wooden door in an ivy-covered wall. Eleanor slid back the bolt. "My grandmother designed this garden in the English style. She had visited your country and was much determined that Laragh be as splendid as any English estate."

Garrett pushed open the door for her to enter ahead of him. It was warm within the garden. The air smelled of moist earth and ripe ivy berries burst by the sun. It was quiet save for their crunching footfall upon the walkway of crushed shells. Here the wind was silent; the noise from the yard was muted. The garden path idled between high, thick evergreen hedges, and though its summer splendor was faded, there remained a richness of color in the deep green ivy clinging to stone, to brick and mortar and tree trunks, the brilliance in the golden yellow of the changing leaves, and in the bright orange berries of the sallow thorn.

The path opened into a space where a sundial perched atop a granite pedestal. It was the center of the walled garden, Eleanor explained to Garrett, and the only area that had no particular name, every other walkway and quiet corner having been assigned an appellation according to a distinguishing feature or some unique event. There were three paths which they might chose to leave this natural room at the center of the garden, and Eleanor led them round the sundial to the farthest one. It was called *Aislinn's Treasure*, she told him.

"There is something I would show you. 'Tis something every visitor to this garden sees."

Again they strolled a narrow green corridor formed of high trimmed hedges, and again they entered a sort of garden chamber, this one notable not for a sundial but for the abundance of rose vines weaving through trellises, climbing brick and mortar, and running along the top of the garden wall.

"This is the *English Rose Corner*," she said, "but it was not my grandmother who brought the clippings to Laragh and nurtured the roots. It was my mother, who brought them as a young bride from her father's fortress in the high hills, where the bushes had been flourishing for nigh on three hundred years."

"How then is it you call them English roses?" Garrett asked.

Eleanor smiled. He was no different from any other visitor; the question was always the same. "My mother was born at a place called Baravore, at the very northernmost reach of a wilderness called Glenmalure, a place where English soldiers dared not venture, and where O'Connor chieftains had ruled since the ancient tribes first came into Leinster from Kildare." She hesitated, wondering if this man could truly care one way or the other how it was that Laragh's roses were English.

"Go on," he encouraged. "I would hear more."

"It was nearly three hundred years before when those English roses were planted in the soil at Baravore; three hundred years past when Lady Aislinn was the chieftain's wife. She was the daughter of Sir Roger, lord and commander of the king's garrison at Killoughter, and she wed Bran O'Connor in the days when the parliament at Kilkenny ruled this land."

Garrett nodded. "I have heard of the statutes that outlawed all contact between Irish and English."

Lady Olivia had told him of the statute that had forbidden marriage, fosterage, and concubinage between the races. It had been punishable for the English or even the Irish living among them to speak Irish, and anyone of English blood was required to dress in the English style, adhere to English law and customs, even to ride an English saddle.

"You know something then of our true history?"

Eleanor's question was a reminder of how far apart she believed them to be. In her eyes he was a stranger, one of the enemy, and Garrett knew it would not be a simple matter to change her opinion. *It is to be my history now as well. Sooth, it has always been mine, and someday, God willing, you will believe and understand.* Oh, that he might shout the words for one and all to hear. Yet it was too early for the whole truth. Indeed, it might be many months until she might believe any such words from him. "I know something of the past," he said. "Enough to understand what you speak of. Tell me more of this Lady Aislinn and her English roses. Was she punished for marrying her Irish chieftain?"

"Nay, Bran and Aislinn made their life at Baravore, where English knights dared not trespass. It was her father who knew the ire of the crown. Sir Roger was stripped of his title, his holdings were seized; it was not, however, for his daughter's defiance, but for his own. Like Lady Aislinn, Sir Roger had followed his heart, and despite the statute, he wed for love; his third wife was an Irish woman, and together, Sir Roger and Lady Bebinn fled Ireland, leaving Killoughter to a new English lord. Thus it was that Bran raided the English, not for coin or horses, but for clippings from the garden in which his beloved Aislinn had played as a child."

" 'Tis a splendid history. A treasured memory," Garrett remarked. "One to be told and retold."

"Prithee, sir, can you imagine the scores of Irish lasses who have drifted to sleep o'er the centuries to dream of a husband only half as bold and romantic as Bran O'Connor?"

Garrett would write of this to Lady Olivia. He imagined her pleasure at reading how he had found a young woman who cherished memories as deeply as herself; he imagined this whilst conveniently overlooking how displeased Lady Olivia would be to learn the circumstances which had brought them together. "I have a dear friend who would love to hear of your Bran O'Connor, the Irish chieftain who raided an English fortress for rose clippings."

"Not only for these roses, but for medlar and quince and holly," Eleanor added, then caught herself before she might continue. His mention of a dear friend was a reminder that she knew nothing of him. He was not a familiar acquaintance with whom she might pass a mild autumn morning in idle conversation. He was a stranger, one of the English, who were not to be trusted. Her smiled faded, and without preface she asked, "How do you come to have the acquaintance of those two men who were riding with Rowlestone's dragoons?"

"We met in Dublin." Garrett crafted a careful reply. "It was business that brought us together."

"And is it true what they said, sir? You are an associate of one of the Commissioners?"

"To some degree, they speak true. Corbet and I have a mutual acquaintance; we have been introduced, and we have dined in one another's company, but he is not an associate. Indeed, Corbet is not a man whose company I would seek."

His honesty unsettled Eleanor, and in her mind, she heard the words he had spoken last night. *Aye, Captain Rowlestone, I am come to claim this forfeited estate, and I celebrate this night . . .*

Slowly, very slowly, she asked, "It was not all lies last night, was it?"

But it was not so much a question as a statement begging denial.

Garrett did not say anything right away; instead he savored the sight of Eleanor bathed in sunshine, her raven hair an iridescent halo, wisping about her face, her shoulders, giving her the appearance of a woman whose beauty and spirit were but delicate, transitory entities. She needed someone to watch over her, to shield her, and he wished to be that someone, yet he was about to shatter her world. There was no other way for him. "No. It was not all lies."

"Please," she said. It was a quiet, almost breathless plea. "You must tell me."

"Do you know what business was being conducted in the coffeehouse?" he asked.

Something cold scraped along Eleanor's spine. It was odd how one's brain worked when searching for answers, hideous how the pieces of a puzzle might fall into place. "I know Ireland abounds with profiteers who would reap their futures from the disadvantage of others. I know there are men who intend to call their own that which has been stolen." He uttered not a word, but the expression in his eyes, in those lovely green eyes, turned cold and sharp. Panic rose in Eleanor. Panic and dread. "You must tell me the truth."

This was it. *The truth.* Whoever said truth alleviates rather than hurts was a fool. Everything was about to go from bad to worse, but it was the only way for Garrett. He had no other choice. Someday she would be able to understand, someday when she knew the whole truth, and while she might never be able to forgive him, perhaps she would not hate him. He took a step closer to her, lest she faint. She stepped back, the wall was behind her, and she stopped, staring up into his eyes. He wanted to break their gaze but could not, and lest he surrender to cowardice, he hurried into speech. "It was not all lies. I am the new owner of Laragh. I hold the debenture for this estate."

# Chapter 16

❦

**I**t *was not all lies.*

From somewhere deep within Eleanor, there came a whisper from the past.

*A lady such as yourself deserves more than this.*

In a flash of pain and joy Eleanor recalled trust, exquisite pleasure, and drifting to sleep in the arms of a man she had known since the beginning of time.

*It was not all lies.*

Somewhere deep within Eleanor a door closed ne'er to open again.

*It was not all lies. I am the new owner of Laragh. I hold the debenture for this estate.*

Eleanor did not flinch at this truth, nor exclaim aloud in horrified dismay.

A single tear welled up in the corner of one eye. She leaned full against the wall, turned her face until her cheek rested against its rough, cool surface, and blinked away that single tear before she returned her gaze to his. She would not cry; she who never cried would not allow this man to be the one to change that.

"My mother is not buried beside my father. She is in the hills with her father's fathers at the old O'Connor fortress. She is at Baravore, where the English roses from Killoughter have grown for nigh on three hundred years." Her words flowed as if she had taken up in the middle of an earlier conversation.

" 'Tis not much above two months' time since my mother died, yet there are days, there are moments it seems she has been gone forever, when it seems none of them were ever here, and I have always been alone." She noted a flickering in the depths of his eyes, a darkening of that lush green hue, but in the space of a heartbeat it passed, and she could not imagine how her words might have affected him.

"Each morning I awaken to wonder if this is the day the English stranger comes to dispossess the children of Sir Thomas Archebold from their forefather's land. I cannot allow that. *I will not allow it.* 'Tis a pledge I made on my mother's grave. No English will take Laragh from the Archebolds, and *there is nothing I will not do to uphold that pledge.* 'Tis why I went to Dublin. To raise funds through the sale of my father's books."

"But Whalley cheated you."

"How could I forget? You know what happened." She heard the sympathy in his voice, and it angered her, confused her. It broke her heart with yearning. There should be naught save loathing and animosity betwixt them, yet once for the space of a few hours there had been something more, and somewhere in a far dark corner of her soul those moments of passion, of tenderness and fused souls, still lived. She wanted to look away from this man who knew her deepest secret, who knew more about her than her dearest friend, yet knew nothing of her at all. Some part of her wanted to get back that which she had given him, while another inner self had entirely contrary thoughts. She sighed, exhausted but not defeated, and met his gaze direct. She would do anything to save Laragh; anything to save what remained of her heart and soul.

"You know, do you not, Sir Garrett, that parting with my father's books was not the most difficult thing I was forced to do in Dublin? I did what was necessary in order that I might return with sufficient funds." Eleanor paused, but did not release him from her gaze. "In the end there was no depth to which I would not sink."

Garrett knew why she stared at him in that damning way. Mistress Eleanor Archebold wanted Sir Garrett Neville to realize *he was the most lowest depth* to which she'd been reduced.

"Prithee, mistress, might you tell me to what purpose you required those funds?" he asked, as if her enmity did not bother him.

She almost laughed aloud. Her grand scheme now seemed silly, ill planned, and wholly inadequate, but she revealed none of her disgrace. She was not yet defeated, and with a proud tilt of her chin she stated, "It is my intention to buy back Laragh from the Englishman who would presume to be its owner."

"And why would this Englishman be willing to entertain such a transaction?"

"Because there are tories in the high hills, and Laragh is too close to those hills for an English stranger. It is not safe here for such a man. The barracks at Baltynanima were torched, and if it is not safe for the soldiery, nowhere is. I would urge that he consider which he valued more: his life or planting in territory that abounds with pestilence and famine. I would ask whether he would rather risk an uncertain future at Laragh, or accept instead enough money to return to England in considerable comfort."

"Well thought, Mistress Eleanor, and well phrased. 'Tis a persuasive strategem, and it would be almost perfect were it not for one thing. What if the man who holds the debenture cares not for gold? What if he departed England in comfort? What if he seeks nothing more than a place he might call home?''

Eleanor trembled. He spoke of himself, and she knew she was doomed.

''Perhaps you would have something else to offer such a man.'' His voice fell to a beguiling whisper. ''Something to make an exchange more appealing.''

Her chest contracted, a piece of her soul ached, and she prayed that God and the angels might forgive her. Indeed, this one man had taken everything from her. ''No, sir, I would not be willing to offer anything more appealing to such a man.''

''Ah, yes, I see.'' He was willing to accept this refusal, for there was a much bigger prize he desired. He did not merely want her assent to a similar arrangement as their previous transaction. He wanted more, much more. ''Nothing but the money to consider then.''

She drew a ragged breath. ''I have nothing left of any value.''

Her voice cut him to the quick. *I have nothing left of any value.* God's wounds, how Garrett despised this. He had done this to her, and wanted nothing more than to fold her in his embrace, to comfort her, and let her know that she was a creature of immeasurable value, that she alone with no estate, no maidenhood, was a woman to be prized and cherished. With one hand he tilted her face upward, searching her gaze, hoping she would see beyond what she heard. ''And if this gentleman agreed to your terms and the transaction took place—the money in exchange for the debenture—you would expect that fellow to ride away from Laragh and never look back?''

"That is what I want."

"Prithee, Mistress Eleanor, what do you imagine will transpire in the spring when Captain Rowlestone and those same dragoons ride down the lane to make certain the Archebolds are gone from Laragh?" His smooth, coaxing voice had turned blunt, hard.

"I will show them the debenture and ask that they remove their persons from my land."

"And they would laugh at you, if they did not kill you first."

"But the debenture would be mine."

"Only in your eyes. They would confiscate the paper, assign Laragh to someone else, and force you on the road to Connaught. Cromwell's proclamation is not merely an order for dispossession, but for transplantation. You would, indeed, do well to heed the fate of William Spenser of Kilcolman."

"The Spensers are of the new English," she said, disdainful and showing too much of her own pride. "The current earl's estates were bestowed upon his grandfather by your Queen Elizabeth." Everyone knew of Edmund Spenser, the poet, who had written with such hatred of Ireland and her people; everyone knew of the family's alliance with the Tudors and their unwavering allegiance to mother England. "Captain Rowlestone must be ill informed. It defies fundamental logic that the Spensers might face—"

She stopped mid-sentence. It defied logic that William Clare's ownership of Killoughter was not safe, or that Rosanna might be reduced to coshering with a widowed servant in a room above the stables. Cromwell had reduced the world to one in which insanity and the devil reigned side by side. "What has happened in Cork?" she demanded. "Are the rumors true? Has Spenser received a notice of forfeiture?"

"He has." It was another truth that could not be denied.

"And your friends, the Commissioners, surely they have granted him an exemption."

"Nay, his petition was denied. Spenser and his household have already left for the west afore winter settles o'er the land."

The shock and horror Eleanor had aforetime controlled erupted into an awful sensation of falling through endless space. She was tumbling, tumbling through a place where there was no sound, and time stretched to an eternity. Her fingers tightened round vines upon the wall, a thorn cut her palm, but she sensed nothing save a vague awareness of someone calling her name. Was it her mother? One of her brothers? The voice was insistent, stern, but not unkind, and it persisted as if calling her back from very far away. Eleanor blinked. There was a tear in her eye, moisture on her hand, and she glanced down. It was blood on her fingers, not a tear. She looked away from the bright red stain, directing her gaze toward the voice, and she saw the English stranger, who had owned her for a night, but would own Laragh for a lifetime.

"You must heed me well in what I am about to say, Eleanor Archebold." He set his hands on her shoulders, hoping to command her attention, grateful she did not shake him off. "If I depart this place, you will not be left in peace. Laragh will be assigned to another man, and whosoever that man may be, he will make no such pledge as I do."

"What pledge is that?"

"I will not harm your family. That I promise you. That is my pledge. And I will do everything to ensure no harm comes to this household or to your people from any quarter whatsoever."

"Why do you care? You, who steal Laragh! You could evict us. Abandon us. "

"But I will do neither. I will not evict you, nor abandon you."

"How convenient that you might steal my home, but cast yourself a hero. You will not sell me what is mine; you will keep it—all in the cause of saving me from someone more selfish than yourself."

"Sarcasm does not become you."

"Your opinion matters not."

"It should."

"Is that a threat?"

"Nay, 'tis no threat. I would not harm you, mistress."

*Ah, but you do harm me. You have harmed me,* the words were on the tip of her tongue. Aloud, she said, "Do you not intend to evict us?"

"Nay, I do not."

"You will allow us to remain?" She was wary.

"Of course. How else to uphold my promise?"

"In the great house?" He gave an affirmative nod, and somewhere deep inside herself Eleanor dared to hope, while at the same time somewhere else within her soul a piece of her dignity was sore tested. She asked, "We would be your servants?"

"Nay."

"What then?"

"You will stay at Laragh and be my wife."

Eleanor's heart lurched. A cascade of defiance and denial tumbled through her. Disbelief marked her face. Of all the ways to save Laragh, of all the schemes she had rejected, of all the circumstances she might imagine with this man, she had not once considered marriage.

"You will have Laragh, sir. Why must you have myself as well?"

"Were I to allow you to remain as a servant, there

would be little to protect you, should Captain Rowlestone be of a mind to force you from this land.
Being wed to me is a way to guarantee your safety.''

"What of Rowlestone's warning to yourself, sir?
What of your own security?''

"You are correct to remind me, mistress. None of
us is entirely secure, and I must be cautious. You
have my assurance I will be cautious for the both of
us.'' Garrett waited for her to say something, anything, and after an awkward silence, he realized
there was more he must do than offer the assurance
of his caution. He gave an awkward cough. "Forgive
me, Mistress Eleanor. I forget myself. Would you,
will you accept my hand and agree to be my wife
and the mistress of Laragh?''

She angled her head, wondering why he dropped
his voice to a tender whisper, why he had spoken
those words as if she were his own true love, as if
he were offering his hand in faith and true devotion
until death might them part. He knew he had won;
she could not refuse him. Why then did he make
mockery of that which might never be hers? Eleanor
fought back tears. She who never cried felt the sting
of salt beneath her lids. There was a bitter taste in
her mouth, and she swallowed it before speaking. "I
will accept, Sir Garrett, but on one condition.''

One of his ink black brows arched upward in
query. "A condition, you say? And what might that
be?''

"I will not share your bed.'' Her parents had
shared the massive bed in the chamber that was reserved for Laragh's lord and lady, and Eleanor could
not bear to share it with this English stranger.

"Do you say you will not consummate our marriage?''

Her heart seemed to stop completely. She managed a reply. "Nay, I will do what must needs be done to make our union legal."

"And you will give me children?"

"I will. But beyond necessity, I will not share your bed, although you may come to mine as you see fit.

"Garrett knew why she spoke as she did, and he would allow her the security of such an arrangement, for he knew it would not last. "You will be my wife, Eleanor Archebold, and I will not deal harshly with you. Who knows—as time passes you might find something to like in me."

"You speak as if we might one day be friends."

"And why not?"

"Why not," came her choked exclamation. "If this were a stage drama, the audience would not tolerate such an improbable fiction. We share nothing in common, sir, and I would rather that we might be better strangers."

"By my faith, mistress, you are cruel. Do you so soon forget there is one thing you already find pleasing about me?"

"I cannot recollect what that might be."

"Do you not?" he drawled. "Then you must allow me to remind you."

The sensual ripple in his voice set off a warning bell in Eleanor's head, but it was too late. Before she could slip past him and down the path, he set his palms on the garden wall, one on either side of her head as if capturing her, and he leaned forward until their bodies were almost touching. Eleanor pressed backward, but there was nowhere to go.

His lips brushed her cheek. They feathered along the line of her jaw, nibbling, teasing.

"Nay, you are mistaken." Her stomach fluttered. She turned her face to escape his mouth. "I do not find such things pleasing."

"Do you not?" His fingers ran along her shoulders

to the back of her neck, then threaded through her hair as his mouth moved to her exposed neck. "What of this?" His lips caressed her, seeking the hollow of her throat, and upon sensing that she had relaxed, albeit only a very little, his tongue stroked her bare skin.

A soft moan rose from her core; liquid heat seeped through her. Her skin was on fire beneath his touch.

"And what of this?" he whispered, soft and taunting, and with a fingertip, he turned her mouth to his.

In that instant, a familiar flash of heat tore through her, sending a ring of fire round her belly, stealing her breath, making her pulse quicken, and her body ache with desire. Energy flowed between them as vibrant as it had been in his lodgings, and in that instant, Eleanor hated herself as much as she did him. Her eyes fell.

His gaze raked over her. Although she tried to hide the misty sheen of passion in her eyes, she had not been quick enough. He smiled, and rubbed the pad of his thumb across her parted lips. He heard her tiny gasp, and his smile turned to a certain, knowing grin as he lowered his mouth to tease hers. It was a tender kiss, and he held her chin when she tried to turn away from his caress. It was a kiss that did not stop. Gently, he increased the pressure of his lips. It was a seductive kiss, unhurried, persuasive; at length he sensed her leaning closer, sensed her lips softening to his, and he pulled away.

Eleanor stared at him in shock and betrayal. Her blood was coursing through her. She heard it thrumming, sensed it pounding, and for a moment, she feared she would faint. Not again! She took a steadying breath, and knew that somehow she must protect herself from this man. She wiped her mouth with the back of her hand. "Hear me, Sir Garrett, and hear me well. I will wed you, but I do not like your wicked kisses. I swore on my mother's grave I would do anything to save Laragh, and if marriage is what you expect of me now, then I comply. But that is the only reason. Do not imagine we will become friends. Do not imagine there will be any pleasure for me in fulfilling my marital vows. You are the anything to which I must stoop."

He didn't believe her. She was lying. The huskiness in her voice betrayed her as did the flush upon her cheeks. Still he didn't like to be told he was the lowest act to which a lady could stoop. "Hear me, sweet mistress. We will wed, aye, that we will. You will be my wife. I will treasure you. And I will wait for you." She was silent, and he went on, "I must be gone for several days. Upon my return we will wed."

"So soon?"

"Aye, so soon. I do not wish my bride to be showing a swollen belly."

"What say you, sir?"

"You could be carrying my child. Could you not? Have you had your woman's flux since Dublin?"

"To answer yes or no accounts for nothing. My body is different these days," she protested, shaken by his suggestion. She was at once thrilled with prospect of a babe to suckle at her breast whilst horrified by the responsibility of bringing an innocent into this unforgiving world; so, too, was she uncertain how her family, especially her brothers, might react to the notion of a wee life born of herself and one of the English. "My diet is poor of late, and there are many anxieties that demand my attention, too much work, and not enough rest. I am no different than most of the women of Ireland."

"Or it could be a babe. Our child. We will wed as soon as I return." The back of his hand slid along her jaw, and he held her chin with two fingers.

"What do you do, sir?"

"I would have a proper kiss from you to seal our betrothal."

His mouth came down on hers, demanding, searching, and he parted her lips to his tongue. It was a drowning kiss that commanded her every sense, stole away her breath. She gasped for air. Her chest was heaving, her skin grew warmer, and the core of her was melting, yearning. "I do loathe you, Sir Garrett Neville," she said on a sort of low underbreath, knowing it was yet another lie.

"Do you?" he drawled. His brow lifted. He grinned, bold and shameless, and held her waist to prevent her from going anywhere. Quickly, he wedged his knee between her thighs and raised it as high as he might, forcing her legs to part, and pulling her forward until she straddled him. He heard her sharp intake of breath, and grinned even more shamelessly as first one of his hands, then the other moved from her waist to cup her buttocks. Holding her this way, he controlled her. She couldn't go anywhere. There was no escape, and any movement on her part caused her sex to press against his thigh. With his hands on her buttocks, he began to rotate her torso in a slow, circular pattern that forced her to move upon his thigh in a sensual caress that tortured him as surely as it must inflame her. He didn't want her to forget him. He wanted her to think of him each night she crawled into her lonely bed, and each morning she awakened he wanted her to wonder if this was the day he would be returning to Laragh.

"Let go of me," she ordered. "I do loathe you. Do you hear? Loose me."

"Loathe me? I think not, mistress mine. Loose you? I am not ready to do so," he murmured against her lips, aching for more of her. She was soft, and she trembled at the feather-light caress of his lips at the edge of her mouth, quivered as he dragged her forward, away from the wall and along his thigh; she didn't resist when he lowered his knee until she was standing against him with one leg between his. Again, he grinned cocky and shameless as his thighs closed about her leg, powerful muscles capturing her, and he bent his knees that he might stroke her with his hard, swollen arousal. He sensed the heat rising in her, and knew if he kept on, he could have Mistress Eleanor here and now; he could press her to the wall, support her on his thighs, and pump into her hard and furious, or he could turn her round to sink into her from behind, deep and swift.

But he would wait.

The next time Garrett rode Eleanor to the peaks of pleasure, there would be nothing to taint their joining. Giving herself to him was the lowest depth to which she'd had to stoop, but the next time he had her, Garrett wasn't going to allow her any reason to attach such sentiments to their lovemaking.

"Mark my word." His lips brushed the tender flesh behind her ear. He inhaled the sweet scent of her, and he ached for the day his words might be true. "One day you will awaken to find yourself sleeping in my arms, your head cradled on my shoulder, and when that morning dawns you will be at my side because it is what you want. Because it is where you choose to be."

# Cradle-Tale
## The Middle

〜〜

... **T**here was nothing for him save to call upon the Lord. The end was anear. He ceased his struggles, savoured one final look at the world, and sorrow-stricken, closed his eyes. The end was upon him, and he had ne'er known pure love.

"Sir, yer hand. Over here. I would be taking yer hand."

He harkened the voice, but saw no one. 'Twas a trick of those sidhe, no doubt, for though the words were English uttered, the sweet voice carried the lilting melody of one whose birth tongue was Irish. He laughed despite the cruelty of this game.

"Too late, my ladies lovely, I do fear 'tis too late for your pleasures. I cannot dance with thee this night."

The voice came to him again, "Sir! Reach behind yerself, if ye canst. I've tossed a length of wool toward ye, sir. Canst ye not be grabbing hold it?"

Being no fool, the young man betook himself as the voice commanded, and soon he was gliding across his grave. Soon he scraped against a rocky surface, rolled to his belly, and pushed to stand on firm ground.

Lo, afore him were hands. He saw them, slender and delicate, reaching through the mist, beckoning to him. He staggered toward those hands, tried to touch them, hold onto them, but they were beyond his reach, and did not stop his fall. Down he went, knees folding beneath him as his mind and being descended into nothingness.

Out of the mist, a maiden emerged. Black as raven wings her hair was, and though she moved with the light steps of an airy spirit, she was human. O, how human she was, owning a tender heart and trusting nature. She was Órla, only daughter of the O'Toole chieftain at Castlekevin, descended from the great warrior Finan and his lady wife, Isabel, daughter of Bran of Baravore and Aislinn, daughter of Sir Roger Clare, knight of Killoughter. And to the people of that glen she was as exalted as any princess of Windsor could e'er be.

Crouching beside the man, Órla set fingertips to his brow. His crashing through the underwood had been a hullallo to wake the dead. He must be one of the strangers who would steal her family's land, and whose king enacted laws against Irish civilization. His name was Henry, that king of the English, who so despised the people of these hills that he ordered his earls to kidnap Irish children for adoption in England, to expunge every vestige of Irishness in their hearts and souls, and to extirpate those that could not be schooled to proper obeisance.

Órla's family guarded her well. To be sure, this was the first stranger she had gazed upon, and he was a clever man to her eyes, tall and straight and fair-favoured in his making. Not so different from one of her brothers or cousins, she was thinking, for she saw nothing to affright her. Sooth, the grief that had marked his countenance upon being trapped in the bog had touched a chord within her.

This stranger must love the world as much as myself, thought she, and the Lord would not be wanting me to let such a rare man perish.

Órla brushed wet hair from his brow. His eyes opened, dark, yet bright, and she gazed upon him in wonderment.

*An invisible arrow embedded itself in the fastness of her pure and tender heart.*

Light of Grace, he was as beautiful as he was manful, this stranger of the English.

*The young man stared at the maiden. She had not the yellow hair of the sidhe, but whether she was mortal, he could not be certain, for he had ne'er seen such a maid of grace. How entrancing were those ebony curls about her lovely face. He did not stop himself reaching for them, and he smiled, for they were as soft to his fingers as they looked to his eye. His other hand moved to where she touched his brow, and threading his fingers through hers, he brought them to his lips. Soft, he kissed her fingertips, the top of her hand, the inside of her wrist.*

*'Tis said the sound of flutes and harps filled the misty glen as they lay upon a bed of sweet clover-grass and moss. The hawthorn shuddered, its white petals spilling to the ground, and nine months later a babe was born at Castlekevin. Wee Órla, she was called after her mother, who waited patient to introduce her lover to his child, but wee Órla's father ne'er held his daughter. A mysterious sickness took him before he might return to the glen, and her mother—that girl who had given pure love to the young stranger of the English—died of a broken heart when she saw her newborn growing not into the image of her lover, but of her own good self.*

*The babe was a dark child of the hills, and ten summers were gone before . . .*

# Part III

Part III

# Chapter 17

The town of Wicklow was not much improved in the mere five days since Garrett had disembarked from the *Prestissimo*. Disease and misery still hung above the mean straggling back lanes, grim and threatening, but along the waterfront it was much changed with the first wave of adventurers arriving to claim their property. The harbor was clogged with barques and other vessels lying at anchor, awaiting their turn to unload their cargo, and the quay was aswarm with soldiery, for additional militia had been assigned to the Wicklow garrison to protect the strutting new landowners. They were a jubilant, noisy lot, and eager to take up residence in their new homes before harsher weather settled over the countryside.

Garrett stood below the sign of The Cock and Boar, and addressed the man who exited the tavern in his wake. "Your list of improvements for the ironworks appears thorough and sensible, Master Blacknall."

"But ye'll be checking the site yerself, Sir Garrett?" James Blacknall was stooped with age, and he tilted his head to one side that he might look Sir Garrett in the eyes whilst speaking to him.

"Aye, Master Petty and I travel to Shillelagh as soon as our business here is done, and should we find anything else in need of attention, we'll get word to you."

"To be sure, 'tis in good order ye'll be finding it, says I. A sound investment is the ironworks. Ye'll not regret heeding Lord Egerton's advice. It was a thriving profitable operation afore, and will be so again. Ye've my pledge on that, Sir Garrett. That ye do."

Garrett set his cockade hat atop his head, and extended a hand to James Blacknall, who had managed the ironworks in better times and would now be doing so once again under his ownership. Although Sir Egerton had vouched for Blacknall's honesty and had provided Garrett a letter of introduction, it did not require a man of much sophistication to discern that the old Irishman did not trust Garrett. But why should any Irishman trust a stranger such as himself? Garrett suspected the old man had not been altogether forthcoming regarding the folk who lived near the ironworks. No doubt there were many secrets in these parts. Indeed, Garrett had more than one of his own.

Having agreed to meet Blacknall at a later date, Garrett proceeded toward the far end of the quay where Edwin Petty was overseeing the loading of two wheelless wagons for Laragh. There was a trunk containing Garrett's personal possessions, official papers, his clothes, and the like, as well as several large items, among them a life-sized portrait of Lady Olivia; mostly it was seeds for planting in the spring, sacks of grain and other foodstuffs to tide them through the winter, plus building materials for repairs and improvements. Lastly, there were a dozen hens and two roosters, a ram and four ewes, six piglets, a milk cow, and of course, the two teams of horses that would pull the slide-cars.

"Our paperwork is in order, and the final transfer of goods from the quay should not take long," Edwin Petty called out at Garrett's approach. The voyage from Dublin had gone without incident, and Wicklow was an agreeable town with harbor masters less greedy than those on the Liffey quays. "We are almost finished."

"Good, for I am anxious that we might depart this afternoon."

Edwin glanced toward the western horizon. The sun was low in the sky. "You would not rather wait until morning?"

"The sooner we are about our business in Shillelagh, the sooner we can return to Laragh. I am eager to show you my new home," he said with a smile, thinking not about Laragh but about its mistress, and of how it would please him to see her again. Indeed, he could not suppress a smile to think how it would please him to introduce her to Edwin. While he had informed Edwin of his somewhat peculiar betrothal to the mistress of Laragh, he had not told Edwin who that lady was, nor had he mentioned any ulterior motives beyond those he had shared with Eleanor.

There would be time enough to reveal the truth when they were headed up the final stretch of lane to the big house; he would not tell Edwin Petty a moment too soon, for his friend would surely roast him for his weakness and the audacity with which he was taking what he desired under the guise of nobility. "You are going to like Laragh, Edwin, and the people thereabout. Indeed, there may be a bride for you to be found in the foothills round Clara and Annamoe."

Edwin turned a wry smile on his friend and part-

ner. Though Garrett had spoken but once of his betrothal, Edwin Petty knew there must be far more
reason for the arrangement than he had revealed. A
man of Sir Garrett's means and stature did not
marry unless it was his choice. The mistress of Laragh must be a most remarkable woman. It might
even be possible that she accounted for the change
he had observed in Sir Garrett. Gone was the young
man who had sat in Dick's Coffeehouse night after
night focused upon one purpose and one purpose
alone. There was little trace of the gentleman who
had near overlooked one of Dublin's finest whores,
and somehow Edwin did not think it was the prospect of fresh country air that made Garrett smile for
no apparent reason.

The last of the wooden cages with the squealing
piglets and clucking hens was secured.

Garrett had hired Aidan Lawless and two other
men from Annamoe to escort the goods back to Laragh.

"I ask you one final time, Aidan Lawless. You are
certain you do not wish me to engage two or three
soldiers to serve as your escort?"

"Och, now, Sir Garrett, a fool myself never was."
Aidan Lawless accepted the musket and bandoleer
Garrett held forth to him. Lowering his voice, he
added with a twinkle in his eye, " 'Twould be a far
more dangerous journey to travel in their company."

"I understand." Garrett nodded. Of a sudden his
attention shifted. Something had caught his eye, and
he turned to Edwin Petty. "Edwin, look you over
there."

They both regarded a tall man with a gold-tipped
cane. It was the peacock who had stood out among
the crows in Dublin.

" 'Tis the fellow from outside the Essex Bridge
Tavern," Edwin said.

Garrett gazed away from the man with the cane, and stared past Edwin Petty toward the sea, but he saw not the vessels lying at anchor; instead it was a ship sailing out of this harbor that drifted before his mind's eye. He had a vision of a lass standing at a ship's rail. She was alone, more alone than any child ought ever to be, and a wind smelling not of home, but of the sea, blew ink black curls about her small, pale face; she swiped at the curls, tiny trembling hands pushing away the stray hair, nothing must block her view of the shore. There were tears in her eyes, eyes as green as the lush hills from which she had been stolen, but she did not cry. Garrett's chest tightened, for he knew this child never cried.

The ships in Wicklow harbor came into focus, as did the certain knowledge that at least one of them was soon to be bound for the Indies or the Massachusetts Colony. A hideous, sickening truth sliced through Garrett. Slavers were conducting their evil business in Wicklow town. What had the different licenses granted? Three hundred women. Two hundred young girls. How many lads? Garrett had seen how sparse was the population hereabout, and he knew the men-stealers would have to sweep wide and deep toward the hills in order to fulfill their contracts. No one in the countryside would be safe, not even the folk who lived as far inland as Laragh. The fleeting images of Eveleen and Grace, of Rory, wee Maeve and her two brothers, of Rosanna Clare and Róisín O'More, and of the lovely, brave Eleanor, who did not cry, tumbled across his mind's eye.

"Edwin, our plans change," he said, urgency in his voice.

"We wait until the morn?"

"Nay, we postpone Shillelagh and the ironworks

altogether. Now I would ask you to go ahead of me with the others to Laragh, and please to convey my instructions for the household. Indeed, I would ask that you oversee Laragh's security in my stead."

"Of course, Garrett. As you wish," Edwin replied. There was more, much more than what Garrett spoke aloud, but instinct warned Edwin Petty to wait rather than ask for details. Garrett would tell him in good time. "You know best what is needed at this time."

"As for myself there is a matter here to which I must attend," Garrett said with a note of authority, although his plans were not formed. The man with the cane must be watched, that much Garrett knew; he must discover the details of his business, and if his suspicions were correct, he would do what was necessary to impede the man's affairs. If need be, Garrett might return to Dublin to seek Lord Egerton's counsel; if need be, he might find himself even taking James Blacknall into his confidence.

He glanced at the ships in the harbor, his mind echoing with the imagined cries of two hundred frightened women forced below deck, and with a deep-etched sober frown, he turned back to Edwin. The two men did not speak. Indeed, the silence between them seemed at once as forbidding as it might be sacred, and studying Edwin's expression, Garrett knew his friend's thoughts mirrored his suspicions. "You will not forget that as I am betrothed to Mistress Archebold, the welfare of her family and people are mine."

"And my concern for their security will be no less than were she my own sister, and the lot of them my closest and dearest of kin. How long will you be?"

"Four or five days mayhap, a sennight at most, then I will return to Laragh, and to my bride."

Eleanor sought solace in her father's library. By day and by night, she sat at the desk, reading across the centuries in Nuala's annals; sometimes pausing to stare at nothing in particular, mourning she was, regretting the loss of the books she'd taken to Dublin, and sometimes staring out the window, watching the empty lane and the yellowed dead grass, listening to the wind, and waiting.

It had been a fortnight since Sir Garrett had declared his intention to wed her, a fortnight less a day since he had departed Laragh, and a sennight had passed since Rosanna had returned to Killoughter, and Edwin Petty had arrived with two wheelless slide-cars laden with supplies, and a letter from Sir Garrett.

A sennight gone by, and the mere thought of that letter provoked Eleanor no less than when she had first read it.

Oh, how mild those opening sentences had been, how considerate, even warm. For a moment, Eleanor had imagined marriage to this Englishman, if it actually came to pass, might at least be distinguished by civility, friendship, and some measure of respect.

"... Along with my good tidings, I send my most trusted friend, Edwin Petty, who has pledged himself to you, your people, and to Laragh in my absence. Be assured of his trust, loyalty, kindness, and honest nature, and please rely upon Master Petty as you would upon myself. Do not hesitate to solicit his aid in any and all matters of concern to you and the household. As you will see, Master Petty brings an abundance of supplies for your inspection that they may be used in accordance with your discretion. . . ."

How quick the weans were to spread word of Garrett's generosity, and the people were so grateful when the lads and Edwin Petty had distributed the seed and grain among them; indeed, they anticipated his return with the hope that he might choose to stay among them. What he had done for them should bring a smile to Eleanor's face, but thinking of him produced naught but a peevish scowl. She did not like feeling in debt to this man. For some reason, her thoughts strayed to the *céilídh* when everyone had accepted Sir Garrett, and in doing so had somehow excluded her. Laragh was her home by birthright; this land held her heart and soul, and it was hers to ensure its future. It mattered not in her thoughts that he held the debenture, and that she had agreed to be his wife. She was still mistress, yet somehow a man, a stranger who was not even present, was taking control, and Eleanor did not like that.

She yanked open the middle drawer of her father's desk.

There it was. *His letter.*

While it may have started mild and promising, the tone and message had altered with the second paragraph.

*Mark well, what I write . . .* his firm, dark handwriting had commanded. Whereupon Sir Garrett had proceeded to dictate rules of conduct to her.

She was not to go beyond the stable yard alone; not to walk out of sight of the great house without Edwin Petty at her side; she was not to go to the opposite shore of the lough, nor down the lane to the orchard, nor into Annamoe, nor along the footpath to Clara without Edwin Petty. And under no circumstances was she to travel to Tansey Close or Killoughter. Of course, it mattered not that the weans and entire household were to be held to the same rules. He had addressed her personally; indeed, he had stressed how she must set an example for all to follow, and his tone had been most distasteful.

*". . . If you proceed in any disobedient actions . . ."*

"You have read this letter?" she had asked Edwin Petty. Her hand had trembled; there was a faint scent of sandalwood in the air. It had been the afternoon he arrived at Laragh, and by some small kindness of fate, there had not been anyone else with Eleanor when Maeve had showed him to this very room. Her stomach had dropped when he had walked through the door. In a heartbeat, she had recalled herself back in the coffeehouse hearing his proposition in behalf of Sir Garrett, hearing Whalley's cruel laugh. The awkward silence in her father's library had made it clear Edwin Petty was recollecting the same.

Sooth, the sudden color upon his cheeks had surely been as bright as the blush that had scalded Eleanor's. Along with embarrassment, a thousand emotions had swept her mind. Dignity. She had sat with her back erect, trying to stop her hands from trembling that she might pour him some refreshment. Panic. Did he know of Sir Garrett's marriage proposal? Had he told anyone of what he knew? Somehow, she had found the composure to act a proper hostess. Finally, she had found her voice.

"You must tell me something, Master Petty."

"If I can, Mistress Archebold."

"And I would that your reply might be as honest as Sir Garrett asserts your good self to be."

His expression had been decidedly nervous.

"Do you think me a woman of reckless morals?" she had asked.

"You wish an honest answer, mistress?"

"Aye."

He had glanced away from Eleanor, and her stomach had lurched anew as Edwin Petty's regard roamed over her father's library. She had held her breath as he had stood and crossed the room to look out the window. It had seemed to Eleanor he had stayed there an eternity before turning to face her. In a quiet, even voice, he replied, "Nay, Mistress Archebold, I believe you must be a lady of prudent courage."

She had exhaled. Another miracle. *Edwin Petty understood*. In sympathy, she had said, "It would appear we are both caught by surprise."

"In fairness, I believe Garrett intended a different introduction than the one circumstances forced upon us."

"Mayhap." Eleanor's doubt had been evident. "Did Sir Garrett tell you he had pledged not to speak of our arrangement until his return?"

"And he asked that I assure you we are the only three who know."

"Very well," Eleanor had allowed, then waved Sir Garrett's missive in the air. "You have read this letter? You know what he writes?"

"I am familiar with its contents."

"And the arrogant manner with which Sir Garrett treats me?"

"He has his reasons. Very sound ones, in truth."

*Aye, sound reasons founded on experience*, had been Eleanor's silent retort. Resentment and anger darkened her eyes; her lips tightened into a thin line. *He knows of what I am capable, knows the depths to which I will stoop. Truth to tell, he has decided he cannot trust me.* "Why do you look at me like that?"

"Because you appear capable of drawing blood, Mistress Archebold. Forsooth, you do not forget I am but the messenger?"

A rare smile had washed away Eleanor's bitterness. "If I am to have a keeper, Master Petty, 'tis glad I am it is your good self."

"Would that you might come to consider me friend. 'Tis what Garrett would prefer, I am certain."

Although Eleanor's initial reaction had been to resist whatever Sir Garrett might *prefer*, Edwin Petty was an agreeable gentleman. "And I hope you will one day come to call Laragh home."

Outside one of the hounds barked, Rory called out to Broc Cavanagh, and Eleanor's attention returned to the present. It was time again for her poem. She picked up a goose quill pen, dipped it in the inkwell. She had been composing in her head, and this time the words came easily.

They were bleak.

*. . . Mist there tumbling from branches, unstirred by night and by day*

They reflected her mood, and the gray silence of coming winter that was settling over the land.

*. . . Darkness falling from heaven, our fortune has ebbed away*

She set the edge of the sharpened quill to the paper, and began to transcribe the lines that filled her head.

> *No sound of duck or geese there,*
> *Hawk's cry or eagle's call,*
> *No humming of the bees there*
> *That brought honey and wax for all,*
> *Nor even the song of the birds there*
> *When the sun goes down in the west,*

*No cuckoo on top of the boughs there,*
    *Singing the world to rest.*

*There's mist there tumbling from branches,*
    *Unstirred by night and by day,*
*And darkness falling from heaven,*
    *For our fortune has ebbed away,*
*There's no holly nor hazel nor ash there,*
    *The pasture's rock and stone,*
*The crown of the forest has withered,*
    *And the last of its game is gone.*

She set the pen aside. It was not done. There were more images and thoughts, more phrases and words weaving and sprouting in her mind, but they were not yet ready to be written out.

November faded to December. The redwings, fieldfares, and wild geese arrived from colder climes, and the great holly trees that framed the entrance to the big house were bright with clusters of ripe red berries. The Christmas season would soon be upon them. Eleanor and Sibéal encouraged the weans to prepare the house with greenery as if this year's celebration would be no different than when their parents and brothers had been with them, and each evening as the days grew shorter and the night wind blew icier, Eleanor sought solace in her father's library sitting, pondering and mourning the past, fretting and fuming the here and now, and waiting for Sir Garrett Neville's return.

It was not that she yearned for his return, nor that she waited in hopeful expectation for her wedding day; rather she wished for nothing more than the opportunity to inform Sir Garrett Neville that while he might own Laragh he did not own her. She wanted to stand before him and tell him that whilst he might make her his wife she would never submit to his whims and orders as if she were a creature of no sense or rational ability to call her own, and if she wished to go traipsing about the countryside on her own she would do so.

# Chapter 18

~~~⌒⌒⌒~~~

**T**he wise woman was away seven years with the faeries.

That was how some folk said Biddy O'Fierghraie
had come by her healer's powers. The wise woman
always had a smile to hear that, for whilst she let
folk believe what they might, she knew her cures
were not the stuff of faery magic, but owed to two
score year of hard work and learning.

It was more than fifty-six winters Biddy
O'Fierghraie had been gathering plants and roots
along the footpath to the Raheen. No matter the
harshness of the seasons or the passing of another
English army, this stretch of rocky hillside never
failed to yield the necessaries for her cures. The purple *dwareen* and *camal-buide* had been picked mid-
summer, and the *bainne bo bliatain* were gone until
next spring, when rains would push more mush-
rooms up from the moist earth, but there remained
an abundant source of *dub-cosac*. The speckled dark
green lichen grew on the schist and granite outcrops
near the top of the hill, and a wise woman could
never have enough *dub-cosac*. And hazel rods. Biddy
always kept a ready supply of hazel rods.

A common sight Biddy was, moving through the
woods, her bright red druggit skirt tied about her

head, a large basket hanging from one arm. There had always been a wise woman living in the cabin below Brockagh Hill, and it was a comfort for folk hereabout to see her walking the hills as always. She was their wise woman. Many neighbors and kin might have been taken from this land, but their wise woman had not been driven away. It was a blessing, for her skills were sore needed in the high hills beyond the old ring fort where young men like Luke and Conall Archebold had been forced to hide.

This day Biddy was accompanied by Rory Archebold and Broc Cavanagh. As did Biddy, the lads carried baskets, and they scampered like puppies, first running ahead of the wise woman, then behind her before returning to gather lichen at her side. Every now and again, the wind carried her vexed voice as she scolded them to attend to their duties. It was help she was needing, not having to tend broken bones should they tumble from one of the rocks.

Upon reaching the Glenmacnass, the trio did not turn back, but forded the river with the wind at their back and the sun warm on their faces; they continued toward the ruins of Saint Kevin's ancient monastic settlement at Glendalough. Here within the shadows of Tonelagee and Camaderry was the edge of the wilderness that had once stretched down the hills, far into the valley, and all the way to the sea. Here an Englishman still dared not venture without armed escort, for it was here the Irish still commanded what had been theirs since the beginning of time.

It was a steep, uneven climb to the caves above the upper lough wherein the tories had found shelter from English soldiers and hungry wolves. The old woman and lads were forced to use their hands to steady themselves as they made their way to the entrance of one of the caves. Situated some thirty feet

above the black cold waters and concealed behind a
tangle of yew, it was not discernible until one was
upon it. Biddy made a high trilling noise in imitation
of a redwing. The yew shook, and she showed the
lads where to slip behind the evergreen branches.

"*Go de mur ta sib uile ann so?*" Biddy inquired
upon entering the dim, smoke-filled chamber. *How
are you all here?*

There had been sixteen young men and women
huddled here last time she had visited, and she
hoped for sight of each of their familiar faces. They
could not be well in so dank and cold a space. A
bone-penetrating chill issued forth from the ground.
It was the kind of cold one could not chase away,
the kind that invaded a body to sicken the lungs.
Indeed, the first sounds Biddy heard were ragged
coughing, and the unmistakable wheeze of strained
breathing. It was a merciless penetrating cold that
rose beneath Biddy's skirts, and the old woman
shuddered.

"*Go m-beannuighe Dia dhuit*, Biddy O'Fierghraie.
Welcome, and *may God bless ye.*"

"God save all here," she replied.

Two gaunt men stepped forth from the shadows.

"Conall! Luke." Rory embraced his brothers.

Conall held the lad at the distance of an arm. "Do
not be telling me this is our Rory."

"Nay, it cannot be," Luke rejoined. "Rory was a
wee one last I saw of him."

"A wean, to be sure."

"Far too small to be venturing into the hills."

"Or to be visiting tories."

The twins continued their teasing, while Rory
bobbed up and down before them as if to verify he
had, indeed, grown in the few months since his
brothers had left Laragh. They tousled his hair, and
he grinned, but there was no mistaking the serious

query marking Conall's features when he looked to the wise woman for an explanation.

" 'Tis owing to the English dragoons, my good young sir. They be everywhere, and I need more eyes and ears than the good Lord gave to myself," she said. "I durst not cross the Glenmacnass without someone to be keeping watch for myself. I durst not go abroad lest I be leading yer enemies direct to yerselves. But I durst not stay away any longer, it being a full forenight near gone since I was last bringing victuals into the hills and tending to the ailing amongst yerselves."

Conall nodded in understanding. "Our sister approves?"

"Mistress Eleanor knows nothing of this," Biddy revealed, as she motioned for the lads to set their baskets before her.

"Which is just as well, for then you'd have to contend with our Eleanor trying to take over for your good self, Biddy O'Fierghraie," said Luke. The hint of a smile touched the corner of his mouth.

*"Bhfuil nuaideact air bit leat?"* Roger Clare stepped forward to greet Biddy and inquire of the goings-on at Killoughter. *"Do you bring any news?"*

"To be sure, I have seen yer own dear cousin, the Mistress Rosanna, and herself is well."

"But what of my uncle? Has he returned from Athlone?"

"Ye've heard then?"

"Of the English upstart who would stake a claim to Clare land? Aye, I have heard of this candlestick maker who makes my cousin sleep in the stable." Malice hung on his every word.

"What would ye be intending, Roger Clare?"

"The devil's cure to him. I intend to drive him off Clare land and out of Ireland. And if it means torching my own home and watching it burn to the ground then so be it."

Agreement rippled through the cave. The tories would stop at nothing to free their land.

"And what of the Englishman who my sister welcomed as a guest?" inquired Conall. "What business brought him to Laragh, do you know?"

Biddy said nothing. Whilst she did not know what had brought Sir Garrett Neville to Laragh, she did own a very good suspicion what was going to bring him back. She had seen the way he had placed his body before Mistress Eleanor when the English horsemen had ridden into the banquet hall, and she had seen how the weans had regarded him. To be sure, they believed it was their charm had brought Sir Garrett to Laragh for their sister, and although Biddy knew the bogbine blossoms and verse had no real power, she was not so certain of whatever bewitchment the young mistress herself might have worked on the English stranger.

" 'Twas no business brought Sir Garrett to Laragh," offered Rory.

"Do you say?" Conall humored the lad. "And what would you be knowing of the stranger's affairs?"

Biddy held her breath.

" 'Twas not business, but charms," he declared, with a voice of authority.

"Charms?" Luke chuckled. "And who might be charming him, and to what purpose?"

"For love and marriage. Sir Garrett is come to Laragh to wed our sister, Eleanor."

Luke's chuckle turned to laughter.

The lad looked to Biddy, and saw the wise woman was avoiding his gaze. Too late did he remember her warning never to speak of what she had taught him and his sisters. He wondered if his careless tongue had angered the *sidhe*. No doubt he had angered Biddy, and he hastened to add, "Of course, I know not for certain how or why he comes, but he likes our Eleanor, to be sure, and he is different from the other English. He is not one of the stiff-necked people."

"Aye." Broc Cavanagh added a childish voice of endorsement. "Even me own sister, Maeve, and Róisín O'More like him."

"Do they now?" Once more Luke laughed aloud. "To be sure, that is a commendation most honorable."

Conall, however, did not laugh. "Is it true this Englishman protected the priest?" he asked the wise woman.

" 'Tis true as true can be," confirmed Biddy. "And at peril to his own good self."

The twins looked doubtful.

"He can be trusted?" asked Conall.

"To be sure, he can, says myself. And should he be choosing yer sister, and staying at Laragh, ye could not want for a better gentleman."

"And how is the way of that, pray tell?"

" 'Twas the light, Conall Archebold. I saw it clear as day. Brilliant white it was, encircling his person when himself stepped before the captain of the dragoons to speak up for the priest."

Nothing more need be said. Everyone knew the wise woman had the sight, and if she had seen the white fire about Sir Garrett Neville, there could be no questioning the goodness of his intent. No matter his name, nor the country of his birth, if Biddy O'Fierghraie had seen the light, they would do him no harm.

"It is the candlestick maker with whom we will deal," said Conall.

"*Is eigin a cur amac*," one of the tories declared in voice deadly, hard. *He must be put out.*

"And the pair who are said to be roosting at Castlekevin like greedy crows."

"Every last one of them." There was unanimous agreement in the cave. "Every last one of them will be put out."

With that, the fate of Nehemiah Stubbs and the London grocers was sealed. There had been no lengthy debate, nor jury of their peers, nor even a single judge. In a land where the rule of law was injustice, there would be no public execution for Nehemiah Stubbs, but an unexpected incident some mild afternoon.

Sadness sat heavy upon Biddy's heart. Nothing had changed. Fifty-six years afore it was not Cromwell, but Mountjoy who had made war on Ireland, who had terrorized her people, and wrought injustice upon the land; fifty-six winters ago O'Byrnes and O'Tooles, MacMurroughs and O'Connors, had been fighting the English as their father's fathers had been four hundred years before them. This was the way of war, and it would never end until every single one of the English had left Ireland.

The wise woman frowned as she crouched to empty the baskets. With care, she removed the top layer of fresh-gathered *dub-cosac* below which her other cures and food had been concealed. Everyone knew where Biddy went when she crossed the Glenmasnass, and anyone with something to spare set it aside for the brave lads in the hills. There were hen's eggs from Laragh, apples from Tansey Close, cheese and a bottle of Spanish port from Sir Nicholas Comyn, three small bags of oats, a large honeycomb had been left anonymously outside Biddy's cabin, and there was even a bit of sausage from Róisín O'More, though how the young widow-woman had come by it Biddy could not venture to guess. Lastly, there was paper and ink for Nuala O'Byrne.

"Nuala? I'm not seeing the girl. Where is herself?" Biddy asked, dreading to hear the answer.

"Over here, Biddy O'Fierghraie," came a thin whisper.

Biddy moved into the shadows, and saw the same pale face that had gazed at her from beneath the sheltery nook of an old thorn. She sank down beside the girl and took her hand in hers; it was stone cold and twig thin and shaking, though whether from a chill or fever, Biddy could not tell. Briskly she rubbed the girl's hands between hers.

"*Ta fuact orm anois,*" Nuala said as if she were apologizing. "*I am cold now.* All the time. All the time."

And Biddy, who thought she had seen the worst, felt her heart breaking all over again. Taking her own druggit skirt, she wrapped it round the girl, tenderly, tucking her thin, trembling hands beneath the wool. She listened to Nuala's labored, shallow breathing, then sat back on her haunches and set about mixing honey and elecampane syrup for the frail girl who was but a ghost of her former self.

The weight of centuries, the despair of generations past was in this cave, and the old woman prayed for the unborn Irish children yet to follow. She made the sign of the cross, and whispered, "*Ó a Dhia dan trocaire orainn! A Mhic na hÓighe go bhfaighe r n-anam!*"

She prayed that the future might be different than the past, that it might be different from the present. *God have mercy upon us. Son of the Virgin receive our souls!*

This was the way of war, and there could be no choice for these young people except to continue. Biddy remembered her own dead sons; her father and his brothers, all executed by the English. She thought of the warriors who had fought for this land for nigh on five hundred years, and she knew that until Ireland was free, her people would never be at peace.

# Chapter 19

❦

"**T**homas Powell, I baptize you in the name of the devil." Eveleen's childish voice was cold, each word was uttered clear and precise. Her expression was somber as she looked at the other children.

All six weans were gathered atop the round tower. November had turned to December, when the days grew short and the night winds lingered past dawn. Three Archebolds and three Cavanaghs, they were crouched in a tight circle around an old brazier Grace had found amongst the many items stored in the old fortress.

Eveleen nodded at Rory. The lad tossed a handful of beech mast into the brazier. A thick white cloud wafted upward, the wind blew it over the ramparts.

Next came Grace's turn. She held forth a bundle of fresh-gathered hawthorn and mistletoe for the other children to see, then she raised it high above her head, and repeated, "Thomas Powell, I baptize you in the name of the devil."

The bundle was passed around the circle; each child spoke the words in turn.

It was up to charms, they were once more, but this time it was not a love potion for Eleanor. This time their intent was maleficant. It was a purpose so

231

wicked they had dared not seek Biddy O'Fierghraie's advice. Zzzzzz. A high-pitched hissing emanated from the brazier; it grew louder, more shrill, then came a series of quick pops. Zzzzpft. Several bits of scorched nutshell shot upward.

"Ooooh," exclaimed wee Maeve. Her eyes were wide-rounded at this proof their magic was powerful, and mumbling a blessing in Irish, she crossed herself.

"Your turn," prompted Eveleen.

Maeve blinked several times. She pinched her small face into as grave an expression as Eveleen's. They had sworn on the eternal purity of their Christian souls never to utter a word of what they did this afternoon to another living being. Sooth, their intent was murderous. In a trembling voice, Maeve said, "Methusaleh Waring, in the name of the divil hisself do I baptize ye."

Broc held up a second bundle of hawthorn and mistletoe. He spoke the same words as his sister had, and passed around the clump of greenery in order that each child might hold it whilst repeating the devil's curse on Methuselah Waring.

When each child had taken part in this ritual, the youngest Cavanagh lad tossed a handful of mast into the brazier.

Silence fell over the children. They held their breath as their thoughts were focused on the two men who were at that exact moment seated with Eleanor in the small parlor. It had become their practice to ride through the neighborhood to inquire upon the goings-on at every cabin and bothy, but it was not the welfare of the people that concerned them; it was their obedience. Thomas Powell and Methusaleh Waring had an orderly, English vision for Castlekevin and Tomdarragh. The open lands were to be fenced, hedges were to be planted along both sides of the Annamoe lane, and the people who lived on their estates would be welcome to remain as tenants provided they paid the rents, did not harbor priests or celebrate mass, ceased speaking Irish, and reported to the authorities the whereabouts of all felons, sturdy beggars, dispossessed landowners, and tories.

This was not the first time the grocers had visited Laragh. Each day their circuit concluded with a call at the big house, but they did not come to pay their respects to Mistress Archebold; their interest was in making certain that during Sir Garrett's absence the Archebold family behaved in a manner befitting their dispossessed status. Methusaleh Waring and Thomas Powell were boorish, to be sure, when they looked down their noses at Rory as if he were a horse boy; their tone was overbearing when they criticized Eleanor for allowing her sisters and brother to run wild with those *bogtrotting little savages* as they called wee Maeve and her brothers.

" 'Tis a corrupt practice, is it not, Thomas, the manner in which the old English have married with native Irish?" Methusaleh Waring had asked his companion, as if the children standing before them could not hear, or perhaps did not speak English well enough to understand.

"Aye, 'tis most depraved," Thomas Powell had agreed, then he had addressed Eleanor. "Is it true? Was your mother Irish?"

"My grandfather was the O'Connor chieftain of Baravore."

The grocer made a clucking sound. "Whilst the blood of thy Anglo-Norman ancestors has been befouled, dost thou not desire to cultivate thy more civilized being, Mistress Archebold?"

"A proposal most excellent, Thomas. Prithee, mistress, hast thou no family in England, an aunt or an uncle, mayhap, who might take thou and thine siblings into their household to be schooled in proper English ways before it is too late?"

The grocers were ignorant, narrow-minded men. It was themselves who ought to be taught some manners.

*Zzzzpft.* The second fistful of mast exploded. A cloud of smoke rose.

"Aaaah," came the children's reaction.

"It is time," said Eveleen. She leaned forward to set her bundle on the brazier. Maeve did the same as six pairs of eyes watched.

Some children in Carlow had rid their village of four soldiers. A witch's curse had been used, and the same was said of how the adventurer who had taken up residence in the big house at Tullagher had vanished. Weans like themselves had been bold enough to do the devil's work. It was true. Rory and Broc had heard tell of it on one of their visits to the cave at Glendalough, or at least it was true enough to serve as a mighty source of inspiration. The lads had told the others everything they had learned from the tories, and it had not been long before the six were in agreement; they must at least try to do the same as the children in Carlow and at Tullagher had done.

Tiny flames began to flick at the effigies. A gust of wind swept over the ramparts. The children rose upon their knees as if at prayer. A rook's harsh cry pierced the silence, and in a flash, a great ball of fire spewed forth from the brazier. It was dangerous work trafficking with the devil, the children knew this, and thus they did not watch as flames consumed the bundles; instead they raised their eyes heavenward, making the sign of the cross, and whispering in unison, "In the name of the Father, and of the Son, and of the Holy Spirit, Amen."

\*   \*   \*

"The dwelling is an eyesore," proclaimed Methusaleh Waring. He addressed his remarks to Edwin Petty, not to Eleanor. Whilst he might sit in her mother's small parlor and drink her father's Portuguese wine, there was nothing, be it matters of society or business, he wished to discuss with the daughter of a felon.

"It is a hovel, and must be taken down," added Thomas Powell.

"And as swift as possible, for Sir Garrett would no doubt be displeased if anyone were to remark on the questionable condition of any aspect of his property."

Eleanor's back stiffened. It was difficult to remain civil when these two came to call. Each day their behavior grew more presumptuous, ever bolder, more arrogant. Edwin Petty had cautioned Eleanor to practice patience. *Garrett will deal with them upon his return,* he had assured her more than once. But this assertion seemed more a reminder that someone other than herself was in charge of Laragh, and it did not produce a calming affect upon her; rather it made the task of holding her tongue to silence even more difficult.

"Master Waring and I have held lengthy counsel regarding the numerous dwellings scattered between here and Castlekevin."

"It wouldst appear every one of them is in sore need of removal."

"We, however, are willing to offer a work party to attend the task." Thomas Powell finished his second glass of wine and set it before Eleanor. With his free hand, he pulled at his close-fitting felt collar whilst he opened and closed his mouth like a fish gulping for air.

"Is something amiss, Master Powell?" inquired

Eleanor. Her pleasant expression did not waver as she poured another glass of wine while studying him close. The man had been twitching like a chestnut on a scorching hearth stone for some time.

" 'Tis nothing, Mistress Archebold." He continued to fidget with the collar, his shoulders twitching.

"You are certain, sir?" She could not help but notice the high flush upon his face. It was not hot in the small parlor, yet beads of sweat popped out on his brow. "Perhaps a breath of fresh air—"

He rose in haste. "Indeed, if thou wouldst excuse me, I will take the air. Master Waring, thou dost not object to concluding our interview?"

"Nay, sir," Waring replied. "Please seek thine comfort."

"Good day." Thomas Powell scarce got out the words as he made his way to the door.

Eleanor glanced at Edwin Petty in query.

He mouthed a single, silent word of explanation, *"Fleas."*

A bubble of laughter rose in her throat. She closed her mouth before it might escape.

Methusaleh Waring watched his distressed companion exit the small parlor, then turned back to Edwin Petty. "Tell me, good sir, what remedy dost thou think Sir Garrett will endorse with regard to that unsightly hut beyond the lane? He will agree with our position, will he not? And will be pleased with our efforts to remove the blight in his behalf?"

"It is not for me to speak for Sir Garrett."

"Dost thou not act in his stead?"

"Indeed, I act in accordance with his wishes, but I do not presume to speak for him regarding matters we have not discussed."

"Surely, thou dost not imply Sir Garrett would deal with this creature in a way that was less than swift, or that he would fail to—"

"Creature!" Eleanor could not contain herself. "You are not speaking of a hound or ewe, Master Waring, but of a young widow-woman. Her name is Róisín O'More, and that eyesore is all that she has left in this world. It is her home."

"Mistress," Methusaleh Waring retorted, sharp and censorious. He peered down his long nose. "In England a lady of virtue maintains her silence, and dost not intrude into matters—"

Eleanor drew herself up very straight, and ignored the warning glance from Edwin Petty. "Sir, this is not England."

Waring did not even acknowledge this outburst from Eleanor. Angling his shoulder to her, he addressed Edwin Petty. "Indeed, 'tis not England as long as the countryside is rife with savages, which is why we seek to remedy these ills, and would enlist Sir Garrett's cooperation in our noble enterprise."

"Noble?" Eleanor's voice demanded attention. She held her head high, and did not care what anyone's opinion of her might be. "There is no nobility in evicting a woman from her home in order that your view of the landscape might be unspoiled."

"Prithee, I cannot imagine how Sir Garrett would tolerate such insolence." He spoke to Edwin Petty as if she were not there.

"Can you not?" a deep voice inquired. "Then you must ask him yourself."

The occupants of the room turned to the doorway.

"Garrett, 'tis good to set my eye upon you, friend." Edwin Petty was the first to break the silence. "And to see your journey ends safe."

"Greetings, Edwin, I thank you for your welcome."

"Sir," sputtered Methusaleh Waring. A sickly pallor settled upon his countenance. "I was not informed thou wouldst be here this day."

"I was not expected, Master Waring." He turned from the grocer to Eleanor, and bowed. "Mistress Archebold."

She whispered a reply, finding to her surprise that she was pleased Sir Garrett was here. It was more than the disapproving gaze he fixed upon Methusaleh Waring, more than the sense that an ally and defender had entered the room to be at her side; it was the gentleman himself that gladdened her. She recalled how he had taken care of her that first night in his Dublin lodgings; she had not forgotten how he had fed her and treated her with gentleness. Her mind abounded with images and memories the most notable of which had nothing to do with broth. How quick her body warmed at the memory of the intimate caress on her bare skin, of his hands, his lips, his tongue. Deep within her something stirred, for her thoughts came alive to think of how his mansword had filled her.

Her heart quickened, a rush of heat colored her cheeks, and the urge to cross the small parlor to greet him tugged at her. She remembered what he had said in the walled garden. *One day you will awaken in my arms. You will be at my side because it is what you want.* So, too, did she recall the certainty in his voice; the bold gleam in his lush green eyes.

Quick, she glanced downward; she forced herself to remain seated. Soon enough her betrothal to Sir Garrett would be common knowledge, and when that time came Eleanor was willing to accept the stares and whispers. Anyone whose opinion she valued would know why she had agreed to such an arrangement; as for the opinions of others like this adventurer, it was up to Eleanor to demonstrate that while Sir Garrett might own Laragh, he would never own Eleanor Archebold.

"Insolence?" Garrett strode into room, looking like he had traveled a fair distance. There was a layer of dust upon his bucket-top boots, and a leather saddlebag was slung over one shoulder. Maeve hastened in his wake collecting his cloak and plumed hat and gloves. "Did I hear correctly, Master Waring? Was insolence the word you used to describe Mistress Archebold's behavior?"

"Sir, 'tis a most woeful truth, and if thou hadst been standing upon the threshold long enough thou would have witnessed the same."

"Ah, but I have been here *long enough*, and I witnessed not insolence, but a fair and charitable woman speaking with kindness." He looked to Eleanor. "Róisín O'More is the young widow woman whose cabin lies beyond the lane on the Annamoe road?"

Eleanor nodded.

"And she is one of Laragh's people?"

"She is."

Garrett turned back to Waring. His face was set in rigid lines. "Have you explained your concerns to Edwin Petty?"

"We have, indeed, Sir Garrett."

"As well as their proposed solution," put in Edwin.

He nodded and frowned. There was a visible darkening in his vibrant green eyes, and for an instant, it looked as if his thoughts had strayed far away, mayhap to another time and place, so odd was the expression that came over his countenance. At length, he spoke. "It shall be left then for Edwin to tell me the whole of it, and I promise to give the matter due consideration. Now if you will excuse me, sir, my journey has been long and tiring. Maeve will show you to the door."

Something in Garrett's tone of voice, or perhaps it

was the way he looked at Methusaleh Waring, chilled the edge of his polite words. He left no doubt the interview had concluded. Methusaleh Waring made a perfunctory bow in Eleanor's direction, bade the gentlemen farewell until next time, and was gone.

"Some refreshment, Sir Garrett?" Eleanor inquired, finding herself in need of some activity to distract her attention from his tall male form.

"I see they have been enjoying your father's wine." Garrett set the saddlebag on the floor, picked up the wine bottle from the refreshment table, and tilted it to one side to inspect the contents. He frowned. "And it would appear they have made more than one visit."

"Daily," said Edwin.

"Their discourse runs similar?"

"Without fail. The countryside abounds with blight that must needs be brought to your attention."

"Not the best sort of neighbors," remarked Garrett.

She held out a glass for him. Their fingers brushed. There was a stirring in her belly, ribbons of heat in her legs.

"They are trying to win your favor," Edwin stated the obvious.

"If you will excuse me, Sir Garrett," Eleanor rose on unsteady legs. She must leave. She needed to be alone and compose herself, to erect some sort of defense between herself and this man. "I will make certain Sibéal knows you are returned."

"Nay, mistress, do not leave. I would like you to stay." He put out a hand to stop her.

Eleanor caught her breath. He had not touched her this time, but the mere motion in her direction sent a wave of sensations flowing through her. She stared at his hand, and swallowed twice so that she might speak. "Your room must be prepared, and to be sure, you would like a private interview with Master Petty."

"Aye, but I would like an interview with your good self, not with Master Petty."

Another ripple of heat washed through Eleanor. She swayed, or at least she imagined her body was of a sudden light enough that it moved of its own accord.

He reached into his cloak pocket and withdrew two envelopes sealed with wax. One was a letter from himself, the other was from Lord Egerton. He held them forth to Edwin. "Would you see to it that these are delivered to Captain Rowlestone this evening?"

"It will be taken care of immediately."

Garrett smiled. "You will excuse us then, Edwin."

His voice touched Eleanor. It was smooth and low, faintly husky, and she shivered. Edwin Petty replied, but she did not hear his precise words; indeed, it mattered not what he said. He was leaving, then he was gone, and finding herself alone with Garrett, Eleanor busied herself gathering the empty wine glasses. It was the best way she might devise to put a small distance between them.

"Please, mistress, we are not strangers; do not step away from me as if we were."

She trembled. His words tumbled through her mind. *We are not strangers.* Past and present mixed as one. . . . *There is one thing you already find pleasing about me.* He moved closer, and she did not step away.

"I have something for you."

"You have been generous with provisions for the household. There is nothing more I need."

"I speak not of necessity, mistress. 'Tis a gift."

*A gift.* Her heart leapt; she wished it did not. A

fleeting memory of the thrill and joy she had known as a young girl visited her; she wished it had remained buried. Such pleasant emotions were part of the past, not of the present or of the future, and she did not wish to be reminded of everything that was lost to her. She tried to sound disinterested. "A gift, do you say? For me?"

"Is it not usual for the groom to give his bride a gift on the eve of their wedding?"

"On the eve of—" She could not finish. A chill seeped through her, then slow, melting heat as the significance of his words stole her breath away.

"You are not going to faint on me?" he asked in a drawl soft and tender. His hands went to her waist. There was a glimmer in his eyes that teased and beckoned her as surely as did his words. "Go ahead, mistress. Would that I might catch you in my arms, and consider it a fine welcome to have you in my embrace."

Eleanor leaned into him. It was impossible to stop herself despite the warning bells in her head, despite the ache in her heart. Once before this man had taken from her, and she knew how important it was to protect herself from him. She knew, but it did no good. There were not enough wise words beneath the heavens that might empower her to resist the promise of his smooth, deep voice, and to ignore the exotic scent of sandalwood that clung to him.

His hands caressed her waist. Even through the fabric she was aware of their size and strength; even the heat in his fingers touched her as if there were no barrier between their flesh. His gaze focused on her mouth, and she swallowed in a throat gone dry. Desire marked his features, it burned in his eyes, and an energy, thrilling, hot and wild, leapt between them. She uttered a tiny sigh, her eyelashes fluttered closed, and her tongue darted out to moisten her lips.

He was going to kiss her, and she was not going to stop him.

# Chapter 20

───◦◦───

**L** avender and sweet woodruff.

The delicate scents permeated Garrett's senses. They were Eleanor, beguiling, feminine, and they aroused him as sure as did the softness of her body beneath his hands, as swift as did the sight of her dark lashes feathering against fair skin while her pink tongue darted out to moisten her parted lips. Each lonely night away from Laragh he had dreamed of this return, of holding her in his arms, and this was everything he had fancied.

Sensory images were stirring throughout his body. His mouth watered to recall how her silky inner flesh had tasted. Blood pooled in his groin as he remembered pleasuring her. He drew a second, deeper breath, and another image awakened within him. It was an image neither of the past, nor present, but of a time yet to come. There were children seated in a sunny nook of Laragh's walled garden listening to a story; it was Órla's tale they heard, and Garrett knew it was himself doing the telling.

His chest tightened. He could almost hear the wee voices as they repeated the story amongst themselves.

The promise of everything Eleanor held for him was intoxicating.

He pulled her against his chest, heard her sigh, and the unguarded sound struck a chord within him. His own, low moan echoed hers. With one arm hooked about her waist, his other hand began to slide up her back, and Eleanor arched like a cat wanting to be stroked. His hand lingered, fondled, then skimmed across her shoulder, going higher to cup her chin. He lifted her face for his kiss, heard the catch in her breath as his lips brushed across hers, so soft, delicious. They trembled at his caress.

"I am glad to be returned to this place." He nibbled at the corner of her mouth as he spoke. "My journey is at last ended." There was more meaning in his words than Eleanor would ever understand, and Garrett could not help wishing he might hear her welcome him home. Of course, it was impossible. While she might be willing to concede his ownership of Laragh, Garrett was willing to wager she didn't think it was his home. Garrett, however, had not come such a distance in time and space to settle for anything less than the whole of his ambition, and he would hold fast to the hope that such sweet words of welcome would one day accompany Eleanor's sighs. Someday she would know the truth of who he was, and why it was he had come to claim this land. Someday the distrust and barriers she maintained between them would be gone.

His tongue traced the fullness of her bottom lip, and another little sound escaped her. Heat poured through him. Fire ignited between them, and he sensed its energy rushing back and forth between them, picking up speed, its flames building in intensity, licking hotter, deeper. Garrett teased, he nipped, he tasted, and she opened fully to accept his delving, stroking tongue. He moaned; she sighed. His hands traveled over her; she snuggled against him, pliant, soft, and warm.

Despite Eleanor's assertion that she found no pleasure in his touch, despite her claim to have no fondness for his kisses, this sensual energy that flared to life between them belied her every protestation. This alchemy was as vibrant and volatile, as palpable and compelling, as it had been that first night outside the coffeehouse. Indeed, Garrett believed it could never weaken, and he dared to whisper, "I was correct, it would appear."

"Sir?" She floated back to conscious thought, aware of how easy it would be to surrender to him.

"Our marriage is not to be as chilling an arrangement as you stipulated."

His words made no sense. Confusion made Eleanor shiver. She must never let him know the truth, must never give him anything that might allow him any more power over her than he already possessed to hurt her. "Clarify your meaning, if you please."

"I speak of the condition you attached when you agreed to be my wife."

"What notion do you entertain?" A frown creased her brow. "Naught has changed. Beyond necessity I have no more intention of sharing your bed now than I did three weeks ago."

"Are you certain, mistress?" he asked on a velvet whisper. "Mayhap you acted in haste to attach such a condition."

She bristled. "Of course, I am certain."

"Are you *very certain*?" His thumb caressed the corner of her mouth. He murmured, "I have heard it said, *Act in haste, repent in leisure*. You would not want to find yourself *regretting* in leisure."

"I am not oft mistaken, and shall have nothing to regret." She angled her face to escape the touch of his thumb. His hand fell away, and she was emboldened. "I find no pleasure in your kisses so wild."

"Is that so?" Garrett reached for her hand, and raised it to his mouth, set his lips to the inside of her wrist. She quivered when he kissed her; he had known she would, and he chuckled on an under-breath. "I stroke, and you purr."

Eleanor's body betrayed her. She swayed as the fire between them reignited. A scorching white heat sprang to her cheeks; it ran along the back of her legs, it shot to the core of her belly. Her breath was suspended.

"Your skin burns, mistress. Your senses are inflamed, for I am as flint to your kindling."

She released a silent breath, tried to move away. She knew a touch of panic. She must get away from him.

"Your pulse races when I beckon your body to mine. Your blood—"

"Oh!" She cut him off with a gasp before he might say another word. "Your pride begets vanity, Sir Garrett. Is humility not one of the almighty English virtues to be taught to the Irish?" She yanked free her hand, and turning toward the door, stepped away from him.

"*No.* Do not leave." His arm shot out, and even though he did not touch her, he managed to halt her exit. "I still have not given you your bride gift."

"Can it not wait?" she asked without looking at him, focusing instead on the outstretched arm blocking her way to the door. She was too much of a coward to meet his gaze. He was correct. His affect upon her was potent. The mere sight of his hand caused her to relive every exquisite detail of how he had rolled down her stockings and cupped her foot in his palm; how he had unlaced her gown and slid it off her shoulders; how he had massaged her back,

kneading, playing, teasing all the way down her
spine with that very hand until those fingertips had
dipped into the cleft between her buttocks. Oh, how
she yearned for that again, for all of it, for everything, and oh, how acute was the shame of her
weakness. She had little willpower where he was
concerned, and even less dignity; she had to get
away before he tried once more to prove his point.
He would succeed, she did not doubt, and then all
would be lost to her.

"No, it cannot wait. We are to be wed on the morrow."

"It is necessary that we wed so soon?" was
Eleanor's thinly controlled reply. She needed more
time to prepare herself, especially for their wedding
night. If she could not control her body from sur-
rendering to him, she must at least be able to shield
her heart and mind. She was not yet capable enough
to endure intimacy with this man, and not yearn for
more than his touch. Very simply, she did not know
how to keep her heart from aching. "Must it be tomorrow? There have been no preparations. Who will
perform the rite?"

"Ambrose."

"It will be legal?"

"Though I do not expect to ever hear it admitted
aloud, I know that Ambrose is the Capuchin Stephen
Kirwan. He can perform the ceremony, and aye, in
the eyes of God, it will be legal."

"But are you not a Protestant?"

"To the contrary. I am baptised in the true faith
same as yourself."

"But what of civil law? Is it not against the law
for the English soldiers to marry with Irish girls?"

"That it is, but I am not a soldier." He grinned.
"Furthermore, I have obtained the necessary legal
documents. My friend, Lord Egerton, made certain

they were signed by the most unimpeachable officials, and that all the appropriate legal authorities were paid a handsome gratuity for their advice on the matter of my marriage."

She forced herself to meet his gaze as she tried one final time to delay the inevitable. "I would like Rosanna to be here. Surely you can wait a few days."

"I could wait, but I do not wish to do so. It will be as I say. Tomorrow we will wed. Now you will stay in this room. Be seated."

"Is that an order?"

"It is my pleasure to give you your bride gift this night and to watch you open it."

She made no move to turn away from the door, nor to sit as he had decreed. He looked at her as if expecting her compliance, and when she did nothing, Eleanor saw the muscles along his jaw go rigid. They did not relax until he spoke.

"But if I must order you so that I might have my pleasure, then aye, mistress, 'tis an order."

Eleanor's back stiffened, her nostrils flared. *'Tis an order*. The words provoked her, as had the list of rules he'd sent to her in his letter. She might have no choice except to wed this Englishman, but she would never be the dutiful English wife whose husband might boast of her silence. "What will you do, if I disobey?"

His expression hardened. His gaze narrowed to match the uncompromising tenor of his reply. "Do not even consider such a thing. There will be no disobedience in this household."

"How, how d-dare you?" She was humiliated. Sir Garrett had not spoken to Methusaleh Waring or Captain Rowlestone in such an overbearing tone as he did to herself, the woman who would be his wife. It was unthinkable. Her father would never have treated her mother in such an arrogant fashion; the chieftains at Baravore would never have spoken to their wives as if they were chattels.

"I dare," he drawled the simple confirmation of his action. An icy edge sharpened his domineering tone of voice. "You will do as I say. *Sit*."

She did not obey, and while she uttered not a word, the defiant tilt of her chin revealed her resentment, the glow in her eyes revealed anger.

Their gazes locked in challenge. Silence stretched between them. Neither Eleanor, nor Garrett appeared to blink. Neither of them appeared to draw a breath. From the long gallery came the chime of the clock, and with this interruption, Garrett was the first to draw back.

"Please, mistress." He motioned to the chair, then ran his fingers through the hair at his temple. It was a weary sort of motion.

Eleanor tilted her head to one side. A tiny line creased her brow. What was that she had heard in his voice? She tried to discern his expression, tried to make sense of what she had heard. Had it been incertitude? *Never*. Or supplication? *Impossible*. Yet for the space of a heartbeat, she imagined vulnerability played upon his features.

"Please remain and accept my gift on the eve it was intended to be given." His voice softened. "If possible, I would that our marriage might commence on a footing which might foster harmony. Such may not be an easy path to follow, but I would that we might face that direction rather than toward discord."

It would have been easy for Eleanor to defy an order, but his words chased away her anger and resentment. She could not naysay him. Defiance was unthinkable. She, too, hoped for harmony; indeed, she hoped their marriage might be more than a mere arrangement; to have such a limited relationship would cause pain, and she could not bear the prospect of the lonely future ahead. She gave a little cough to regain her voice.

"Your gesture does not go unappreciated, sir. I will accept your gift in the spirit in which it is offered." She sat down, and set her folded hands upon her lap. For a moment, it seemed he might speak. She looked at him, waiting, but he said nothing. Instead, he nodded in acknowledgment, then bent down to his leather saddlebag, lifted the flap, and retrieved a small square package, which he held forth to her.

Twine secured brown wool about the contents, and as Eleanor untied it a tickle of awareness skirled up her spine. He was watching her, his gaze steady. She sensed its heat, its singular intensity, and the skin at the nape of her neck tingled. She paused to glance from beneath her lashes. Aye, he was watching her, and the look in his eyes stole her breath away. It was akin to the moment outside the coffee-house when he had caressed her face, that passing instant when she had glimpsed what it must be like to be adored by a man.

Somewhere in the vicinity of her heart, something twisted, and the pain was almost more than she could bear. Quick her gaze returned to the package. She continued to pull away the string, then with care she unrolled the wool to reveal two books. Her hands trembled to hold this gift that had been wrapped with such care. They were two of her father's volumes that she had sold in Dublin and thought lost forever. Hot tears burned her eyes, they stung her nose; indeed, there seemed to be an over abundance of them, and in another heartbeat, she feared one might escape.

"You did this for me?" she asked on a whisper.

"I did."

More tears gathered. She tried to blink them away, yet they continued to increase until she could no longer see the books clear enough to read their titles, but she could feel them in her hands, and as a sightless person might explore a precious object, her fingertips traced over the leather covers, down the bindings, across each vellum page. At length, she was done with this exploration, and she held the books to her as if embracing a dear, long lost friend. Tears flooded her eyes. She sniffled hard, but failed to contain them.

A single tear escaped from the corner of one eye, then a second and a third, a fourth followed to mark slow, wet trails down her cheek. For the first time in many years, there were tears for Eleanor Archebold. She swiped at them with the back of her hand, and was grateful he said nothing to her. He offered no trite comfort, no false platitude, nor any observation that likewise as she was mistaken about his kisses, mayhap she was mistaken about her fortitude.

"Thank you, Sir Garrett." She raised her eyes. "To be sure, this is the most kind gift I have ever received. You could not have selected any gem or bauble or treasure that would hold greater value to me than these books. Thank you."

He smiled. That was what he had intended, what he had hoped she would feel, and when she returned his smile, he had never seen anything so enchanting. It was the first genuine smile Eleanor Archebold had bestowed upon him, and he wanted her more than ever. His need for her was fierce, consuming. He wanted all of her, body, heart, and soul, and would not be satisfied with anything less. He desired a wife who would share more than his name and a place at his table, and he was willing to give the whole of himself in return. Devotion. Passion. Respect. Joy. Laughter. Companionship. Fidelity.

Love. They would be hers, if only she would allow. If only he might win her. Garrett intended to court and claim the affection of his wife, and this was a favorable beginning.

"I am glad you are pleased. 'Tis good to see you smile."

"But how?" she wondered aloud how he had obtained them.

"There is nothing to tell," he replied with a dismissive shrug.

Again, she smiled, knowing full well the books had long ago been auctioned and dispersed. "Thank you again, Sir Garrett." She could only imagine the trouble and expense to which he had gone to obtain them for her. The enormity of what this man had done worked its way into her heart. "You are a most considerate gentleman."

"Would you not call me Garrett? 'Tis not an order, but a most humble request. It would please me to hear you use my name without any formality of address."

"Thank you, Garrett," she said, finding it in no way awkward or strange to drop the Sir from before his given name. "You were right to make me stay to receive my gift this night."

"Then you agree, 'tis possible that we might start our marriage on a path toward harmony?"

She stared at him, considering her reply with care. She knew it would be almost impossible to protect her heart from this man.

"Well, mistress, what say you?"

Eleanor's answer was soft-spoken, and full of promise, "Aye, Garrett, all things are possible."

# Chapter 21

**" . . .** **I**f any man and woman are joined together otherwise than as God's Word
allows. . . ."

The priest recited the rite as it had been spoken in
Ireland for hundreds of years. Eleanor had heard the
words many a time. As a child, she had yearned for
the day they would be meant for her; now that day
was here, yet her mind wandered, bursting not with
thoughts of her future, but of the past. Eleanor suspected this was not the way of most brides as they
stood with their bridegrooms before the priest, but
then, she was not like most brides. She held her
trembling hands at her waist, and glanced downward, staring at her satin slippers but not seeing
their toes peeking from beneath the hem of her
cream velvet gown. Her thoughts were of days and
people gone before. Scores of images played through
her mind: she recalled the night she had waited outside Sir Garrett's lodgings; heard her mother singing
as she trimmed her roses in the walled garden; saw
her father galloping up the lane with a troop of
brave Irish soldiers riding in his wake. Her immediate surroundings faded as her thoughts continued
to stray backward in time.

"Stitched by angels, to be sure. 'Tis soft as the

clouds, and could only have come from heaven,"
Eleanor had marveled. She had been six years old,
and wonderment had laced her voice. She had never
set her eyes upon anything as beautiful as the cream-
colored velvet gown her mother took from the linen
cupboard and unfolded before her. It was magical.
Hundreds of pearls studded the fabric, and edged
the neckline. "And look! There are even stars."

Lady Moira had smiled. "Nay, 'twas not angels
who sewed this gown, but a seamstress in the royal
household of King Phillip. And 'twas not heaven,
but Spain from whence it came. Go ahead," she had
encouraged her to touch the costly garment with its
wide, pleated skirt and brocaded petticoat.

"Spain is far from Ireland, is it not?"

"Aye, 'tis across the seas beyond the shores of England and Flanders, beyond even Rouen and Bor-
deaux." Lady Moira had set her hand beside
Eleanor's. Together, mother and daughter had
traced the satin ribbons woven into the bodice. "This
gown was brought on a ship trading Spanish wines
and salt for Irish woolens and hides. It will belong
to you one day."

"You will give it to me?"

"As my mother gave it to me, and her mother
gave it to her good self before that. Aye, it will be
yours. The lady who first wore it was my mother's
mother, your great-grandmother. *Nóirín Dubh* she
was called. *Dark Noreen.* A Maguire from Ferman-
agh, and being the only daughter of the lord of Ballyshannon, naught but the finest would do for *Nóirín
Dubh.* 'Tis true as true, the tale of how the lord of
Ballyshannon parted with a full dozen of his finest
wolfhounds to acquire this gown. *Nóirín Dubh* gave
it to her daughter—who was to be my mother—
upon the occasion of her betrothal to Rory
O'Connor, the chieftain of Baravore; my mother

wore it the day she wed, and upon my betrothal to your father, she gave it to me as I will give it to you, Eleanor. You will wear this gown when you wed, and one day your daughter will wear it."

The promise of that velvet gown had many times repeated itself in Eleanor's daydreams over the years. One day she would wed a man steadfast and brave. A handsome man who would be tender yet strong. A horseman, a poet, and a warrior as fearless in the face of death as her father. Everyone in the countryside would attend. Her kin from Baravore and Killoughter would be there, even folk from as far as Delgany on the coast, and from across the mountains in Kildaire would make the journey to Laragh. No formal invitations would be sent—that was not the Irish way. Neither would the guests bring gifts, for it would be their good presence to witness and celebrate the wedding which was desired above anything else.

Lo, what a celebration it would be with toasts and music in the banqueting hall, and dancing in the garden led off by the newlyweds. So it was that Eleanor had dreamed of wearing the gown, and of dancing in the arms of a fearless Irishman, who would lean close to whisper, "Wife."

Eleanor unclasped her hands, stretched out the fingers, brushing them over countless pearls to rest her palms against the velvet. She listened to the priest.

". . . Honor and keep her in sickness and in health, and forsaking all others, keep thee only unto her, so long as ye both shall live?"

"I do," Garrett replied, and Eleanor's heart did a queer little somersault as another wave of memories washed through her.

While she had oft indulged in daydreams of her wedding, she had never been able to decide which one of her brothers' friends or which of the soldiers who fought with Sir Thomas would be the one to call her wife. The MacMurrough brothers were braw lads, all seven of them, and a splendid thing it would be to live in the fortress near Enniscorthy; there was a captain from Carlow with a teasing smile who had once taken her fancy, and another time, at the grand age of eleven, she had imagined herself in love with one of the Fitzgeralds.

"Each one of them would make an exceptional fine husband for any girl," Lady Moira had assured Eleanor.

"But, mother, how will I know which one to choose?" If only one of them might have been more like Bran O'Connor, then it would have been clear.

"You will know, my dearest daughter. When the time is right, you will know the man who touches your heart as a woman's heart is meant to be touched, and who charms your body as a woman's body is meant to be charmed."

She had stared at her mother in bewilderment, thinking that her answer was not an answer at all. *Touching hearts. Charming bodies.* Eleanor had frowned hard and thoughtful, then said, "There is one thing of which I am certain."

"What is that?"

"Whomever it is, I will not wed him at harvest time, else be cursed to a life of gathering."

"Ah, you have been listening to Biddy O'Fierghraie. What else does the wise woman tell you?"

"That I am one of the *bean-draíocht* with a destiny, and a grand destiny it is certain to be. *An incarnation of the past, a guardian of the present, and a bridge to the future,* those were her words, and I should be hoping to hear the cuckoo's song on my wedding morn. 'Tis a promise of luck, and destiny to be fulfilled."

But no such favorable omen had been Eleanor's this day.

The cuckoos had long since left Ireland for the winter, the morning had dawned gray and cold and dank, and by mid-morn snow had started to fall, heavy and steady. Indeed, her wedding day was nothing like her girlhood imaginings. There were no guests come from far and wide, no throng of friends and kin; there was but a handful of people, who assembled not in Laragh's banqueting hall, but in its kitchen, where the familiar aromas of burning gorse and peat from the hearth-fire warmed the air.

"The kingdom of Heaven tolerates sieges," recited the priest.

"Alleluia," the bride and groom and their witnesses replied in unison.

"And the forceful take it."

"Alleluia."

Eleanor closed her eyes, and waited, breath suspended, heartbeat thrumming in her ears. In another second, the girlhood dream would be gone forever. The words that came next were familiar to her, and once they had been spoken the last, slim thread of hope that she had refused to relinquish would be taken from her. She heard the priest speaking, and held her breath as if it were possible to stop herself at this very moment in time for always and forever.

The priest spoke *the words*. "I pronounce you to be man and wife."

She exhaled. It was done.

Mistress Eleanor Archebold of Laragh was wed, she was no maid, but wife, though not to a Fitzgerald or MacMurrough. It was not a fearless Irish officer with a teasing smile whom she would call husband. All the Irish boys were gone. It was an Englishman whom she had vowed to honor and obey, to love and to cherish.

*"Go ndéana Dia díon dár dtigh, dá bhfuil an istigh, dá bhfuil as amuigh. Claíomh Chríost ar an doras go dtí solas an lae amáraigh,"* the priest blessed the dwelling in which the newlyweds would reside. Eleanor and Garrett repeated in English, *"May God be the roof of our house for all within and all without, Christ's sword on the door till tomorrow's light."*

"You are marked with the sign of the Cross of Christ." He raised his right hand to make the sign of the cross. "Length of life and sunny days, and may your souls not go homewards till your own child falls in love. Peace be with you into life eternal."

All replied as one, "Amen."

"Sir Garrett, you may now give your lady-wife the kiss of peace."

Eleanor did what was expected. She knew what came next, and raised her face to the man who was now her husband. His eyes were focused on her mouth, her gaze went to his, and for a moment she could not draw a breath to think of how those full masculine lips had known her in a most intimate way. He was a dangerous man, this husband of hers. Dangerous for the affects he had upon her, dangerous for the threat he posed to her. To be near him was explosive. Like a burst of flame in the hearth, reason and passion collided within her, and her strength of will proved weaker than the powers of her heart. With stunning clarity she knew the dreams of a steadfast, fearless husband were not dead as she had thought they were. They were more poignant, more vivid than ever.

*All things are possible,* she had told him last night, but she had spoken too quick; one dream was not possible. It might not be dead, but it was not possible, and Eleanor knew what would happen if she failed to protect her heart. She must never allow that to happen; if she hoped to be strong for Eveleen and Grace and Rory, she must never forget that while he might own Laragh, he did not own her.

But when he set his hands on her shoulders her knees went weak.

When he drew her closer for his kiss, she trembled with emotions that threatened to overwhelm her resolve.

There was fear no less vivid than her longing; desire as powerful as her resentment; an abundance of confusion, anger, and hope. Each tried to triumph over the others; all tried to dominate her heart and soul and mind. Her trembling began to worsen, but she controlled it as she forced herself to stand tall in the manner befitting the mistress of Laragh. She met his gaze and did not flinch as she awaited the kiss that was his to take.

Garrett looked down at her upturned face. Golden, soft light from the hearth and flickering wall sconces bathed her features. She was an exquisite vision, a delicate, appealing woman, and she was his. His gaze traveled over her, slow and hungry. He had not been able to contain his more prurient thoughts since he had seen her descend the broad oak staircase wearing that cream velvet gown, her glorious black hair flowing free down her back, curling in soft patterns about her face and neck. He did not know what brides thought of during their wedding ceremony, but Garrett was certain he was not different than any other groom; his thoughts were on bodily passions and on what the night ahead held for them once they were alone.

For a moment, he sensed a trembling beneath his hands, and he glanced to her face, but saw no sign of any such weakness. To the contrary, he witnessed how she straightened her shoulders to stand tall and brave and ready. This was Eleanor as he had first come to know her; this was the young woman forced to accept responsibilities beyond her years. This was Eleanor in need of someone to watch over her. This was the young woman who would do anything for her family, and he knew what she must be thinking.

She stood before him not as his wife, but as a sacrifice; she was the human offering given in exchange for favorable treatment of her family. There was about her such an aura of purpose, pure and resolute, one might almost believe the angels had blessed her; indeed, it seemed to Garrett she must be one of them.

"An angel," Garrett whispered. Longing roughened his voice, for whilst she might be an angel she was also a temptress. To Garrett's eye the cut and design of the gown were in no way ethereal. Styled with a long, pointed waist-seam, and a snug, low cut pannier-bodice, it accented her small waist while displaying her breasts in a most tempting manner. Some might regard her dressed in that gown of velvet and pearls and be reminded of soft clouds and bright white starlight, but Garrett saw a confection of sweets and spun sugar. This was Eleanor as he had always known her, a woman who was at once as fresh and innocent as she was sensual and alluring. She was almost good enough to eat, and wanting a taste, he lowered his mouth.

"I have taken an earthly angel for my bride," he murmured, as his lips brushed across hers. He wanted to ravish her, to devour and possess her, and she was his to possess, but he would never win her heart, if he took from her before she was willing to give. She would never come to him of her own will; he would never hear her welcome him home. The pads of his thumbs made tiny circles at the corners of her mouth. Again his lips feathered back and forth across hers, lightly.

Eleanor's eyelashes fluttered closed. She tried not to react, tried to remain distant and indifferent, but failed. Little ribbons of heat skipped along the backsides of her legs and upper back, across her chest. A small sigh escaped her. Oh, his kissing produced the most wonderful sensations. Even in a room full of onlookers she could not prevent her body from responding. Her belly warmed when he nibbled at her bottom lip. The tip of his tongue slid back and forth over the seam between her lips, coaxing her to relax, to yield, to open to him. She sighed a second time when his mouth pressed more firmly, and she swayed against him when the light caresses turned to a slow savoring kiss.

Those little sighs and that swaying motion told Garrett everything he needed to know. It was clear that no matter what she might insist to be the truth, she was his. He had already won sensual command of her body. Now he must win her heart and mind. She sighed again, and he did not hesitate to hold her tighter as his tongue pressed into her mouth to stroke and play with hers.

A spark of energy passed between them. Not a soul in the kitchen failed to witness the way Eleanor melted in Sir Garrett's embrace, nor how tenderly he cupped her face, and how eagerly their mouths melted one to the other. It was a kiss the likes of which the poets sang.

Rory let out a jubilant yell, and Garrett raised his mouth from Eleanor's as the weans rushed to embrace their sister. Everyone began to speak at once, pressing round the bride and groom to offer their well wishes, and Eleanor could not help marveling how they accepted Garrett. It seemed as if he had always been one of them.

Last night Sibéal had not batted an eyelash when Eleanor had announced her intention to wed Sir

Garrett. The old woman had displayed even less reaction upon learning that Sir Garrett was Laragh's
new owner. It was almost as if Sibéal—and everyone
else for that matter—was privy to a secret. A secret
no one had confided to Eleanor. Even the weans had
not acted in the least surprised. Indeed, they seemed
to be under the impression that Eleanor's marriage
to the English stranger somehow meant all was
right, and the troubles of the world would bypass
Laragh.

"I believe 'tis tradition for the bride and groom to
dance the first dance," Garrett said to Eleanor.

"A dance may be customary," she replied, more
than a little confused. She was not feeling at all like
herself. Their kiss might have ended, but as she
gazed up into his eyes, a warm, smoldering sensation lingered in her core. She was not feeling like the
young woman who might control her emotions, who
might mask her reactions with ease and skill. "But
we have no music."

"Have we not?" he said, as if pondering a riddle
most perplexing.

Grace giggled.

Rory elbowed his sister as if to silence her.

"Mayhap there is a solution." He gave a nod to
Róisín O'More.

A bustling ensued as Archebold and Cavanagh
children scurried about the kitchen. They set about
moving benches, and reaching behind the bins and
cupboards that lined the length of one wall. Prior to
Eleanor's entrance into the kitchen they had concealed a variety of items which they now retrieved,
but did not reveal.

Róisín O'More went to stand before the hearth.
The children took their places on either side of her.
The girls positioned themselves to her right, the lads
to the left, and when Róisín signaled, they brought

forth their hands from behind their backs. The two
Cavanagh lads were each holding a bodhrán; Rory
and wee Maeve had flutes; Grace had a goatskin
tambourine; while Eveleen, who stood closest to
Róisín, handed an Irish harp to the young widow-
woman.

"Music for dancing? How is it possible I should
be so blessed this day?" exclaimed Eleanor. "There
is no doubt Róisín can pluck naught but the most
sweet, lingering notes from her harp, and Eveleen
has a singing voice as pretty as a thrush in full summer. But Rory Archebold, when was it you were
learning to play the flute?"

"Since Garrett taught me."

"He and Róisín taught a song to all of us," added
Grace.

" 'Twas not barn work my brothers were about
this morning, Mistress Eleanor. But learning music
ourselves we were doing, and every one having a
part for our verra own," said wee Maeve, who no
longer scowled at Sir Garrett, nor scurried out of his
way in terror, but gazed at him in open adoration.

Róisín cradled the harp in her arms, and plucked
the introductory notes of a tune. The children ceased
talking to take up their instruments and await her
cue. She gave a signal to the lads, and they began to
keep beat with their bodhráns; next Rory and Maeve
joined on the flutes; lastly, Grace took up the tambourine as Eveleen began to sing.

Garrett bowed to Eleanor in formal invitation,
then held out a hand. He gave her his most charming smile. "Mistress mine, would you dance with
me?"

His expression was warm, seductive. Irresistible.
She returned his smile, and set her hand in his as
they faced one another. His gaze seized hers, deep
emerald probing the depths of her brighter, luxuri-

ant green eyes, and drawing Eleanor ever closer, ever deeper into his thrall. Sandalwood and tobacco flooded her senses. She focused on naught but him, and her feet moved through the steps of the reel with no instruction from her conscious mind. If he had set out to seduce, she did not think he could have done so with more skill.

Music filled the kitchen. It was a light, airy reel with a perfect tempo for dancing, and Róisín carried the melody while the children played their various accompaniments.

*"Ní chela: ba hésium mo chridesérc,"* Eveleen sang "Líadan's Love Song." The tender words had been written eight hundred years before. *Conceal it not: he was my heart's love.* They told the story of the poetess's love for the poet Cuirithir.

"Thank you," she whispered. "Líadan's Love Song" had always been one of her favorites. There was no other tune she might have picked if the choice had been hers alone. "Thank you, Garrett," she whispered his name because she knew it was what he wanted. To call him Garrett was the least she might offer in return.

The sound of his name falling from her lips pleased Garrett. He began to speak, but hesitated when he heard knocking at the kitchen door. He did not look toward the sound, but focused on her as she glanced toward the door. The warm brush of her words faded all too fast, and Garrett could only hope it was not the last time he would hear his name fall softly from her lips, he could only hope she would not forget what she had said to him last night.

There it was again. A firm but friendly rapping. A visitor. The children, too, glanced toward the door, but continued playing. Ambrose nodded to Garrett, then went to answer the knock.

Eleanor smiled at Garrett. It would appear the household did indeed have secrets of which she was not aware. Lovely secrets, she decided as she listened to the music, and wondered who that might be knocking for entrance. Had he sent a message to Rosanna? To her brothers? Although Eleanor did not like to think they would take such a risk, she knew Conall and Luke would come out of the hills to wish her well this day.

The door opened. A chill wind swirled round the kitchen, and Captain Rowlestone was revealed on the threshold. He entered as if anticipating his welcome. There was no hesitation in his stride as he handed his hat and cloak and gloves to Ambrose. Another man entered behind him, not a soldier but a Puritan; his close-fitting black skull cap and flowing preacher's gown were covered with snow.

Garrett sensed Eleanor's reaction. It was immediate. Her hand went stone cold in Garrett's, and she tried to pull away from him, but he would not let her free. He leaned close to murmur, "Smile, my lady. You must give our guests a most warm welcome."

"I must? Our guests?" she answered, in a voice meant only for him, drawing out the final letters in "guests" until it seemed a scorching sound that might burn as surely as would a hissing piece of burning turf. In that instant, it was as if Lady Moira had never taught Eleanor anything about hospitality. All she could think was the man who called himself her husband intended to welcome her enemy into their home on this day of all days. All she could think was the celebration was ruined. "Smile? And why should I do such a thing, if I am not pleased?"

"You are my wife and have vowed to honor and obey me. That is why."

"That is an order?" Her heart plummeted.

"If it must be."

A chill ran through Eleanor. The dream had survived for but a few cruel moments. It was well and truly crushed. She whispered, "I will obey, and I will smile this day, but I will not forgot this, this betrayal. And you, *Sir* Garrett, must not forget that whilst you may own Laragh, you will never own me."

Her expression was forced, brittle. The light in her eyes burned with anger, and Garrett knew she would remember this moment more than the music and the dance, more than the books. It could not be helped. There had been no other choice for him, not if he hoped to guarantee the legality of their marriage, secure his position with the authorities, and perhaps discover who among his neighbors would deal with the slave traders.

Marriage between a Protestant and Catholic was permitted, if the ceremony was peformed by a preacher, not a priest, and if the Catholic converted. That Garrett and Eleanor had been wed by a priest in the faith of their fathers' fathers would never be told by those trusted witnesses in this kitchen. In the eyes of the authorities, they would be wed according to English law.

Someday, God willing, Eleanor would understand.

"Captain Rowlestone, welcome to Laragh." Garrett stepped toward Rowelstone, bringing Eleanor with him at his side.

"Welcome, good sirs," she forced herself to speak. "The afternoon is cold, and our fire is warm."

"Mistress, Sir Garrett. 'Tis is an honor that thou wouldst invite me, Sir Garrett, and wouldst seek my assistance." The captain bowed. His companion said good afternoon in a tone as dour as his expression.

"I am pleased you accept my invitation." He extended his hand. "It is a poor day for travel."

"Thou didst not think I wouldst ignore thy request?" Rowelstone accepted his hand. "What, I doth ask of thou, is a little snow? As an officer of the Commons, I am pledged to uphold English law, and by thy example thou ease the burden of my work. I am grateful that thou demonstrates how an Englishman may chose to live among these people, yet not defy the will of the Commons." He motioned to the man who accompanied him. The Puritan stepped forward.

"May I present Nathaniel Peters, chaplain and late a resident of Sheffield, but now residing in and preaching from the pulpit in New Castle. In adherence with the laws of the Parliament of the Commonwealth of England, Master Peters will perform your marriage service, Sir Garrett, and by his mouth you and Mistress Archebold will be made man and wife."

# Chapter 22

E leanor sought solace in her father's library, isolated from the rest of the wedding party by her own choice. She stood before a window gazing at the terrace, where the ground sloped down to the lough. It had been snowing these past four hours, and the landscape was well buried beneath several inches of light, dry snow.

*Ideal conditions for sledding*, Garrett had proclaimed, and while no one at Laragh had seen sledges mounted on runners as were popular with English children, they were familiar with sliding down snow-covered hills on planking or old doors. Everyone had agreed, sledding it would be, and they had bundled up to leave the kitchen. Edwin and Rory had rummaged through the old tower for appropriate sledding vehicles; even Captain Rowlestone had accompanied the group outside and had helped set a bonfire at the top of the hill, where the sledders might warm themselves between runs.

Only three persons remained indoors. Eleanor, Sibéal, and Nathaniel Peters. The Puritan preacher devoted three hours daily to reading his Bible, and had not once in the past twenty years, he asserted, neglected this discipline. Sibéal was busy in the kitchen; there would be many hungry mouths to feed this night. As for Eleanor, she was in no mood for merriment of any sort. She did not feel frolicsome; her pleasant mood had been destroyed before that first dance had been done. Sooth, she was feeling bitter and most vexatious, and as she was wont to do at times such as this, she had retired to her father's library. But the familiar room had not offered the usual solace.

She glanced over her shoulder to where Master Peters sat a comfortable distance from the hearth. Sadness marked her expression as she recalled repeating her wedding vows twice in one day. She understood the necessity for doing it, but not how she had become aware of the arrangements. Garrett did not have to explain the realities of English rule. In every aspect of their lives, they must comply with Cromwell's laws, and to be married by a Puritan preacher with a captain of the English dragoons as witness was, she conceded, more than a way to ensure the legitimacy of their marriage; it was a brilliant device to further protect them all. She did not, however, understand why he had not told her of this plot before the two men had arrived to ruin the dancing and music. By virtue of keeping her uninformed, he had chosen to disregard her; he had not chosen a path toward harmony. To her mind, this was no better than ordering or demanding her obedience.

The man who was her husband had not confided in her, and for an Irish wife that was deeply hurtful. She tried to remind herself that Garrett did not understand Irish ways, but nothing eased the hurt, erased the unfortunate truth that her husband had not confided in her because there was no need for him to do so. Garrett knew she would do anything to stay at Laragh, anything to protect her brother and sisters. It was not necessary to extend even the most basic courtesy to her. She would do whatever was necessary, and he knew that only too well.

There were voices in the hallway, coming closer. A man and a woman were engaged in animated discourse. She heard their laughter outside the library door, and turned in that direction.

The door opened. It was Captain Rowlestone with Róisín O'More on his arm. The cold air had put a pretty pink upon her cheeks, her eyes sparkled, a length of wool was wrapped high around her neck for extra warmth, and her dark hair rippled over it like a stream cascading downhill. Whether it was the preacher, who looked up from his Bible, or Eleanor, who stepped away from the window, who was more surprised by the sight of this odd couple it would have been difficult to gauge. Both were astonished.

"Goodwife Neville," said the captain, addressing Eleanor not as Mistress Archebold, but as the married woman she had become. "We are here to inquire if thou wouldst not change thy mind, and join us after all."

For a moment, Eleanor stared at the officer, and said nothing. *Goodwife Neville.*

"Please, mistress, will ye not change out of yer gown and come outside?" asked Róisín.

Eleanor focused on Róisín, and startled to realize the captain had been addressing herself.

"Come, mistress, there is yet time before night falls. Snow-sliding is great fun, and we are challenging one another to races," added Róisín.

It was Eleanor's intention to repeat her earlier refusal, but the conversation flowed on before she might speak; Captain Rowlestone addressed the preacher, and she held her reply.

"And thyself, Master Peters?" the officer prompted his fellow Englishman. "Thy company is requested as well."

"Nay, captain, I will remain here." He patted the Bible resting upon his lap.

"Do not say Puritans frown on snow-sliding. 'Tis such a simple, harmless pleasure," Róisín remarked. It was not often she spoke to one of the English, and even rarer that it was anything more than a curse she might mutter beneath her breath. Mayhap it was true what was said about the effect wedding celebrations had on some people: even the coldest hearts could be revived.

"Aye, simple and harmless, and a Puritan maid is denied not the enjoyment of such a pastime." The preacher's response was not an answer to her query, but a reprimand. "So, too, a Puritan maid would not allow her hair to be unbound and in such a state of disarray as thine, nor would she allow her person to flush with such excitement as thou display. Thou art a widow woman, I am told. Surely thou should behave with more decorum than a Philistine."

The color upon Róisín's cheeks faded. It had been a mistake to let the captain help her keep balance as she had trudged back up the hill, a mistake to accept his arm, and an even greater mistake to engage in discourse with him while they had warmed their hands at the bonfire. She did not look at Captain Rowlestone whilst she spoke. For a few moments this officer had made her laugh, and regret oozed through her. She had consorted with her Declán's enemy, with her beloved Ireland's enemy. It had been a mistake to be his partner, a mistake to accept his invitation to accompany him to the library. Róisín, who was quick to see the error of her ways, was also quick to mend them. The rare light in her eyes that had brightened her countenance was replaced by the bland, almost dull-witted expression it was her habit to wear in the presence of English strangers.

A shudder passed through Eleanor. She could scarce believe the moderate, agreeable tone in which Master Peters spoke. The words made something inside her recoil, then strengthen, and while she still had no interest in merrimake, the unwarranted rebuke prompted her to say, "You are kind and thoughtful, Róisín, to encourage me. Indeed, to see your good self is to know what fun there is to be enjoyed this day. Please let the others know I will come to the terrace as soon as I am changed into something more sensible." She smiled at Róisín, expressed her thanks to the captain, then excused herself from Master Peter's presence, and went to change.

A few minutes later, Captain Rowlestone and Róisín left the library beneath the watchful, reproachful eye of Master Peters. Their exit was far more restrained than their entrance. In silence they made their way down the long gallery.

The corridor seemed longer than it had when they had hurried along in laughter. The captain gave an awkward cough. "There is nothing sinful about thy coloring, Mistress O'More. The winter air colors thy complexion. There is nothing wrong in that. You must not take Master Peters's remarks to heart. Thou art neither a barbarian nor a Philistine, Mistress O'More."

"Thank ye, sir," she said on a quiet whisper. "A man such as the preacher does not dishearten myself, sir. I'll be taking not a dram of offense at his insult to my good self."

"Good thou will disregard him, then."

"Not altogether, for I willna be forgiving him, nor will I be forgetting the kind of man himself be."

"Prithee, Mistress O'More, what manner of man is that?"

"A weak and ungodly man filled with hatred and

bigotry. Why, 'tis the same verra hatred such as his—hatred of people who have done him no harm—which puts a chill to my bones.''

He did not dispute her, but nodded, then walked awhile before adding, "Forsooth, Mistress O'More thy appearance is most appealing. 'Tis a fine thing to witness happiness.''

Róisín held her breath. Was the English officer complimenting her as a man compliments a woman? She forced herself not to glance in his direction as they continued toward the end of the long gallery.

"I remember seeing thou, Mistress O'More, on the night we rode into the hall." The truth was he had not forgotten her. He he had not forgotten any of the terrified faces. Fear was a dreadful emotion. It would be sensed, sometimes almost touched, and he had felt her fear that night when he had ridden around the hall, peering into each face as he had searched for the priest. Her fear in particular had touched him, for he had seen more than fear in her wide eyes, more than hatred; he had seen despair and loneliness. She had not meant to reveal herself to him, and if asked, he would have not wished to see; nonetheless, this young widow woman's pain had been visible to him, and it had touched him as sure as her fear and loathing. " 'Tis a fine thing to know I am not the cause of anyone's fright this day. And 'tis an even finer thing to see thyself at ease, mistress.''

She slowed her pace, and tried not to look at him, but she could not help herself. It was no more than three steps before she angled her head to stare at Captain Rowlestone as if seeing him for the first time. There was a gentle light in his eyes, and the lines upon his brow at the corners of his mouth were softened.

"A terrible spectacle we must have presented, and

especially myself, for I do not take light the duties I am pledged to uphold, and I was more determined than ever that night to fulfill my responsibilities, no matter what they might be." His voice faded away. None of the Irish would care there were times aplenty when he doubted the righteousness of what he was required to do as a captain of the dragoons; they would not care about his loneliness, nor about the desperate need to fulfill his duties in an honorable and speedy manner so that he might once again be with his son before the child was grown to a man and had never known his father. None of the Irish would care, yet for a moment this afternoon he had imagined this woman might be able to see him as a man, not an Englishman or Irishman, and thus he was bold to say, "I am not a wicked man."

Róisín came to a halt, and looked Captain Rowlestone full in the face. "Are ye not? Ye're captain of the dragoons, and 'twas yer dragoons took away my Declán, leaving myself alone with a babe on the way. There's some might say it was an act of God or faeries what happened next, but yer dragoons it was who kilt the wean in my womb, says I."

With her back straight and her head held high, she hurried across the entrance hall to Laragh's large, double front door. She reached out, but his hand came from behind to grab the handle first.

*"Go de is mian leat a raga liomsa?"* So great was the distance she put betwixt herself and the English officer that without forethought she spoke first in Irish, then repeated in English, *"What do ye wish to say to myself?"*

"I am sorry, mistress." He opened the door for her. ". . . To know of thy loss."

"And what would ye be knowing of such suffering?" She stepped outside, and readjusted the length of wool about her neck.

"Dost thou imagine it is only Irish who suffer?" he rejoined. "This is not the only countryside to be swept by war and famine. My son has been motherless since the hour of his birth."

Awful shame flooded Róisín. Her face flushed, and her eyes and nose stung as if she might cry. She had been wrong; she had made the error of thinking of this man as less human than herself. Indeed, it made her no better than one of the English. Her voice softened. "I should not have spoken in haste. How old is the lad?"

"Five years this past summer. My wife was visiting her family in Colchester during the seige."

"He lives with kin in England?"

"Nay, he is not so far away. He has been in Dublin these past three years in the care of a preacher and his good wife. It is my wish the boy know something of family living, and be near that I might visit when possible."

"A wicked man would not be doing such a fine thing for the lad."

"I would do anything for his sake."

"*Ululu*," she cried, soft. It was the mourning lament of the Irish. " 'Tis seeing the way of it now, I am."

Captain Rowlestone smiled. It was not a happy expression, but one of slight satisfaction, for Mistress O'More understood, and at that moment, it seemed more than he might have dared to want. She did not smile in return, but matched her pace to his. Together, they walked the final distance in companionable silence.

The last snowflakes had fallen from the sky. A blanket of white covered the trees, the lane, the yard, and the hills beyond the house. Everywhere was clean, unsullied. There was no hint of war, nor of the famine and death that were as much a part of Laragh as the giant sycamores that towered above the south side of the stables. Footsteps in the snow marked a path around the house, and Eleanor followed them to the terrace. Ambrose and Edwin stood before the bonfire, sharing a story and laughing. The children were scrambling up the hill. Even the wolfhounds were enjoying the last hour of daylight, galloping up the hills, chasing dried leaves and twigs, and kicking clouds of snow about themselves.

" 'Tis Eleanor. Look! Eleanor is here!" one of the children exclaimed, whereupon everyone was calling her name and dashing toward her in welcome.

Garrett brought up the rear with wee Maeve on his shoulders. "Your arrival is most timely, mistress wife."

"Pray, why is that?" A blush warmed Eleanor's cheeks, and she glanced at him from beneath her lashes, liking the sight of him, tall and dark, with the small girl perched on his shoulders. A light wind blew the soft snow from the branches of a nearby yew. Several flakes settled on her cheeks, cooling them; another gust of wind, and snowflakes fell on her eyelashes; she blinked them away.

"My partner is abandoning our effort," he said, with the sort of exaggerated frown a child employed to win favor.

Wee Maeve slid from his shoulders and edged between two adults to get a spot close to the bonfire.

"You must agree to take her place. Mistress Róisín and Captain Rowlestone have challenged me, and I would hate to forfeit for lack of a partner."

"And the object of the challenge?"

"To travel the farthest distance from the top of the hill," he replied. Then, as if she had already agreed to participate in the contest, Garrett led Eleanor toward the starting point. "They will go first, and we will follow; whichever team slides the farthest is the victor. Are you willing?"

"Was there ever an Archebold who did not like a challenge? Of course, I am willing. You must tell me what to do, for I am determined that we might win."

He explained the basic technique, pointed out how the captain and Róisín shifted their weight as they went down the hill. The children cheered in excitement as the sled went the entire distance to the lough, then veered to the left and continued along the shore, coasting to a stop by a snow-shrouded clump of gorse. It was a significant distance, given the uneven nature of the hillside, for while one might use the many dips and rises to one's advantage, one could as easily be stopped by them before reaching the bottom.

Ambrose acted as race official and urged the second team of contestants to their mark.

Eleanor sat down in the middle of the makeshift sled. Garrett would sit behind her, but before doing so he adjusted and readjusted the starting angle of their sled in the hopes of going farther than the clump of gorse. Satisfied with the starting angle, he sat behind Eleanor, wrapped his arms around her, pulled her close to his chest, and braced his legs against hers. In order to see and navigate where they were going, he rested his chin on her shoulder.

"Ready," Garrett asked.

"Aye."

Ambrose yelled, "Go!"

They took off down the hill.

"Oh, my!" gasped Eleanor. They seemed to shoot straight out in the air. She held her breath.

They sped through a dip.

"Ooooh!" she exhaled.

The sled dropped down then soared upward with the next rise, her stomach flying skyward, then plummeting with each undulation in the hillside. She turned her face against his chest to shield it from the wind. Snow flew in the air as they raced onward. A final dip, another rise, and down, down, down.

*Hills.* This was the feeling of hills. They rolled upward from the pit of her stomach. *Hills.* She sensed them in her chest, in her heart, lifting her up, up, and she opened her eyes.

"Oh, no!" she gasped.

They were headed for the lough. The ice was not thick enough to support herself and Garrett.

"Noooo!" she screamed.

"Lean with me to the side," Garrett shouted. His grip tightened about her waist.

She leaned with him, the sled went to the left, and they sailed away from the lough, sailed on toward the clump of gorse. Safe, but for the moment. Another obstacle was in their path.

"Saint Brigid, save us," Eleanor cried.

They were going to collide with Captain Rowlestone and Róisín.

"*Oh, no!*" she shrieked.

Garrett yelled, the captain pulled Róisín from their path.

The sled careened off the course, and acting on instinct, Eleanor covered her face with her hands. In the next instant, the vehicle slammed into something beneath the snow, perhaps the exposed root of an ancient oak. Eleanor gasped as she flew off the wooden sled. She landed on her back. The impact stole her breath away. She tried to move, but could not. There was a heavy pressure on her chest.

It was Garrett, face down. He had landed atop Eleanor, and he tried not to move until he knew whether or not she was injured. He watched as she took her hands away from her face; her eyelashes fluttered open, and her lush green eyes stared up at him not in pain, but mild confusion. He smiled down at her, reassuring, gentle, and slipped a hand beneath her head to lift her out of the snow.

"You are not injured, I trust?" he asked.

She blinked. "Stunned. That is all."

"Stunned and lovely." He leaned close and kissed the tip of her nose, brushed his mouth across hers.

She blinked again. He licked the outline of her mouth, and she sighed as he slid his tongue between her lips. Her mouth parted beneath his warm caress, his lips tugged on her lower lip, and she sighed again as his tongue retraced her mouth. Her blood sang to his touch, her lips nipped at his, she swayed toward him, and when his tongue slowly, sweetly stroked hers, she sighed a third time. A kiss tender and tempting it was, and her eyelashes fluttered closed in anticipation of more.

"Thank you," he whispered against her lips, but he did not kiss her again.

"You are welcome, Garrett." Her eyes remained closed. She raised her face wanting the delicious sensations wrought by his lips on hers. "Did we win?"

"Ah, you misunderstand, mistress mine. 'Tis not the contest for which I owe you thanks."

"Pray what, then?" She met his eyes, angled her head to one side.

He rolled off her, and taking her hand in his, he pulled her to standing. She wobbled a little, and he steadied her in his arms. "You are to be thanked for refraining from complaint upon the arrival of Master Peters, and for participating in the second ceremony without incident. Thank you for your cooperation."

Eleanor glanced away. *Thank you for your cooperation.* The moment was ruined. He spoke in the tone one might use when dealing with a merchant; he spoke of a subject which festered within her, and as if to make it right, he offered thanks, but it was not his thanks she desired. He had ignored her, and she wished that he might recognize that, wished that he might apologize. That did not happen. He did not admit his oversight, nor ask for her pardon; instead, he had treated her as if she were a good, obedient hound. Disappointment and sadness returned to her.

In the high hills, a wolf howled. A second beast replied, then another echoed closer to the house. From the nearby woods came a frenzied barking. Garrett and Eleanor looked toward the rising cacophony. The wolfhounds paced in agitation, whining. All eyes scanned the hills, the open fields, and the wood, coming to rest upon the same sight.

To the north a ribbon of bright orange edged the gloaming sky. It was a familiar sight, the red and gold reflection of flames glowing along an Irish horizon.

*"Diá ár sábbáail!"* cried one of the women. *God protect us!*

"Fire! Castlekevin, it is burning," declared Rory with an unaccountable measure of satisfaction. "The grocers are burning."

No one disputed this, nor the lad's gruesome sentiment.

No one spoke aloud the truth.

It was tories, to be sure, raiding the district, and doing what they might to drive away the English strangers. Róisín stepped away from where she stood beside Captain Rowlestone, quietly moving back, moving closer to Ambrose and the others of her kind.

"You ride out, captain?" Garrett asked.

"Without delay. Wilt thou accompany me, Sir Garrett?"

Garrett agreed, and within minutes, the two men were saddling their mounts. The wedding party gathered in the stable yard.

"I will be back soon, mistress mine," Garrett whispered for Eleanor alone, but she had no reply.

It did not seem her wedding day could get any worse, but it had ended in the worst way imaginable. It was not that she must bid farewell to her newly wed husband on her wedding night. It was the painful reminder of the distance betwixt them that could never be bridged. Her husband would ride this night at the side of a captain of the dragoons, accompanying English soldiers in pursuit of tories, in pursuit of her brothers.

"Come, Eleanor," he whispered. "Give your husband a proper farewell and wish me luck that I might return swift and whole in order that we may consummate our marriage vows." He pulled her against his chest, and his mouth swooped down to hers, eager, hungry, possessive. His moist tongue seared hers as it stroked within her mouth. He crushed her to his male hardness, and clearly wanting her to know of his passion, he pressed his loins to hers. He murmured against her lips, "Ah, mistress mine, you must know I do not abandon my rights this night willingly, and whilst we are apart I will think of little else save our reunion."

His lips lingered at the corner of her mouth. He growled deep in his throat, and drew back to meet her eyes again. "I have not forgotten the intimate fit of your body against mine. I have not forgotten your potent eagerness for my man-sword, and I am most eager to enjoy the delights of your velvet sheath once again."

"Whist!" Eleanor cried, soft and breathless. "You must not speak aloud of such things." Trembling, she had a sudden awareness of how cool the snowflakes were upon her skin. She was burning up.

She felt the warmth that surely colored her cheeks, and she saw the approval in his eyes. He chuckled, low and soft. Those eyes, alight with the slow burn of his desire, held hers. "I must not speak of such things, do you say? Ah, but, mistress mine, to the contrary, I must speak." His voice fell even lower. He was teasing her, tempting her. "I must because I want you to think of me in my absence; I must because I want you waiting and ready for my return."

He afforded her no chance to speak, and swung into his saddle. Without a backward glance, he rode down the lane.

# Chapter 23

Eleanor tiptoed down the staircase, one hand on the banister, the other holding a tallow-wick lamp above her head. The big house was dark and silent except for the slight sigh the wooden stairs made beneath her feet. The household had retired more than two hours before. Outside, the wind howled like a hideous dullaghan hiding in a church-yard and ready to snatch the head off a human child. Inside, everyone was snug beneath mounds of wool-ens and furs, nightcaps upon their heads; they were safe from the winter storm, safe from the dragoons, fast asleep and dreaming.

Everyone, that was, except Eleanor, who had tossed and turned atop her down-filled pillows. She could not sleep. There was something she must do.

She hurried toward the library, and closed the door behind her, even though there was little warmth within to contain. The shutters rattled. Frigid air passed through unseen cracks, it seeped through the floors, down the flue of the chimney-piece. The fire in the hearth had burned to embers, and it would not be long before Eleanor began to shiver. She took Nuala's annals from the high shelf, and having secured the metal box beneath one arm, went to the kitchen, where she might sit in comfort for awhile.

Although the *Annals of Finnén* had been left in her possession for safekeeping, not so that she might write in them, Eleanor could not sleep until she had recorded the events of the day. She did not imagine Nuala would object as long as she wrote the truth.

Opening to the first blank page, she took up a pen, and the familiar whisper of quill on paper rose to her ears as she began:

> A.D. 1653, *December, the bean-draíocht, Eleanor Archebold of the old English family of Laragh, granddaughter of Rory O'Connor, the last chieftain of Baravore, was wed to the stranger, Sir Garrett Neville, late of England and title-holder by Cromwell's law to Archebold lands.*

Eleanor glanced around the cluttered kitchen. Extra benches had been brought from the banquet hall to seat everyone for the evening meal; musical instruments sat atop a small table, and everywhere cloaks and woolens, mittens, caps, and other snow-sodden articles of clothing were draped to dry. The faint aromas of boiled eel, oatmeal, and rye cakes hung in the air. Not even a full day had passed since she and Garrett had exchanged vows, yet it seemed a lifetime had elapsed.

With a sigh she added the lines to the annal:

> *Those tenants and people who survived the Curse of Cromwell witnessed the ceremony, and celebrated this union through which the bloodlines of the most noble and ancient families of Leinster would continue to inhabit this land for another eight hundred years.*

A sudden gust of wind shook the door to the yard. Eleanor paused again.

Snowing it was anew, the night wind was whistling wicked, and they were out there. Her brothers, the tories, the O'Byrne sisters. And Garrett. Sooth, Eleanor worried for him as sure as she did for Conall and Luke. It was true that she owned not a wife's loving affection for her husband, but she was not so petty a creature that concern for his welfare would depend upon the direction of her heart. Despite his dealings with her, Garrett had shown himself to be a fair and decent man, and she would not wish her worst enemy to be lost in a storm as was howling out of the hills this night. She had heard tell of how entire herds of cattle could be frozen in their tracks and buried until spring. In storms such as this, a body might wander lost through the blinding white until the cold claimed one's fingers or toes, mayhap even the tip of one's nose; there were other souls whose whole person vanished without a trace, and it was not *sidhe* that whisked them away on a night such as this.

Her final entry read:

> Also this same day a great snow swept out of the north, tories rode down from the hills, and the O'Toole fortress at Castlekevin was set afire.

Another gust of wind shook the big house, and above the rattling shutters came an insistent rapping upon the door. Was it Garrett returned? Eleanor rose to investigate. Only a desperate man would travel on a night like this.

She cracked the sturdy door. Whirling white had stolen away the black of night, snow was drifting high, and a small figure wrapped in ragged woolens huddled on the stoop. Eleanor opened the door wider, and recognized the same eyes as Nuala O'Byrne's peering back at her. She grabbed the girl's outer garment to pull her inside.

"Eleanor," the child gasped in obvious relief that friend not foe stood before her. She continued in Irish, "Glad I am 'tis yourself who answers my knock."

"By all the company of heaven, Cait. You must be ice cold. Come out of the storm."

The girl hesitated. "Is it safe?"

"Aye. *Na biod eagal ort.* Come now," she switched back and forth between Irish and English. "*You need not fear.* Hasten, inside with you."

"First, I must tell the others." She began to return to the storm.

"Who is with you? I will go." Without waiting for an answer, Eleanor pulled Cait into the kitchen and secured the door. "You must come inside."

"Nuala is out there, and my other sisters. She's not well, Nuala isn't, and we are all four of us come to accept your hospitality. It was the only way, for there was no getting Nuala to leave the hills on her own."

"You must sit up to the fire and warm yourself." Eleanor removed the girl's wet woolens, and led her to the bench before the hearth. "Where are they?"

"The cow byre."

Eleanor secured a cloak about her shoulders, then stepped into a pair of boots by the door. Remembering that there was a kettle of oatmeal remaining from the evening meal, she turned back into the room, retrieved the pot, and hung it in the hearth to warm before going into the storm.

Already Cait's footprints had been blown away. Eleanor did not cut across the yard, but hugged every available wall, making her way around the base of the tower, along the far side of the walled garden, and behind the stable to the byre.

"Nuala?" she called. The shed smelled not of cattle, but of mice. There was a scuttling from one corner to another. There was another noise, weak and pitiful. Somewhere in the dark, cold byre a child was crying. It tugged at Eleanor's heart. "*Na bi gul.* Nuala? Aislinn? Isobel? *Do not cry.* 'Tis Eleanor, come to bring you inside."

"Over here we are," replied a small voice. The child sniffled. "Please, can you help? Nuala cannot rise to standing on her own."

Moving closer to the voice, Eleanor saw the little girls and how they shivered. "Go on, the both of you, now. You know the way to the kitchen. I'll see to Nuala, and be bringing her straightaways."

The girls went ahead as Eleanor bent to secure her arms beneath Nuala's and lift her to her feet. Her friend weighed no more than wee Maeve, and supporting her against her body, she heard the dreadful rasp that Nuala's breathing had become.

"*Deanam anois,*" she urged her to walk. *Let us go now.*

Nuala moaned.

"Only a wee bit more," Eleanor whispered in encouragement. "You're going to be fine, Nuala. Only a few steps more, and then you won't have to move until the quicken-trees flower come spring."

"Eleanor?" The young woman's voice was hardly human. "Is it yourself?"

"And who else would be fetching Nuala O'Byrne out of the byre on a night such as this?" Eleanor tried to brighten her voice, tried to disguise her despair upon seeing Nuala's condition. " 'Tis only a wee bit of a distance to the kitchen, then you'll be out of the storm, and up to the warm hearth with some oatmeal."

" 'Tis safe? At Laragh?"

"Aye." Eleanor held her friend close as they made their way behind the walled garden, and around the tower.

"The captain of the dragoons?"

It did not surprise Eleanor that Nuala would be aware of the comings and goings at Laragh. No doubt there was not a Puritan who sneezed without tories knowing of it. As they neared the kitchen, she said, "The captain was here earlier, but he is gone. The only stranger at Laragh is a Puritan preacher."

They reached the kitchen stoop. One of the younger girls had been watching for them, and opened the door.

"A preacher, do you say?" Nuala asked, her words were coming very slowly. The effort of walking from the byre had sapped the last of her strength, and she gasped for a breath of air between each syllable. "It is done then?"

"*Go de an munmur sin ort?*" This time, surprise jolted Eleanor. They entered the kitchen, and she searched her friend's eyes for an explanation, but saw only the light of fever. "*What muttering do you make?*"

"That you have spoken your vows. You are wed."

"How?" It was not necessary to say anything more, not necessary to phrase the whole query.

"Even in the caves we have heard of the English stranger who came to Laragh, and who protects the priest, and would marry you."

"Luke and Conall know of this?" There was a trembling in her voice, a thickening as if she once again fought off tears. Eleanor had wanted to be the one to tell her brothers; she had wanted to explain, and to ask them to forgive her, to understand and accept what she had done.

Nuala allowed Eleanor to take the wet cloak from her shoulders, then she sank upon a bench, and leaned against the hearth wall. "They accept what you have done. No one speaks ill of you. He is a decent man, 'tis said. Biddy O'Fierghraie saw the light round him, and told them so."

Eleanor turned to hide her uneasiness, her uncertainty. As had happened before, she was struck by the way everyone accepted Garrett. Everyone with the exception of herself. She wondered how she might feel, if she had not met him in Dublin. She wondered how she would feel if his physical person did not arouse such intense reactions within her; how she would feel if she did not sense the need to protect herself.

"I think you are very brave, Eleanor Archebold."

Glancing down at her friend, Eleanor saw how Nuala's gaunt face strained with each word, how her coloring faded to gray, and her chest heaved with the effort required to breath. "Nay, Nuala. There is no bravery in what I do. 'Tis yourself and your sisters who are brave. Come, you must eat something, and then I will fix a place for you to sleep."

"Ah, but you are wrong, Eleanor. There is bravery in each of us. Each of us has a role to play. Each of us makes a sacrifice, a commitment, and though we may follow different paths, our destination is the same."

"*Go raith maith agat, Nuala,*" Eleanor whispered in reply. The simple words of thanks would never express how deeply Nuala's words eased her. *Thank you.* "That gives me great comfort."

"*Nil aon focal breige ann.*" With a nod, Nuala closed her eyes. *It is perfectly true.*

Cait brought a dry blanket to drape across her sister's shoulders, then she slid beside her on the bench, and closing her own eyes, wrapped her arms about her older sister. Isobel and Aislinn sat close to the fire warming their hands and feet, casting wary glances about the kitchen. No one spoke a word while Eleanor ladled oatmeal into wooden bowls, and set a large hunk of rye bread atop each serving. Isobel, Aislinn and Cait needed no encouragement to eat, and before Eleanor's hand had surrendered a bowl to theirs, they began using the bread to scoop up mouthfuls of oatmeal.

Eleanor pulled up a stool to sit and feed Nuala. Her friend did not protest this attention; indeed, she did not even open her eyes as she ate. Her younger sisters emptied their bowls, and helped themselves to more, but even with Eleanor's help, Nuala did not have the energy to eat more than a few spoonfuls.

"Have you enough for now?"

Nuala answered with a nod.

"It is best to put you in the old tower. The big house is full this night, and for now I do not think your arrival should be wide known."

The sisters agreed it would be wisest not to announce their presence, especially while the Puritan preacher remained at Laragh. Eleanor led the way to a chamber on the middle level of the tower. It was stocked with a plentiful supply of woolen blankets and fur rugs. There were two braziers set with peat bricks; Eleanor lit them.

As Lady Moira used to do, and as her father had done since Eleanor's earliest memory, she kept this chamber in readiness for travelers needful of a secure place to bide their time. Within these walls many an enemy of the English had prayed to the Lord that they might live to see another sunrise, and the O'Byrne girls were no less grateful than the numerous priests, outlawed noblemen, and rebel poets who had found shelter at Laragh. The small tower chamber seemed a royal palace after the cave the sisters had called home since mid-summer.

For the first time in months, they slept through the night.

The storm did not relent. Snow and wind continued through the next day, and all those who had passed the night at Laragh knew it would be at least another day before they might depart for their own homes. Thrice Eleanor slipped into the tower to check upon her special guests, and during her second visit, Nuala and her sisters talked of what had happened at Castlekevin.

The decision to burn the O'Toole fortress to the ground had been a solemn one. Castlekevin was one of the oldest strongholds in Wicklow, built almost four hundred years before the English had named this land. For centuries, Castlekevin had been fought over, and had changed hands numerous times. In some ways it had become a symbol of the struggle to drive the English out of Ireland, and there was not a man or woman among the tories, Irish or old English, who did not claim kinship to the ancient clan that held hereditary rights over those lands. Most recently, the English under Ludlow had seized the fortress upon the capture of Colonel Luke O'Toole. More than three hundred years before O'Tooles had burned the fortress whilst it was being used as an English garrison.

The tories were in agreement. Whatever means were necessary would be employed to force the strangers from their land, and as in times past, the Irish had agreed to burn one of their ancestral strongholds to the ground rather than see their enemy claim it as theirs.

As planned, no one had remained in the caves; everyone came down from the high hills, everyone would bear witness to the torching of the ancient fortress. They had departed Glendalough at dawn, men and women, boys and girls, and every single one of the two score plus six who had left the caves would return to the hills before dusk. If there was any trouble alternate routes and shelters had been identified ahead of time.

The roads between Annamoe and Laragh and Castlekevin had been observed for more than a sennight, the daily habits of the grocers were known as was the routine of the English patrols. It was a well-planned raid, but two unanticipated events had transpired to impede it. First was the blinding winter storm that had hindered a speedy return to the hills; the second was a change in the dragoon's routine. Whilst Captain Rowlestone had gone to Laragh, his men had visited the grocer. To the tories' surprise, the soldiers had been inside the stronghold when they'd set it aflame.

Chaos had ensued.

There had been fighting, musket fire, and hand-to-hand combat, but whether anyone had been killed or captured, the girls could not tell Eleanor. They did not know who had made it back to the hills, or if anyone had been injured.

The only certainty was that Castlekevin had been reduced to a smoldering ruin. The grocers were without a home; they had not even a stable or cow byre with a roof to cover their heads.

The storm ended sometime during the second night, and the morning dawned against a backdrop of blue skies. There was not a cloud to be seen, not even the tiniest whisper of wind, and the sun shone brilliant upon the white landscape. The last time there had been a storm of such severity had been many years afore.

Eleanor remembered how the sun had shown with the same blinding brilliance, and how her father had ridden out on a morning such as this to check upon his people, and the villagers in Annamoe. If Garrett were here she would urge him to do the same. While most of Laragh's people had passed the storm in the big house, there were a few folk who had not come to her wedding, and whose well-being was the duty of Laragh's lord, especially at a time such as this. In his absence, Garrett would expect Edwin Petty to act in his stead, but Eleanor could not allow that; Edwin Petty was not Laragh's lord, and the people were not his. It was she who must check upon their welfare, carry some victuals with her, and offer the shelter of the big house to one and all.

Eleanor confided in Sibéal. She told her about their guests who had arrived in the night; someone would have to check on Nuala and her sisters while she was gone, and Sibéal understood the importance of discretion. She told her about her intentions to check on the people, and with the old woman's help, they planned a route that would take her the distance to Biddy O'Fierghraie's cabin, and home via Annamoe before dusk.

She set off mid-morning with two wolfhounds, a pistol, and a bandoleer with powder hanging beneath her outer cloak. The closest cabins were empty, their occupants being at the big house, and she was exhausted by the time she reached Cormac MacMurrough's bothy. All inside were well. Aidan Lawless was there, too, and a warm greeting they had for Eleanor, who expressed pleasure that they had survived the storm, for she would not like to think she'd heard the last of their pleasant music. There was adequate peat for warmth, and the family declined Eleanor's invitation to Laragh. It was likewise at each occupied bothy. All were well, and were content to remain in their own home.

At the approach to Biddy O'Fierghraie's cabin, the

wolfhounds began to bark. It was not an agitated howling to warn of danger, but one of excitement with the familiar, and Eleanor knew a similar exhilaration when the wise woman opened her shutters. It was not only a joy to find Biddy well, but also to discover that she had sheltered tories during the storm, and Eleanor was blessed again that Conall and Luke had been among them. Her brothers were alive as was Roger Clare; as for the O'Byrne brothers, they had taken a different route in their flight to Glendalough, and no one had known whether they were safe.

" 'Tis late, young mistress, should ye not be biding the night with auld Biddy?" she asked when Eleanor prepared to leave.

"There is time and enough, if I hasten. I dare not stay away. Sibéal has too many responsibilities already. I should be there to attend to Nuala and her sisters, especially Nuala."

"Worsening the lass is, I hear tell."

"Sibéal says she'll not be with us to celebrate the coming Christmastide."

The wise woman mumbled something beneath her breath. She went to the corner of her cabin where dried flowers, branches of holly, and other assorted greenery hung from the ceiling. Breaking off a few twigs of this, some roots and leaves of that, she invoked an old Irish blessing for healing, "Pain and sickness be in the earth's depths, fly with the birds of the air, be upon the river's currents cascading to the sea."

She put the curative herbs in a pouch, and gave it to Eleanor. "These should ease her breathing, and clear her lungs. Camomile, celandine, and pennyroyal. Boil a strong brew, and with honey thicken it, the more the better. A full cup, it is ye should be having her drink, five times each and every blessed day. Be keeping her warm. Away from chills. And praying I'll be for the lass to celebrate many a Christmas yet to come.''

Eleanor secured the pouch at her waist, hugged the wise woman farewell, and then with a promise to visit again before the New Year, she headed down Brockagh Hill.

At the Annamoe crossroads it was obvious the dragoons had resumed their patrols. A wide path had been trampled in the snow, and Eleanor, who was more exhausted and cold than she had imagined possible, found herself for once grateful to the soldiers. She was passing Róisín O'More's cabin when she saw a horseman approaching from the opposite direction. The wolfhounds commenced their friendly barking and bounded ahead of her.

It was Garrett, and Eleanor quickened her pace. She was glad he did not ride with the dragoons, glad he had fared well these past two days, and the hint of a smile edged up at the corners of her mouth.

"Mistress," he called out, when he was close enough to be heard.

She waved. Anticipation tumbled inside her. She recalled his parting words, his parting kiss, and was thankful the cold air already colored her cheeks.

They met where the lane to the big house joined the road. She looked up at him as if to speak, but what he said rendered her silent for a moment.

"You are disobedient."

This was not the greeting Eleanor had expected. She tilted her head and stared up at him, wondering if she had misheard. She blinked twice and forgot his parting kiss, his parting wish. "What?"

"I said: You are disobedient."

"There is no need to speak to me in that manner, sir. I am not an errant child."

He grinned, finding it hard to stay angry at her, finding it impossible not to gaze upon Eleanor and desire her. "Ah, sweet mistress, I would never call you a child."

"What of errant?" she demanded, wishing his expression were not quite so hungry, not quite so sensual. He was flirting with her, and she was not certain which angered her the more: that he would call her disobedient, or that he would flirt instead of answering her question in a straightfoward manner. "Explain yourself."

"Most gladly. Did I not give strict orders you were never to travel without Edwin Petty?" Garrett wondered if she had any notion how enticing she appeared, this lovely wife of his. Her beautiful face was framed by the same hooded cloak she had worn sledding, her eyes were sparkling, her face was flushed with exertion, and her red lips were parted as her breath made soft, pale clouds about her. She stirred his soul, aroused his loins, and unleashed fear for her in his heart. "This countryside is no less dangerous than the back alleys of Dublin; mayhap more so, for the perils are not as apparent. Where have you been? What do you do?"

She hesitated, confused. Did he speak of wolves? She had the two hounds. Surely, he knew the reputation of Irish wolfhounds and how their name owed to their ferocious skills in fighting wolves. Besides, there were no wolves in Dublin, the only predators were man and his greed.

"Do you hide something from me?" he demanded.

"Nay, sir. I have nothing to hide."

"Then answer my question."

Again she hesitated. That he dared order her to answer tempted Eleanor to defy him. The trouble was she did not wish to argue with him; she had not abandoned her wish that their marriage might one day be tolerable, if not civil.

"Answer me, if you please."

His voice had gentled, and looking back at him, she sensed that he did not wish to argue any more than she did. She coughed, then spoke, "I have been checking on my people. The storm was severe, and as Laragh's mistress I wished to assure myself that no one had suffered, nor was in want."

Garrett had the grace to acknowledge that had he been here, she would not have had to do this. He was Laragh's lord, and it was his responsibility; they were his people now, these people whose father's fathers may have known his father's fathers. "Everyone is well?" he inquired.

"Everyone is fine. Even the wise woman who lives up Brockagh Hill. The worst was a bit of thatch missing from a roof."

But Garrett knew something far worse than missing thatch had more than likely befallen some unsuspecting souls along this road. It was even conceivable that the people she had visited a few hours before in their cabins were no longer there, and would never return. How could he tell her what he had seen this day? He could not bring himself to speak aloud the cruelty he had witnessed; her knowledge of the world was already far too harsh, and Garrett wished to protect her, not only from danger, but from sadness and despair. He asked, "Did you see the dragoons?"

"No, but the path they cut through the snow goes the distance to Annamoe, and at the crossroads continues toward Castlekevin." At mention of the old fortress, she said, "Tell me, please, what happened there? At Castlekevin?"

"By the time Captain Rowlestone and I arrived, the tories were gone. There had been fighting, two soldiers were dead, another two were wounded."

"And the tories? They were already gone, you say, but how many had been killed? How many were arrested?"

"Not a body was to be found, and none were taken prisoner. As for the fire, it was out of control, and naught could be done to save the fortress. Powell and Waring were in a state, accusing Rowlestone of dereliction of his duties, and demanding the dragoons ride in immediate pursuit. Rowlestone knew it was a fool's mission, but saw no other choice when the grocers' ire was coupled with his men's desire to avenge their fallen comrades. I rode with Rowlestone, and we were ambushed on the Arklow road; the captain himself was wounded, he lost two more men, we fell back as the storm worsened, and were fortunate to find shelter in an abandoned holy house on a hill above the village of Kilcarra."

"That is where you passed the storm?"

"It is."

"And Captain Rowlestone? How does he fare?"

"He was taken to Arklow where a physician might attend him."

What Garrett did not tell her was what the soldiers had done once the storm had passed. None of them had forgotten that they had been driven by vengeance for their two comrades killed at Castlekevin when they had ridden forth in the first place, and now two more were dead. The number of English lives for which the Irish owed them had risen to four, and as everyone knew, it required many Irish lives to equal the value of a single English one. The dragoons intended to exact their pound of flesh from the Irish; any man, woman, or child would suffice, and those living in the village at the bottom of the hill were an obvious target.

Rowlestone had been unconscious during this unpleasant discourse, and Garrett had tried to talk them out of what they intended. He had tried to steer them on another course, and had even warned them that they could be disciplined, that their actions without direct orders from their commander might be considered mutiny.

He spoke in vain. Nothing would turn them back from what they intended, especially not after one of the soldiers pointed out that if they did not kill the villagers, they could be sold to the merchants at Arklow harbor. The idea had caught their fancy. Their bloodlust had been coupled with greed, and the round up had begun.

It had been easy. Garret had watched from the holy house as they stormed the village capturing every man, woman, and child for the slave traders. Whilst two soldiers with loaded muskets guarded their weeping, frightened merchandise, the others had ridden off in the direction of Laragh. Garrett had not been far behind them, fearful of what he might find in their wake. He had seen nothing, not a living, breathing soul until Eleanor, and there was a sick twisting in his gut at the thought of her fate had she come walking down this road earlier.

"Come, mistress." He held out a hand to hoist her behind his saddle.

"I can walk the rest of the way," was Eleanor's reply. She did not wish to ride with him and began to cut a path through the snow.

His horse ambled alongside her.

Eleanor kept walking, shoulders straight, head high, but with each step the snow seemed deeper. She stumbled, listed to the left, then to the right. The energy that had sustained her through the day was fast ebbing, and her sodden skirt hem was weighing her down as if small rocks had been sewn within the garment's seams. Each step was harder than the one before; she stumbled again, and by some miracle managed to keep herself from falling flat on her face. But the third time she was not so fortunate, and as her knees buckled, she let out an unladylike oath born of frustration.

"By the Holy Virgin," she cried, waiting to experience the sensation of sinking into the deep snow. Instead, a strong arm encircled her chest and her feet left the ground as Garrett lifted her.

"Do not be stubborn. You cannot be here without an escort; I am your escort, and I am hungry, cold, and tired. I wish to be home sooner rather than later."

At his mention of being hungry, cold, and tired, Eleanor's determination dissolved. Like Garrett she was hungry, cold, and tired; too tired to resist another moment, too tired to refuse his assistance.

In silence, they rode down the lane. Eleanor had not realized how sore and exhausted she had become until she was off her feet. Indeed, she felt lightheaded, and the thought that she might again faint on this man made her giddier. *Nay, I cannot, I must not faint on this man another time.* Perched behind him on the saddle, she wobbled a little, then held fast about his waist to prevent herself from sliding off.

The last thing Eleanor recalled was resting her cheek against Garrett's back as if it were a large pillow.

# Chapter 24

The wolfhounds raced through the snow, rousing here and there a great-winged black rook from its perch atop the branches of one bare tree or another. By the time Garrett led the horse into the stable yard the household had been alerted. The front door flung wide, and six children spilled from the big house along with the other hounds. Sibéal poked her head out to see who was there, waved in greeting, then closed the door against the cold. Róisín came around the corner from the hen house with a basket. Everyone talked at once.

Garrett shifted his weight on the saddle in preparation to dismount.

"Take care, sir, with my sister," called Rory. The lad dashed the final distance to reach Sir Garrett and Eleanor.

"Greetings, Rory." He smiled at the lad, then leaned back to ask Eleanor, "Would you like to take Rory's hand and slide off first, mistress, or await my assistance?"

She did not reply. Indeed, Garrett had a sudden awareness that she wasn't sitting straight, but was supporting her weight against him as if she had . . . *God's wounds*. Was it possible? His smile deepened, and he almost laughed aloud at the possible explanation. *It could not be.* "Tell me, Rory, your sister has not fainted, has she?"

The lad tilted his head to one side, then to the other, and frowned. "Can't tell."

"Herself appears to be fast asleep, sir," said Róisín. "Let us be helping." She handed the egg basket to wee Maeve, then she and Rory supported Eleanor to prevent her from toppling to the ground while Sir Garrett dismounted.

One of the Cavanagh lads took the reins, and in the next instant, Garrett scooped Eleanor off the horse. He strode toward the front entrance with his sleeping wife in his arms.

The children began to follow, but Róisín held them back. She whispered to wee Maeve in Irish, "Forget not yer duty, lass."

The girl ran ahead to hold open the door.

Garrett entered the big house, and gazed down at Eleanor. She had not awakened. The hood of her cloak had fallen back, her unbound hair spilled over his arm. It was a familiar sight, those dark, feathery lashes lying against skin as fair as fresh cream, those soft, full lips the color of summer-ripe plums parted in temptation. It was a delicious sight, and he smiled at the sudden urge to kiss the tip of her nose. There would be time aplenty for such caresses, and more, much more. He reached the top of the great wooden staircase, and his smile deepened to a grin.

In anticipation of Eleanor's return, the hearth fire had been lit in her chamber, and Garrett closed the door behind him to prevent any warmth from escaping. He sat her atop the bed with her legs dangling over the side, and holding her upright with one arm, unfastened the closures on her cloak; he unwound the garment that had been double wrapped about her, then eased her upper body backward until her head rested upon a pillow. His one hand lingered for a moment on the soft, curling black hair that floated about her head and shoulders. He brushed a stray curl away from her face before pulling out the cloak from beneath her. Her legs still dangled over the edge of the bed; Garrett placed them atop the mattress.

None of this stirred Eleanor. Her slow, even breathing remained undisturbed, and Garrett having removed his hat and great coat, set about removing her outer garments. First, he pulled off her woolen mittens, and finding her hands were like ice, he brought her stiff fingers to his mouth to thaw them with his breath, and rubbed them between his palms until they warmed.

She gave no sign of awakening, and he proceeded to her boots. The leather was wet, proof of how much time she had spent in the snow, and he marveled at the sense of duty that compelled this young woman to walk the distance she must have covered this day. It was the same sense of obligation that had compelled her to travel to Dublin, and do whatever was necessary that she might not return empty-handed.

Something tightened in Garrett's chest when he considered what could have happened to her on the road. His blood chilled to think what could occur at any time. Garrett intended to watch over her, to guard her with his life, if need be. There was only one obstacle.

It was impossible to protect Eleanor from Eleanor. Despite the evil in the world around her, she remained far too innocent and generous, far too independent.

He tugged at the boots. The wet leather did not move, and he tugged again.

How was he to protect Eleanor, if she would not follow orders?

He gave another, sharper tug.

He could not be at her side every moment of every blessed hour. It was not practical.

Using both hands to take firm hold of one boot, he gave a hard, quick jerk, and the leather gave up its hold on Eleanor's leg. He jerked again. The boot moved a bit more. At last, it was peeling off, and with it, her wet, woolen hose.

He applied the same technique to the other boot, and soon both wet boots and hose were lying in a pile on the floor.

Why did she disobey? Did she not trust him?

He knew the answer, and it was not what he wished it to be. He tried to push it to the back of his mind. It would be best if he could concentrate on nothing more than taking care of her. He noticed the bottom of her skirt was sodden, and he tried to focus on that, but his thoughts wandered.

*His wife did not trust him.*

Anger and frustration got the better of him. He yanked off her skirt as that most displeasing truth echoed through his mind.

She had trusted him as a stranger; she had trusted him not to hurt her, but for reasons Garrett did not comprehend Eleanor did not trust him as her husband. What wrong had he done?

He swore an oath beneath his breath. Mayhap she would never trust him; perhaps there was nothing he could do to change that.

None too gently he undressed her, venting his spleen and frustration on her bulky tunic and a pair of men's pantaloons, both of which he tossed to the growing pile on the floor. Beneath it all her chemise and underskirt had remained dry. The fine fabric revealed the shape of her thighs, the swell of her breasts. Garrett gazed upon her sleeping form, watched the gentle rise and fall of her chest as she breathed, and his anger began to abate. He could not resist the urge to brush the back of his hand against her waist. So delicate, so feminine, so vulnerable. His hand followed the contour of her hip, traced the outline of her thigh.

Her slender leg was like ice beneath his hand. Indeed, the lower he moved down her body, the colder she was, and in response, Garrett wrapped both his hands around one ankle. He started massaging upward, his hands briskly moving to her knee, then gliding across to her other knee to work down the other leg. Firm, but gentle, he kneaded her toes, her feet, her calves until her skin warmed beneath his touch. Soon one foot flexed in reaction, then the other.

It was a tempting sight, those pretty feet pointing and flexing, and holding her heel in the palm of one hand, Garrett trailed a fingertip up her shin. There was a small catch in her breathing. He glanced upward to see if she opened her eyes, but she was still asleep. It must have been his imagination. His fingertip continued onward, drawing little circles up and down her leg. How smooth her skin was, how soft and inviting, and his pulse quickened. He wanted to feel more of her, and his fingers wrapped around her leg, the palm of each hand spread wide to press flat against her flesh. His large hands circled her slender legs, while his thumbs stroked the sensitive area behind each knee.

This time, it was no mere catch of her breath Garrett heard, but a sigh, soft and full. This time, it was no trick of his imagination. She could not control her response. He caressed, she sighed, and he knew a thrill of perverse satisfaction that at least in this one way, if in no other, he commanded her obedience. He sat beside her, and his hands continued to caress her legs. Once more she sighed.

She made another little noise that bespoke enjoyment, and Garrett grinned that he could draw this response from her. He might not be able to protect her against slave traders or even against herself, but he could at least make her sigh with pleasure; he could at least transport her for a short space of time. His hands moved upward over her knees, deliberately, he fondled, his palms stroking her inner thighs, his fingers massaging, kneading. Again, a noise escaped her, and this time, it was a definite moan as his caresses became firmer. Her legs relaxed beneath his touch, and her head rolled from one side to the other.

This emboldened Garrett. His hands went higher, slowly, he explored; his fingertips brushed against the soft triangle at the apex of her legs, but he did not linger there. His hands continued to circle over her hips, down her thighs, then up her inner thighs again.

Higher his hands glided, the hint of warm moisture between her legs drawing his fingers like nectar drew a bee. He allowed his hands to brush across the outside of her sex as they circled over her hips and down thighs. Her body arched upward, and this time, her legs parted as his hands slid back up her inner thighs. This time his fingers did not graze across the top of her sex; this time they slid up the seam. Her reaction was immediate. Her whole body seemed to quiver, and as it did his fingertips slipped between her outer lips. He groaned to discover the dew within her. God's knees, she was wet, and he became aware of his own hard, throbbing response.

With one finger he stroked her, slow and sensual. She made a little whimpering noise, the moisture increased, and her inner muscles tightened, then released on his finger.

There was a knock upon the door. Little voices.

He pulled his hand away, and knew an unfamiliar rush of shame. Soon he would have taken what he desired from Eleanor without any consideration of her sensibilities. He coughed to clear his throat that he might speak. "Enter."

The door opened. Eleanor's two sisters entered.

"We bring food for you, and something hot to drink," said Eveleen. She set a tray on the chest against the wall.

"Look, she still sleeps," Grace whispered. "Should we wake her to eat, do you think?"

"Nay, let her rest," Garrett replied.

"And you, sir, would you like to retire? I will sit with my sister," said Eveleen.

"That is not necessary. I will stay." He took a slice of cheese from the tray, and sat in a large chair.

The girls giggled.

"Do you forget I am her husband?"

"Nay, sir, how could *we* ever forget that?" They exchanged a knowing, secretive glance. "Are you tired, sir? Mayhap we should leave you and Eleanor alone."

Garrett did not finish the piece of cheese, and returned it to the tray. "Sooth, I am tired."

"You must lie down then, sir," encouraged Grace.

"Without further ado," said Eveleen.

Although the girls giggled, their expressions were most sincere, and before Garrett knew what they intended he allowed them to pull him from the chair.

"But not there," said Grace. "No sleeping upon that chair."

"You must sleep upon this bed, as is a husband's proper place," added Eveleen with firm conviction.

They propelled him around the far side of the bed that he might lie next to Eleanor. Garrett did not protest. He was indeed tired, and had no wish to argue with any female who seemed as certain as these two were about what it was he ought to be doing. He sat upon the edge of the mattress to take off his boots.

"Allow us to help, sir," said Eveleen. She and her sister removed them for him.

He thanked the girls, and noticing how they waited to see what he would next do, he reclined on the bed beside Eleanor. They were still watching, so he pulled a woolen blanket over the both of them, then closed his eyes. The last thing he saw was their smiles of approval. He heard them whispering to one another, heard the door opening, and their voices fading as they went into the corridor. The door closed behind them, and Eleanor's gentle breathing filled the quiet room.

Opening his eyes, he turned on one side to face her. He wrapped an arm about her, slid the other beneath her shoulders to bring her close to him. Here, in this well-appointed sleeping chamber, holding this beautiful woman who was his wife in his arms, it seemed the events he had witnessed this morning were years not hours past. Here, it was possible to believe there was no evil that might come between himself and his lady-wife, and he sighed, wishing there might be more moments such as this one. He set his lips to her brow.

Eleanor stirred. Her body lengthened like a cat stretching. Her eyelashes fluttered. He did not release her, but kept his eyes fixed upon her face, waiting for her to fully awaken. He wanted the first thing she focused upon to be his face. He wanted her to look into his eyes and know she was safe.

She blinked twice, focused, and gave a little, startled, "Oh." She met Garrett's gaze, confused, but not frightened. "Where—What—?"

"You are in your own bed in your own chamber, mistress."

"But how?"

"I carried you from the yard."

"The last thing I recall was sitting behind your saddle. Pray, sir, I did not faint again, did I?"

"No, you did not faint again," he said with the hint of a gentle smile. "You were sound asleep by the time we reached the big house."

"Who was it undressed me?"

"Me."

Deep pink suffused the skin of her chest. It spread up her neck, and the whole of her face.

"Why do you blush? I am your husband," came the soft whispered words.

The color upon her cheeks deepened. "Yet you are still a stranger in some ways."

"You would like to know about my family? My parents?" He knew she did not mean stranger in the way a bride would ordinarily intend the word, and he wanted to tell her his whole story, but part of him remained uncertain. He could not, would not risk her disbelief. The truth must be revealed in pieces, slowly; it must be built upon like the foundation of a massive cathedral, little by little, each piece supporting the one before. He began with the simple, the obvious. "Have I any siblings? No. Where I was raised? In Kent, at the estate of Lady Olivia Turbeville. Being orphaned in infancy, I became the lady's ward. Was I schooled in university? Yes, I read the law."

"That would be a start."

"Oh?" He cocked an eyebrow in query. "Is it that you wish to know me better? Or that you wish to understand me?"

She glanced at him from beneath her lashes. Her pulse was racing, and she required a deep breath before she could reply. "I wish to be at ease in your presence."

Her honesty touched him. "You are ill at ease around me?"

*Ill at ease*. Eleanor almost laughed aloud. Verily, he made her act like some other woman; he made her abandon common sense. She whispered her reply as if it were a confession, "Somewhat."

"And why is that?"

"You must allow that the manner of our introduction and betrothal are not in least bit . . ." She required a few moments to decide upon the proper word. "Usual."

"Usual. Unusual." He weighed the words, and could not help but grin at her with that knowing, wicked grin she had seen many times afore. "I would call our introduction and betrothal memorable. Memorable and most remarkable. Just as I would call the passion betwixt us memorable. And most remarkable."

"P-p-pas-sion." She mangled the word. Her heart skipped a beat.

"You do not still deny it?" Garrett's hand drifted from beneath the blanket. His fingers cupped her chin to tilt her face up to his. "You do not still deny the attraction? This?" His voice fell to a deep murmur. It resonated with a sensual quality intended to seduce as surely as his words could charm, as surely as the penetrating heat in his eyes could beguile. He lowered his face until his lips grazed hers while ever so lightly he spoke, "You do not still deny this? This energy?"

A small moan escaped her lips. Her eyelids fluttered closed, and she held her breath waiting for his lips to brush hers, wanting his touch again.

"These flames that flare and pull us close until we melt?" With each syllable his lips brushed back and forth on hers.

He spoke the truth.

Garrett's power over her was dizzying. He had only to lean near enough that she might be seared by the heat of his body, and she began to melt. He had only to whisper low enough that she might be enticed by the warmth of his breath, and she began to tingle. He had only to trace the tip of one finger on her skin, and it would begin. Liquid fire flowed through her veins and stole away her common sense; liquid fire made Eleanor yearn for the intimate invasion of his hardness. There was no resistance in Eleanor; there was only need, and when he pulled her closer, the fire began to flow through her. Her arms went around his shoulders.

"Ah, mistress mine." His tongue caressed her lower lip, lightly gliding, licking. She sighed, and every nerve ending in his body came alive. The ache in his loins was fierce. Once, twice, his lips tugged on her lower lip, then he sucked the soft flesh. "During the long, lonely storm my thoughts were of you, Eleanor. I dreamed, and hoped, and prayed for a thousand tomorrows. I do not forget how captivating was your response to arousal, how intoxicating was your surrender to ecstasy, nor how intense was my own pleasure to guide you to such heights."

She shuddered to hear him speak of such things, shuddered not in shame or repugnance but with the arousal of which he spoke, and knew so well how to kindle in her. She shuddered again as his hand slid down her back to her buttocks. He squeezed them, and she moaned.

"You were in my mind's eye, Eleanor. A hundred thousand images clear and vivid. You at the *céilidh* dancing free as the wind on the wild sea. You in your brocade gown as green as your eyes. You in Dublin proud and brave. Mostly though it was the vision of you standing beside me in the kitchen, wearing the velvet gown stitched with pearls, the cloud lit by stars, an angel vowing to be mine." Garrett's voice was thick with desire. "My wife, my angel. Over and over have I reminded myself 'tis possible for this marriage to be more than a civil agreement."

His hand slid below her buttock to lift her leg over his hip and expose Eleanor's sex.

She gasped. Firm, but gentle, his palm pushed against her backside, tilting her closer to him as she began to throb with need. His swollen man-sword nudged against her, and she was aware of how the wetness within her increased. Eleanor moaned as if half-asleep; she arched and rocked her hips forward until his full length rested against the lips of her sex.

Garrett groaned at this exquisite agony. "And to see you this afternoon . . . every bit as beautiful as the image I held fast in my memory, every bit as desirable, as innocent, fresh, and lovely. . . ." His lips claimed hers in a hard, deep kiss.

He rocked toward her, then backward, and his swollen desire slid back and forth along her dewy cleft. Eleanor gasped at the ribbons of heat that shot straight to her core, that made her respond with a moan, made her slide her leg higher up his hip.

"You must swear a solemn oath to me, mistress mine." He murmured against her mouth. "You must swear you will always obey me."

A chill tore through her. The misty, dreamlike state was shattering like a delicacy made of spun sugar.

"You must promise me you will not leave the big house without my permission and that—"

"Nay," she cut him off before he might finish. She slid her leg off his hip, and leaned away from him. She shook her head. "No."

"Your obedience," he said. There was an unfamiliar edge to his voice, harsh and impatient. "I will have your obedience, Eleanor."

"I will make no promises to you at the expense of my duty to my people, or my family. Nor will I make any promises I cannot keep because they come between me and my brothers." She disentangled herself from his embrace, and got off the bed. "You may own Laragh, Sir Garrett, but you do not own me. You will never own me."

"In the eyes of both God and state, you are my lawful wedded wife." Rage mixed with Garrett's utter disbelief. He was as disheartened as he was furious. "You have not so soon forgotten your marriage vows?"

"Nay, sir, I forget nothing, least of all your agreement to the condition *I* set forth to our marriage."

He stared at her, hardly believing what he'd heard.

"As you appear somewhat confused, allow me to remind you of what it is I speak. I will not share my bed with you; that was my condition. This is my chamber, this is my bed. I have no desire to share either with you, and thus I ask you to leave me to my privacy, if you please."

Garrett swung upward to a sitting position, lunged to the side, and grabbed her wrist. There was a cold, almost deadly quality in the way she spoke, the way he gazed upon her. "Mayhap 'tis *you* who are confused. As I recollect, you agreed to share my bed to consummate our vows, and beget an heir. I fear you speak in haste, madam."

"You would not dare," she gasped as he pulled on her wrist. She resisted his attempt to unbalance her that she might land on the bed beside him. "You would not force me."

His grip upon her wrist tightened, and his gaze held hers as a wolf might hold its prey. A long, loaded silence stretched between them. His lush green eyes darkened to black, hers the bright green of a faery bog flashed with resistance.

He saw defiance and opposition in her eyes, and he did not want to hear the words that went with that contempt. He did not think he could bear to hear her say, *Do not imagine there will be any pleasure for me in fulfilling my marital vows. You are the anything to which I must stoop.* Somehow it had all gone wrong before it had even started. He dropped her wrist, and raked his fingers through his hair. He was tired, very tired.

"You are correct. I would not force you." He rose from the bed, retrieved his boots from the floor, and walked to the door. "Good night, mistress mine. Enjoy your lonely bed."

# Chapter 25

The days at Laragh settled into an uneasy pattern as Christmas approached. For the children and Ambrose it meant keeping watch for dragoons, or a tory passing in the night in need of aid or having a message to relay to one of his comrades. For Róisín and Sibéal, it meant seeing to the needs of a full household. Every bed in the big house had at least one occupant. Added to this were the O'Byrne girls hidden in the tower, whose presence was supposed to be a secret, but which with each passing day was becoming known to more and more persons; lastly, there was Nuala, who needed special care.

As for Eleanor and Garrett, theirs was the most uneasy pattern of all. Garrett did not make any overtures toward her, being loath to finding himself insulted or rebuffed by his wife, while Eleanor bristled like a hedgehog at her husband's every word, and regarded his every move with suspicion.

Yet everything was not grim. Christmastide would not be a season of want this year. Every day Garrett's and Edwin's efforts restored Laragh closer to its former glory. The cow byre and the beehive-shaped hen house were again filled; the *mucais* squealed with pigs, and there were geese and sheep in the barn. Ambrose and the boys gathered greenery to deck the halls with ivy and boughs of holly. Sibéal and the girls devoted several days to baking. There were currant cakes frosted with almond icing, heart-shaped stroans, oaten cakes called faery rings dipped in honey, and Columcille cookies shaped like letters of the alphabet and named for the ancient saint whose mother had baked a cookie for him each time he mastered a new letter. The larder was full, and baskets of baked goods were distributed to the people. The finest development was with Nuala. Biddy O'Fierghraie's tea of camomile, celandine, and pennyroyal had eased her fever. The young woman's lungs had begun to clear. She would be celebrating Christmas with them.

One afternoon dragoons galloped up the lane. Several of Rowlestone's men, who had raided Kilcarra, were among them, and a squat, round-faced Puritan identified himself as their captain. His name was Uprighte Phillips, and he asked to search the grounds for tories, although Garrett suspected they would do so with or without his permission. They were looking for outlaws, who had participated in the raid on Castlekevin, four young boys named O'Byrne. Five pounds for each of them, dead or alive, the Puritan officer told the Cavanagh lads in his most soldier-of-God voice, mayhap to entice them to treachery or terrify them with the prospect of their own fate should they dare to turn outlaw.

"Where is Captain Rowlestone?" asked Garrett. He liked neither the well-fed looks nor overbearing demeanor of Uprighte Phillips.

"His wound festered, and he lies abed in Arklow," replied Phillips. "I have charge of his command at present."

"I am sorry to hear that. Please tell the captain I wish him well."

"Thy message will be conveyed, Sir Garrett. Now, may we proceed with our purpose?"

The soldiers searched the grounds, and when they had satisfied themselves that there were no rebels in the stables, other dependencies, or walled garden, Garrett escorted them to the dwelling house.

They entered through the kitchen where the number of girls at work had increased by four since midday. Three of them were scrubbing pots with wee Maeve, and the fourth, a frail wisp of a creature, was seated before the hearth fire, her pale fingers plying a needle over mending. Garrett did not recognize their faces, and knew there must be some relationship between the dragoons searching for tories and their appearance. He nodded to each of them as if nothing were out of the ordinary. Could it be the O'Byrne lads were hiding at Laragh disguised as girls? He studied them with a discreet eye. Nay, these lassies were not laddies in skirts. But were they O'Byrnes? That would explain their sudden appearance, and wee Maeve's frantic expression. Garrett hid a grin. The English, it would appear, were embarked upon a wild-goose chase.

The girl seated by the hearth began to shiver, and while the soldiers searched the larder and pantry Garrett took a cloak off the peg by the door and draped it around her shoulders. The girl said nothing, but her eyes as green as a faery bog met Garrett's, and he was certain he detected the faint light of a smile.

Eleanor appeared as the soldiers were going into the banquet hall. She walked with Garrett and Uprighte Phillips, and assisted the soldiers as they opened cupboards and trunks for the captain's inspection.

"Goodwife Neville, the size of thy household differs from my expectation."

"Prithee, captain, how might that be?"

"I was led to believe there were but eleven souls residing at Laragh, but thus far I have accounted at least a full dozen more than eleven."

"You are correct, captain, we are grown since the great snow," said Eleanor. "They are widow-women or others who would be living on their own."

"My wife is very tender-hearted, captain, and most graciously offered shelter to any of my tenants who did not wish to pass the winter months in solitude."

"What explains the abundance of children?"

"What of the children?" Eleanor coughed to disguise her panic.

"Are they orphans?" Uprighte Phillips inquired as if being alone in the world without one's parents condemned them to some unknown fate.

"Many are kin."

"But are they orphans?"

Garrett did not like this interest in the children. There was something sinister about it; indeed, he was reminded of how Commissioner Corbet had spoken at Lord Egerton's about the enslavement of children being for their own good. What Garrett next said, he phrased with care in the hopes his words would humor Phillips, "Orphans or otherwise, such a distinction matters not. They are good, hard-working children who enjoy lives of purpose and honest labor at Laragh."

"Excellent. 'Tis goodlie news." Phillips appeared well satisfied with Garrett's reply. An hour later he was likewise satisfied with the results of his search.

As soon as the dragoons rode away, Garrett summoned Eleanor to a private interview.

"How long have you been hiding the O'Byrne girls?"

"Girls? Captain Phillips is searching for lads."

"Aye, that is what he said, but he will never find them. You know that as well as I do."

"You know? How?"

"It was not difficult to discern, especially with the unannounced arrival of four girls in the kitchen. How long have they been here?"

"Since the first night of the storm. They arrived long after you had left."

"The night of the fire. Then they were at Castle-kevin, and Phillips was correct in that much."

She studied his grim expression, and tried to read its meaning. "What do you intend? I will not turn them out, no matter what you say."

He frowned. "All this time, near a fortnight sheltered at Laragh, and you said not a word to me. I am master here. Should I not know what takes place beneath my own roof?"

"I confided in no one save Sibéal, and we agreed it best that as few persons as possible should know."

"You chose a prudent course." He could not deny there was wisdom in how she had handled the situation.

"It gladdens my heart that they have come out of the tower. 'Tis right they should be part of the household," Eleanor whispered to Garrett, as they entered the kitchen. She introduced him to the three younger girls. They had remained to help wee Maeve with her chores, and were whispering and giggling while they worked. It was how young girls were meant to pass their time with laughter and smiles upon their faces, not hiding from dragoons or sleeping in dank caves.

His gaze searched the kitchen. "There was another girl."

"Nuala. The eldest."

"Where is she?"

"Returned to the tower," said Eleanor. She led the way to the chamber.

The effort of walking to the kitchen had taken its toll on Nuala, and when they entered she was propped on her pallet, the cloak from Garrett still about her shoulders, and a book upon her lap. She smiled.

"You have been ill," Garrett said when Eleanor left them alone. He hunkered down beside Nuala.

"I am much better," Nuala replied, liking at once this Englishman whom Eleanor had wed. He was as tall and dark and handsome as one of her brothers, and had a way about him that put her at ease.

"What do you read?" he asked.

"Actually 'tis not reading, but writing I am."

"You are a poet?"

"Nay, a scribe of sorts. 'Tis the *Annals of Finnén.* The true and accurate history of these hills and vales, and since the summer of 1399 my family—the O'Byrnes of Aghavannagh—has recorded the births and deaths, the triumphs and defeats, the joys and mysteries of the people. Each of us, sons and daughters alike, are trained in scribing and reading. I am honored to be the keeper of the annals."

"You carried it with you in the hills?" He noticed for the first time the dark ink stains on her thumb and two fingers.

"For a short while, and when I became concerned for its safekeeping, I brought it here to Laragh."

"Eleanor hid it for you?"

"Aye, she did, and gave me paper and ink and quills that I might make entries to deliver to her."

"May I see it?"

She handed it to him, eager to share and proud of the history within.

In silence, Garrett perused the pages with great care. The oldest ones were of heavy yellowed parchment with grand, intricate designs upon the borders. A.D. 1020, *A great comet passed across the skies*. His fingers touched the paper, traced over the lettering; some of the entries were in Latin, some in Irish. A.D. 1597, *Hugh McShane O'Byrne, grandson of Redmond, dies at Gabhal Raghnaill . . . his son Feagh is chosen by the people to be chieftain*.

"A treasure," he said with undiguised awe. "This is, indeed, a treasure, and your work is most noble, Nuala O'Byrne." Emotions surged through Garrett to consider this moment wherein Órla and her memories had at last been reunited with their whole. "Tell me, please, is there mention in your annals of a young girl named Órla, who was stolen by the English from the O'Toole's?"

"Aye, there was such a lass," came her whispered reply. His reverence touched her deep, and she knew this man was not what he appeared. "She was taken from her grandfather's lands during the time of the king Henry, but how do you come to know of Órla?"

"Mine was an upbringing most uncommon," said Garrett. He told Nuala about the lady who had cared for him since infancy. "Lady Olivia was raised upon her mother's and grandmother's memories, and it was those cradle-tales and songs, those stories of Cuchullain and the *Táin*, of Cathair Mor, and Conn, and of the Fianna that she imparted to me."

Nuala was fascinated by everything Garrett said. She hung on his every word, and had many questions which he answered, but he did not tell her the whole tale. He did not explain why he had been the ward of a spinster lady, who was not blood kin. He omitted any mention of his own ancestry.

"You have come to the place of your childhood cradle-tales," mused Nuala. "If only everyone of us might be likewise blessed. Tell me, Sir Garrett, is our

Ireland a faery tale come true? Is it everything you expected it to be?"

"If you mean did I recognize the hills? Aye, they were as I had dreamed as a child. But as for a faery tale ending, nay, this is not true."

They were both quiet for a moment.

"And where is Órla's great-grandchild now?" asked Nuala.

"Safe and secure at High Knole, I trust."

"But that you are here, while her good self remains in the stranger's land does not seem fair."

"Lady Olivia is not young."

"All the more reason that you must bring her to Laragh come spring."

"Her health is poor. She might not survive the journey."

"Think upon it in this light, Sir Garrett. What if she survived but only for a heartbeat's glimpse of Ireland, would that not be better than to die in the stranger's land? Oh, say that you will bring Lady Olivia to Ireland, Sir Garrett." Nuala smiled. "It makes my spirits soar to think of the entry I could record. Imagine being able to bear witness to and then record the return of Órla's great-grandchild. Why, to bear witness to Lady Olivia arriving at Laragh to gaze up at the high hills for the first time would be a living testament to the value of truth and history, to the importance of the annals, and to the enduring miracle that is Ireland."

"You have a way with words, Mistress O'Byrne," said Garrett as another surge of emotions swept through him. "Aye, you have my promise to bring Lady Olivia back to Ireland."

That evening Eleanor and Garrett returned to sit with Nuala. They brought Edwin Petty, and by the first week of January, the tower was where Edwin spent most of his free time. Edwin and Nuala shared an enthusiasm for chess, and the two passed many hours seated on the floor facing one another with a chess board set between them. Indeed, Sibéal had been heard to say that the gaining color in Nuala's cheeks owed nothing to Biddy's tea, but all to Edwin Petty's gentle smile.

"We were speaking of Lady Olivia," Nuala said to Eleanor when she came to visit one afternoon. "Edwin says Garrett has asked him to begin making arrangements for her to travel."

"Lady Olivia is coming to Laragh?" A queasy, uncomfortable feeling beset Eleanor. It was obvious Edwin Petty and Nuala knew more about her husband and the woman who had raised him than she did. "But I am told she is frail and elderly."

"Do you not agree it is only right that the great-grandchild of a stolen Irish child be returned?"

Eleanor's queasiness worsened. These two did, indeed, know much more than she did. While Eleanor knew her husband had been raised by Lady Olivia Turbeville, she had not known the lady was Irish. Once again Eleanor pondered Garrett Neville; he was not the man he appeared to be, but who he might be she knew not. Eleanor had a thousand questions, a hundred doubts, and more than anything, she wanted to understand. She wanted to look upon him with a clear gaze, not with confusion or doubt. She wanted to be able to trust him as she had once before.

The door burst open. Cait rushed in. There were tears streaming down her face. Garrett had caught her on the Arklow road, and was going to punish her, if she ever left Laragh on her own again. He had threatened to use a switch on her. To beat her!

Garrett strode into the room looking for all the world like an angry parent.

"You have no right to discipline her," said Eleanor, going to stand before the girl.

"Tell me, mistress, if I allowed her to wander into harm's way, would that be right?"

"Harm's way? Are you speaking of men-stealers again?"

"Is that doubt I hear in your voice, Eleanor?" he asked as if mocking her. "Do you think I fabricate these things?"

"Nay."

He glowered at her. "Pray, what is it, then?"

Eleanor forced herself to voice aloud her deepest, darkest fear. "I wonder why it is you know so much about their affairs."

Garrett had never imagined hearing such words from Eleanor. They were as good as an accusation, and his heart became very heavy. "If that is what you wonder, Eleanor, then I fear there is no answer which would satisfy."

"That is unfair," she whispered.

"Is it, now?" He paused. "Mayhap then you know a little of how you have made me feel."

Without another word Garrett left; he descended to the ground level and exited from the tower to the old bailey. A few moments later Eleanor departed, and made her way via the passageway into the big house.

The distance between the lord of Laragh and his lady-wife was getting wider.

# Chapter 26

January passed, and the weather began to turn. Rain in February was welcome as it softened the earth, and encouraged the hills to green. The days were lengthening, warming. In a good year, in the time before Cromwell, when every bothy was occupied and fathers and sons had not been arrested or forced into the hills, there would be men in the fields at sunrise every morning; the annual tasks of tilling the soil for planting would begin, and early booleying—moving cattle from the valleys to higher grazing—would commence.

It was Saint Brighid's Day, the first day of spring. The lads had spent the morning gathering fresh rushes. They spread some on the kitchen and entrance floors, and the girls used others to weave enough Brighid's crosses that one might be hung over the door and window of each stable, byre, and dwelling place on Laragh land. Weaving the *cros Bríde* was an ancient tradition. The charm had worked many a time, keeping a house and its occupants safe from harm, especially from fire and lightning. They were finishing the last of the crosses when an unexpected, but most welcome visitor arrived at Laragh. It was Rosanna Clare, galloping down the lane, black cape flying behind her like the wings of a great bird.

"You did not travel here by yourself, I trust?" Eleanor embraced her dear friend.

"Nay, I rode with Uncle William. He had business to which he must attend, and left me at the end of the lane."

"What manner of business?"

"He escorts a surveyor, a Puritan, who is not familiar with the countryside hereabout."

"Another survey," Eleanor exclaimed. "Will the English never be satisfied with their accounting of our lands?"

"This time I believe 'tis people for which they account. The Clares will retain their title to Killoughter in exchange for the services my uncle renders the English." Rosanna frowned. "It is shameful trickery. My heart is heavy with the knowledge that I sleep in my own bed because Uncle William will help the English determine who has or has not obeyed Cromwell's edict to transplant."

"You must not trouble yourself with such thoughts, Rosanna. No one would imagine you approve of such behavior. The kind of man Sir William Clare has always been is well known to one and all."

"But I will remain while others must leave to confront untold hardships," she said in a stricken voice.

"Is that guilt you suffer?"

Rosanna nodded aye, but could not admit so aloud.

For a moment Eleanor wondered if she should feel guilt that her own fortune had changed for the better, then she recalled what Nuala had said. "You know, Rosanna, staying at Killoughter does not guarantee yours will be an easy path. Each of us faces our own challenge, and each of us must do what we can to aid the struggle for Ireland. Those of us who remain must dedicate ourselves to ensuring the past survives through our memories; we must not allow those who could not stay to be forgotten. Our task is a noble one. We must make certain the Irish endure in their own land."

Rosanna thought of the dear ones already gone, and of the familiar faces soon to leave. She began to cry as she vowed not a single one of them would ever be forgotten as long as she lived.

A few hours later William Clare arrived with the surveyor.

"I would like to meet your husband," he informed Eleanor, as if she were a servant.

Garrett joined them, but his greeting was cold. He had no smile for Rosanna's uncle, and did not extend a hand to either man in greeting, but merely tipped his head in the slightest nod when Eleanor introduced them. He had recognized the two men drinking wine in the small parlor. One of the men was a peacock, the other was a crow, and he had seen them before outside the Essex Bridge Tavern in Dublin.

In his search for the man with the gold-tipped cane, Garrett had not thought to visit Killoughter. He had never imagined this would be the answer. The landowner, who would do business with men-stealers, was Sir William Clare, and his companion, the so-called surveyor, was David Selleck, ship owner from the Massachusetts Colony.

"We have met afore, have we not, good sir?" Selleck addressed Garrett.

"Not that I can recollect," Garrett lied, hoping as he did that Selleck's memory was indeed as vague as it seemed. If Clare wished him to believe this man was a surveyor, he would not be the one to unveil the truth. Not yet. He turned to Sir William and spoke "I am told there was some confusion about your property and a candle-stick maker insists he is the rightful owner. How goes it at Killoughter?"

"There is no confusion. My niece and I are back in the big house once again."

"You are most fortunate. I am told the Spensers of Kilcomman were not."

"I am perhaps more clever than Spenser."

"Oh?"

"Land is not the only thing the English desire in Ireland."

"And what might that other *thing* be?'

"Maps. The English put great store by maps, you know. There is no map of this area."

"You are a cartographer?"

"I am assisting Selleck with his survey."

"You were *surveying* today?"

"You might say that."

"Well, I would like a good map of this area myself. May I see what you have done?"

Rory burst into the small parlor. The Cavanagh lads came in his wake, and the three of them were yelling and talking in an hysterical garble of English and Irish. Grace, Eveleen, wee Maeve, and Nuala's sisters had gone with Róisín to her cabin. Why did they go? Why, to hang a *cros Bríde* above the door. Yes, it was a disobedience, they knew that, but they had not thought any harm could befall them on such a fine day. As for danger, they had been thinking wolves, and had not been suspicious when the dragoons surrounded the cabin. The lads had been in the uppermost branches of a giant quicken tree; from there, they had seen everything, but had not been seen themselves by the dragoons. The soldiers had seized Róisín and the girls, captured them like felons.

"Where are they now?" Garrett asked.

Rosanna and Eleanor sat closer together, and

stared at Rory hoping against all odds that his answer might be better than what he had already described. Both young women had become pale, and they wore identical expressions of horrified disbelief.

"The soldiers tied their wrists with rope, loaded them in a wagon, and drove toward Arklow."

"Find Master Petty and Ambrose, and whatever the three of you lads do, you must stay together. You must always be with myself or Master Petty, if you go out of doors. You must trust no one else. No one. Off with you now. Tell Ambrose and Edwin to meet me in the kitchen," he instructed the lads. They dashed from the room, and Garrett turned on Sir William. "William Clare, you are as vile and contemptible a man as I have ever had the misfortune of meeting. Neither yourself, nor your companion are welcome in my home or on my land."

Eleanor gasped at Garrett's insult. His increasingly inhospitable behavior on top of the shock of what had befallen the girls was almost too much. She held a hand to her heart as if she might faint.

"Indeed, madam, your husband is most rude," Sir William declared to Eleanor in his most self-righteous manner. Then, assuming a most innocent tone, he said to Garrett, "I cannot imagine why you would make such a remark to myself or Master Selleck."

"Can you not? You may play one game with your niece and your neighbors, but I am not so naive. I have been in Dublin of late, and in Wicklow. Earlier, I spoke false. I have, indeed, met Selleck, and another of his kind, a Captain Bingham, and I know what *business arrangements* you would make with Selleck. Indeed, I know his business has naught to do with surveying."

Selleck rose. "Come, Sir William, 'tis evident we are not welcome here, and as there is nothing more to say betwixt thyself and this man, let us leave."

Garrett blocked Selleck's way to the door. "I will hold you and Clare personally accountable for every hair on the head of each of those girls, as well as for the life and well-being of Mistress O'More."

"Do not meddle in matters of which you know nothing, Sir Garrett," Clare said. "Matters which are not your affair."

"Not my affair? Do you claim them to be yours, then?"

"Aye, I have papers."

"As do I. Signed by the Commissioners."

"What? What kind of documents can you possess, Sir Garrett? Show me!"

"Nay, they are my affair. In the same manner that your affairs are yours. That is, as long as they hurt no one else." Garrett paused. "As long as you do not profit at the expense of others."

Eleanor, who had been listening to every word, but did not yet comprehend what these men were discussing, finally spoke up. "Prithee, Garrett, Sir William, what are you talking about? Will not one of you enlighten myself and Rosanna?"

"Ask Sir William how he saved Killoughter," Garrett told Eleanor.

"I must be on my way," said Clare. He grabbed for his niece. "Come, Rosanna."

"How did you save Killoughter?" Eleanor asked, loud and clear. A trembling started deep inside her before the last word had been spoken. There was evil in this room, although she did not understand its form.

"I do not have to tolerate this. Come, Rosanna. Where is that little servant? The wee girl who took our cloaks? Where did she put them?"

"*That little servant* is trussed up like a felon and

on her way to the Arklow wharf. Answer her, Clare. Answer my wife."

"How, uncle?" Rosanna spoke for the first time, her voice choked with tears. She had become very pale, and she bit her lower lip to hold it still. When her uncle did not reply, she turned to Garrett. "You must tell me, sir. I must know. How did my uncle retain our right to Killoughter?"

Everyone in the room looked at Sir William Clare and waited to see if the man had the courage to speak for himself. He did not; Sir William headed toward the door.

Garrett spoke for him, "With the flesh and blood of Irish women and children."

The words echoed through the small parlor, hideously magnified. Rosanna swayed, and Eleanor grabbed her arm to prevent her friend from swooning face first onto the floor.

"You are no surveyor, then, Master Selleck? Your business is not pacing and measuring?" Rosanna asked. Her voice was composed, though she did not sound like herself. She did not break down into tears, she did not gasp for air between words. Of a sudden, there was a stark, emotionless quality to the way she spoke, the way she regarded her uncle.

"He is a merchant."

"Do not look shocked, Rosanna," her uncle sneered. "We do what we must, and as for me, I do not intend merely to survive, but to win. Now come along."

"Nay, uncle, I will not walk at your side, and I shall never return to Killoughter as long as you reside there. Nay," she corrected herself, "I shall never return as long as you draw breath."

"Bravo, niece," he drawled in derision. "Quite the dramatic performance. You make the perfect martyr.

Fine. Have it your way. Do not return. Do not appreciate what I have done for you."

"Done for me?" she rejoined. "Do not deceive yourself, uncle, for you do not fool anyone save yourself. It is wide known: William Clare has never done anything for anyone except for William Clare."

Rosanna rose and turned her back on her uncle. With her shoulders square and her back straight, her chin high, she left the room without a backward glance. It was evident she had spoken to and gazed upon her uncle for the last time.

Eleanor remained in the small parlor only long enough to say her final words to William Clare. "I agree with my husband, Sir William. Neither you nor your companion is welcome at Laragh. Not now and never again. Farewell to both of you."

She, too, quit the small parlor without a backward glance. Clare and Selleck departed without delay. Garrett went to the kitchen, and after conferring with Ambrose and Edwin, he sought out Eleanor.

"What are we to do?" She burst into speech without waiting first to hear what he might say. "Can my sisters be saved?"

"It is possible." He did not want to give her false hopes.

"We must, at least, try."

"And so we will. I have a plan, a carefully crafted plan, for I feared something like this might come to pass, and wished to be prepared." While in Dublin he had sought Lord Egerton's counsel on a number of legal issues other than his marriage; how to deal with men-stealers had been one of them. "It is a good plan with every chance for success, if we can catch up with them while your sisters are still on Irish soil."

She stared at him.

"Something troubles you?" he asked.

"How—how—how is it you would know enough of these things to have a plan?"

"To know of these men and their activities is not to condone them, nor abet them. Indeed, it has been my intention since my first day in Dublin to foil them if I could. I met the merchants, Selleck and Bingham, in Dublin at the residence of a mutual acquaintance. I have always had a loathing for men who deal in flesh, and found their attitudes particularly repugnant. By happenstance I saw them a second time in Dublin in the company of a man I did not yet know was William Clare."

Garrett told Eleanor of seeing the man with the gold-tipped cane in Wicklow and of his decision there and then to disrupt any business the merchants and their collaborator hoped to conduct. "I intended to make my home and my future in this countryside, and I did not intend to live in a place terrorized by or or indifferent to men-stealers. The only problem is: I failed. I did not stop them, nor did I protect the most vulnerable members of my household. For that I ask your forgiveness."

"You ask for my forgiveness?" Shame flooded through Eleanor. She forced herself to meet his gaze. "Nay, Garrett, 'tis I who should beg for yours. You spoke of a path toward harmony in our marriage, and I claimed to share your feelings, yet I failed to honor my solemn vows."

"Do not be hard on yourself."

"How can I not? You have been generous and kind and patient whilst I have been stubborn, petty and mistrustful. Can you ever forgive me?"

"You need not ask. It is done." His voice was laden with regret that this moment had come to pass out of calamity; indeed, there might yet be greater tragedy ahead for them "I hope it is not too late."

"Too late?" Her heart raced. She blushed, and

lowered her eyes. "I have never been one to admit defeat."

He set the back of his hand against her cheek. It was a tentative, almost shy caress as if he might still be uncertain of her. She looked up at him, and he smiled.

"It is too soon to declare failure, Garrett. Far too soon for us, and for my sisters and the others." She returned his smile. "You say there is a possible way to save them. Tell me about it. What must I do?"

"Will you take me to your brothers?"

Eleanor looked up at Garrett, and knew that if her sisters and the others were to come home, this man could make it happen. "I will do anything, Garrett. For my family. And for you."

Gazing down at his wife, Garrett knew she spoke true, and he thought he had never heard more sweeter words than those.

# Chapter 27

**E**leanor and Garrett traveled along the footpath to Glendalough. Copse gave way to wood, and gray mist settled over the trees as they moved deeper into the hills. The sun was setting behind the mountains by the time they made their way to the upper lake. Eleanor's satisfaction with their swift progress was crushed, however, when they discovered the cave was empty. The tories were gone. At least, there were no signs of a struggle. It did not appear they had fled in haste, but had made an orderly move to other quarters, leaving behind a small cache of supplies should anyone need temporary shelter.

"We must hasten to Baravore," said Eleanor. "The nearest pass is a short distance north of here. It is a rugged crossing, but direct."

"No, we go nowhere. Not now. Not tonight."

"But there is so little time to get help for my sisters and the others."

"We have no choice but to remain here. Night falls, and you know as well as I, the weather could turn against us without a moment's warning."

Eleanor did not argue. Garrett was right, and while he crouched to light a fire, she made a pallet from the assorted blankets, ragged cloaks, and old pelts left by the tories. They sat before the fire side by side, and when he offered to let her lean against his shoulder, she accepted. It had been a hard, fast climb up the Raheen and into Glendalough, and for a while they were content to relax in silence.

Dusk gave way to night, the light in the cave faded. Soon they were in total darkness except for the golden fire. Garrett whispered into the darkness, *"Come hither, handsome sir. Won't ye be dancing?"* a *chorus of pretty voices beckoned. "A fine night for frolicking it is. Won't ye be coming closer now?"*

"What is that?" asked Eleanor when he paused.

"A cradle-tale of adventure, enchantment, and pure love. Of stolen children, and memories preserved."

"Is it Irish?" she wondered aloud.

"It is."

"Please, go on."

He did, and Eleanor found herself transported to a faraway time and place.

*"A dust cloud whirled past his good self. The nearby hawthorn shivered. He'd heard tell Irish faeries had a fondness for hawthorns. Mayhap 'twas nothing more than the wind in the trees turning the merlin's cry to girlish voices, stirring up the dust, and making the branches tremble. 'Twas dusk, and in the gloaming light the tangle of brambles. . . ."*

When he had finished Órla's story, Garrett explained why it was he had been entrusted to Lady Olivia's care.

Tears scalded Eleanor's eyes. For the second time that day Nuala's words echoed in her thoughts. Eleanor blinked, and the tears fell. Even far away, even across the sea in England, men and women dedicated themselves to truth and justice. Even across the generations there were sons and daughters of Cathair Mor who had never set eye upon these high hills, yet they embraced their past, and each shared a part in ensuring memories never died.

At last, he explained why he had come to Ireland.

"You are an O'Byrne, then?"

"I am."

Her tears increased. Garrett had not come to steal Laragh, but to do what he might to save it. He was not a stranger, but was one of them. That was why the people had trusted him, and it explained many things she had not understood. Another tear slid down her cheek. She had never before experienced such wonder and sadness, such grief and hopeful expectation at once. Garrett had come home, but there had not been any welcome for him. There was a painful, hollow ache deep inside Eleanor, and another tear chased the ones that had gone before.

"Would that I might start anew, Garrett, and that you might allow me a second chance," she whispered.

He nodded in understanding. "For each of us there are things we would do differently, if only we had a second chance. As for myself, I am sorry to have failed in my pledge to keep you safe."

"When did you pledge that?"

"Before I even knew your name."

"I do not understand."

"That first blessed night when you fainted in my arms. Your lips enticed me, mistress mine, but it was your innocence, your courage, and your utter determination which captured my heart. Later you were gone from my lodgings, but you had not left my thoughts. Over and over I could only think a lady should not make the kind of choices you had made. A lady such as yourself should have someone to watch over her, to protect her and guard her. I could not get it out of my mind that there should be someone for you to take the weight of your burdens onto his shoulders to spoil and protect you."

In that instant, Eleanor was back in her mother's bedchamber in those final moments before Lady Moira had ascended unto Heaven, and it seemed her heart stood still. *There will be someone for you. A loving man to cosset and protect you, and to take upon his shoulders the great responsibility you are ready for this day.* When Eleanor spoke, hope laced her voice. "A second chance is yours, Garrett, if you would grant me mine."

"I would grant you a hundred, thousand chances, mistress mine."

"We start this very night, then." She put her hand in his, and trembled, a little shy. "I will be yours for the night, my husband."

An outright declaration of love could not have been sweeter to Garrett's ears. Entwining his fingers with hers, he turned over her hand to kiss the sensitive underside of her wrist, and was rewarded by her soft sigh. With his other hand, he traced the lines of her cheekbones and jaw, and found the little pulse beating like the wings of a bird in her throat. He set his fingers beneath her chin, tilting her face up to his, rubbing his thumb along her lower lip. Her mouth parted, and her breath kissed his thumb in sensual invitation. He could not resist that proposition, and he slid his thumb into her mouth and along the inside of her upper lip.

"For this night, and for ever more." Desire roughened his words. "You are my wife to cherish and adore, to watch over and to love with my body and my soul until the end of time." He sealed this promise with a kiss like no other they had shared before. His lips teased and nipped, erotic, and beguiling. It was a kiss that transcended passion and fire; it quivered with aching, sweet tenderness. His tongue swirled in her mouth, seductive, possessive.

Eleanor bent within his embrace, pliant, willing, wanting, and as full of burning need as he was. He wrapped his arms about her, pulled her upward, and she followed his lead, rising to her knees before him as he knelt before her. Their kiss continued long and deep, a drowning, consuming kiss; he devoured her lips, the whole of her mouth, and their tongues fused in a slow, thorough dance that trembled with unbearable longing.

His mouth began to travel. He leaned into the column of her slender throat, his lips eager to brush across her soft, warm skin. He pushed her cloak off her shoulders, and sought the wooden buttons that fastened the bodice of her gown; his fingers fumbled with them, and her hands joined his. Together, they opened the gown to her waist, baring her full, round breasts to the moist night air. He heard her little sigh when his hands cupped one breast; the soft flesh filled his hands as he massaged and lifted it. He lowered his head to lick the beautiful, feminine globe in a circular pattern, making each circle smaller than the one before until he had reached her rose petal, soft peak.

His tongue lapped across her sensitive flesh, and a rush of expectancy shot through Eleanor. She was aware of how her breathing quickened, aware of the ache in her breasts, and the one between her legs. Her nipples began to pucker, and when they were hard as pebbles he took first one into his mouth, then he suckled the other. His tongue flicked over the stiff nipples, he tugged at them with his lips. Eleanor's aching intensified, heat flooded her. His hands kneaded her sensitive flesh, he pressed her breasts together, and his tongue slid along the line of cleavage. There was a throbbing at her core, and she could not deny the hunger, the need to be touched by this man.

"Spread your legs a little," he rasped.

She heeded his words, and he settled between her thighs.

Her legs parted. Their embrace tightened. They rocked inward, each rubbing against the other. He fit the swollen evidence of his desire to her softer sex, and through their layers of clothing, Eleanor felt the heat of his body sinking into her.

A shudder of pleasure coiled though Garrett; he needed more. His hands disappeared beneath the hem of her skirt, skimmed along her calves, and up her thighs. Up they went, higher, all the way up until one hand cupped her backside, and the other one delved between her legs, where she was warm and moist. His fingers spread the petals of her deliciously ripe sex, fondling her plump outer lips, working their way up the crease in search of her most sensitive nub. He found it, rubbed gently with two fingers, and she moaned as he concentrated his caresses there, spreading her abundant dew with small, controlled strokes, heightening her pleasure with occasional, quick, gentle pinches.

A shivering sensation worked its way through her, and into him. They both moaned, low and soft. She widened her legs to him, and a jolt of lust exploded in his loins.

"Free me," he murmured. "Touch me as I touch you."

Eleanor needed no more encouragement. She had not forgotten a single detail of their night in Dublin; nor could she deny the pleasures he had given her, and the liquid cravings that flowed through her now were as irresistible and compelling as they had been before. She wanted to touch him, wanted to feel the hot hardness of his man-sword; she wanted that powerful strength to fill her as before. She unlaced his breeches, and as the material loosened, his erection seemed to push it aside and stand up of its own. She touched him as he had asked, and the tumescent male flesh in her hands excited her.

He slid one, then two fingers into her sex, and she trembled. Her fingers found the drop of moisture upon his tip, and she spread it around in a tiny circle. His fingers stroked deep inside her, then slid out and in again, whilst her hand was wrapped around his shaft stroking up and down, keeping pace with his fingers.

He sat back upon his ankles, and hoisted her to straddle his thighs. With both of his hands on her buttocks, he spread her open as he positioned the head of his throbbing erection against her moist lips. His grasp on her buttocks was gentle, yet firm enough to encourage her to lower herself on his shaft, but she needed no such assistance or instruction. Garrett let out a low, guttural groan as her lush feminine ripeness encased him.

Flames of pleasure licked through Eleanor as the head of his man-sword parted her lips, and pushed inside. A long moan trembled forth from her as she slid, lower, lower, as far as she might go until she rested upon him. He was in her to the hilt, and Eleanor did what seemed natural; she closed her eyes and surrendered to the urges of her body, grinding her hips in a titillating circle.

Urged on by his hands on her buttocks, she began to raise herself up, and then lower herself down again. She lost herself in the excruciating, taunting slowness of sliding up the length of his shaft until only the tip remained within her, and then going down, taking him within her again, making it almost as exquisite as the first entry.

There was great beauty in this coupling, this joining. Together they created an act of such intense ecstasy it could only be called love. *This* was what her mother had meant when she spoke of *charming the body* and *touching the heart*. In a brilliant flash of clarity Eleanor knew that even if there had been no need to save Laragh, she would have chosen this man. Somehow across the span of time and space, they would have found one another; their hearts and souls had been destined for each other. Somehow she would have found him even if it had taken centuries. He moaned. She felt his man-sword contracting, then expanding within her, and she knew her movements teased him as much as herself.

She clung tightly to him through this dance, and in response, his powerful thighs flexed and he thrust upward. Her hands clenched his shoulders, she met his upward thrusts, grinding down on him. She was a pagan goddess, wild and unrestrained. Her head fell back, long black curls trailing down her back, over his hands, her buttocks, his legs. Her breasts bounced and swayed. Their potent passions surged in tandem. Their tempo increased. He was panting hard; she gasped with each thrust.

Faster, harder. The friction was intense, the sensations vivid. A little spasm seized Eleanor at almost the exact moment she sensed the sudden tautness within him that occurred in the heartbeat before he thrust upward to explode. Deeper, louder. Another spasm tightened within her, and then it began to crescendo. He let out an exultant cry as his hot seed emptied into her. He thrust again, and again. Harder. A cry of sheer ecstasy burst from her lips; convulsive sensations rocked her, wave upon wave radiating outward from deep within her core. He thrust a fourth and final time, and her inner muscles milked him until every bit of his essence filled her.

They were both shaking, quivering. There was a thin sheen of moisture on her breasts, across his shoulders. Garrett did not withdraw, and holding her to his groin, he shifted both of them at once, bringing her to lie beneath him on the pallet. He was ready for her again, and gently he began to pump in and out of her slick, tight sheath. Her arms went about his shoulders, her fingers threaded through his hair, and she arched up to him. They made love again. This time, slow, languorous, but no less intense, and when they finally slept, their limbs were entwined, her upper body was cradled against his chest, and his man-sword nestled between her legs.

For the space of a few hours they had both allowed themselves an unfamiliar luxury. In a rare moment of self-indulgence they had set aside the world and its troubles, responsibilities, and demands. Nothing had mattered this night except their passion; nothing had mattered except the fusing of their bodies and souls. Garrett had wanted nothing more than to make her his, to fill her with his essence. Eleanor had wanted nothing more than to be his as surely as he would be hers. In emptying himself into her, Garrett became hers, and through the act of receiving Eleanor gave herself to him for all time. And in that moment nothing else mattered.

Eleanor awakened at dawn. Two men were standing at the entrance to the cave.

"*Nac gcuala tu an nuaideact?*" It was Garrett who spoke. *Did you not hear the news?* "There is a new captain of the dragoons. Rowlestone was wounded after the raid on Castlekevin."

"That is what I heard tell. What is he called?"

"Phillips, and I do not trust him to obey anyone's law except his own."

"*Ir éol dam a ndognaitm,*" replied the other man. *I know what they are up to.*

Eleanor recognized the voice of her brother Conall

as he conversed with Garrett. She fastened the bodice of her gown while she listened.

"Two birds with one stone," said Garrett.

"Aye, 'tis not greed alone that makes them steal women and children. They play at politics, and think to stop us in the hills, if they clear the countryside of anyone who might share a crust of bread with us, carry a message for us, or conceal us for a night."

"You are right, Conall."

"They will fill the holds of their ships until they can barely push down the hatch to lock them within."

"We have not a moment to idle," declared Eleanor as if she had been a part of the conversation all along. She gathered up her cloak, and stood.

Conall embraced his sister, then answered her unspoken question. "Luke is fine. He is outside keeping watch with James FitzDermot."

Eleanor kissed her brother on the cheek, then glanced from Conall to Garrett, then back to Conall. "Has Garrett told you of his plan?"

"Only that we are needed to help locate the women and children who have been captured." He looked to Garrett. "Once we know where they are, what is next? The men are fine soldiers; any one of them is worth at least two of the English for bravery and endurance."

"It is my hope that we avoid a fight."

"And why is that?"

"If we take back your sisters by force, then they can be declared stolen property. We must get them legally."

Conall laughed, a short, cynical sound of disbelief. "Legally? And how do you propose that? I heard tell you have the light; so says Biddy O'Fierghraie, but she said nothing about being able to perform miracles. Or mayhap you know something of sorcery."

"There is trickery of a sort in my plan." Garrett smiled, and reaching inside his great cloak, where a pocket had been stitched into the lining, he withdrew several sheaths of paper folded together as one. "On my last trip to Dublin I had several legal documents drawn up. First, there was the title to Laragh, which in the event of my death conveys to my wife or her next of kin. Lord Egerton and I toiled over that until it was worded in such a way that allows Archebolds, regardless of politics or religion, to remain at Laragh in perpetuity. It is a clever piece of legal work, and already several others have acquired similar documents with Egerton's assistance. Come spring not everyone will be headed for Connaught; moreover, they will have legal documents signed by three Commissioners to protect them."

"The second document was our marriage contract. That, too, was endorsed with the signatures of three Commissioners. And finally, there is this." He held up the papers. "It is my list."

"A list? What kind of list?"

" 'Tis a list of property to which I am entitled. Women and children captured to be sold as slaves are property, are they not?" He unfolded the papers. There were four of them, and each of them was the same. At the top was a statement of ownership, at the bottom were the Commissioners' signatures, and the large middle space was blank on three of the four. On the fourth was written the following:

> *Róisín O'More, widow-woman,*
>     *aged twenty-two years*
> *Eveleen Archebold, orphan, aged eight years*
> *Grace Archebold, orphan, aged seven years*
> *Maeve Cavanagh, orphan, aged six years*

*Aislinn O'Byrne, orphan, aged fourteen years*
*Isobel O'Byrne, orphan, aged eight years*
*Cait O'Byrne, orphan, aged eleven years*

"Once we have found them, I will need you to identify anyone else who may be with them so that their names can be added to the list. When the list is complete, I will approach the dragoons with two men, present my covenant of ownership sanctioned by the highest authority in Ireland, and if all goes well, I will retrieve my property—at which time your help will again be needed. This time to assist us in as swift a return as possible to Laragh. What think you, Conall Archebold?"

" 'Tis a brilliant piece of trickery," was his reply.

"And should some of your comrades linger behind to deal with the dragoons as they see fit, there will be no one to naysay them once we are a safe distance away."

Conall laughed. "Aye, 'tis brilliant, especially that last part about lingering behind."

"We leave then without any further delay," said Garrett. He turned to Eleanor, and his voice dropped to a whisper. "My thanks to you, mistress mine, for trusting me, and for second chances. And thank you for last night."

She blushed, and found herself glancing up at him from beneath her lashes like a maiden. She smiled. "Thank you, Garrett."

He returned her smile, then leaned close and kissed her, hard and quick. "James FitzDermot will see you home to Laragh. Godspeed, mistress mine."

"What?" Her expression was as incredulous as was the astonished query in her voice.

"When I go with the tories, you will return to Laragh. You are not coming with us."

"Why not?"

"Have you forgotten my vow to watch over you? 'Tis far too dangerous."

"Everything is dangerous these days."

"All the more reason to stay out of harm's way when you have a choice. I would be derelict if I did not make certain you were secure in the relative safety at Laragh."

"If I have a choice, then mine is to come with you."

"Nay, you do not have a choice, and you may not come with us. You will return to Laragh," he repeated. "And that is not an order. It is a request. A most humble request. I do not wish to fail in fulfilling my pledge, and if something goes awry, I will be comforted by the knowledge that you survive. You are the *bean-draoícht*. Indeed, for that reason alone, if for no other, you must return to Laragh. You are to be the bridge to the future, and you must survive."

A strange sensation was o'ertaking Eleanor not unlike the one that had rolled through her stomach when she'd been sledding with Garrett. She was not ill. It was not a bad feeling, but it was most unfamiliar.

"You speak of surviving," she said, very slowly, not liking the direction in which this was going. "Does that mean you fear you may soon encounter death?"

"Nay, I do not fear death. I regret it. I respect it, and know that it can always be around the next bend in the road. I respect death, and would surrender to it, if doing so might contribute toward a higher goal."

*Hills.* That was the sensation o'ertaking her.

Eleanor stared at Garrett, her eyes wide in astonishment as his words repeated themselves in her head. *Hills.* She was on that sled again, speeding down the hill, and she could feel the world rolling up from the pit of her stomach, through her chest, to her heart.

With those words he had told her everything she ever needed to know about him. With those words she realized what it was to love. This undulating within her, this soaring in her spirit, this was love. Her husband was indeed the man she had dreamed of wedding, and Eleanor knew that she loved him and no other. At that moment it mattered not whether he felt the same for her. Like Bran O'Connor, the ancient chieftain of Baravore, Garrett was a man willing to give his life for her, for her sisters, for Laragh. Garrett Neville, Baron Aylesbury, was as worthy as any other Irishman who had ever walked these high hills. Out of respect to him, she would obey him and return to Laragh; out of hope for the future, she would pray for the success of his mission, and await the safe return of her family to their home.

"I promise to bring your sisters back to Laragh safe and sound," Garrett pledged to Eleanor at their moment of parting.

"*Se do beata,*" she said to Garrett, then she repeated the same to her brother. *God save you.*

Conall smiled at his sister. "And I promise to make certain your husband returns home safe and sound."

# Chapter 28

**"T**hy name. I wouldst have thy name," barked the Puritan soldier. He was seated at a table beneath a tree, and before him were paper and an ink well. In his hand he held a pen as he awaited the lad's response. Behind the lad was a line of children waiting for their turn to stand before the table and answer the questions. "State thy name, and without further delay."

The child trembled like a hazel tree before a storm.

"Speak! And of a loud enough voice to be heard," the soldier bellowed.

The small boy opened and closed his mouth, but not a word came forth. All around the air was rent with wails and sobs of distress, and he glanced first over one shoulder, then the other to get a better understanding of this place to which the soldiers had brought him. What he saw was not reassuring.

Mayhap, once upon a time, this had been a pretty spot, situated as it was in a clearing above the sand dunes with a view of the strand and ocean beyond. Askintinny it had been called for centuries, less than a mile south of Arklow town, and once upon a time, there had been a village in this clearing. Mayhap then it had been a happy place, but the dwellings had been burned, the people who had once called this home were gone, all sign of their habitation vanished. Nature had even reclaimed the herb gardens and fields. Now it was a maze of stockades, a sort of open-air prison wherein several hundred women and children were being processed and confined.

A little girl, who was in a stockade several yards distance from the table, called out to the soldier, "If you would allow, sir, may I speak for my brother, please?"

"Ain't an idiot, is he?"

"Nay, sir, he is not an idiot. He is frightened, and cold and hungry."

"Everyone must speak for his or herself. 'Tis a test. Whosoever cannot answer the questions, 'tis proof of idiocy. In which case—" He raised his hand and drew it across his neck in a slicing motion, making a dreadful gurgling noise as he did so.

"Ignatius, sir," blurted out the lad. "Name's Ignatius."

"Speak up. Thy full name, young Ignatius, and thy place of residence as well as thy age."

"Ignatius Stacpool of Clonsilla, six years of age."

Twice today the dragoons had returned to the clearing with more captives, and the English, liking order and liking lists even more, were making a detailed record of each person in their charge. Eventually, the manner of their disposition at the Arklow wharf would be recorded as well as the price they fetched.

A second soldier eyed the lad up and down as if inspecting merchandise at a fair. He took stock of the child, and dictated to the man at the table, "Flaxen hair, full face, low of stature. No visible scars, nor any mark of the pox. All limbs whole and present. His every facility functional. No impediments noted to a goodlie day's hard labor. Recommendation: transportation."

The soldier at the table wrote this on the piece of paper before him, then pointed to the stockade wherein the lad's sister was being held. "Over there, boy."

The boy hurried to join his sister. Reunited, the youngsters embraced, then huddled on the sandy ground as another child was brought to stand before the census taker. There were several stockades each of them filled with many more children than adults.

From beyond the clearing came the snarling of dogs, soldiers yelling, shrieks of terror, the retort of muskets, more dogs. One of the children began to wail, then a second, and a third as another group of captives was marched into the clearing. The little girls from Laragh were in one of the stockades, and they cried as hard and ceaseless as did the others.

A greasy-faced soldier turned on the children. "Silence. Cease thy wailing."

This only made it worse.

"Silence, else I will do the silencing, and it will be permanent," he threatened.

Róisín understood the man's meaning, and she gathered the girls to her. "*Eist, eist, mo leannas*," she crooned. *Hush, hush, my dear ones.* Eveleen and Grace, wee Maeve, Cait, Isobel, and Aislinn crowded about her, clinging to each other, tiny hands straining to make what contact they might with Róisín's shawl, or the fabric of her skirt. They crowded, they reached, but they did not quiet. This was not the first time Róisín had tried, but there was nothing more she could say to comfort them. There was nothing she might do that would made any difference; they knew this as well as she did.

The afternoon when the wagon had lumbered away from her cabin, the girls had not doubted Róisín when she had told them that before the sun set, someone would rescue them. Even though help

had not come, Róisín's certainty had not wavered
during the second day; it had been easy to explain
the delay, and the girls had kept faith with her. But
now four days had passed, and each day took them
farther away from home; Róisín had herself begun
to lose faith, for whilst she believed they had not
been forgotten or abandoned, she feared they were
beyond the reach of those who cared.

It was only another day or two before they would
be taken to the ships. Róisín had heard the soldiers
speaking about their plans. The license they held entitled them to take three hundred Irish women and
children, and there were nearly that many in the
stockades.

"*Feach!*" whispered wee Maeve. *Look.* "Mistress
Rosanna's uncle! Do ye see him, Róisín?"

"Aye, 'tis Sir William."

"Look, they have Sir William. The soldiers have
Sir William," the girls whispered to one another.

"Nay, he is not their prisoner. See, his hands are
not bound."

"Then he is come to save us."

Now the little girls embraced. They cried tears of
joy.

"Here, Sir William, over here," Eveleen called out.
"We are over here, sir."

Sir William Clare did not answer. He turned his
back on the girls in the stockade as if he had not
heard Eveleen.

"Sir William, it is Grace and Eveleen Archebold,"
Grace added her voice. "Eleanor's sisters, Sir Thomas's daughters."

"Can you not help us?"

He turned and stared, then spoke to one of the
soldiers, who crossed the clearing to the stockade.
"The goodlie gentleman says thou art mistaken. He
does not know a family named Archebold."

Eveleen and Grace gasped.

Róisín's stomach knotted, her entire body went clammy.

" *'Tianam 'on diabhal,'* " Cait cursed him. *Your soul to the devil.*

"Speak not thy heathen tongue," the soldier commanded her.

Cait did not flinch. She stood taller, her sisters on either side of her, and wee Maeve before her; Róisín stood behind, Eveleen and Grace were to one side.

"Hear me well, Sir William," Cait called out, despite the soldier's warning. A hush fell over the clearing as she spoke. The children in the other stockades quieted. All ears listened to the girl who dared to speak; all eyes were upon the well-dressed gentleman who had turned to face her. "Although you pretend not to know us, Sir William, 'tis no more than a deception. You look away, and think to deceive us, to deny us. But you deceive no one save yourself, William Clare. What you do this day does not go unnoticed, and whilst we may be powerless, you know as well as does anyone else born and raised in these hills that there are others who have noticed, others who are all-seeing and all-powerful. Others who will one day seek you out, and when that day comes, justice will be served."

The gentleman with the gold-tipped cane said nothing in reply. His complexion had become a putrid shade of yellow, and it seemed he could not stop his hand, which grasped the cane, from shaking.

It was then that the *caoine* began. The thin, high-pitched wailing rose up from the stockades. The lament came from the women and children.

They were mourning for Sir William Clare.

Eleanor had not expected Garrett to return with her sisters the first day, but she had hoped to hear some time before sunset that they had found the girls and would soon be home. On the second day, it would not have surprised her if they had come up the lane; indeed, that they did not was the worse surprise. On the third day, it had required some effort to hold fast to her optimism, but she had not begun to despair. The next day was a disaster.

By the fourth day, no one could bring themselves to talk of the missing girls or of Garrett. An awful silence descended over Laragh, and Eleanor retreated to Sir Thomas's library, where the spirits of Ireland's patriot poets kept vigil with her. There was comfort in the distinctive scents of leather and ink; security in sitting at her father's desk; hope in leafing through the manuscripts, especially the ones Garrett had given her as her bride's gift.

The fifth morning dawned an exceptional spring day, mild and sunshine bright. Eleanor sat by an open window reviewing the poem she had been composing since harvest time. She read it aloud several times, tinkered a bit, made a few revisions, and then concentrated on what must come next.

Thoughts of Garrett's journey home filled her head, and she had an image of the land, of Laragh, waiting here for the Archebolds to return. That was how her poem must end; it must speak of coming home. She rose to fetch paper and ink as Sibéal opened the door to announce that Captain Rowlestone had come to call.

"Good afternoon, captain. Welcome back to Laragh." The first thing Eleanor noticed was his limp. "Please, sir, be seated."

"Thou art a most gracious hostess, Goodwife Neville." He sat in the chair opposite her. "I do not interrupt thy work, I trust?"

"Nay, 'tis a welcome diversion to have a visitor. You are not wearing your uniform, I see. Did you come to bid us farewell? Are you leaving Ireland?"

"Although I have decided to resign my commission, I am not leaving Ireland. I have been offered a post at Dublin Castle. My son and I will make our home within the old town walls." He paused. "I have come to inquire about Mistress O'More."

"Róisín is not here." Eleanor stared at Rowlestone, and could not help noticing how nervous he was.

"She has returned to her cottage?"

"Nay, captain, she has not returned to her cottage."

"Thou speaketh of Mistress O'More in a tone most grim. What has happened? She is not injured or abed with illness?"

"Would that it were so. I fear her condition is far more serious than any injury. Róisín, my sisters, and several other young girls were taken away."

"By whom?"

"Dragoons."

His features curled with distaste. "Did Phillips ride with them?"

"We know not for certain. The lads did recognize some of the soldiers who had been with Phillips one day when they searched Laragh."

"How long ago was this?"

"It has been five days now."

"So many." He made as if to rise.

She laid a hand on his arm, and nodded in a way that urged him to resume his seat. "There is nothing for any of us to do except wait. I know not where they are, nor even if Garrett and my brothers have found them, nor whether they have been able to proceed with Garrett's plan to rescue them."

"Sir Garrett rides with the tories?"

"He does." She said in a soft voice uncertain how he would react to the revelation. "What choice did he have, Captain Rowlestone, if he harbored any hope of rescuing Róisín and the girls?"

"Fear not, mistress, 'tis not my place to disapprove of what Sir Garrett does to aid his family, nor is it necessary that I repeat anything thou may tell me. Be assured, mistress, Sir Garrett did the right thing. I would have done the same were I in his position. With God's blessing they have found them already and are headed home."

"Thank you, captain."

He nodded. "Thou must know, mistress, that I have neither the heart nor stomach to enforce the will of England upon people who have committed no crimes, who have not sinned against God. My purpose for remaining in the army was to insure that I might have the means to support my son in Dublin, where I had hoped to visit him, but I did not see enough of the boy, and have missed him too much already. 'Tis why I came to call upon Mistress O'More."

"I do not understand."

"It was perhaps a foolish idea on my part, but I will need a housekeeper, and I had thought to ask Mistress O'More if she might wish to come to Dublin. Tell me, Goodwife Neville, dost thou think Mistress O'More might be willing to join my household?"

Eleanor smiled. "I cannot answer for her, captain."

He looked more anxious than ever. "Let us hope Sir Garrett and thy brothers are successful, and Mistress O'More will be able to answer for herself."

"Aye, let us hope and pray. And until we know what has happened I offer you the hospitality of Laragh. You will stay with us, I trust."

"I would be most honored." Indeed, he thought to himself, he had nowhere else to go, and once again it tested his convictions that these people who had been treated with such cruel injustice might yet extend a kind hand to himself.

Garrett stood before the table while two officers perused the document he had presented to them.

" 'Tis a list."

"And signed by Corbet and Fleetwood as well as by Cromwell's own son."

"What dost thou make of it?"

"I know the signatures. These are authentic." His voice dropped to a whisper.

Garrett waited while the two soldiers conferred in voices that could not be overheard. He did not look toward the stockades. Róisín and the girls had seen him when he'd ridden into the clearing, and the quick, sharp look he had given them had silenced them. The document listed property, not beloved kin and friends; there could be no joyous reunion here.

The soldier handed the document back to Garrett. "Thou will read of the names of thy property, sir, and if they are among these people, they will be released to their rightful owner."

Garrett nodded, and went to stand in the middle of the clearing. He began to read from the list. "Róisín O'More, Maeve Cavanagh. . . ."

One by one, the girls from Laragh walked out of the stockade to stand behind Garrett. The last of seven names had been read aloud, but there were still names on the list, and before reading the next one, Garrett looked to the nearest stockade and fixed his gaze upon a young woman with a blue petticoat hanging from beneath her skirt. He did not know her name, had never seen her before, but his eyes did not waver from hers when he called out, "Sorcha O'Kane."

He saw the query upon her face, and without

moving his head, he lowered his eyes for the briefest moment as if nodding, *Aye*, then he called out again, "Sorcha O'Kane."

The young woman raised her hand. She was released from the stockade, and went to stand behind Garrett as he read the next name, and the next. Twenty-five more names, and when he had reached the bottom of the list, he quietly led his property out of the clearing.

He wished there might have been a hundred names on his list, but this was the most for now without raising suspicion. Tories were lingering in the woods on the other side of the clearing. They were waiting for the signal that would let them know when Sir Garrett and the others were a safe enough distance away that they might do what they could to set the others free.

Dusk was settling over the countryside, and as the day remained unseasonably warm, Eleanor had gathered the household residents on the terrace above the lough. She had finished the poem and wished to share it. Edwin, Nuala, and Rosanna were on the bench in front of her, Sibéal and Ambrose stood to one side, Captain Rowlestone sat on a chair, and the lads were gathered on the ground at his feet.

She began to recite the lines she had committed to memory.

> *What shall we do for timber?*
> *The last of the woods is down.*
> *Kilcash and the house of its glory*
> *And the bell of the house are gone,*
> *The spot where the lady waited*
> *Who shamed all women for grace*
> *When earls came sailing to greet her*
> *And Mass was said in the place.*

*My grief and my affliction*
   *Your gates are taken away,*
*Your avenue needs attention,*
   *Goats in the garden stray.*
*The courtyard's filled with water,*
   *And the great earls, where are they?*
*The earls, the lady, the people*
   *Beaten into the clay.*

*No sound of duck or geese there,*
   *Hawk's cry or eagle's call,*
*No humming of the bees there*
   *That brought honey and wax for all,*
*Nor even the song of the birds there*
   *When the sun goes down in the west,*
*No cuckoo on top of the boughs there,*
   *Singing the world to rest.*

*There's mist there tumbling from branches,*
   *Unstirred by night and by day,*
*And darkness falling from heaven,*
   *For our fortune has ebbed away,*
*There's no holly nor hazel nor ash there,*
   *The pasture's rock and stone,*
*The crown of the forest has withered,*
   *And the last of its game is gone.*

And the final verse that she had penned this day.

*I beseech of Mary and Jesus*
   *That the great come home again*
*With long dances danced in the garden*
   *Fiddle music and mirth among men,*
*That Kilcash the home of our fathers*
   *Be lifted on high again,*

*And from that to the deluge of waters*
*In bounty and peace remain.*

That was it. Eleanor Neville ní Archebold's poem was finished.

Silence greeted her. She searched their faces, and did not think it was a bad silence.

Nuala was the first to reveal her reaction when she raised her hand to catch a tear at the corner of one eye. She was crying. "It is beautiful, Eleanor. More beautiful than I can express."

In a hushed voice Captain Rowlestone agreed, then Ambrose and Edwin added their praise, and then came the thunder of horses approaching. Everyone looked toward the lane, but could see nothing, for the big house blocked the view. Eleanor was the first to move, lifting her skirt about her ankles and dashing across the grass. Rory and the Cavanagh lads were right behind her, and in a matter of seconds. They were running ahead, reaching the yard first.

Eleanor's heart was in her throat, tears already burned her eyes, and when she rounded the corner of the dwelling house, they began to flow down her cheeks at the sight before her.

They had come home.

There was Garrett holding wee Maeve before him on his saddle; Conall and Luke had Grace and Eveleen behind them on their horses; the O'Byrne brothers carried their sisters; Róisín rode with Roger Clare; and there were many other tories she did not recognize, each of them having brought a woman or a child to the safety of Laragh.

"Garrett," Eleanor called out as she rushed to him. She smiled through her tears.

There was much laughter and crying, tears of joy and long embraces.

Nuala hurried toward her as their sisters leapt down. Wee Maeve slid to the ground, as did Eveleen and Grace, to be embraced by their younger brothers. Captain Rowlestone helped Róisín dismount, and Rosanna embraced Roger.

Garrett dismounted, and stepped toward Eleanor. He held his breath, wanting to embrace her, wanting her embrace, but holding back, waiting to see what she might do.

"Your plan was indeed a fine one." She stepped up to him, and rising on tiptoe, she cradled his face in her hands. *Hills.* They were there deep within her. She felt them in her heart, and smiling, soft, she kissed him full on his lips.

"Thank you," Garrett rasped in a voice full of emotion. Eleanor's kiss was not one of gratitude, but a tempting kiss, full with the promise of passion.

A horse nickered. One of the tories called out to the others. It was time to return to the hills.

"Not so soon," said Sibéal. "To the kitchen, each and every one of ye now, for a hearty, good meal."

"Nay, we must not. We dare not linger."

Already several of the men had wheeled around their mounts to head back to the high hills. Eleanor had but a quick glance at her brothers as they departed, before she looked back to her husband.

Garrett gazed down at Eleanor and thought he had never seen a lovelier sight, but it was her words that thrilled him above all else. Eleanor spoke the sweet words he had longed to hear.

"Welcome home, Garrett."

"Ah, such sweet, sweet words. You make me a very happy man."

"Welcome home, my husband, my love."

"My love?" In a rush, Garrett sensed the whole of his life arriving at this moment.

She smiled. "Ah, did I neglect to tell you?"

"Tell me what?" he asked, but he knew. How could he not when his own heart loved her most dear?

"I love you, my husband."

Garrett let out a whoop, a great joyous exclamation that turned to robust laughter. He pulled her to him, kissed her light, then gazed deep into her eyes as the lush green of the hills fused with the bright light of a faerie bog. For the first time in his life he did not doubt there would be a future for him.

"That pleases you?" she asked, flirtatious.

"Aye, it pleases me."

"And why might that be?"

Again he surrendered to laughter. It was a jubilant sound. "Because I love you, Eleanor Neville ní Archebold. I love you, bold, determined, beautiful, valiant, and stubborn woman that you are. Now, kiss me. That is an order."

This time, it was Eleanor who laughed, and this time, without a word of complaint, she obeyed.

# Epilogue
## *A Cradle-Tale Ends*

∿∿∾◯∿∿

**T**he babe was a dark child of the hills, and it was
··· ten summers gone before English came once
more into the glen.

The strangers closed their ears against the whispering
sidhe, and made for Castlekevin with purpose. They
searched for the child of an English knight who had one
time lost his way in the hills, and they found Órla.

Their purpose was to make certain the daughter of Guy
Turbeville of High Knole, Kent would be raised in a civilized household. This daughter of an English knight must
be cleansed of her hedge-ways, and schooled to proper obeisance. Órla was stolen from beneath a hawthorn tree at
the edge of a bright green bog. Alack, she was taken
against her will across the sea, and in time, made to wed
a Turbeville cousin, but she ne'er forgot Ireland.

In time wee Órla, far from her beloved home and living
among the English, had a daughter, and she named the
child Órla, not for herself but for everything she had lost.

In time, she told that child about the glen and the
O'Tooles, about Castlekevin and the sidhe, the hawthorn
in spring, the flutes and pipes, and she taught her daughter the language she'd learned at her grandfather's knee.

*The time came to pass when Órla had a daughter of her own to whom she imparted her mother's everlasting memories, and although this little girl was not named Órla like the mothers afore her, the good Lord blessed her with the same dark beauty of a child of the hills.*

*This last girl's name was Olivia, born in England, but with the blood of Ireland, and she waited for the day she might tell her child about the glen and the O'Tooles and Castlekevin, waited for the day she would teach her child the language her mother had taught her in secret. She waited for a child to whom she would impart grandmother Órla's memories and the knowledge grandmother Órla had learned at her own grandfather's knee in Ireland.*

*Time and again Olivia was reminded, "If you do not know your history, then you have lost your memory, and you must do your part to make certain Ireland does not lose her memory."*

*As her mother and grandmother before, Olivia would preserve history; she would hold it sacred. Not for herself alone, but for the centuries to come . . . Cuimhead . . . Ireland must never be without its history, no Irish child must ever be without memory.*

"They are come! They are come!" Rory shouted from his watch atop the ramparted roof of the old tower.

A chaise carriage was wheeling down the lane. It was an elegant vehicle designed for comfort. Someone special was arriving at Laragh this day. There were outriders fore and aft, and Garrett rode at a walk alongside the carriage that he might converse with its occupant.

Children dashed out of the tower, they burst through the front door, more careened round the corner from the terrace. Adults poured forth from the big house and stables to gather at the stoop. The entire household was there, and more. There were the villagers from Annamoe, Laragh's people, and there were others, too, not out in the open by the stoop, but hidden, unseen in the orchard or walled garden, behind the hen house, and in any place where strangers could not see them. Conall and Luke were there, along with Liam and Cahir O'Byrne, as well as other tories who had come out of the caves to witness this moment.

The carriage rumbled to a stop. Garrett dismounted, opened the door, and reached a hand inside.

Everyone watched as a thin hand slid into his.

Eleanor stood at her husband's side.

The occupant of the carriage put one foot on the box, and stepped out. She was tiny and frail, but she carried herself with pride and strength, and her eyes were as vibrant as a faery bog. She lifted her pale face to Órla's schist and granite mountains, her smiled deepened to see the lush green fastness, the rugged peaks, and from those lush green eyes tears began to flow. They glistened silver, and color blossomed upon her cheeks as she heard her mother's voice reciting the cradle-tale:

> This last girl's name was Olivia, born in England, but with the blood of Ireland, and she waited for the day she might tell her child about the glen and the O'Tooles and Castlekevin, waited for the day she would teach her child the language her mother had taught her in secret. She waited for a child to whom she would impart grandmother Órla's memories, and the knowledge grandmother Órla had learned at her grandfather's knee in Ireland.

"Welcome, Lady Olivia," said Eleanor. "Welcome to Laragh."

The elderly woman smiled at Eleanor. "Go raith

*maith agat*," she whispered in Irish. *Thank you.*

"Nay, thank you, Lady Olivia, for your love and devotion to Garrett and to this land. Thank you, for in preserving the past, you have given me my future."

Lady Olivia nodded. She understood of what the younger woman spoke, and most gladly went into her welcoming embrace.

Lady Olivia Turbeville, daughter of Órla, descended from the O'Tooles of Castlekevin, born among the English and raised at High Knole, had fulfilled her destiny.

She was one of the *bean-draoícht*, and she was home at last.

Dear Reader,

As you're getting deeper and deeper into the holiday hustle and bustle, don't forget to take some time out for yourself—by indulging in an Avon romance! Is there any better way to enjoy a precious few moments of time for yourself?

Avon's Romantic Treasure for December comes from Karen Ranney, whose emotionally intense and wildly passionate love stories are sure to warm up the coldest December night! In *Upon A Wicked Time* a young beauty transforms a wicked English duke into a man worth loving. This is a story that will go straight to your heart!

Contemporary readers won't want to miss Patti Berg's delightful *Looking for a Hero*. What would you do if a devastatingly handsome man washed up on your beach and into your life? And what would you think if he insisted he was a real, live 18th Century *pirate?* Fans of warm, wonderful, magical love stories won't want to miss this "keeper!"

Readers just can't get enough of *The MacKenzies* by Ana Leigh, and the latest MacKenzie is here—*Peter*. These heroes are hot, and Ana Leigh's writing is filled with the passion and humor—and western setting—I know you all enjoy!

And if you like your romance stormy and sensual, then don't miss Margaret Evans Porter's *Kissing a Stranger*...where a beautiful heroine travels to Regency London, desperate to marry for money. But she ends up with more than she ever bargained for...

Until next month, happy reading.

Lucia Macro

*Lucia Macro*
Senior Editor

# Avon Romances—
## the best in exceptional authors and unforgettable novels!

THE HEART BREAKER     **by Nicole Jordan**
78561-7/ $5.99 US/ $7.99 Can

THE MEN OF PRIDE COUNTY:     **by Rosalyn West**
THE OUTCAST
79579-5/ $5.99 US/ $7.99 Can

THE MACKENZIES: DAVID     **by Ana Leigh**
79337-7/ $5.99 US/ $7.99 Can

THE PROPOSAL     **by Margaret Evans Porter**
79557-4/ $5.99 US/ $7.99 Can

THE PIRATE LORD     **by Sabrina Jeffries**
79747-X/ $5.99 US/ $7.99 Can

HER SECRET GUARDIAN     **by Linda Needham**
79634-1/ $5.99 US/ $7.99 Can

KISS ME GOODNIGHT     **by Marlene Suson**
79560-4/ $5.99 US/ $7.99 Can

WHITE EAGLE'S TOUCH     **by Karen Kay**
78999-X/ $5.99 US/ $7.99 Can

ONLY IN MY DREAMS     **by Eve Byron**
79311-3/ $5.99 US/ $7.99 Can

ARIZONA RENEGADE     **by Kit Dee**
79206-0/ $5.99 US/ $7.99 Can